SPECIAL MESSAGE TO READERS

BOTH OF YOU

Leigh Fletcher, happily married stepmum to two gorgeous boys, goes missing on Monday. Her husband Mark says he knows nothing of her whereabouts. She simply went to work and just never came home. Their family is shattered.

Kai Janssen, married to wealthy Dutch businessman Daan, vanishes the same week. Kai left their luxurious penthouse and glamorous world without a backward glance. She seemingly evaporated into thin air. Daan is distraught.

DC Clements knows that people disappear all the time — far too frequently. Most run away from things, some run towards, others are taken but find their way back. A sad few never return. These two women are from very different worlds: their disappearances are unlikely to be connected. And yet, at gut level, Clements believes they might be . . .

ADELE PARKS

BOTH OF YOU

Complete and Unabridged

CHARNWOOD
Leicester

First published in Great Britain in 2021 by
HQ
An imprint of HarperCollins*Publishers* Ltd
London

First Charnwood Edition
published 2021
by arrangement with
HarperCollins*Publishers* Ltd
London

*A catalogue record for this book is available
from the British Library.*

ISBN 978–1–4448–4755–0

Published by
Ulverscroft Limited
Anstey, Leicestershire

Printed and bound in Great Britain by
TJ Books Ltd., Padstow, Cornwall

This book is printed on acid-free paper

For Abdu Mohammed Ali.
Tech genius who saved the day.

1

Tuesday 17th March 2020

I am engulfed in emptiness. I'm not in my bed. I am not in any bed.

In the instant my eyes flutter open I know there is something wrong. Seriously wrong. It's dark. I'm suspended in a threatening, airless blackness. I'm lying down but am disorientated because I'm on a cold concrete floor. A floor that looks as though it's waiting to be tiled, but something immediately suggests to me it never will be. My mind is lazy and unable to process why I think this. I can't remember when I last slept on a floor, a million years ago when I was a student and would bunk in another student's room if I was too drunk to get home. I try to sit up; my limbs feel heavy, my head sore. I try to stand up but as I do so, I am yanked back down, my left hand is tethered. Chained. I hear the rattle of the chain at the same time as I feel the cold tug. Am I dreaming? My head pulses, swells and then bursts, I close my eyes again, my lids are like sandpaper scratching, I open them for a second time, giving them a chance to adjust to the darkness. Is it my dizziness that's leaving everything unfamiliar? Shaky? I feel slow, behind myself.

How much did I have to drink last night? I try to remember.

I can't. And then — this is terrifying — I realise I

1

can't remember last night at all. I feel sick. I can smell vomit, suggesting I have already been sick. I should not be waking to the smell of vomit. Where is the smell of my husband's early morning breath? There is no smell of toast from the kitchen, no traces of the Jo Malone Lime Basil and Mandarin room spray that I sometimes wake to. I'm somewhere dusty, not damp, a little overwarm. Am I in a hospital? No. What sort of hospital makes patients lie on the floor, chains them? There are no sounds. My boys are not arguing in the kitchen, the TV is not blaring, no doors opening, slamming, no demands, 'Mum, where are my football shorts?' I wait, sometimes I wake to something more serene. Sometimes it is Radio 4 and the smell of coffee.

Nothing.

Alarm and horror flood through my body. My organs and limbs turn to liquid and I can't coordinate my movements. None of us are that naive anymore. The news doesn't always enlighten or inform, often it terrifies. My foggy mind realises I must have been drugged. I have been abducted. The terrible thing that you read about that happens to someone else — someone other — has happened to me.

Panicked, I tug hard at the chain, there's no give. I scramble about in the darkness. Trying to understand my environment. I can't move far because of the chain, which is attached to a radiator at one end and through a zip tie that is tight around my wrist on the other. The chain is about a metre long. As my eyes adjust, I see that I am in a room that is about three metres long by just over two, like a standard guest room. The walls are manila. It is clean and bare. I am not in a derelict warehouse or abandoned cottage. It's bland to the state of anonymous. I imagine that is the

2

point. I could be anywhere. There's no furniture in the room. None at all. Not a bed, a mattress, a lamp. Nothing to soften or comfort. Just a plastic bucket. I realise what this is intended for and my stomach heaves. I can see the outline of a door and a boarded-up window. I can't reach the door as it's in the far corner, or the window as that's at the end of the wall opposite the one with the radiator I am chained to.

I go to check the time, but my Fitbit has been removed. Not knowing what time it is, or even what day it is for sure, sends spikes of isolation and confusion through my body. Still, I have my voice. I can shout and maybe attract attention. I fleetingly consider that shouting will attract the attention of whoever it is that brought me here. He could do a lot worse to me than chain me up, but I have no choice.

'Help! Help me! Help!' My voice shatters the dead, unnatural silence. I yell over and over again until I become hoarse. The pain in my tender head intensifies.

No one comes.

No one responds.

The silence stretches. I stop yelling and listen. Hoping to hear something, cars in the distance, people in the street, birdsong, as the light has started to eke around the boarded window. A new day, but which day is it? Nothing. It's like I'm in a vacuum. Then, I hear footsteps coming towards the door.

'Please, please let me out,' I whimper. I'm crying now. I'm not sure when I started crying. Tears and mucus pour down my face. I don't want to be weak. I want to be strong, brave, resistant. That's what you imagine you'll be in a situation like this but it's beyond me. It's a ludicrous fantasy. I am just terrified. I will

3

beg, plead, implore. Anything to stay safe. Anything. 'Please, please don't hurt me. Please.'

Then I hear the distinct sound of the keystrokes of an old-fashioned typewriter being pounded. A sort of shuffling rat-tat-tat. Slow, precise. Like a hostile countdown. Next, the hurried juddering whirl of paper being forcefully pulled out of the machine's roller. It is incongruous, this passé sound is the domain of busy newspaper rooms in decades gone by. Who has a typewriter anymore? There is rustling, as the piece of paper is pushed beneath the door. I stretch to reach it, but it is tantalisingly out of my grasp. I lie on the floor and carefully, oh so slowly, edge it nearer with my toes until I can drag it close enough to snatch it up.

I am not the villain here.

2
Leigh

Sunday 15th March

Sunday. The boys are out. All three of them. I probably shouldn't refer to Mark as one of my boys, not really. It's a bit infantilising and he's not that sort of man at all. He's very capable. Strong. Powerful. It's just shorthand. And it sounds a bit formal and pedantic if I say my husband and sons are out.

Plus, not strictly accurate.

My husband and *his* sons are out. The thought flickers into my head, nips hard and cruel. Even now. This sudden and brutal distinction wounds. Although, it hasn't been sudden, has it? Not really. I might as well be honest with myself. It's always been there. An imbalance that we are both aware of and try not to acknowledge ever. An imbalance that has been impossible to ignore for these past few months, Oli has started being insistent on highlighting the difference.

They *are* my sons. I always think of them as my sons, I love them as though they are. I couldn't love them more.

I really couldn't.

I have done everything a mum can. I have bathed them, nursed them, fed them, shopped for them, I have played with them — oh the endless, mindless games! I have taught them. Not just their alphabet

5

and how to tie their shoelaces, I've taught them how to swim, ride their bikes, measure out cooking ingredients, fasten buttons, tie knots, tell the time, cross the road. I try to teach them everything I can about the world. I want to stuff them full of knowledge and fortitude and curiosity because these qualities will sustain them when I'm away from them. But sometimes — maybe it's all the time — kids are not pliable. They don't note or understand your grand motivations. They don't know you are trying to keep them safe, help them grow. They just think you are the strict parent, the one that obsesses about homework and teeth cleaning.

They *are* my sons. No matter what Oli says.

It's breaking my heart. Everyone warned me that this stage would come, somewhere in their teen years when they test boundaries, want to develop their own identities, set their own agendas, create new worlds, generally turn into little shits. My best friend Fiona jokes that Oli could be doing far worse things than calling me Leigh. He could be ditching school, shoplifting or getting high every night. I should be grateful, she says. I'm not, I'm heartbroken. Because this is not a stage, it's a protest. A point. It is true I'm not their biological mum but I'm the only mum they have, so you'd think he'd accept I'm doing my best. We used to be so close.

We had another row about it this morning. I filled out a parental online form about his Prom night. Just stuff about allergies (he has none) and giving him permission to get the coach that's taking the kids on to the afterparty (I agreed). Nothing controversial. He said I had no right. I'm paying for the bloody party.

Mark just said it wasn't the day to get into it. He

6

always says that. We shouldn't get into it on a school day because kids doing GCSEs are under enough pressure, we shouldn't get into it during the weekends or holidays because it will bring the mood down. We shouldn't get into it on a day ending in 'y'. Although we are always into it. Oli seethes. Grunts. Sulks and is monosyllabic a lot of the time.

When they go out — look, this is an awful thing to admit — but sometimes, when the door slams shut behind them, and I know there are walls between us, the silence changes. There's often a silence that's claustrophobic and accusatory but I feel freer. Without anyone's gaze on me, it is easier to think.

They are visiting Mark's sister-in-law. Mark has stayed close to his first wife's family, her sister in particular. Usually I also go along to see Paula and her family, when Mark and the boys go, but today there are a number of reasons why I thought it was best that I leave them to it. I pointed out I have some phone calls to make, there is a stack of washing up to be done and the kitchen floor needs mopping. Sunday lunch has been quite eventful. While we were eating, our cat, Topaz, jumped onto the counter and paddled in the discarded, greasy baking trays in the kitchen, leaving a trail of oily footprints everywhere. He's a big, greedy cat and somehow, he managed to pick up the chicken carcass and throw it onto the floor, where it slithered and slid, leaving a trail of smeared poultry fat. Finding the cat hunched over the chicken carcass, gnawing on the bits of remaining flesh, led to a mini crisis as Seb panicked that the cat was going to choke on a chicken bone. He didn't, he just spat and clawed aggressively when I separated him from his prize. I'm not especially house proud. Before I was a mother

7

and wife, I used to keep my flat neat enough but then one day I read a fridge magnet that said, *A clean house is the sign of a wasted life* and I realised I agreed with it more than almost anything else I had ever read.

I can't bear waste.

Especially wasted time.

However, even with my fairly relaxed standards, I couldn't leave the kitchen swilling in bird fat; the boys would walk it through to the carpets, Seb — who is a bit clumsy — would no doubt slip on it. So, I said I'd stay behind and make everything shipshape.

Besides I hate graveyards.

Today is the anniversary of Frances's death. Eleven years to the day since they lost their real mother. Mark's first wife. My predecessor. The forerunner. Mark is taking the boys to visit her grave. Frances's sister, Paula, her husband and their three daughters are going too. Frances is buried just minutes from Paula's house and Paula often visits the grave — keeps it tidy by weeding and supplying fresh flowers. Paula's three girls visit the grave so frequently that they talk about it in the same way as they talk about visiting their nana or going to the playpark. 'Shall we go and see Aunty Frances?' they cheerfully ask on a regular basis. I think it's because they like buying flowers at the florist — what little girl doesn't? Paula's kids weren't even born when Frances died but Paula keeps her alive for them, and for my boys too. She is forever telling Oli and Seb stories about Frances. She's in a unique position to do this and I think it's important for them to feel comfortable talking about Frances. I don't think she necessarily has to be the main topic of conversation every time they see their aunt, sometimes it might be nice if Paula talked to the boys without

8

breaking off mid-sentence to exclaim, 'You like chocolate fudge cake? Of course you do, your mother loved chocolate fudge cake' (well, who doesn't?) or 'you remind me so much of your mum when she was your age. The spitting image.' The boys actually look like their dad, but I suppose they might have mannerisms inherited from Frances that I'm unaware of. I am not disrespectful of Frances. I understand that by all accounts she was a wonderful woman. Kind, patient, funny, clever. No one has a bad word to say against her (which honestly, I find a little hard to swallow — none of us is perfect). I also understand some people get a great comfort from visiting graves, they like to show their respect and demonstrate gone but not forgotten. I think grave visiting is morbid. And in this case, a power play.

It's just a fact that Paula and I are not close. We don't argue but we don't gel. Never have. We are polite with one another. I suppose her cool detachment towards me is understandable. Mark could get a new wife; she could never get a new sister. I realise if Frances hadn't tragically died of cancer, I would never have become Mark's wife, Oli and Seb's mum, because they were not the sort of couple that would ever have split up. They were happy. Mark would never have noticed me.

But Frances did die.

It takes a lot of strength and determination not to think of myself as second choice. Second place. I am constantly reminding myself, I'm not Plan B, I'm just a different path. I do visit her grave with them on her birthday and even Christmas Eve, just before we dash off up the M1 to see Mark's parents — although that drives me mad, because there are a ton of things that have to be done on Christmas Eve and all of them are

9

time-sensitive. I just think making a thing out of the death anniversary is a bit much.

I'd rather wash the kitchen floor.

I am going to do the housework first and then settle down to my telephone calls, catch up with friends and family. It will be my treat after the drudgery. I'll make plans for the coming week, discuss bars and restaurants that are worth a visit, remind myself that there are more ways to validate my life than my success — or otherwise — in parenting Oli and Seb, being Mark's wife.

Don't get me wrong. We're a very happy family. More often than not. Very happy. It's just sometimes — and any mother will tell you this — sometimes being a mum seems a bit thankless, a bit hopeless. Well, if not hopeless, then certainly outside of your control. I think that's the hardest lesson I have had to learn as a parent; no matter how much I try, I am not able to guarantee my sons' happiness and success. There are constant outside forces at work that disrupt things. Forces that matter to them more than I do. Friendship groups, strict or nagging teachers, Insta likes and follows, whether or not they are picked for a team or invited to a party, whether they think they are tall enough, too fat, too thin, too spotty. Whether they are the best at something, at *anything*. It was easier when they were younger; a cuddle, a colourful Elastoplast or an ice lolly solved just about everything.

I like to listen to music when the house is empty. Two reasons. One, to fill the void that is normally owned by the noise of video games beeping, music blaring and the TV streaming, and secondly because when the boys are home, I rarely get to pick what music is played. Oli likes hip-hop and rap, Seb pretends to like

10

these things because he lives in awe of his big brother and tries to ape his every move — adopting his style, claiming his tastes in music, food, TV shows — much to Oli's annoyance. Because both the boys like hip-hop and rap, the angry lyrics and heavy, insistent beats tend to thud through our rooms whenever they are about; my preferences are not considered. No one would call me a muso. I stopped following bands when Oasis and Blur started to slip down the charts. Most of the music I like is blacklisted on Radio 1, but I do like dancing. I like a beat thrilling through my body. I guess I'm the musical equivalent to that person who says they know nothing about wine, except what they like to drink.

Sometimes I'll hear a track that Oli and Seb are listening to and I'll say, 'What's this? This is good.' Up until about six months ago that would make Oli smile; he'd excitedly show me some incomprehensible YouTube video and tell me facts about the singer: they've been in prison, they've performed on a yacht to crowds on the shore, they gave away ten million in cash in their local hood. The worlds he describes are alien to me; I remember when the most surprising thing a pop star could do was wear eyeliner. But I liked to listen to him enthuse. I liked to see him animated, I felt honoured that it was me he chose to share his excitement with. I miss that. I miss him.

I once made the mistake of commenting that after hearing Taylor Swift on Radio 1, I considered her my spirit animal — because if you listen to her lyrics, she writes the things I feel. Well, felt, when I was young and vulnerable. It appears those things don't change for a woman no matter how woke a world becomes. It was around this time that I noticed Oli change towards

11

me. When I said the spirit animal thing, he didn't get the sentiment, couldn't see my joke or my attempt at connection. He was horrified. Suddenly furious that I might encroach on his world of youth and possibility, crushes, and illicit under the covers (solo) activity.

'You don't even know what a spirit animal is,' he snapped. 'Another person can't be your spirit animal.'

'I know, I was making a joke!' I said, smiling, trying to get him to engage. 'But she is brilliant, isn't she? It's as though she understands everything there is to understand about secret longings, triumphs and mistakes.' After hearing her on the radio, I had downloaded her latest album. I pressed play on my phone. 'Listen.' I began to dance around the kitchen. We first bonded over dancing, me and Oli. He used to climb onto my feet, and I would step with him, in a strange slow shuffle dance, the way my father had once moved with me. Obviously, he's far too big now. He's taller than me! He's a great dancer. I like watching him. It takes a confident teen to dance anywhere, let alone in the kitchen with his mother. That day, when I said the thing about Taylor Swift, I waited for him to join in, but Oli just scowled, said Taylor Swift was crap and then disappeared to his room. I can't remember him dancing with me since.

Wallowing in the luxury of an empty house, I pump up the volume and listen to her touching lyrics and dazzling melodies whilst I mop the kitchen floor. She sings about young love and irresponsibility. Mark and I never had that. He was a father when I met him and I became a mother the day I agreed to be his girlfriend — or at least a stand-in-mother, an almost-mother. Yet as I listen to the words, I am flung even further back into days defined by spectacular failures, magnificent consequences. I like to dance, it's a great source of joy to me. I adore the sheer extravagance of it. The alone time on a Sunday afternoon seems deliciously illicit, indulgent. I start to sway my hips, move my feet, click out a beat. Soon the lyrics and rhythm infiltrate my body like a stranger. I give in to it. No, that suggests resistance — I jump in to it. I let myself go. I let it all out. I'm normally in control of everything: myself, my family, time. I'm relatively self-conscious, constantly aware of the impression I make. But when dancing, that drops away. My arms and legs loosen, I shake my hips and my head. I start to use the mop as a fake dance partner and spin and twirl.

Outside, the sky dips from bruised grey to a dark indigo as I clean and dance. Mark texts to say that he and the boys have gone back to Paula's for supper. Decision made. I'm not being consulted, just kept up to date. But I was only planning a sandwich tea, it's not like I can complain. When the floor is clean, and all the surfaces are gleaming, I put away the mops, cloths and bucket but — a regular Cinderella determined to go to the ball — I continue to dance. My stomach becomes clammy with sweat, my hair sticks to the back of my neck, and I am loving it! The pleasure, the freedom is absolute.

That's why I am so angry with Mark and the boys for taking it away. The pleasure. The freedom.

I hear them. Their laughter. Loud and unruly. It is pitch black outside now and I have the light on in the kitchen, it is as though I am on a stage, performing but also exposed. Mark, Oli and Seb are stood at the glass patio door, laughing like hyenas. I wonder how long they have been watching. They pile into the house, still laughing. Carelessly ridiculing me.

'Quite the performance,' says Mark. He kisses me briefly, his cold lips bite against my blushing cheek. 'I forgot my key, so we came around the back.'

'God, Mum, you dance like Grandma,' says Seb. I don't. Their grandmother still does the twist — to her credit — I'm a little more 90s. Yes, stuck there, probably but it is not the twist, it's a lot of jumping up and down and arm waving. Still, I understand the point Seb is making. Hurriedly, I pull my arms to my sides. If I could chop them right off, I would. I imagine reaching for the carving knife, clean and gleaming on the kitchen unit.

'Wash your hands. Thoroughly. Sing 'Happy Birthday' twice, like we've been told,' I say. No one responds.

'You are such a loser, Leigh,' mutters Oli. Barging past me, he grabs an apple from the fruit bowl I've stocked, bites into it aggressively. He shakes his head. Not the way I did when dancing, not with joyful abandon, but with despair. Disgust. 'Embarrassing.'

I turn to Mark and plead with my eyes for him to say something, I know he understands me, but he just shrugs. His eyes say, *don't bring me into this; it's your battle.* Sometimes being a wife and mother feels like death by a thousand cuts. I straighten my shoulders, force out a smile, albeit a small one — no one is going to think I am deliriously happy right now, but I don't want to cause a scene. Or maybe I do, but Mark doesn't. I am master over my own body. I choose what to reveal. I keep my face relaxed, my brow unfurrowed, my chin stays high. Unreadable. You are not meant to feel like an outsider in your own tribe. It's unnatural.

'Can we get a dog?' Seb asks.

'No,' I snap. He's been asking this question on and off for about six months. Normally I'm more serene and make an effort to let him down gently but I don't have the patience, the energy. How would a dog fit in with my lifestyle?

Seb looks startled, his face is shadowed with a hint of worry. I instantly feel guilty. Twelve-year-olds shouldn't worry about their parents. He's an observant and kind kid. Funny and light-hearted himself, he wants the same brightness in everyone's world. 'What's wrong?' he asks.

How do I tell him everything is wrong, except perhaps him? Although even loving him is complicated. There is no pleasure in my life that is absolute. I am entirely to blame for that fact.

'Nothing, I'm just tired. Look, why don't you go and have a shower? I'm going to call Fiona. I'll come up and see you before you turn your lights off.' He nods, dashes off obediently, willingly, wanting to believe I'm just tired.

I pour myself a healthy-sized glass of wine and tell Fiona about Oli's loser comment. I try and fail to make it sound like I think it is no big deal. She knows me too well to be fooled. I'm glad, I don't want her to ignore the situation, the way Mark does. I need her to sympathise, to affirm that it's unfair, that I don't deserve to be treated this way. There's been a suggestion that Oli and Seb ought to see a grief therapist. Actually, the idea has been mooted more than once. I think Fiona was the first one to bring the idea to the table and she does so again tonight. She's my best friend. I love her, she means well but her timing couldn't be worse.

'Why would the boys need therapists?' I demand.

15

'To process their grief.'

'What grief?'

'For their mother.'

'I'm their mother,' I assert hotly.

'Their birth mother,' she replies patiently.

'She died years ago. They were practically babies. I've been their mother for nearly a decade.'

'Yes, that's my point, they were very young when they lost her. Too young to process it. Maybe they need help in doing so now.'

'I'm their mother,' I say again. 'I don't want some therapist poking about in their minds disturbing things.'

'What's the matter, Leigh? I know something is up with you.'

She doesn't ask if it is Oli. Is it work? She leaves it open-ended and suddenly the question seems wild and dangerous. What if I told her? What if I confessed? The question opens up a wide chasm of longing. I wonder whether I'll ever be able to close it down.

I can't answer that question.

3

Leigh

Ten years ago

It's a Saturday afternoon, and the sun is shining. Outside of London postcodes hot days are without doubt, no qualms, heaven-sent. An opportunity to stride or cycle across the downs and through national parks, to set up deck chairs in the garden, maybe throw a few sausages on the barbie, go to a country pub. For a couple of thirty-three-year-old heterosexual women who share a poky, second-floor London flat, hot days are a moment when their lives feel exposed. Unsatisfactory. Like Christmas, Easter and Bank holidays. When it's hot and the sun streams through the windows showing they could do with a wash, Fiona and I feel claustrophobic, trapped. Failing. Our flat which can look kooky, quirky — with its IKEA shelves and string of multicoloured chilli-shaped fairy lights hanging around the kitchen cabinets — is uncovered as cramped and juvenile; the damp patches may have dried out, but the drains smell awful.

We both know we should be somewhere else. Further up the food chain. Maybe we should be lolling outside a bistro eating plates of watermelon and feta salad with our boyfriends, or wasting the afternoon in B&Q arguing with our fiancés about which Farrow and Ball paint shade will be most statement on the walls of our newly renovated kitchen; maybe we

17

should even be pushing a pram around a park, or dipping a toddler's feet into the fountain at Trafalgar Square. We've both missed the beats that so many of our friends seem to have effortlessly hit. On gloomy wet days we can hide this fact from the world and ourselves by staying indoors, watching crap reality TV and playing on our phones. When the weather is good, there's an unspoken demand that the flat must vomit us out, that we must find a place in the outside world. Somehow squeeze into it.

'Shall we go to the park?' I suggest tentatively.

'The local one?' asks Fiona. Fiona is the closest thing I've ever had to a sister. It's not just that we get along great, which we do, we know one another inside out and often, that's even more important than getting along.

'Yeah. The local one.'

'Shouldn't we go to like one of the proper ones?' I know what Fiona means. I always do. Sometimes she can be bossy and yet I know she's uncertain about herself, which is why she can occasionally come across as irritable or demanding. Dismissive. I don't mind. Men do. She means sitting on the local green — which backs on to the railway track and is framed by a number of small but busy roads — seems defeatist. The local park will be full of local families, and that's OK for them, because exhausted mums and dads can't be expected to go to Hyde Park to rollerblade or Alexandra Palace to skateboard or Richmond to spot deer — the most that busy parents are expected to do is dress and drag their kids outside. But people like Fiona and me, women in the prime of our lives, who are still looking for our soulmates, should muster the energy to get out there. If we don't, we are basically

18

acknowledging that we've given up.

I stare at Fiona, she knows all this as well as I do. It doesn't need to be articulated. 'If we stay local, we can come back and use the loo if we want to,' she points out.

I nod. It's as though neither of us ever went to Glastonbury and used the portaloos from hell.

We do at least make an effort with our picnic. Food is something we've started to pay more attention to in the last year or eighteen months. I guess as we've had less excitement on the dating sites, we've looked to replace that emotional hole at the local deli. Our deli has huge brine-cured hams hanging from scary-looking hooks swaying in the window, ripe cheeses sweat and swell, there are about ten different types of olives to be purchased. It's intimidating, and that sort of excites us. We spend as much in that deli each month as we spend on our rent. We might not have boyfriends, mortgages or children, but we do have hefty chunks of salty pig. Today, we buy three good cheeses and a selection of charcuterie. We buy an overpriced, ready-prepared summer berry salad, but the convenience justifies the inflated price tag. We glance at one another half guilty, half encouraging and then add a four-pack of luxury chocolate brownies to the basket. At the till, I slip a packet of caramel popcorn in too and Fiona adds some hand-cut vegetable crisps. It's a family-size pack, but we'll make a heroic effort. Finally, we buy a large bottle of sparkly water and a decent prosecco. By the time we leave the shop, we feel in better spirits.

As predicted, the park is full of families with young kids, but it's a relief to note there are no loved-up couples. They are the worst. I guess the loved-up couples

19

still have the impetus to get on the tube and haul their asses to London's central parks which looks significantly more impressive on Facebook. Social media impact is a new but important part of dating. Equal to physical attraction and only a fraction below potential earning-power. I sigh, frustrated with how increasingly complex the dating scene is becoming. My mother and father met one another through friends who 'thought they might click'. It seems quaint, being set up by mutual, interested parties. No one does that now.

Probably because most people shag all their vaguely attractive friends throughout their twenties, and so passing them on seems vaguely inappropriate. *Hey, I didn't think he was quite, you know, but maybe you will* . . . No one likes sloppy seconds. Thinking about sex takes my mind in a different direction. I suddenly doubt the loved-up couples of London are bothering with parks at all. Maybe they can choose to shun the sun, loll in bed, tangle themselves in sweat and sheets. As couples they have the confidence not to care if they are 'wasting the day', not to believe they are, since they are wrapped in one another. The thought of these imaginary couples makes me feel horny and depressed at the same time.

Fiona and I spread out the picnic blanket. Settle. Whilst we eat and drink, we swap the odd comment but don't commit to a conversation.

'Oh my God, that brie.'

'Good?'

'Heaven.'

'Tear me off some bread, will you?'

'Top-up?'

We don't feel the need for constant chatter. We have

20

known one another for twelve years. We don't have many surprises to offer each other. There are few, if any, stories we haven't shared. This week's news and gossip from our respective offices has been dissected. It doesn't matter, the silence between us is comfortable, companionable. We met just after we graduated, in the waiting room of a recruitment agency. Both of us clueless. I didn't know much more than I wanted to work 'in an office'. Fiona wanted to work 'in fashion or interiors, something not boring'. We struck up a conversation and then after we'd both registered and interviewed we went for a coffee, eager to share our dreams and admit to our insecurities. We just clicked, easily and instantly became close. Thank God I have Fiona. I think I love her more than anyone else in the world. I don't want this to be the case. I want to love my husband and my kids more but since neither thing exists, I'm grateful I have Fiona to love.

We first flat-shared years ago, then went our separate ways. We both broke up from serious relationships around our thirtieth birthdays, neither of us could afford our own place, or bear to be alone, so we got a place together again. It was convenient, often fun. It was supposed to be a temporary measure, we didn't buy, not wanting to tie up our cash. That was three years ago. Property prices have gone up so much since then. We should have bought.

Fiona puts on her headphones and closes her eyes. I reach for my paperback. I open it where the bookmark nestles but don't start reading. The sun is glaring, the glass of prosecco I've already downed is oozing around my bloodstream. I keep losing my spot on the page, rereading the same paragraph over again. I let my gaze drift to those around me. I like people-watching. I always have. In fact, I secretly feel considerably more comfortable observing than participating. Sunglasses offer a benefit. No one can tell if you are staring at them too long, too hard, trying to work them out. That is my habit. Working people out. Trying to solve the puzzle of who they are and what makes them tick. I've been told it makes me a little intense. It's just I believe that there are people in this world who are simply better at living and being involved than others. They have the knack. A zest. I'm not one of them. I think maybe if I stare at such people for long enough, I'll learn, discover the capability of being adult, of fitting in, maybe even thriving — something that seems eternally elusive to me.

I'm not deluded. As I glance about I see that there are cranky, cross parents squabbling with one another because one of them is fed up of pushing their offspring on the swing, whilst the other has their phone glued to their ear. Some are bickering, others have nothing to say to one another. Family life isn't a guarantee for happiness. God, I know that. But I also see the families that are the goal. The ones that laugh at the cuteness of their chubby toddler doing something mundane like picking a daisy or petting a dog. The ones that hand over enormous ice creams to grasping pudgy hands and bask in the beam that the child throws out in return. I know it's a habit I need to kick. This professional voyeurism. It's unhealthy. I need to get involved, not ceaselessly hover around the edges of life. If I could afford to see a therapist, she'd most likely want to talk about me confronting my fertility issues. I wouldn't want to talk about the matter. It's probably a good thing I can't afford a therapist.

His hair is thick and black. So black I think he must dye it because I'd put him in his late thirties, early forties and most people that age are fighting grey, right? Fleetingly, I think less of him for it. A man carrying such vanity seems off-putting. Which is a) stupid because this man I'm staring at hasn't asked me to ogle him and probably doesn't care *at all* what I think of his grooming habits and b) it's deeply hypocritical of me, sexist, because I dye my hair, always have. Since my teens, for fun and fashion. And — for about the past three months — for what I think of as necessity. Holding back the tide. Prematurely (I like to think) some nasty white hairs (not grey — straight to white — I'm that extreme) have suddenly started to sprout around my hairline like mushrooms in a boggy autumnal field.

But his eyebrows are dark, and the hairs on his legs are dark too so maybe he doesn't dye it. He has a great jawline, strong, definite. He's tanned. A lot of London men spend long hours hunched over laptops and it shows. This man looks like he spends a significant amount of time outdoors. This handsome man is only average height, five ten, maybe eleven, but he looks especially strong and purposeful. He's muscular, he picks up his boys and swings them onto his shoulders with ridiculous ease. Both boys at the same time, like someone performing in a circus! I don't think he's trying to draw attention, but he is. He's compelling. I notice a number of women take furtive sideways glances, even the ones with their own husbands and children. The boys look aged about two and five years old. They both look like their father. Stocky, strong, easy-to-tan golden limbs. They ooze a boyish energy and ferocity. They each have a mop of dark hair, like

23

their daddy, and although I'm not close enough to know for certain I imagine thick long lashes, the sort that can create a breeze when they blink. The only difference between them is that the younger kid looks open and light — he's quick to smile and laugh — the eldest has a furrowed brow, like his father. He's serious-looking.

I'm looking at this very handsome man and whilst appreciating him and enjoying that, I'm also stung by a familiar but always uncomfortable emotion. I feel jealous of his wife. Not that she is anywhere to be seen. He's playing with his two little boys alone, no doubt giving her an afternoon off. Maybe she's having a manicure, drinking chardonnay with her girlfriends. I imagine him saying, 'Go on, darling, you deserve it, you have them all week. It's my turn.' I hate his wife. I mean obviously not really; I don't know his wife.

But sort of.

It happens in a flash. A moment that's over before it's begun and yet is instantaneously tattooed on my memory in slow-mo, forever. He only looks away for a nanosecond. The eldest boy calls, 'Look at me, Daddy!' He is standing on the swing, bending his knees inexpertly to try to create some momentum. The chains of the swing rattle.

'Sit down at once,' the father instructs. Concern making him sound ferocious, old-fashioned. The boy's face flickers with worry, he was showing off, doing something adventurous and remarkable, he doesn't quite understand why he is in trouble. 'You will fall!' yells the father for clarity. 'Do you want to give me a heart attack?'

Then, as the elder boy follows instructions — slowly, precariously bending his knees, the swing wobbling as

24

he finds a safer seated position — the little one impatiently slips his hand out of his father's and tries to set off down the slide alone. Instead, he tumbles over the side. He plunges head first towards the tarmac, as though he is diving off a board into a pool. His chunky little body rushing after. Creating momentum, even though the fall is less than two metres. The smack of his baby body hitting the ground shakes my bones.

Nose, lips, head bleed the most.

I'm up in a flash. Running towards them. Normally, I'm someone who hesitates but not now. The father is just staring at the kid. Frozen. He hasn't instinctually bent to tend to him, which is odd. I guess he's shocked. The child isn't howling, which would be reassuring, normal. Is he unconscious? My hand tentatively touches his warm little arm and he blinks. He's not unconscious but stunned. Why isn't he crying? He looks at me wide-eyed, trusting. I have no idea why the kid thinks he can trust me. I don't know about children or injuries or what to do. I don't know anything and yet, he needs me. He's looking at me as though I'm all he's got and as his father is frozen, temporarily useless, I am.

'It's OK. It's OK. It's all going to be fine. I've got you,' I murmur as I pull out my phone and call an ambulance.

I am wearing a vest top with an open shirt over it. I quickly shrug out of the shirt and press the cloth around the gash on his head. I have no first aid training (why the fuck haven't I got first aid training?!) but instinctually I feel I need to slow the bleeding. The older boy has run to his father's side now. They both watch me, but stay distant from me and from each other. I haven't got time to be annoyed or to wonder

25

why. They watch, fearful and I see something in their gaze. They are people who have seen tragedy, who expect the worst. They are terrified.

As we wait for the ambulance, I continue to murmur soothing things to the father and both boys. I tell them it looks worse than it is (I don't know this). I promise I'll stay with them, because the father asks if I will and I can't refuse him. Fiona looks on, shocked. She's not used to me taking control, being able. There is a small crowd of onlookers gathered around us, they keep asking if anyone has called for an ambulance, someone puts their jacket over the injured little boy, someone else asks if he wants a drink, yet another person says he can't eat or drink anything, 'Just in case.' Then the crowd starts to move on, parents don't want their children seeing this, they nod at me and mumble, 'You seem to have this covered,' as they melt away. I don't know whether to move the child. I'm certain you shouldn't with suspected concussions and yet somehow, he shuffles his head on to my lap. The blood from his wound seeps onto my white broderie anglaise skirt. I gently stroke his arm, hold his hand, his big brown eyes stay latched on mine the entire time.

'What's your name, angel?'

'He's Sebastian,' says the father.

'But we mostly call him Seb,' adds the brother. 'I'm Oli,' he adds as an afterthought.

'Hi, Oli.' I smile but he doesn't smile back.

When the ambulance arrives, I am mistaken for Seb's mother. I explain I'm not, the paramedics are efficient, kind, empathetic but obviously don't want to lose any time. 'Who is coming in the ambulance?' they ask brusquely. Seb's fingers tighten around mine.

26

His father notices.

'Can we all come?' the father asks.

'Not really allowed.'

'Please.' I guess the paramedic sees the same desperation and fear in the face of the father as I do, as he reluctantly nods.

I don't hesitate for a moment. I hop in the ambulance. The doors close on Fiona's amazed expression.

'I'm Leigh Gillingham.'

'Mark Fletcher.'

It should feel odd. It doesn't. I feel protective, useful, needed in that moment in a way I've never felt before.

I discover two things about visiting a hospital with a child. The first is that the staff are considerate, efficient, reassuring and knowledgeable. The second is that nonetheless the process is horrifying. Seb is taken away to be X-rayed. Mark is repeatedly questioned about how the accident happened. I guess with children's injuries, health workers can never be too careful. I reiterate seeing Seb fall from the slide. 'It was a split second. He just launched himself, fearless.'

'Yes, that's children for you,' comments the nurse, not unsympathetically.

Mark, Oli and I are asked to wait in a small room that is cheerfully decorated, specifically to distract children. Rainbows are painted on the walls. There are plastic toys scattered about and a basket full of books. Oli does not seem interested in any of them. He sits staring after the door where Seb was taken. Forlorn.

'Don't worry, the doctors know what they are doing. They are taking care of him,' I say with false brightness. The air conditioning in the room is brutal but I don't want to put my shirt back on, even though it's been returned to me, as it's covered in Seb's blood.

'What do you think they are doing in there?' Mark asks me.

I have no idea, but I realise Mark needs more than that. 'Stitching him up, X-rays. Like they said. It won't be long now. Someone will come out and tell you what's going on.' Mark nods. I find it bizarre that they both seem to believe me.

'Should I call your wife?' I've already checked out his left hand. It's just habit. The solid, steady gold band is of course nestled on his ring finger, as I expected. I mean, of course this man is going to be married, he has two kids with him. I just don't understand why he hasn't called her already. Does he think she's going to blame him because he was in charge at the time of the accident? A number of my friends have kids, I've seen that some parents do judge one another's parenting styles. 'He's so rough, when he plays with them.' 'He can't put a nappy on to save his life. I mean there are sticky tabs, how hard can it be?' But I don't know any parent that wouldn't want to be called if their child was being X-rayed. Or is it possible this man genuinely is in shock and hasn't thought that calling his wife is the next logical step?

He looks at me confused. 'I don't have a wife.'

'Oh.' I see. A weekend dad. He's divorced. Some part of my brain does a small mental high five with another part of my brain. Low, below my tummy button there is an entire conga dance going on. I mentally berate myself. I shouldn't be pleased that the man is divorced. It's sad for the kids, and as he's wearing the ring, I'm guessing he's still raw, not exactly back on the market. Yet I can't help my emotions. I should probably stop looking at his ring. It's rude.

'She's dead. She died.'

'Oh.' I want the ground to swallow me up. I don't know what to say. I'm not good with death. Who is good with death? Apparently, our ancestors were really chill with laying corpses out in their front rooms, but times change. Eventually I manage to mutter the completely uninspiring response, 'I'm sorry.'

'It's all right,' he shrugs. 'Well, it's not, obviously. It's completely shit. One hundred per cent shit, but it's not your fault.'

'When?' I ask.

'Just five months ago.' That perhaps explains why he behaved as though he was paralysed when Seb fell off the top of the slide. Not simply a matter of a useless father, unsure what to do for the best, although maybe it was that, his wife might have been the practical one. But I think it was horror, fear. *Not my boy too. Please, God, no.* After you've lost someone you never look at the world in the same way again, everything is unsure. You expect the worst. That's why Mark Fletcher asked a total stranger to come to the hospital with him. He didn't know how to cope alone with another tragedy.

'How?' As the question spills out of my mouth, I want to punch myself. It's none of my business. I just wondered if it was a fall, an accident, something that might have triggered his extreme response.

'Cancer.' Mark looks away, uncomfortable. I'm an idiot. I've overstepped. The intimacy forged in disaster isn't real, it has no roots. 'Look, thanks for your help but I've taken up a lot of your evening as is. I totally understand you must have somewhere more exciting than A&E where you need to be on a Saturday night.'

29

'No, not really,' I admit. He drags his gaze back up to mine. Perhaps pityingly, perhaps relieved.

At that moment the doctor who took Seb to be X-rayed reappears. He indicates that he wants to talk to Mark alone, that Mark needs to go to Seb now. Mark looks at Oli, clearly wondering what to do for the best, what should Oli hear?

'I could stay, sit here with Oli,' I offer. He looks doubtful. Of course, he must be worried. How can he trust me?

'I'm sane, safe,' I add. I rummage in my handbag, although I'm not 100 per cent sure what I'm hoping to find. I'm unlikely to have a certificate endorsing my sanity stashed in there. I pull out my wallet and then retrieve my driver's licence. I offer it to him. 'Look — Leigh Gillingham, this is my address. You can hang on to it whilst I hang on to your kid.' As I hear myself make the offer, I realise I've almost certainly convinced him I am nuts, although I was hoping to reassure. I'm needy. He can probably smell it. I like kids. I like him. I want to help. I rummage in my bag and retrieve a business card, it's a bit creased at the corner and dusty. I should probably buy one of those wallets designed specially to hold my cards but I think business cards might be a thing of the past soon. 'I'm a management consultant,' I say. Although when has that ever made anyone trust me more? I fish in my bag once again, this time I pull out a packet of M&S chocolate-covered raisins. 'Does Oli like raisins?' I ask. Oli glances at the packet, then at his father, then without waiting for permission, he reaches out and snatches them from me with considerably more keenness than his father is demonstrating. 'I'm starving,' he asserts, ripping the packet open with a dexterity

30

that I think is impressive in one so young. I wonder if he has had to do more for himself than other kids. Kids with mothers. He immediately tucks into them.

The exhausted-looking doctor says firmly, 'I really need you to come with me, Mr Fletcher.' Mark's gaze hurriedly bounces from me to my driver's licence and my dog-eared business card. He picks them both up. 'If you are sure.' He's already on his feet, following the doctor.

I grin at Oli. 'Would you like me to read you a story? There's a whole basket of books over there that I think anyone is allowed to root through.'

He shrugs. 'If you want.'

'Yeah, I want.' As I read, his head starts to droop with tiredness. He allows it to drop to my shoulder. I carefully put my arm around him.

'Can I climb on your knee?' he asks.

I nod, not able to find the words because my heart is singing so loudly.

4
Leigh

I was slow to sex. My mother demanded too much of my time and attention for me to develop a real relationship with a real boy. I was busy trying to fill the space of my father, who had left us when I was nine. Until I was twenty, my romantic life was mostly limited to my imagination, to crushes on popstars, movie stars and other inaccessibles such as my university tutors or gay men. I didn't keep a diary; I knew my mother had no personal boundaries and would not only feel entitled to read it, but most likely want to discuss the contents of it with me too. I stayed in my head. A vivid and filthy place to be. Depending on my mood, a labyrinth of desire, fear, hope, longing. I plotted elaborate trysts between myself and the current object of desire, I wrote poetry, I deconstructed the lyrics of love songs.

I had no idea.

I didn't have sex until I was twenty-one and then it was with a man whose first words afterwards were, 'You need to get going because my girlfriend will be home from work in an hour.' A girlfriend had not featured in my fantasies or his conversation. I was stunned to watch his casualness morph into cruelty in just moments.

The shock, disappointment and shame left me spiralling. My self-esteem plummeted. After that I didn't really hold an expectation that any man would date me exclusively; even if he claimed he was, I'd be dubious. I expected betrayal and complexity — not a great way to view the world. I'd grown up keeping everything close, not confiding my inner feelings and so didn't have a gaggle of girlfriends who could have normalised the shitty behaviour of men in their twenties, or a cheering mum who would promise me it would be all right in the end, that there were plenty more fish in the sea. Fish that were, more often than not, caught in their thirties when they'd grown up a bit. I confided some things in Fiona, but she didn't have much experience either so was unable to offer context or consolation. When I recounted a relationship disaster to Fiona, she would roll her eyes and say, 'Oh God, and you are so pretty. If men fuck you over there's no hope for someone as ordinary as me.' She'd half laugh as she said it, but I always got the feeling she wasn't entirely joking.

So, I realised that people played fast and loose with hearts and hymens, that it was best to stay a little secretive, protect yourself. If you had to choose then it was better to hurt than be hurt. Obviously. And the world as I saw it, was one where you had to choose.

Throughout my twenties I dated a series of different men. There was nearly always someone on the go. Sometimes relationships lasted a matter of hours, a couple lasted eighteen months. However long or brief they were, they followed a pattern. For all the years before my father left, I had watched my mother trying to make herself attractive enough to persuade him to stay as he always had one foot out of the door. She rotated through fad diets and punishing exercise and beauty regimes. Her tactic of being pretty and pleasing and pleasant (at least to him) was an unmitigated disaster and yet, without any other model, that was the mode I slipped into with men too. On dates I tried to be pretty, pleasing, pleasant. Young and still experimenting with my sense of self, I was happy to pursue the pastimes of my dates, I didn't have any hobbies anyhow. So, if a new boyfriend wanted to play tennis, ride a motorbike, swim in the sea, play video games, watch horror movies — I agreed. I found myself agreeing with their politics, or at least not speaking up if they contradicted mine. I even wore the clothes they liked to see me in, and so swapped between preppy, grungy, jeans and hoodies, floral dresses. What harm did it do? There are much worse things to be than a people-pleaser. Besides, having spent years being my mother's confidante in relation to how unhappy my father had made her, I find I'm a good listener. I don't judge and I'm sympathetic to others' struggles and problems. I get close to people quickly. There's nothing weird about being interested in other people's hobbies, families and lives. Not really. Maybe more people should try to be more accommodating. Maybe the world would be a happier place. Only I fell into the habit of moulding myself into their ideal. I was a chameleon. I gave each boyfriend the part of me I knew they would find palatable, but I never gave the whole package.

I guess I'd present myself as uncomplicated. Men adore uncomplicated. But I'm very complicated.

Mark is different. His life experiences are so much more profound than those of anyone else I've ever dated. He simply seems more grown up. He is thirty-nine, six years older than I am but besides that, he is a father and a widower. He hasn't got time or patience for games. He is straightforward, honest, sincere. Not that he's dull, far from it. It's just his sense of humour is old-fashioned, non-satirical. He likes things that are borderline corny; he loves a bit of harmless slapstick. It's pretty lovely.

Being with him is easy. These last six months have been refreshingly direct and purposeful. We have not played games. There are the boys to think about, games would be callous. The four of us left the hospital together. We shared a cab home. Relieved that Seb was glued back together. The thought, *it could have been worse* travelled with us in the cab. It turned out that we only lived ten minutes apart from one another. As I climbed out of the cab, he thanked me for everything I'd done and asked, 'Would it be all right if I call you tomorrow?'

'I'd like that.'

And he did call. He invited me over for tea. 'The boys have been asking after the nice lady who helped,' he told me, I guess making it clear that it was them who wanted me rather than him. He wasn't the sort who would want to give the wrong impression. This wasn't a date. It was fish fingers and chips, served with peas that were chased around the plate but hardly eaten. I was offered a choice of apple juice or water to drink.

'Sorry, I made the mistake of promising Oli he could choose what we'd eat,' said Mark as he apologetically put the plate in front of me. It was a noisy and disjointed evening. Mark hardly managed to get a sentence out uninterrupted but somehow, I still managed to find out more about him than I ever discovered about the closed and secretive men I'd dated in the past. Mark told me he had a sister who lived in Chicago, parents who lived in York. His best friend was called Toby and they'd been mates since secondary school. He went to university in Brighton, he dreamt of owning a boat but had never actually sailed anything other than a dinghy. He was a landscape gardener, which explained the tan and muscles, he admitted his business was struggling a bit because of juggling childcare since his wife got sick and then died.

'People have been great. Frances's parents live in the Midlands. They offered to move here but it was too much to ask of them. They need to stay near their friends in Frances's childhood home — I mean, they lost a daughter.' He shakes his head. 'Her sister, Paula, has been very good. A big help. She's north London.' People think losing a child is the worst thing that can happen in the world. I glance at the young boys — who are absorbed in trailing Lego cars through apple juice puddles and therefore not listening to our snatched and whispered conversations — and wonder if the worst thing in the world is losing your mother. I suppose it depends on the age of the person who dies. It isn't a competition. Grief seeps everywhere. 'Her friends from the various baby groups have been very kind. They've done a lot of pick-ups and drop-offs but there comes a point when everyone has to get back to their own lives.' He shrugged. Not self-pitying. Just a fact. He dug out a pea that Seb was trying to put up his nose, he reached for the kitchen roll, mopped up the apple juice, refilled Oli's water glass. 'Tell me about you? What do management consultants do exactly?'

I realised he needed a change of subject. Talking about death is exhausting, even for the bereaved. I started to tell him about efficient supply chain management, integrated IT systems and maximising efficiency with human resource. He laughed and told me I sounded like a corporate brochure, but he wasn't mocking, he was kindly, interested. 'Tell me exactly what your day looks like. Talk me through it.'

So I did. Blow by blow. Each telephone conversation, the endless research behind the presentations, which I sometimes don't get to present anyhow because someone more senior takes the credit. I told him about the long hours and weeks being sent away from your home. I told him how intense it gets with the people on your team, how we're like a family for a few short months, living in one another's pockets but then, when we are seconded elsewhere, we might never speak again. I confessed that it is a little lonely, working in this nomadic way.

Mark listened carefully asking the type of questions that proved as much. 'Wow, I'm so impressed. I just couldn't work in an office. I'd go mad. But I'm always so in awe of people who get their heads around business stuff,' he laughed, good-naturedly. It was refreshing. Often, I have to play down my work because some men are threatened by a woman with a higher earning capacity than theirs. 'Do you enjoy it?' Mark asked, as though this was all that mattered.

'I do, on the whole. It is stimulating. It pays well, which is great because it means I can treat my mum to the odd holiday. We grew up just the two of us, so I still sort of feel responsible for her happiness a lot of the time. And her bills. Earning well goes some way towards helping with that.'

I don't know what made me admit this. Normally I go out of my way to hide my mother's neediness. Mark just nodded. 'That's kind of you. Do you travel abroad at all with work?'

'No, mostly in the UK. There are opportunities to transfer to overseas offices, but that's never appealed to me. Well, again, my mum.' I shrugged. 'UK travel is disruptive enough. I haven't bought my own place. I suppose I could afford something but it's more of a question of where do I put down my roots?' I realised that I might just have confessed to waiting to find the right man, to help me make the decision about the right place and so I hurried on. 'I'm gunning for a senior manager role at the end of this year. If that promotion happens, a decade of hard graft will have been worth it.' I wanted to ask what Frances did for a living, if she worked out of the house, that is, but there is no reason to assume she would because she had two young boys. I held back because I thought it might seem impertinent.

'Frances was a teacher,' said Mark, as though he had read my mind. 'Although her career was a bit stop-start. Interrupted by two maternity leaves, two bouts of cancer.'

After tea Mark and Oli kicked a football around the garden. Seb wanted to join in, but Mark was being cautious because of his wound. Seb started to cry with tiredness and frustration. I instinctively picked him up, hitched him onto my hip and he rewarded my boldness by immediately settling, nuzzling into my neck. Mark looked relieved, grateful. I left just before the boys' bathtime.

The second time I went around for tea, we had lasagne and a glass of wine. Quickly, visiting Mark and the boys became the thing I most looked forward to.

'Are you dating him?' Fiona wanted to know.

'No.'

'But you want to?'

38

'Yes,' I muttered. I didn't want to look as though I was dissatisfied with our friendship, because I wasn't. Not exactly. I was enjoying what Mark was able to offer, I couldn't expect more. 'But it's not like that. He's grieving. I'm — '

'Handy.' I scowled at Fiona. 'Well, you *are*. Let's be honest, an extra pair of hands at bathtime and bedtime. Least the kids' bedtime,' she added with a wink, letting me know she didn't want to cause offence, she was just looking out for me.

'We're friends and I'm fine with that. I like going to the swimming baths and the park with them at the weekend. It feels really comfortable being around them all.'

'Just don't let yourself be friend-zoned. Mark is really hot and there aren't many hot men around. All these non-sexual playdates might be sending out the wrong message.'

After two months of 'playdates', Mark kissed me. We had been to Legoland and the boys had fallen to sleep in the back of the car on the journey home. We put them to bed clothed, not bothering to wake them to clean their teeth.

'Stay for a glass of wine.' I couldn't tell from his tone whether it was a question or an instruction. It didn't matter, I wasn't going to say no. He got the wine out of the fridge but before he even opened the bottle, he marched over to me, put one of his hands on the back of my head and pulled my lips onto his. It was intense, explosive. The sort of kiss that oozes energy, purpose. In seconds I was bent over the breakfast bar, my knickers around my ankles. It was the right side of rough. It was fast, dirty, exciting.

Not friend-zoned then.

5

Leigh

'Mark is a good man, one of the best.' My mother's voice oozes approval and relief. I smile, also relieved to have pleased her. Passed the test that neither of us thought I was ever going to get to sit. A man wants to marry me, a good man. I will be a wife. I've made it. 'You are so lucky,' she adds, a hint of wistfulness in her voice. I take a deep breath; the room has no oxygen. Never before has my mother called me lucky. I've longed for her to but the pronouncement, now it has come, seems bitter.

For as long as I can remember my mother has firmly asserted that we are unlucky. She and I. She said it often when I was growing up. Repeatedly. Small inconveniences would weigh on her disproportionately, but at the same time she seemed to expect and certainly accept the bothers, upsets and troubles, never challenging them or offering solutions, because she considered us unlucky. It was just the way it was. Not something to be contested, or even resented, something I ought to accept. My unluckiness. Goods arriving through the post, faulty or damaged, never got returned, she didn't trust the retailer to send a refund so she would make do with whatever she'd received. When she discovered damp or insufferably noisy neighbours in a rental, she didn't question landlords but instead shrugged and just complained of endless chest infections that she said were expected — and

40

indeed they were under those conditions. I did not get into the outstanding comprehensive school in my catchment area but had to get on a bus to travel to a much bigger, rougher one several miles away, however she didn't appeal the decision, the way some mothers successfully did, instead she just accepted it.

Then when, aged nineteen, I got mumps which led to the rare complication of viral meningitis, which in turn was identified as the reason for me having the rarer still case of early menopause at just twenty-four, my mother simply said it was unlucky that I had been born at a time before regular MMR vaccinations were the norm for schoolchildren. Just unlucky. She didn't say the early menopause and my subsequent infertility was devastating, soul-destroying, catastrophic.

Just unlucky.

I have been waiting my entire life to hear her call me lucky — it is contrary of me, then, to resent the implication once the words have been delivered. She doesn't think I deserve him. Not quite. My own mother. She thinks good luck, not good management, brought me to this point. She is secretly wondering, will my luck hold?

'It's a shame about the weather,' she adds. This morning when I woke up, it was drizzly and not the bright summer day of my imaginings. I'm trying to ignore the fact. 'Do you think that marquee will be waterproof?'

'Yes,' I reply firmly.

'If it rains heavily no one will be able to hear you say your vows. That's not something you'd have had to worry about if you'd married in a church.'

I reach for my phone. Check the weather. 'It's supposed to dry up in the next hour or so.'

41

We're getting married in Mark's garden. Our garden! We decided not to marry in a church because the last time the boys were in a church was at their mother's funeral and Mark and I did not want to prompt any difficult memories. Mark has no problem with the fact we are skipping a church service, he is not religious; if ever he believed in a God he stopped after watching his wife die of cancer when she was just thirty-two. I consider myself vaguely spiritual, although not crazy about dogmatic patriarchal doctrines. I suppose I had probably always thought I would marry in a church — if ever I was to marry at all — not for me so much as for my mother.

My mother is a regular churchgoer but she stopped trying to drag me there when I was nine; she was embarrassed in front of the other churchgoers by my open lack of enthusiasm for the prayers, recited by rote, that seemed to fall on deaf ears. That was around the time my father left us. My mother's response to his departure was to up the ante with God. No longer satisfied with weekly visits she went to mass daily; it wasn't clear who she was praying for — my father or herself. Despite not attending personally, my mother's beliefs — and her guilt and fear — have permeated my entire life. I have a very acutely developed conscience and actively choose to do the right thing whenever I can, even if it is inconvenient, boring or genuinely hard. It was difficult to know what the right thing to do was in the case of deciding where to marry, considering my mother's desire for a church wedding but playing that off against the boys' trauma. I briefly wondered whether I could simply find a church that was completely dissimilar to the cool, grey-stoned, nineteenth-century one Frances's funeral had taken place

42

in. Mark pointed out that modern churches don't make for great photos anyhow. I backed the boys. My mother is delighted she's going to be a grandmother but irritated that I didn't marry in a church because she thinks the whole thing seems a bit improper.

Not sanctified. I put a lot of energy into not letting her view get inside my head.

'Today, darling, try not to resent how much attention the boys will get.' I mentally roll my eyes at her but outwardly work hard to keep every muscle in my face still. For as long as I can remember I've aimed not to let her know what I'm really thinking. Focus. *I'm getting married. I will have a new family. I don't need to care what she thinks or says anymore.*

'Why would I resent it?'

'Well, no one would blame you, darling, if you did,' she says hurriedly. Identifying her mistake, a moment after she's made it. Situation normal. 'It's just that traditionally brides expect to be centre stage and command all the interest.'

I've insisted that the boys are very much centre stage throughout. I was the one who suggested that they invite their friends, that they should stand with us as we say our vows. That they wear navy blue linen suits, that echo their dad's. If I tell her all of this, it will sound as though I'm over-explaining. Somehow my sincerity will sound contrived. I simply add, 'It's really important that they are a big part of the celebration, that they know we are all in this together. I'm more than happy to share the oohs and aahs with the boys.'

Luckily at that point, before things could get heated, Fiona calls up the stairs that the car is waiting to take us to the wedding. If we don't get a move on, we'll be late. 'You don't want Mark thinking you've changed your mind,' Fiona yells.

Our wedding is a happy, chaotic, boozy, child-friendly affair. It flashes by as everyone warned me it would; a series of Technicolor images, clinking glasses, broad, sincere smiles. I expected to be the one who oohed and aahed the loudest over the boys but in fact when I saw the three of them stood at the top of the aisle waiting for me, I was swept away by a far greater emotion than considering how cute they looked. I cried. Big, gulpy, happy tears rolled down my face, ruining my make-up but making Mark's day. When I reached the top of the aisle, I could hardly stutter out my vows, I was that overawed. *That* damned happy!

Our guests look elegant, healthy, excited, every last one of them. I invited my friends, a couple of work colleagues, one or two of my mum's friends and their families. Naturally, Fiona is my bridesmaid. Mark invited more than twice the number of people I did, not at all kowtowed by the traditions that dictate sec-ond weddings ought to be smaller, quieter. He invited his entire extended family and all his friends. I try not to think of how many of the guests at my wedding were Frances's friends. To be fair, it is impossible to tell because everyone is thrilled for us, for him. I'm showered in compliments and congratulations. If people secretly think Mark marrying within a year of his wife's death is a little too soon, they have the good manners not to say it aloud.

After the ceremony, when we are milling around in happy clusters and I'm straining to keep my weight in the balls of my feet so my heels don't sink into the grass, I stand with Fiona, peaceful, content. I allow my gaze to drift across the scene of celebration and make an effort to lock it in my mind. All day I've consciously tried to hold onto the precious moments: Mark's expression as he first saw me drift towards him, the boys' laughter breaking through the chatter at regular intervals — my ear is attuned to that sound now, I can identify their laughter in amongst other kids' — the beautiful flower arrangements that are everywhere and fill the air with a heady, intoxicating scent, the fizz of champagne on my tongue, although I don't really need alcohol, I'm already drunk on joy. Seb's hot little hand has been firmly wedged in mine for a lot of the day but he slips my grasp and joyfully dashes off to join Oli and some other children who are clustering around the cupcake table.

I am awash with kind comments from my friends, casual as they feel free to dive in amongst this, the most intimate relationship and make a judgement call. *You did well there!* Well-meaning colleagues chime in too, *He's one of the good ones!* He is liked, popular. Exceptionally so. Since I started dating him, I have been somewhat overwhelmed by the constant wave of praise he garners. Before him I largely dated men that people rarely approved of, let alone admired.

He is admirable. I can't argue. Why would I even think of doing so? I have started joking that whilst people like me — they might even think I'm especially lovely, in fact — when they meet him, they like him more and they realise I'm actually the duff half of the couple! I make this joke with a smile in my voice, to show it doesn't bother me. Because what kind of woman would I be if I was bothered that people like my husband inordinate amounts? I am not overlooked. If anything, people notice me more now that I am his, and that I have the boys. He is used to being centre stage. A wife dying so young begs attention, as does being a really excellent single dad. Mark smiles a lot; he likes being liked. I mean, who doesn't? He doesn't have to work at it. Even when he stops smiling, say to have a conversation with the Year 1 teacher about the kid who bit Oli, he's still adorable. I'm so lucky he chose me.

'It's great that the weather hasn't spoilt a thing!' says Fiona.

'I know, right.' I shake my head.

'What?'

'Nothing.'

'What?'

She knows me too well. 'OK, this is crazy, but you know how my mother gets under my skin?'

'What's she said now?'

'Nothing. Well, nothing new. It's just that when I saw the weather this morning I did have a moment when I couldn't help but wonder, if there was a God was there a chance he was a bit miffed with me, feeling the brunt of my snub?'

'Because you didn't marry in a church?' I can hear the amusement in Fiona's voice. It helps. Her laughing at me exposes my silly superstition for what it is. Fear.

I allow myself to smile. 'I guess he's not that annoyed anyway. He hasn't sent a plague and pestilence, just grey skies and a bit of early morning drizzle.'

'Yeah, it's pretty low-grade for a slighted Almighty. Maybe it's Frances showing her displeasure,' Fiona teases, poking me playfully in the ribs. 'She's up in heaven, looking down at you and she's pretty pissed off that you've moved in on her hubby and kids *and* her home quite so swiftly.' Fiona, who does not have a religious belief in her head, laughs as she says this. She squeezes my shoulder affectionately, to show me she's teasing and means no harm at all.

I shiver. It is chilly and my floaty, flimsy dress was designed and picked for a brighter day.

'Look, you're shivering! She just walked over your grave.' Fiona howls at her own joke. I love Fiona, but we're not very alike. I'm all careful and good. Or at least I try to be. She's wild and fun and often makes bad choices. It's part of the reason I love her. It's unreasonable of me to feel uncomfortable. A moment ago, Fiona's irreverence was comforting. It's not her fault she always takes things too far and she's just stepped over to tactless, tasteless. Fiona only ever sees the joke, the joy. She clocks the anxiety in my face and softens. 'Seriously, Leigh, chill. The poor weather is a bit of a shame, but we live in England, crap weather is an odds-on favourite, not a surprise or a punishment.' I nod, bury my nose in my flowers. I want the clean, rich smell of the roses to overwhelm me. 'You do know that if there was such a thing as an afterlife — which there isn't —' Fiona rolls her eyes, dismissively — 'but if there was, and if Frances were looking down, surely she'd be really pleased that her sons have found a new mum to love them.'

'I'm not trying to replace her.' This is something I've said a hundred times in the months since I met and fell in love with Mark.

'I know you aren't, but you will, because the boys will love you and they will forget her. They are only young. It's for the best.'

'How are you so sure?' I mean about the boys retaining memories of their mother — or otherwise — but Fiona misunderstands me.

47

'That there is no afterlife? Well, it's a fairy tale, isn't it? It makes no sense. I mean, what happens when you and Mark die if Frances is already up there holding a seat for him? Are you going to have a cosy little three-some? I don't think a *ménage à trois* is your style.'

She is right, of course; none of the stories about the afterlife make sense. Nor does it make sense that God would punish me for deciding to marry in a garden to save the boys' feelings. If he is a vengeful God, he has murderers, terrorists and paedophiles to pursue. And from what I can gather — watching the news, reading online — those people often go unpunished.

'Hey, Leigh, I'm sorry. I didn't mean anything. Look, this is the best day of your life. You have the family you have always wanted, the family you thought you'd never have.'

She's right. There is nothing to worry about. Everything is going to be OK from now on. I have a family. It's a miracle. I stop even flirting with the idea of there being a God. Or lucky people and unlucky people trapped by fate and predestiny. I decide to make my own way from now on.

Mark is talking to a group of friends. He's laughing along with whatever it is they are saying but I sense that whilst chatting with them, he's also hunting me out. Checking I'm OK, that I'm not alone, that my mother hasn't upset me, that the wedding logistics haven't over-whelmed me. Things I've admitted to worrying about on the run-up to the wedding. We catch one another's gaze; he smiles at me. It's a warm, honest, open smile that completes me. I smile back, he blows me a kiss. I pretend to catch it. We both laugh. Then we each look about us again. Eyes scanning like a beam from a light-house. We simultaneously spot the boys, sat under the cupcake table, faces smeared with cream and delight. We are all having a perfect day. We're going to make our way as a family and it's going to be lovely.

6

Mark

Thursday 19th March 2020

'Where's Mum?'

'Don't know.'

Seb stares at his father, his dissatisfaction with that
answer radiating. 'Why hasn't she rung this week?'

'She's probably been too busy.' It's a low move. A
dig at his wife that pinches at the child but Mark is
furious with her, so he doesn't care.

'She's normally home by now,' Seb points out. He
sounds churlish and concerned. It's clear he doesn't
know which way to go. 'I need her to check my French
homework.'

'I'll have a look at it.'

Seb looks unimpressed. They are both aware that
Mark knows little about conjugating irregular verbs,
probably less than Seb himself and Seb is in the bottom set for languages. 'You're all right,' he mutters
and then slowly makes his way out of the kitchen. He
hasn't finished his breakfast, but Mark can't be bothered to shout at him, insist that he should return to
the table. He hasn't got much fight in him, or at least
what he has he's keeping to vent on Leigh.

Oli does not ask where his mother is, but he keeps
glancing at the kitchen clock. It's twenty-five past
eight. Both boys need to be getting to school. They are
going to be late. Normally Leigh is back just before

50

eight, sometimes if the trains play up, she bounds through the door at five past. The sleeper train gets in at 7.07 a.m. Leigh is always off the train the moment in arrives into Euston. Keen to get back home and see the boys before they go to school, even if it's only for a few minutes. She always calls if the train is running late. Always. She's a stickler for planning and time-tabling. She's forever telling them that her success as a management consultant comes from the fact she is in control of her time, doesn't allow a dead moment, maximises all the time she has, etc., etc. They often tease her about her slightly uncompromising approach but they all reluctantly accept that the structure she places on their lives is largely helpful.

It's definitely odd her not being here. Her not calling all week. Mark should have known the boys weren't going to be forever fobbed off with his unconvincing excuses that she probably had back-to-back meet-ings, that her phone was most likely out of charge, that maybe she'd even lost it.

'Why hasn't she just used the hotel telephone then?' Seb asked.

'She might have forgotten our numbers.'

'What, all of them? Even the house number.' Seb had looked contemptuous. He was twelve not six.

None of them have heard from her since Monday morning. She always works away Monday to Thurs-day, but normally she calls them a couple of times a day, messages on a more or less continuous basis. Messages to remind them what she has left for them in the freezer, what order to eat the organic, homemade meals and how long they take to heat up. She might message to say what time football practice starts or whether there is a permission slip for something or other that needs responding to. Oli in particular is often saying her remote micromanagement is annoying. Mark suspects that, like the time management, Leigh's concern is secretly appreciated. Often her messages are simply: *Hi, hope you've had a good day. Hi, how was the maths test?!! Hi, just thinking of you.*

This week, no one has received a single message.

'I'm not going to school, Dad,' says Oli. 'I think you should call the police.'

★ ★ ★

The doorbell chimes through the house, it seems to everyone that it is louder than it has ever been before. It shakes the walls, thumps the silence that they are stewing in.

'Is that her?' Oli yells down the stairs.

'I don't think it is. Why would she ring the bell? She has a key.' Yet Mark's heart quickens a fraction because he wants it to be. He really does. Deep down somewhere, he feels something more powerful than reason, yearning and regret combined. He longs for it to be her; at the same time, he knows it won't be. It can't be. It would be a miracle. He wants the miracle; the problem is he doesn't believe in them.

Oli, as a sometimes surly almost sixteen-year-old, who spends a lot of time trying to convince his mum and dad that he cares about nothing other than video games and getting his hands on illicit alcohol — and that he cares about his parents least of all — is obviously agitated, no doubt very worried. No amount of shrugging or hair flicking can disguise the fact. Both the boys had refused to go to school. Seb had burst into tears and said if his dad didn't call the police

52

then he would.

'Let's just see, shall we?'

'See what?' Seb demanded. 'She's not here to see! That's the point!'

Mark waited until ten, and then when his calls to Leigh had gone unanswered and they had not heard from her, when there was nothing on the news to explain a severe train or tube delay, Mark had finally called the police.

Hearing the doorbell has brought both boys out of their rooms. They are hovering at the top off the stairs, Mark is at the bottom. A matter of metres but somehow an unbridgeable gulf in that moment. Impassable. Too much. Mark knows he should say something comforting. He can't think what that might be so instead he mutters gruffly, 'I thought you were doing some schoolwork.'

'Couldn't concentrate,' says Oli.

'Got none,' responds Seb.

'Go and find something to do.' Mark has an unfortunate tendency to come over a bit short-tempered when he is stressed. If Leigh were here, she would put a discreet hand on his arm to gently remind him to go easy on their boys. Her big brown eyes would silently plead for patience. *They are frightened too.*

But she is not here. That is the problem.

Oli mutters something, Mark doesn't catch the exact words but gets the gist. Disappointment, disapproval. Fear. The boys stomp off to their separate rooms — hating the uncertainty but appearing to hate their father. Mark's back bends with the weight of it all. He wants to fold to his knees, fall to the floor, but he has to straighten up. What sort of impression would that give the police if they found him prone

53

and sobbing?

Mark opens the door and feels something whoosh around his being. He shivers for no logical reason. It was probably just the cold air getting into the house, the warmth of the house escaping but it feels like it is more than that. Mark's life — as he knows it — rushing out, and trouble charging in.

They tell him their names and show their badges. The woman, DC Clements is the more senior. The man — a boy really — says he is Constable Tanner. Aware that the boys — Oli almost certainly — will be lurking about, still within earshot and straining to absorb everything that will be said, Mark quickly confirms that yes, he is Mark Fletcher and yes, he called them about a missing person, his wife. Then he hurriedly invites them into the sitting room.

Mark finds himself staring at their uniforms — their radios, their torches, bulky belts and heavy boots — which seem dramatic and belligerent in the family front room. The Fletchers' house is pretty standard. Possibly a bit messier than average. Most of the furniture is from Next. The soft things are shades of grey and beige, the various tables — console, coffee, side — are a light rustic oak. Matching. Leigh likes things to match. Not that anyone generally notices what does or doesn't coordinate when visiting the Fletchers because of the mess and clutter. On the other hand, no one is likely to notice that the sofa is a bit saggy, even stained, and the tables have coffee cup rings on them. The war wounds the furniture has picked up over the years — through the boys spilling drinks or not using coasters — are largely covered up by the debris of family life: magazines, newspapers, ironing piles, school bags, books and sports kit. They are the sort of family that gather around the TV most nights. Other than Oli; Oli prefers his own company and mostly skulks in his room unless tempted out by food. A lot of their junk is dumped in the hall as soon as they come home from school and work, but a fair amount makes it into the sitting room too. From time to time Leigh or Mark lose patience with the mess, usually when they've lost something — the remote control, a set of keys — and then they threaten a clear-out. Sometimes, they even get around to it. Mark feels a physical pain in his chest as he recalls that Leigh made an effort and tidied the kitchen on Sunday, but she didn't get to smarten things in here because everything kicked off. The police are still standing.

'Have a seat, take a seat,' he offers. Both officers turn to the sofa and their gazes seem to drift across the mess, a bit helplessly, hopelessly. Mark sweeps at the clutter, carelessly shoving books and trainers off the couch and onto the floor. 'Please sit down.' He sounds overly insistent. An instruction, rather than an invitation, which is regrettable. He doesn't want to come across as aggressive. He wants them onside. He needs them to see him as everyone sees him. Mark is generally known as an easy-going sort of bloke. The secret is, he is not. Not really. Well, not always. Who is? It is just what he is known as. Reputations are not always fair or accurate. Not constant. Some are hard won and easily lost. Others gained easily but harder to shake.

But no one could expect Mark to be feeling easy right now.

DC Clements smiles and sits down. As she does so, she gestures to the chair opposite hers and Mark takes it, obediently. It is his house but it's clear to all of them that she is suddenly in charge. Mark doesn't mind. He needs her to be. He guesses at the police officer's age — he puts her in her early thirties but her brief yet calming smile suggests a cool confidence beyond her years. Mark has been making jokes about the police looking like kids for a while. When he does so, Leigh tells him not to go on that way. 'It ages you,' she insists. Leigh doesn't look her age and avoids admitting to it if she can.

Even though they are sat opposite each other, with a coffee table between them, Mark can smell cigarette smoke on the policewoman's breath and clothes. He tells most people he meets who smoke, what a disgusting death cancer is. People allow him to do that because he lost his first wife and it would seem disrespectful not allowing him to vent. To crusade. He doesn't bother giving his speech to the policewoman. He imagines she knows as much about horrible deaths as he does. Mark thinks that maybe he would smoke too, if he had her job.

'So, you've reported your wife missing.'

'Yes.'

'How long has she been missing?'

'I haven't seen her since Monday morning,' Mark admits.

'It's Thursday lunchtime, sir.' The 'sir' seems purposeful. Ostensibly respectful but in fact distancing, challenging. It's the male officer who says this. He has red acne spots erupting around his jawline, announcing the fact that — in relative terms — he's just crawled out of childhood. It's all ahead of him. The glory and gore of life. 'Why have you waited until now to call?'

'She works away Monday morning to Wednesday

56

and then gets the sleeper train from Edinburgh Wednesday night. We normally see her Thursday breakfast. I wasn't aware she was missing until she didn't show up this morning. She's a management consultant. She's currently working for a wind energy company based up in Scotland.'

'But you've called her place of work to confirm she was at work, Monday to Wednesday so not missing, just not at home, right.' Mark doesn't like the casual way the young policeman makes statements and simply lifts his inflection at the end of the sentence, hoping that passes as a question. Mark thinks he ought to be more formal, more thorough. He shakes his head.

'She didn't show up to work?' asks DC Clements.

'I don't know whether she did, or she didn't. I don't know who to call. I don't have a telephone number for her colleagues or her boss.' Mark feels awkward admitting this. He wasn't actually aware this was the case until he needed to call them this morning. But Leigh is an independent sort, they don't live in one another's pockets. If he needed to call her at work, he'd call her mobile, why would he have ever needed her boss's number?

'There isn't a head office you can reach?' Again, a statement dressed up as a question. Mark bites back his irritation at the young constable's lazy grammar.

'It's different with management consultants. Once they're assigned to a job, they're not contactable through the usual switchboard. If you think about it, people only ever call in management consultants when things are going wrong in their company, they don't really want to shout about it. The process is shrouded in secrecy. I'm not even sure which energy company she's working for.'

The police officers exchange a look. Mark is concerned that they are judging him, that they think he has failed as a husband, that he is uninterested in his wife's career, not enlightened enough. That will work against him. He tries to claw back. 'I've never needed to know the details. Normally we are in touch via phone a lot.'

'You do know the name of her company though, sir?' It is impossible to ignore the note of sarcasm.

'Yes. Peterson Windlooper. She's worked for them for about eight years.'

'We'll look into it,' says DC Clements. Mark smiles at her, gratefully. She doesn't smile back.

Constable Tanner carries on. 'So, you said normally you're in touch via phone a lot. Do I take it that hasn't been the case this week?' he asks.

'I haven't spoken to her.'

'Text? WhatsApp? Email? Anything?'

'No, nothing.'

Their eyes are now bolted on Mark. He can feel the power of their gazes although he's not looking at them but instead staring at the spot above their heads. 'Nothing? No word. And that's unusual?'

'Yes, it is. Of course it is,' Mark snaps. 'Like most couples we normally speak on the phone every day while she's away. She usually rings to say goodnight to the boys, and yes, we message regularly as well.'

'But you waited until now to report her missing?'

He sighs. It's going to come out. It might be important when and how it comes out; he thinks he should tell them straight away. It's never going to look good. 'We'd had a row. I thought she was sulking.' Mark still doesn't look at the police officers' faces. He would like to see their expressions, to judge what they are

58

thinking but he decides he can't risk trading that gain against them reading him and knowing what he's thinking. He imagines the police are trained in that sort of thing. Understanding what is said. Hearing what is left unsaid.

The policewoman nods to the younger officer. He takes out a notebook. It's incongruously old-fashioned, Mark thought they might have electronic notebooks nowadays. 'Constable Tanner is going to take some notes. So, let's rewind, shall we? The last time you saw your wife was when?'

'I said, Monday breakfast.'

'And that's when you had your row?'

'No, we rowed Sunday night.'

'What about?'

'It was silly. Nothing at all.' The officers wait. 'The boys and I had laughed at her dancing.' Tanner snorts and pulls Mark's attention. Mark stares at him resentfully. DC Clements also shoots him a hard look. He straightens his face.

'That doesn't seem like too big a deal, wasn't the air cleared by Monday morning?' asks Clements.

'It wasn't a big deal but, well, one thing led to another. It got out of hand. You know how rows do.'

'Enlighten me?'

'We ended up sleeping separately. Look, is this relevant?' Mark runs his hands through his hair, scratches hard at his scalp. It is a habit he's had since he was a kid; when he is stressed, he scratches his head. There was a time, just after Frances died, when he scratched his head so hard and frequently that he ripped at the skin; his scalp actually bled.

'We're just trying to establish your wife's state of mind.'

59

'Her state of mind?' Mark doesn't know. 'Leigh is not easy to read. She's usually very calm.' Almost cool. It's one of the things that attracted him to her in the first place, to be frank. She's not hysterical in any way. Not overly emotional. Well, not usually. When they met, Mark had had enough going on, enough emotions to handle — his and the boys' — he wouldn't have been able to cope with a sensitive, overly excitable woman. He needed a clear-sighted, dry-eyed, composed wife. 'That's why the row was so unusual. It wasn't like her to overreact the way she had. Yelling at me, at the boys.'

Then at bedtime she wouldn't just climb into bed and let the matter drop.

'I can't. I just can't,' she muttered as she dug out the spare duvet from the airing cupboard. 'I can't sleep in the same room as you.'

Mark didn't offer to take the sofa. Fuck her. She was being a cow.

They hardly spoke a word at breakfast. Just enough to convince Seb that everything was all right. You can still do that with twelve-year-olds, trick them into thinking you are the adult and you are steering the ship. Oli was less convinced; he has worked out that adults are just as lost as everyone else. She made Mark toast as usual, he didn't eat it. He was being a twat, making a point, rejecting her in a tiny pathetic way. He hadn't slept well. He kept thinking she would come upstairs and gently slip between the sheets. That they'd smudge into one another, no need for words, they'd both know it had been a daft row, blown out of all proportion. But she didn't.

At three in the morning, he got fed up of staring at the ceiling. He threw back the duvet and sneaked downstairs to her. Ready to swallow his pride, make the first move. He fully expected her to be wide awake, perhaps reading, perhaps just staring into the darkness as he had been. She was asleep. Her breathing deep and steady. He didn't know why, but her ability to sleep after everything that had been said annoyed him more than if he'd found her crying.

A wave of guilt sloshes into the room. It nearly drags him under. He takes a deep breath. 'She's missing. You should be looking for her, not wasting time sat here with me.'

'In most cases, after a domestic, there's a cooling-off period and then the wife comes home,' says the policeman. He sounds almost bored by this fact.

'It wasn't a domestic.' Mark doesn't like the choice of word, doesn't like where Tanner's mind has gone. You read it in the papers, don't you? *Police called to a domestic disturbance.* 'I didn't hit her or anything,' Mark insists.

'Have you? Ever?' This sharper question comes from the woman officer.

'No!' Mark realises he ought to stop talking. He's conscious that he may very well be making things worse. He's not thinking clearly. He feels like he's thirty seconds behind reality, like when you watch someone Skype on a news report and there's a time delay; they don't seem quite present, quite real. What they say isn't believable.

Mark can't catch up. He can't react quickly enough to save anything. His thoughts are disjointed, severed. It is to be expected considering the trauma and lack of sleep over the past few days. He feels as though he's dragging his body through someone else's life. Thank God he didn't say that out loud. No one should be

61

talking about dragging bodies. He doesn't feel fully conscious, but it isn't like dreaming or even having a night terror; the comfort of those is — however weird or disturbing — you eventually wake up. Mark knows he is not going to suddenly wake up and have his old life back. 'It was just a matter of hurt feelings,' he mutters defensively.

'I presume you've tried to call your wife? Sent her messages?'

'Yes, I called her on Tuesday.'

'Not Monday?'

'Yes but ...' The policeman holds his pen over his notebook. Poised, ready to write down whatever Mark says. Mark has to be careful. Exact. 'I called, she didn't pick up, so I left her a voice message, apologising. When she didn't get back to me, I just thought she was being overly sensitive. A bit, you know, difficult. Making a point. I've sent a couple of WhatsApp messages since, but she hasn't read them. Again, I thought she was making a point.'

'And now?'

'Now I'm worried.'

They ask more questions, quickfire, alternating between them. Mark's head swivels left to right as he responds and tries to keep up. Tries to be clear. Careful.

'Is anything missing?'

'Like what?'

'Anything: clothes, shoes, bag, her passport.'

'No, nothing. I don't think. I haven't checked everything. How would I know? She has a lot of clothes.'

'Have you contacted any of her friends?'

'I called her best friend, Fiona. She saw her on

62

Monday morning. Sometimes if Leigh is getting the later train up to Scotland, they meet up for a quick coffee before she sets off. Fiona says that happened but she hasn't seen or heard from Leigh since.'

'Is that usual?'

'They're very close. They're on the phone to each other all the time. So no, it's not usual. You should probably talk to Fiona.'

'And family members? We'll need a list of names and numbers of anyone she might have contacted.'

'OK.'

'Can we just have a look around?'

'If you like.'

'You mentioned the boys. You have children?'

'Yes, Oli and Sebastian.'

'How old are they?'

'Oli is sixteen next month and Sebastian is twelve.'

'Has she been in touch with either of them?'

'No.'

'You're sure?'

'Yes, I'm sure. They would have told me.'

'Can we talk to the boys all the same?'

'Well, I don't want them worried.'

'But you do want their mother found?'

'Of course.'

'Then it would be best if we talked to the boys. See if they have anything to add.'

Mark follows the officers into Seb's room. He's on his phone. Mark feels a flash of embarrassment, believing his parenting is under scrutiny when Clements comments, 'Oh, what are you playing?'

'Brawls Stars.'

'My nephew likes Subway Surfers, have you tried that?' Seb nods. He isn't fazed by the police; he has been brought up to trust and respect them. 'Are you looking for my mum?' he asks.

'Yeah, we are. You could help with that.' Seb's face lights up. He is a big fan of Sherlock Holmes. More the TV series than the books, much to Leigh's disappointment. She is always trying to get the boys to read more. Mark thinks Seb is most likely imagining working with the detectives following them around, dusting for fingerprints, putting taps on lines.

'Can you tell us when you last saw your mum?'

'Monday morning, she dropped me off at school. She doesn't need to, no one else is dropped off at my age. It's embarrassing.' He blushes. The ongoing family discussion about whether he needs picking up or dropping off is a constant in the house. Mark doesn't believe Seb needs the parental drop-offs and pick-up, Seb can more than manage the tube himself. Mark believes Leigh insists on doing them because *she* needs it. She misses the boys and feels guilty about the fact she is away half the week. She tries to suck up as much of them as she can when she's at home. 'She even picks me up on the days she's not working.'

'Does your dad pick you up when your mum is working?'

The Fletchers have taught their boys not to lie. Specifically, not to lie to people in authority. 'No. Mum thinks he does but I just get the tube home. Dad's always here waiting. It's our secret.'

DC Clements looks at Seb for a long time. Mark can see she wants to ask if they have any more secrets, but she is aware that he's a young boy, worried about his mother. 'Has she sent you any messages while she's been away?' Seb shakes his head, his eyes fill up with tears. He blinks hard. 'Well, here is my card. It has my telephone number on it. Be sure to tell me if your mum does get in touch, won't you? Don't feel you need to have secrets from me.'

Oli is more concerned when the policewoman knocks on his bedroom door and asks if she can come in. 'Hide the skunk,' she jokes. Oli blushes. Both boys inherited the habit of blushing from Mark. They all three turn pink if they are angry, embarrassed or even sometimes simply happy. Mark thinks it's frustrating. It isn't a very manly habit.

Oli isn't blushing because he smokes joints, it's just he finds adults embarrassing.

Clements takes a different approach with Oli than the one she used with Seb. She doesn't chatter about gaming or try to ingratiate herself. She gets straight to the point; she knows how to talk to teens with limited concentration levels or interest. 'Have you seen your mum since Monday? Heard from her at all?'

'Leigh's not my mum,' mutters Oli sulkily.

'Oli, stop it,' Mark warns. DC Clements looks quizzical. 'Technically, Leigh is Oli and Seb's stepmother but she's the only mother they've ever known,' Mark explains.

'That's not true. I remember my real mum,' mutters Oli. There is a darkness in the room. You can almost taste it.

'My first wife died of cancer when Oli was five years old. I suppose he remembers Frances a bit. But Leigh has been his mother since he was not quite seven.' Mark hated this conversation. It made him feel awkward and disloyal, to his first wife, to his second, to his son. Oli and Seb belonged to Frances but they belong to Leigh too. Also, he never knew how old to say Oli was when he and Leigh married. Today he has

65

gone for 'nearly seven' because then the mourning period sounded a little more respectful. Other times he's admitted to six to show that Leigh had picked up the reins a long time ago. It's complicated.

Initially Oli and Seb had known Leigh as Aunty Leigh. Then she became Mummy. She didn't push the title on them. They elected for it soon after the wedding. And for years Oli had referred to Leigh as Mummy, then Mum, but recently he'd started to call her Leigh and insist she wasn't his real mum. It had come up when they were rowing on Sunday. Mark knew this was just a phase his oldest son was going through, he was simply testing boundaries, like teens do. And yes, boundary testing could seem cruel, wounding.

'You should just ignore it. He's doing it for attention,' Mark had said to Leigh.

'I give him a lot of attention,' she pointed out.

'I know you do. Look, it's just a stage.'

Leigh — in a rare moment of showing her emotional vulnerability — had turned to Mark and said, 'It's not fair though, is it? Because being a mum isn't a stage. It's a constant. I'm not allowed to throw my toys out of the cot and say I've had enough.'

Had she? Had she had enough?

Mark is brought back to the here and now as Clements asks, 'Have you heard anything from your stepmum over the past few days, since Monday?' She is precise, persistent. Oli shakes his head. Mark sighs and thinks you would have to know the boy well to see his sadness, to the untrained eye he just looks bolshie, inaccessible. The detective leaves her card with him too.

The officers nose around the house a bit. Clements

66

asks to see Leigh's laptop. 'She has it with her.'

'And phone.'

'The same.'

'We'll need to see Leigh's social media accounts.'

'She doesn't do that stuff.'

'She's not on Facebook or Insta? Twitter? None of them?'

'No.' Mark looks proud. 'Old-fashioned, huh? But also, really admirable. She always says if anyone wants to reach her, they can pick up the phone. She really values a chat.'

'Have you got a photo?'

Mark shows her one on his phone. 'It was only taken on Saturday night.' Less than a week ago but also a time that is firmly in their history. Gone. The family were heading out for a meal. Nothing fancy, just the four of them going out for burgers. Seb had said his mum looked pretty. He insisted on taking the shot. Five days ago, a lifetime ago. Clements uses her phone to take a photo of the photo.

'Can we see the messages you sent Leigh over these past few days?'

Mark willingly gives up his phone. The messages are there, just as he described. There are no blue ticks indicating that they have been read. Just grey ones, saying they have been sent and delivered.

Sweetheart, I'm sorry about the other night. If you call me, I promise I'll be suitably contrite

Then . . .

Actually, it was seriously cool twerking ☺

Mark had added that because he was trying to lighten the mood. He didn't mean it. His wife really can't dance.

It doesn't matter anyway because she hasn't read

them. The messages are lingering in the ether somewhere. That black hole of miscommunications,
broken promises and lies. The messages are languish-
ing where betrayal can hide.

7

DC Clements

The minute the door to the Fletcher home bangs behind the police officers, Tanner asks, 'So, what do you think? Has she done a runner?'

'Maybe.'

'Or is she already dead?'

Clements shoots Tanner a filthy look. He doesn't notice or if he does, he doesn't care. 'Let's hope not,' she replies stiffly.

'Yeah, but it's always the husband that's done it. Isn't it? Statistically.'

'You are getting ahead of yourself, Tanner. Let's keep an open mind, shall we? At the moment we just need to file a missing persons report. And statistically it isn't *always* the husband — that would make our jobs too easy.'

Someone is reported missing every ninety seconds in the UK; 180,000 people are reported missing every year. A whole lot more go unreported. Clements knows the statistics. Around 97 per cent of missing people either come home, or are found dead, within a week. And around 99 per cent have come home or been found dead within a year. The numbers sound OK. You'd bet on them, maybe. Except that a year is a long time. Found dead is a bad result.

And then there is the 1 per cent who remain unaccounted for, sometimes forever. Clements lies awake at night thinking about the ones that don't come

69

home. Their faces haunt her; immortalised in holiday snaps, school photos or dressed in out-of-fashion wedding dresses. The image of Leigh Fletcher is already scorched onto her brain. She glances about, as she and Tanner walk down the street, automatically scanning women's faces; hoping to spot the Fletcher woman. It surprises and frustrates Clements that despite over a million CCTV cameras tracking movements, PIN numbers, databases, credit ratings, bank records, phone records, registration plate recognition, social media, tracking apps, emails, GPS and even bloody nosy neighbours, people can slip away unnoticed.

Or are dragged away?

Clements doesn't let her mind go there yet. It's not rational. Statistically, a missing adult has left of their own volition, although admittedly with varying levels of intentional planning and often more than one cause. She mentally runs through the checklist of why a person disappears and holds it up for inspection against what she knows about Leigh Fletcher. Mental health issues, diagnosed or not, account for up to eight in ten missing adults. Possible. Relationship breakdown is the reason for three in ten to do a runner. Mark Fletcher admitted to an argument, so not the garden of Eden, but one row is not usually enough to make a person leave home. In this case, dementia can be ruled out — four in every ten people with dementia will go missing at some point, often unintentionally. Homelessness can also be ruled out. Leigh has a lovely home. Financial issues? They were not apparent, but Clements will look into it. Abuse or domestic violence? You never know. She'd need to do a bit of digging.

Clements takes a deep breath, a clear, logical head

70

is paramount. She reminds herself something she was told in her training days. You can't let it get to you, you can't let it depress you or drive you mad. She coughs, 'The devil is in the detail, Tanner.'

Tanner shrugs. No matter what the superior officer says, his mind is made up to the way he wants this to go. Secretly, some part of him is hoping Leigh Fletcher is not only missing but chopped up and hidden under the floorboards somewhere. No, not really. He's only messing. But sort of. Because he's never investigated a murder and he's dying to. Excuse the pun.

If Tanner had more experience, he wouldn't be so keen. Murder cases are not glamorous, just sad. 'Let's hope this is something and nothing. That Leigh Fletcher is just cooling off after their argument. That she comes home before the end of the evening,' says Clements. But even as she says it, she can't help but think the absence of a social media platform usually flags a problem. For a woman of Leigh's age, it is unusual behaviour. There were many people who had accounts but don't show pictures, don't share much of their lives and just used it as a way to nose about in friends' and colleagues' worlds. There were many people who had privacy settings turned up to the max. Forty-three-year-old women that had no presence at all, generally had secrets. They wanted to be invisible.

8

Leigh

Tuesday 17th March

I'm parched. My wrist aches. My head too. I massage my wrist to get the blood to flow back into it. The pain in my head is unbearable but of course I do bear it, because what choice have I? I touch my skull tentatively, wondering if there might be a sticky gash. There isn't one but there is a tender bump at the back. Was I struck from behind? Or was I drugged? I think that's most likely. I don't know. I feel drugged, dense and opaque, yet at the same time my heart is hammering at a speed that will split me open from inside. Thinking is terrifying, horrifying. More painful than any physical discomfort. Thoughts of what might come next assault me. Dark and dreadful thoughts but I can't push them away.

Am I going to survive this?

What is going to happen to me?

I do not know what to do. I am without choices and that is alien to me. I always have choices. I am always able to act. But now, at least for the time being, I have to submit. I am locked up by a madman. Of course it is a madman because what sane person locks up another human being? But how mad? What is he going to do to me? My body quivers with shock and fear. I move my left arm and the chain fastening me to the radiator rattles again. I can't get used to the

72

sound. I'm powerless.

'What do you want with me? Why have you brought me here?' My shaky voice sails out into nothing. Into the space which is at once endless and yet claustrophobic. No response. I'm pretty sure he is just on the other side of the door. I can feel him, sense his menace. He hasn't said a word to me yet. His silence scares me. The light around the boarded window is fading. Can I have been here a full day? My fear is overpowering and debilitating. I crawl into a ball and cry.

★ ★ ★

I must fall to sleep and only realise as much when I wake with a jolt. I guess my body shut down as a defence mechanism but I'm furious at myself for losing any sense of time. Sleeping is careless. I should stay alert. I have to. I notice a bottle of sparkling water had been rolled into the room. Unsteadily I crawl towards it, snatch it up and glug too much of it down, too quickly. I don't know when more might next be delivered, I should ration myself. So I stop drinking. Or at least try to but as there is nothing else to do in this room, I find I keep taking sips. I can't stop myself. It seems like some level of control — doing something — even though it is probably the opposite thing to what I should be doing. Self-sabotage. My head is light and I can't think clearly.

Something switches from flight to fight. Whatever it is seems to be out of my control. I'm nothing more than a quivering bag of fear and adrenalin. 'I need some food!' I yell, suddenly furious. Furious more than afraid. 'I'm no fucking use to you dead!' I kick the wall I can reach. I immediately regret my outburst.

73

My foot aches. I'm an idiot to injure myself. I need to stay fit, in case an opportunity to escape presents itself. Besides, how do I know I am no use to him dead? I don't know what this sick creep wants. Maybe starving me to death is his plan. I should be conciliatory. I should be trying to find a connection, that's what happens on dramas on TV. That's what locked-up women do. They try to talk to their captors, find something human and empathetic about him.

It's such bullshit.

Be nice. Be good. Even when you have been abducted and chained. Especially then. I am sore and thirsty and afraid. Mostly that. So fucking afraid. I'm not able to behave as they do on TV. I yank at my chains again. Hard, so I hurt my shoulder. They clank and clash but don't give at all. 'Let me out, let me out!' Silence. I feel like a toddler that has thrown his biggest tantrum and the parent looks on unmoved, but simply — silently — points to the naughty step. I slump. The fight gone almost as fast as it arrived. 'Someone will come for me. They will be looking for me,' I insist.

Then I hear the typewriter again. Rat-tat-tat. The rustling. Paper under the door.

Who will come for you? Your husband?

I read the note and freeze. It doesn't feel like a question. It feels like a taunt.

9

Kai

'How's your mum?'

'The same.'

'Is she responding to the antibiotics?'

'It's too early to tell.' I try not to go into too much detail. Talking about illness — imminent death — is sad, everyone knows that. It is also boring; people don't admit that.

'Try and not worry, hey, darling? You know that Alzheimer's sufferers get a lot of UTIs. She's had them before and pulled through.' I know what that sentence has just cost my husband. This world I have brought to his door is alien to him, a little frightening if the truth be told. He doesn't want to think about my mother's wee. Of course not. I don't want to either. 'You know the delirium is a result of the infection. Her seeming agitated and restless is just a symptom.' He repeats back some of the information I have already given him in the past. Perhaps to demonstrate he listens to me, perhaps simply for something to say on the matter. 'At least they caught it in good time.' I once explained that if a UTI goes unrecognised and untreated for too long, it can spread to the bloodstream and become life-threatening. I don't like reminding him of that fact. It seems too dramatic. A little manipulative to introduce a 'what if' scenario. Nor do I mention that

75

UTIs make Alzheimer's patients aggressive, sometimes unrecognisable. It's all too much. Daan tries to change the subject. 'What is your hotel room like?' He knows, because I've told him I stay in the same place every time.

'It's a Travel Inn, Daan. I think you can imagine.'

'I wish you'd stay somewhere smarter.'

'It's a waste of money.'

'We have money to waste.'

'I know, but — ' I don't finish the sentence. When Daan and I go to a hotel, we only ever go to the very best ones. The ones that feature in colour supplements, that have a media team behind their Instagram account. High-thread-count bed linen and white fluffy robes are a starting point. We go to places where we can sip champagne whilst sharing enormous copper baths, stay in there until our fingers go wrinkly. Daan has introduced me to the sort of hotels that offer a private boat ride to an exclusive island, a clifftop hot tub that offers views of the caves, beaches, crashing waves, where we will be served a plate of fresh oysters. He can't imagine a mean single bed, a synthetic pillow, a bathroom that doesn't have Molton Brown toiletries. He would never stay anywhere less than the finest. He doesn't want me to. I've explained that luxury hotels aren't a part of visiting my mother, they can't be. I would find it obscene leaving a hospice and then sinking under a goose-down duvet. Even if I could find such a place nearby. 'You only want me staying somewhere plush so you can imagine me lying in a big bed,' I say, allowing him to hear the smile in my voice. I need to switch this up. For me, as much as him.

'No, I'm not so shallow,' he says. I can hear the

amusement and anticipation in his response. He knows where we are going. We have a lot of phone sex, we have to. 'I can imagine you in a shabby room, if you want.'

'It's not shabby,' I say defensively. 'It's just functional. Basic.' I have never let him visit my mother's care home in the north-east of England. He has offered to come with me on a number of occasions, of course, but I've never allowed it. The best explanation I can offer him is that there is family stuff that I have to do on my own.

'I don't care what sort of bed it is; the important thing is you lying in it. What are you wearing?' he asks.

'Nothing.' I always say *nothing*. I wonder if he really thinks that is likely or whether he knows I'm really still in my jeans and jumper, sometimes I'm in cosy pyjamas. It is just a game we both know the rules to.

'I wish I was with you.' His voice is low, thick with desire.

'I wish that too.'

'Do you know what I'd do if I were?'

'Tell me.' I do allow myself to lie back now. I unbutton my jeans.

'My hands and mouth will be all over you. My tongue in your mouth. Your little pussy, hot and wet, on my face. Your perfect little arse. My cock rock hard in hand. Your tongue all over it. Then you straddling me and riding it. My hands on your arse, looking up at your beautiful face and perfect tits as you fuck me insanely until I come hard inside you.'

It's blunt. Honest for that, and as usual I feel waves of lust build between my legs, rush through my body. My tits sit up, perky at the thought of being cupped, nipples harden, begging to be sucked. The only thing that I don't quite like is the word pussy. Together in bed, he'd use the c-word, but he never does on the phone. A step too far perhaps. I want to tell him that *pussy* is outdated, somehow dwells in the world of Austin Powers with words such as *groovy*, that can only be used ironically. But he prides himself on his command of the English language and use of idioms, so I don't tell him because I don't want to offend him. He's been using it for years now. It's too late.

Instead I respond by telling him precisely what I will lick, suck, fuck. The hard, primitive Anglo-Saxon words work their magic on my gentle, sophisticated Dutch husband. I hear him reach climax. It's an efficient process, we've been here before, but nonetheless an exciting one that we both value.

'I miss us.' His tone is forlorn. I shouldn't have rung him on a Sunday night. Normally I don't, I encourage him to go to the gym and I just send a WhatsApp message. Tonight, I needed him a little bit more than usual. I listen and hear him walk to the kitchen. I know he is going to pour himself a whisky nightcap. I listen as he opens a cupboard, retrieves a glass, the ice clatters into the glass and then cracks beneath the alcohol. We sometimes do this, just be on the line to one another, in comfortable silence. Especially after phone sex. It makes it seem more normal. If I was with him now, we'd both be having a drink. The preparation of a drink is supposed to be a celebratory sound. If you are drinking with your spouse, friends or family, I guess it is. Alone, the ice sounds like chains clinking. I think of Jacob Marley, dragging around his sins. A wave of sadness swooshes over me. Something telepathic as I sense his loneliness. 'When you are here with me, I feel full, purposeful, vibrant.

78

When you are not, I am a balloon well after the party is over, shrivelled. Used,' he says.

He's a poetic man. Confident that revealing his innermost thoughts to me is not only safe but desirable.

I understand. Things can get lonely in our beautiful, huge apartment. The strange thing is it can get stifling there too, despite the size. I don't have a day job. It's just not possible with my commitments here that are unpredictable but vital and non-negotiable. I constantly battle with feeling torn as it is, putting a third element in the mix — work — is too much. We don't need the money, so it doesn't make sense. However, not being gainfully employed does mean when I am not here, I am often alone in our penthouse. I spend my days going to the apartment gym or pool, but I find the joy of the convenience is negated by the feeling I am trapped. That I have trapped myself. I eat up time thinking about what food I should cook him, what underwear I should buy and parade around in. If you fill your head with enough little things there is no room for the big things. I've managed not to think about anything important at all for four years. I wonder if Daan feels similarly trapped when I'm not there? Most likely not. Not usually. He works in the city and has boisterous companionship all day long. What he feels when I have to be away is most likely less complicated, simply a bit lonely, possibly a bit sulky. I am suddenly swamped and exhausted by my ever-present concern that I am not being fair to him. This situation is untenable and unkind. But I don't have a choice. I have responsibilities.

'I'll be home tomorrow night. Shall we go out or stay in?'

79

'Let's stay in.' I can hear the growl in his voice and my body responds with another pulse.

'And on Tuesday we have people coming around, right?'

'Yes. Everyone has confirmed.'

We like throwing supper parties. Not dinner parties. Inviting people for dinner is a little passé, a little-try-too-hard for our friendship circle. In a similar way, we regularly eat out at the very best restaurants in London, but we rarely talk about going out for dinner. There must be no suggestion that it is an occasion. The whole thing must appear more spontaneous and be undervalued, even if we are visiting the sorts of places where you have to book weeks in advance, sometimes join a waiting list or promise to give up the table after ninety minutes. Paradoxically, casual is the most valued vibe amongst our attractive friends who try so intensely at everything: staying slim, staying on top, staying fit, staying informed, being brilliant, beautiful, the best. The people Daan and I invite to supper are bankers, broadsheet journalists, CFOs who nurtured internet start-ups twenty years ago and have watched them thrive, the occasional actor who has a film breaking in Hollywood. They are the top 1 per cent.

I like them though.

I wasn't expecting to. I'm far more ordinary in just about every way than anyone Daan knew before he met me. That is to say, my education and social background is very ordinary. I was however lucky that my parents' genes collided successfully and — there is no modest way to say this — I've always been considered pretty. Some would say quite exceptionally so. Although not my father, and since my father never

80

said it, I never really believed it or saw the value in it. Until, that is, I met Daan. Then I realised beauty is something I can bring to the table. When he first talked to me about the friends he made at his elite private school and at Harvard University, or the glossy, impressive colleagues and clients he wanted me to meet, I felt intimidated, sure I wasn't going to like them — worse that they weren't going to like me. But I was pleasantly surprised. Yes, some of them are arrogant and boring, others are superficial and vain but many of them are interesting, driven, ambitious. I found listening to their stories about their various roles in diverse industries exciting. I'm not stupid, I can easily hold my own and my obvious interest and reasonable knowledge about the world, combined with my slim frame and high cheekbones, means I fit right in on most occasions.

It's not as though I could tire of Daan's friends, or feel threatened or jealous of any one of them in particular, because while we throw a supper party about once a week, our guests are in constant rotation. I'm not expected to become bosom buddies with any of the chiselled and toned businesswomen or any of the beautiful clotheshorse wives who visit our home. The men remember me as charming but usually politely ask Daan about 'that lovely wife of yours' not bothering to commit my name to memory. Busy sorts, like these people, don't expect intimacy, just stimulation.

While I only expect to see most people every six months or so, often less frequently, I keep a logbook detailing who visits when, what I served (or what the caterers served), who sat next to whom, to avoid the catastrophe of serving anyone the same thing twice. The level of organisation clearly belying the casual

81

'oh you must pop over for supper'.

On Tuesday we are expecting six guests. A female MP and her obliging, smiley, balding husband, and two clients of Daan's who are both still with their first wives, conveniently. It will make for an easy group, which is good management, rather than good luck. Daan thinks about such things. No obvious *faux pas* on the horizon. I can guess the way they all voted at the last election. The clients' wives will no doubt discover they have people in common, something to do with their children's prep schools, most likely. I find I am looking forward to it. Possibly there will be an awkward moment when one of the women inevitably asks how old our children are. And I will explain that we don't have any. Sometimes I add 'yet', to ease the burden of embarrassment that might occur when people hear we are childless. Childfree. Depending on their viewpoint. Some plough on and ask why not? Assuming a desire and ability. Others politely mumble, 'Well, you are still young, there's time yet.' Again, assuming a desire and an ability.

The more polite guests just turn the conversation; they ask how we met, because everyone has a meet-cute story, even if they don't have offspring. It's safe territory. Was it technology or chemistry? Swipe right or eyes across a crowded room? We still make such a big deal about the distinction. As though either method is any less random.

We are often called an adorable couple. We look good together. We're frequently laughing. We do a lot of sport. We habitually urge the other one to finish a story.

'You tell it better!'

'No, you tell it!'

The story of how we met is always mine to tell, though, no debating. The beginning is always the sweetest bit. The forever, never-to-be-taken-back bit. The story that is subsequently shared with friends and family, that gleams and glistens despite the constant retelling. Perhaps it sparkles even brighter as though each time it is told it is being polished — which I suppose it is in a way.

Even ours. Despite everything.

'I miss us too,' I tell Daan.

10

Kai

Four years ago

The sun is shining. I mean, really unapologetically shining and it is only March, so we have no right or expectation of this. Normally the sun shining is an unequivocal joy to me, today it seems like a taunt. Shouldn't it be raining? Shouldn't it be grey and desolate? I can't stay in the office, eating a sandwich, hunched over my desk as usual. I might as well make the most of the fine weather, allow the sun to soothe me, I need comfort. Work is punishing. Everything is punishing.

I have just heard my father is dead. I mean literally just heard, this morning. I can't process it. I can't imagine that he's no longer on the planet. No longer anywhere. Freddie, the oldest of my three half-brothers, called my work landline. I don't know how he got my number. I can't remember giving it to him. I do remember writing it down for my dad, along with my mobile and my home number, years ago. Opportunities to reach out, scribbled on a notepad near the telephone that sits in his hallway. Stiff, restrained. Like everything about my father. Was it possible that the notebook had remained in the same position for all these years and Freddie found it? Or had Dad transcribed the numbers into his address book? I don't know and I find myself thinking about this gossamer-thin strand of longing, or hope, or something, stretching between us.

His death is unexpected. At least to me. I hadn't known he was ill because we are going through one of our phases of estrangement which happen periodically throughout my life. *Were* going through. *Happened.* Past tense. Funny formal word, *estranged.* We throw ourselves into formality, don't we? When we are ashamed, or sad or simply defeated. I don't know when else that word is used except when families splinter: husbands and wives, parents and their children. People who should be closest become *as strangers.* My father and I have not seen one another for over a year. We spoke on his birthday, it went badly, as it often did between us since years of tension and resentment simmer under the surface of our relationship, always threatening to erupt. Until now, I suppose. No chance of an eruption now. Or a reconciliation. Or anything.

My father always liked to give the impression that he was trying, that I was difficult, resistant. The implication was that the disappointing thing about our relationship was that we hadn't found a way to click, when in fact the disappointing thing about our relationship is that we don't have a relationship. *Didn't.* And now can't. My father liked to give the illusion that he was a good father to me, fair, that I stand equal with his three sons. That he worked just as hard to please me as he did them — harder, in fact. That also hurt. Because the truth is, he never had to work hard with them, with them it was effortless.

We've only exchanged a handful of texts since that birthday call. This morning, when Freddie awkwardly passed on the news, my first thought naturally was, *I should have rung more often*, because that is what people think in times like this. Regret is kneejerk. Apparently, the cancer was diagnosed eight months ago. Why didn't Freddie contact me before now? Now is too late. But I don't blame my blond-haired, blue-eyed brother. I never blamed any of them for coming after me, expanding into my space, inadvertently pushing me out of it. To blame takes a level of confidence and entitlement. I never had either thing when it came to my father.

What would I have said anyhow? Those never-happened calls would have been punctuated with long silences, awkward pauses, miscommunications. Recriminations. We have never found it easy to speak to one another, even at the best of times. Whenever they may have been.

I'm not much of a sharer. I don't want to tell anyone at work my news. I know they will make a fuss. Kindness will lead to them insisting I go home but I don't want to do that. Nor do I want to receive their sympathy when I'm unsure whether I'm entitled to it. I have often said that I hate my father — to his face, to my mother, to boyfriends when lying in bed, sheets soiled with fucking that couldn't quite exorcise out the complexes. I did not hate my dad and I have never been more aware of that fact than in the moment that I know I can never tell him.

All morning I carry on at work as though nothing has changed. I've always had a great poker face and a developed ability to compartmentalise. I chair a meeting, send emails, make calls. Then someone cancels my first afternoon meeting, opening up a rare three-hour break in my diary. The gap scares me. I want to keep busy, not to think. I have a mountain of emails to get through and a strategic mid-term project that needs some thinking time but I doubt my ability to concentrate on either, so I tell my PA that I am going to work offsite. My plan is to find a café with internet, surround myself with distracting strangers who I can watch and perhaps swap an unattached word or two with.

I wander along Piccadilly, trying to stay in the moment, trying not to give in to the grief that I can feel ballooning in my chest, making it hard to breathe steadily. I have cried a lot of tears over my father long before he died. Enough tears. Far too many. I don't want to waste any more. I am glad of the sunshine; it has enticed people out of their offices and apartments and so the streets are heaving. I concentrate on weaving in between the hurrying pedestrians. Everyone else seems purposeful, determined. By contrast, I feel as though I am floating, directionless. I glance in coffee-shop windows but my original plan of setting up camp in one has lost its appeal. I drift onwards but my shoes are a little tight, and too high for walking in London streets. Suddenly, the heat is uncomfortable; there is a tidal wave of humanity on the pavements and I am a fish swimming in the wrong direction. I feel sick, a little faint. So I dip into the cool and calmer courtyard of the Royal Academy.

I plonk myself down on the steps outside the gallery and scramble in my bag for my water bottle. I sip at it and then lose some minutes. Find some stillness. I am wearing dark blue trousers, so my shins quickly become hot. I take off my jacket and the skin of my arms soon tingles as the sun scorches. Sweat pools on my back. The shock of the news of my father's death is spreading through me, paralysing me. If it was raining,

I would have probably still been rooted to the steps, drenched, so the sun is a gift.

There are a large number of people sat in the fore-court and I am glad of it. I want humanity buzzing about me. Vibrant, alive. Blocking out what I obviously need to think about, process. Everyone is notably more buoyant than usual because of the unseasonably brilliant weather. I try to decide how much I want to commit to being involved. Striking up a conversation with a stranger would at least pass the time.

Waste time.

The thought makes me more nauseous. I don't want to think about how much time I have already wasted. Time I'll never get back. You only get one life. My father's is over. His death has left us both exposed.

The Royal Academy attracts an eclectic bunch. Mostly, earnest grey-haired types. There are worse things to be. Some people are cheats, or liars. Some people dodge their responsibilities. Some people are stuck in the past and waste the now. There are women wearing brightly coloured skirts and scarves, gossiping with their friends about their grandchildren and daughters-in-law. I spot an elderly gent with a yellow tie and hat from a different era, a girl with a leopard-print skirt, a young man with a purple Mohican. Every detail of this kaleidoscope of humanity becomes tattooed on my brain.

There are schoolgirls picnicking on the steps too, chatty, giggling, breathless. My eyes graze, my ears cherry-pick their conversations about sandwich fillings, boys and homework. They are given a two-minute warning that they need to leave. Their noise level rises as they begin to stand up, look for bins to deposit their waste. They need to find the loos, visit the gift shop, take one last look at . . . As they file past me — untidy gaggles, some still chewing, hungrily, others patting their flat bellies and yet worrying that they'd eaten too much — I am struck by the length of their legs and the smell of them. They look like teens but smell like children: sweat, crayons, paper, chocolate, excitement, a bundle of all that. Something in my heart swells, pinches, then relaxes. Groups of children always leave me with that sense of treasure found and lost. Their skirts are wound up at the waistband, apparently that doesn't get old.

The schoolgirls vanish under the cool arches, leaving the sanctuary of the gallery and spilling back onto the London streets; the packed tube, the chaotic queues, London proper.

I close my eyes and lean back against the low wall near the steps. I think I must drift off to sleep. My body and mind closing down, shutting out. I've always been good at that. Switching off is a survival technique. I don't know if it's moments, minutes, hours later when I wake up, disconcerted. I can smell marijuana.

The earthy, herby, somewhat sweet scent always slightly embarrasses me as I've never tried any drugs in my entire life. I know, extraordinary — and so smelling hash is basically a signal that someone infinitely more daring than I am is in the vicinity. Yet, I am also aware that hash is considered the gateway drug, soft — teens sometimes don't class it as a drug at all — so I also judge marijuana smokers as faintly loserish. I open my eyes, expecting to see an unkempt, beanie-wearing, bloated guy with a chubby roach indiscreetly hanging out his mouth. Instead I am met with the embodiment of sophistication, beauty, confidence.

Love's first imprint is precise. This is the when. This is the where. I will never understand the why.

He is wearing a crisp white shirt, and a dark blue tailored suit, he is lean, tanned. His blond hair is just long enough to suggest rogue, rebel, but not too long so as to alienate his wealthy clients or powerful peers. I think this man most likely does have both wealthy clients and powerful peers, my guess is lawyer or merchant banker. I wonder what he was doing so far from the city at — I check my watch — at 4.15 p.m. The lateness surprised me. I should be back at the office. How have I let time slip away from me? But I don't rise to go. Something about the sunshine, the sweet scent, the sexy smile stops me.

He does have a sexy smile. He is a coiled man, ready to spring.

He holds the roach out towards me, as though we are old friends. He raises his eyebrows questioning, daring. I shrug, all insouciance and take it from him, draw on it. First time ever. The smoke hits the back of my throat, leaving me feeling excited and scared. And I know, just know that this is our pattern carved out right in this moment. Everything that happens from now on will be a repeat of this simple action. This is who I am when I am with him. This is who he makes me be. Who he allows me to be. A woman who tries things, who takes up dares. A woman who smokes a joint, who takes pills, who talks to strangers, who drops to her knees to deliver a blow job in a public loo.

I don't know how I know that the rules have all been thrown out of the window, but they have.

The smoke passes down my throat, wraps itself around my lungs. It is as though I am taking my first

90

breath ever. As I breathe out, I feel the tension pour from me. I look to the ground, expecting a steaming pile of fear or regret. I am surprised to see nothing other than a paving stone, a small insect scurrying, popping up from one crack hiding down in another. I take another drag. The air is warm. A huge cocoon. After an afternoon in the sun the skin on my face is tight, slightly seared.

'Do you want to go for a drink?' he asks. I nod. 'I'm Daan,' he says.

'You have an accent,' I comment clumsily. It could have been worse. I could have blurted that I like accents.

'I'm Dutch.' He nods at the roach, as though his nationality explains everything. He doesn't really believe he is breaking the rules by smoking this in public, although of course he is because the law is different in the UK. His shrug suggests the rules are beneath him, provincial.

'I'm Kai.'

'Cool name.'

He stands up and I note his powerful build, he is way above average height. Six feet four, maybe five. He stretches his hand down to me and pulls me to my feet. He doesn't let go of my hand but threads his fingers through mine and I let him. It should be odd, but it isn't, it's the most natural thing in the world. He leads the way. Mentally I accept that is pattern two set in stone. He leads, I will follow.

He knows a place. I like that. It's refreshing to meet a man who has ideas about what we should do and where we should go. I find myself in a rooftop bar, the view offers flashes of buildings in the throes of regeneration and gentrification. I feel dizzy thinking

91

about how exciting it is to be up above. Looking down. Money allows that, I suppose. By 5.30 p.m. we have already drunk a couple of gin and tonics each. The music thumps around me. I feel it in my head, chest, knees and between my legs. Or is that him I feel inside me? Not literally, of course. Not yet. But I think that is where this is going. Where we are going. There is an immediate and intense sexual attraction, the sort that is rare and coveted. It feels as though he has climbed inside me. That I've accepted him.

Everyone is younger than I am on this rooftop, in their twenties and early thirties. Daan tells me that he is thirty-five, I throw caution to the wind and tell him my age, he seems delighted. 'Ah, an older woman,' he smiles wolfishly and buys me another drink. We move on to tequila shots. We lick salt off one another's hands. Who am I? I don't know. Not myself. No one.

The rooftop quickly fills up, dating couples mostly. Glamorous women with hair and nail extensions, full make-up and scanty dresses; men with groomed beards, obvious intentions, business expense accounts. These people smudge up against each other.

'I love meeting new people,' I tell him, giddy, drunk, high.

'I have such respect for people who do,' he replies. He moves closer to me, bends to close the gap between us, so I can hear him clearly. I feel his breath on my cheek, and it blows my sense away. There is nothing but sex all around us. New and perfect. Old and established. Burnt-out, burning bright, angry, pitiful, grateful, unclassifiable.

'There are so many people. I feel the ache of being only one of them and want to be more,' I tell Daan. It is a dramatic thing to say. Something to do with my

92

father's death, or maybe the hash. Both. A combination. Chicken and egg.

'What do you mean?' He looks interested. I am interesting for the first time in a long time. Maybe ever.

'Well, the problem with being only one person is you can disappear. You can be snuffed out.'

'That's a sad thought.' I shrug but decide not to tell him about my father. How I am entitled to have sad thoughts, this day above all days. I am thinking about mortality, about the meaning of it all. Why are we here? 'Do you fancy another drink?' he asks.

I do, and I feel entitled to another drink. Several. Too many. We talk, he has a lot of interesting stories. He comes from money, made through fibre optics and oil. He doesn't impart this information in a crass way, simply through dribs and drabs, asides to the main tale he is telling and yet I know he is trying to impress me. I'm flattered he's bothering.

'We had to take a helicopter or else I would have missed my mother's birthday bash. She would never have forgiven me, but I was in such a hurry I left her gift on the helipad, so I am a bad son anyway!'

'The Heinekens are old family friends. They are very down-to-earth, really, like everyone else, but their parties never run dry.'

He sparkles. We laugh. At some point, he puts his hands on my throat, tips my head up to his, bends down. I kiss him. A man that I've only just met. Who I know nothing about. I'm not usually a fan of public displays of affection. I expect it to feel strange, wrong. It doesn't. It feels absolutely safe. Correct.

We have sex in the disabled loo in the basement of the bar. It sounds seedy. Awful. I suppose it is, but it doesn't feel awful. It is the right sort of bad. His hands are clumsy, unwieldy, ill-fitting. I like the strangeness. I like the fact he doesn't know how to please me, and we'll have to learn, or I'll leave unsatisfied and maybe that will be for the best. I'd be lying if I said it was great sex from the get-go. To begin with it is good sex, made interesting because it is so wrong, so dangerous. But then something slips or jumps, and it becomes great. The orgasm he pulls from me heats my belly and then rolls through my limbs, chasing the alcohol that has already seeped into every part of my body. The desire will ultimately settle in my mind, the most dangerous place of all. He leaves me feeling light, rather than weighed down, which is good. But I also feel flimsy, rather than substantial. If that is a red flag, I ignore it.

Afterwards, I pull up my knickers, mop up the desire. I have never done anything like this before and I wait for the embarrassment (mine), the dismissal (his). My mind gallops, planning, plotting. Preparing. Modern dating is a minefield. There is ghosting and haunting, being benched, breadcrumbed and kittenfished. Countless different ways for people to hurt one another. These are the new ways, or at least the new names, the old ways are still very much in existence too. Lies, deceit, rejection, regret. I don't want to get involved with all of that. It has been years since I started up any sort of a relationship. A man like Daan: handsome, young, tall, confident, wealthy, will have a pick of women. I can't risk my peace of mind. He will be trouble. I should simply walk away right now. I really should.

He offers to get me another drink. I watch him head towards the bar. He effortlessly cuts swathes through

94

the crowds, people part for him. Men glance nervously upwards, clocking his height, women glance appreciatively, noting his beauty. I like it but I'm afraid of it. I could just slip away now. I can't flatter myself that he'll be too worried. Most likely, he'll just pass the drink to the next pretty, willing woman. Why is he even spending time with me? Novelty? There are so many beautiful, brilliant, younger women to pick from. Yes, I am drunk, but somehow some deep reserve of self-preservation has kicked in, and I know that giving him a way to get into my life, my head, my heart would be ruinous. I will get hurt.

He returns, hands me a glass of champagne. 'How can I reach you?'

It's flattering. A man wanting to see you again after you've shagged him is not to be taken for granted. It's tempting to trust him but impossible.

'You can give me your email, I'll contact you,' I say.

'Email?' He seems amused. 'Not my number or my Insta?'

'Your email.' I like the thought that that ball is in my court. I can contact him if I want to at any point although I'm not planning to. I must leave this here. One illicit night, on the back of an incredible shock. A treat. A holiday from work, my mother, all my responsibilities. Not to be excused but perhaps possible to explain. I've got away with it. I should count myself lucky. I should leave well alone.

95

11

Kai

But I don't leave well alone. I can't. I get home and expect to be able to compartmentalise the incident, consign it to a deep crevasse in my mind. Left alone, not disturbed, not disturbing. I tell myself it was just a flirtation. Exciting, electrifying. Isolated, contained. Nowhere to go. No future. A man like that would simply play with me. Let me down. It is not worth the risk, the inevitable heartbreak. But my real life conspires to be as hard and dull as possible so that he glistens and glitters all the more brightly. There is the funeral to attend, on hearing news of my father's death my mother slips further into decline. She's needy, angry, regretful. Days are lost to cleaning cat sick off the bed, sorting out dark and light wash loads, ploughing through towers of ironing, pairing socks, picking up dry cleaning, paying bills, shopping, cooking, cleaning, answering to my boss, managing my team, each one with their own spider's web of demands and desires. Domestic and professional responsibilities threaten to overwhelm and bring little joy. He was joyful. The ball is in my court and I pick it up, serve a volley right over the net by setting up a new non-work email account and emailing him.

Is there a feeling like it? When the small envelope icon bounces onto your screen and suddenly it's as though his fingers are on you again, in you again? We swap increasingly flirty emails, dozens every day.

I wonder whether he is sending dozens of emails to dozens of women. Probably, but as I'm not planning on meeting up with the man, not allowing him in, it doesn't matter. It's just a game, a distraction. It is flattering, being rediscovered — reinvented even. We don't speak. Our communication is confined to email. He tells me he works mostly from the offices in Amsterdam, that he is only in London once a month or so. I receive this news with relief. See, this man could not have a proper relationship with me. He is like all the men in my history, aloof, unattainable, unreachable. He tells me when he will next be in the UK. He writes that he'd like to see me again.

How many other women have you sent this exact email to?

He sends back the startled, pink-faced emoji. **Just you!!** He uses a lot of emojis and exclamation marks. I try to avoid both. I try not to trivialise or sensationalise. I'm walking a tightrope. He waits a moment. I wait too. His next email pings into my inbox. Heart beating quickly, I open it up. He explicitly tells me exactly what he wants to do with me. It's a good thing I set up this account outside work, as the profanity filter would never have allowed it through. My heart beats even faster, and there's the quickening between my legs too. I email back and tell him I can't see him.

Can't see me or don't want to see me? 🙁

Can't, I reply, honestly. I want to and I won't lie about that.

There's no such thing as can't. What are you afraid of?

He doesn't bother waiting for an answer, not that I would have been able to give him one. He simply adds.

97

See you at 9 a.m. on Wednesday. Breakfast at The Wolseley.

He doesn't email me again and I don't email to confirm whether I will or will not turn up.

I do go, even though it requires me taking time off work. I tell them I am going to the dentist. Breakfast, what harm could there be in breakfast? We eat full Englishes, or at least we order them, but then both of us helplessly push the food around our plates. 'You've put me off my food,' he admits. 'I'm never off my food.' He sounds surprised and a little bit annoyed with himself. I haven't eaten well for two weeks, since we met. I can't deny it, I'm enjoying the hollowness that I feel in my belly. I'm bright-eyed, despite not sleeping. I look suspiciously like a woman falling in love.

We catch a cab to an apartment that he tells me his family own. He's vague, the way rich people who are slightly embarrassed by their glut sometimes are. I call my PA and tell her that my face is too numb for me to come back into the office straight away. That I'll work from home but try to get in later.

His apartment is breathtaking. Not my usual style, because it is minimalist, uber-stylish and functional. My home is stuffed with objects that I've kept long after they've ceased to have a practical use because of the memories they harbour. Still, I find myself admiring it for what it is. Other. The penthouse suite is sixteen floors up. We are surrounded by glass walls affording tremendous views. I am on top of the world. There are much taller buildings scattered across London's skyline: countless offices, some hotels, the Shard obviously towers above us. Yet I think I am tickling the toes of the gods, miles away from being mortal.

'You must get fabulous views of the fireworks on New Year's Eve from here,' I comment. He shrugs, accustomed to privilege, the best views, seats, service, wine. He probably doesn't notice it. I feel silly, gauche. He continues to twist the champagne bottle he is holding, explaining this is the proper way to open a bottle, not forcing the cork with the thumb. He smiles as the discreet pouf sound heralds his success, no uncouth explosion, no mopping of the overspill. Although privately a tiny part of me misses the vulgar, celebratory pop.

He had the champagne on ice. He knew I was coming here. The whole thing feels suspiciously sleek; I try not to think of the women who have trodden this path before me. Or the ones that will come after. He hands me a glass of champagne, a coupe not a flute. Waves of desire throw me off my feet, wash sense out of my head. I barely manage to take a sip before he takes it off me, sets it aside and I fall back on to his bed. He briefly kisses my mouth but quickly moves on to lap the lips between my legs. He does so with such incredible vigour and enthusiasm, something I've always enjoyed, and he obviously loves, so I love it too. I push my hips towards him. Arch my back. Offer myself up. I burn for him.

Afterwards, I stand naked looking out of his window. Too high up to worry about being seen, much more interested in what I can see. London is shimmering. Blue skies and sunbeams bounce on the Thames, transforming the green sludge into a silver slithering snake. Light reflects and refracts off every window of every building. The city gleams. An illusion of frosting or gilding. I can see the Tower of London, London Bridge and HMS *Belfast* stately squatting on the Thames. The Tower is the size of a Lego castle. It is like a beehive with endless streams of tourists buzzing in and out. I watch boats chug from Westminster to Greenwich Pier. I wave at the passengers, but they can't see me, I am far too high up. I am used to being invisible, and this time it is useful.

'The Tower of London is a great thing to see every day,' I comment. He nods. Affable but dazed the way men are after acrobatic sex that ends in rare mutual orgasms. 'It reminds us of our mortality. We're up here, feeling big but really we're quite small.' The trains run below me to and fro; determined, relentless. All of this — the bee-like tourists, the ancient palace, Southern Rail, give me permission somehow to risk everything. To throw my lot in with this man. To dare to see where it goes. Because those things go on regardless of the decisions I make. I am small and want to be bigger.

He gets out of bed, makes me a coffee, not bothering to dress.

I can't take my eyes off his smooth buttocks, his relaxed cock. He hands me a double espresso, no sugar. 'I guessed you would take your coffee strong and black.' Normally I drink sweetened cappuccinos. I took my coffee strong and black when I was a student. His barista skills have somehow stripped me back to that hopeful, experimental, promising person that I once was. I drink the coffee; tell him I have to go. Leave before he asks me to.

I travel back to the office, via tube. He stays between my thighs, wet and full. Long after I'm sat behind my desk, I feel him.

★ ★ ★

100

I do not imagine it will last any length of time. This thing we have. Whatever it is. His youth, looks, wealth will guarantee as much. Every time I am with him, I think it is the last and value it all the more for that. However, I find that we are together even when we are apart, the presence of him stays in my head, on my hips and tits, between my legs. Throbbing, pulsing, like life. Until the next time.

I've given him my telephone number and so now we speak often and message constantly. I lose hours typing flirty messages in WhatsApp. I practically orgasm when I see the word '**typing . . .**' and I know he is across the channel but also right next to me. We only see each other once a month as he still lives and works in Amsterdam. He's busy, inaccessible, important, impressive. I am very certain I am his London booty call. Nothing more. I imagine there are other women in other cities. Maybe one woman in particular. Sometimes, I even wonder if he is married. It is possible. I don't ask. I tell myself I can't be jealous. Such a destructive, hopeless, pointless emotion.

Yet, I am jealous. Eaten up with it.

I find myself googling him in the dead of night. Sifting through his social media accounts. Then — when my eyes are sore and tight with staring at every pixel, reading every comment, reading into every exclamation mark — I look at the accounts of his friends and family, hoping to see his familiar, suave, blond image on their pages. I do not request Friend status, I do not heart any of his posts. I remain invisible, untraceable. There are photos of him with other women. His arm slung casually around tanned shoulders, slim waists. It is impossible to tell if these women are lovers or friends. He is discreet, careful. I am mad to trust him.

It becomes wearing. I can't get a decent night's sleep. My priorities are warped, my responsibilities are neglected. I'm tired, tearful. Unreasonable.

And so, after six months I try to end it. I try to leave.

I force a row, behave brutally, spit out hurtful truths that every couple knows about each other, but they manage to suppress, to curtail, in the name of harmony. I pick at the scab. Make us bleed. I finish it. Or he does. It's nuanced. Unclear who finally ends things as it happens so quickly. In just minutes I tear us apart, which suggests we are only paper thin. I give him an ultimatum, it is in temper and frustration and he probably knows I don't mean it even as I issue it, but I choose a time when he's under pressure at work, rushing between meetings. He hasn't got time to debate or think.

'Meeting up once a month is pointless. How can we have a relationship when you live in another country?' He is confused because haven't I always given the impression that I like the casual nature of what we have? 'You are just stopping me having meaningful relationships elsewhere. You're not thinking of me in this at all. You are spoilt and selfish.' I pull the thread that stitches us together. The space, his absence makes us possible. My words wound, and I'm certain he'll want to bleed out alone.

'We can't discuss this over the phone,' he says stiffly.

'But I want to.'

'I don't.'

'I'm sick of doing everything your way.'

'I wish you would stay calm, be rational, Kai.'

'You are so cold. You are incapable of real feeling,' I snap accusingly. I imagine his upper lip quivering.

Not because he is close to crying — not the sort — he is angry with me for exposing him. For exposing us both. The telephone is a cruel way to end a relationship. He stays silent. 'Haven't you anything to say?' I demand.

'Let's talk about it when I see you next.'

'I want to talk about it *now*.' Because I can't let there be a next time. Every time leads to another next time.

'It's better face to face. It's better if we wait,' he insists, firmly.

'Now!' I all but stamp my feet. 'Now or let's just call it a day.'

He sighs. I hear his breath. Imagine I feel it. 'Then we should call it a day.'

'Fine.' I hang up and relief whooshes through my body, almost knocks me over. I reel.

After the relief comes the agony. I miss him so much. I hadn't expected that. I hadn't realised how quickly he'd been absorbed into my daily routine, my consciousness. The words, whilst being the ones I was looking for, cause me to wander around as though someone has beaten me. I hurt. I feel like I am being ripped apart. Split in two. If only. I call work and say I have flu. I go to bed, pull the duvet over my head. It feels like a sickness. My heart, my back, my head aches. I do not cry. I am too sad to cry. It surprises me how much he matters.

The world becomes duller, as though someone has dropped down a shade. Cut off the light and warmth. I can't find any joy where I found it before, which makes me ashamed. Meeting friends for coffee is melancholy, not uplifting, attending book club is dull rather than stimulating. It feels like I am encased in an impenetrable mist. I can't concentrate at work as I check my personal email account repeatedly, obsessively, every fifteen minutes, every ten. Every three. I recall the things I said. Harsh and impossible to retract. I told him not to contact me: no phone calls, no emails, no messages.

It takes a week for him to decide to ignore my dictate. It feels like a month, a year.

I cry when the text comes. Awash with relief, again. A total flip-flop of thought. Which makes no sense. I had deleted his number but not blocked him. It reads, **Come to me.**

I can't not. I text back within seconds. **Where? When?**

When I arrive at Sushisamba, a Japanese-South American fusion restaurant with stellar views and dreamy interior (because Daan never sacrifices style, not even during times of emotional turmoil), he seems different, changed. Dipped in pain and self-knowledge. Has he missed me too? He must have. Why else get in touch?

'I'm sorry,' we blurt, simultaneously.

'You don't need to be more committed, I'm rushing things,' I add, because I've had time to think about what I can cope with, what I can manage. What he might throw my way. If it is just once a month and there is no contact in between maybe I won't drive myself wild with jealousy. Maybe it will be enough. I don't want to be that woman, but I don't think I have a choice anymore. I could be her.

We talk. We smooth it out as best we can. I try to explain my insecurities but can't explain everything to him. I probably should. This moment of clarity and honesty would be the time to tell him everything about myself, to shine a light on what we actually have going on here. But I don't. I hold part of myself back, it's habit and now necessity. What if he walked away from me once he knew all about me? I know now I can't lose him. The early lunch stretches into the afternoon. But I should be at work, I've taken so much time off recently though, what harm can one more afternoon do? I'll give some excuse about needing a blood test, I'll imply that they are investigating a potentially serious health issue, then people won't pry. I might not be asked for a doctor's note. I'm shocked at how fearlessly I lie to secure time with Daan. I had thought we were meeting for more sex. I imagined him dropping to his knees, pulling my knickers aside and licking me out. Maybe not in the restaurant but back at his apartment. Or I would drop to my knees. Take him in my mouth. Tongues and fingers. Sucking, flicking and fucking.

He does drop to his knees. In the restaurant. 'Marry me.'

'What?' I feel the proposal roar through my body, it doesn't reach my head.

'You are right, once a month is not a relationship. I've requested a transfer. It's all been agreed. I'm moving here to London. There is something about you, Kai, that's different from any other woman I've ever met. You ooze independence, self-containment. I love it. I love you. Marry me?'

I try to process what he's saying. He wants me because he thinks I don't want him as much as other women have done, or do. Just six months, six or seven encounters, his gesture is rash, vain, attractive.

He is holding out a ring box, which he opens, quite clumsily, his hands are shaking and in that moment I feel something so powerful, so tender, it has to be love. I want to stop his hand shaking. I want to make him happy. He's irresistible to me. The pause between us, the expectation, is painfully potent. 'I'm thirty-nine years old, Daan.'

'I know that.'

'Children. There might be —Well, it's most likely to be harder, if at all.'

'I don't want children. They have never been part of my plan.'

'You say that now, but you're young enough to change your mind.'

'I want you.' His green eyes, framed with thick, long lashes bore into me. Insistent, almost impatient. 'Will you marry me, Kai, my beautiful darling?'

'Yes.'

'Yes?'

'Yes.' I nod and hear people around us *oh* and *ah*. There's a slight pattering of applause — people too British to commit — as he slips the ring onto my finger. A heavy ring, three enormous diamonds on a platinum band.

I love it.

12

Kai

It would be sensible if the engagement was at least a year because, obviously, we need to get to know one another, work out each other's habits, needs, routines and lifestyle. To find a way to fit together. Or I could leave. By anyone's standards we are being impetuous. Foolhardy. Agreeing to marry him makes no sense at all. Part of my brain knows this. The other part thinks I have won the lottery. When we spend the night together and I can feel his breathing against my back, I sometimes think that is all I've ever wanted. It's enough. It's everything. But of course, it isn't.

It is not as easy to push our two lives together as Daan assumed it would be. Now that he lives in London, he expects me to move in with him straight away. He is delighted when I tell him I only rent and don't have a flat to sell. He wants to see me every day. That's quite a leap after seeing one another just once a month. I'm overwhelmed by the expectation. The reality. I have to explain that my work takes me away a lot, and my mother is ill. I have responsibilities. Daan, to his credit, accepts my obligations, relishes my independence. I discover he is very easy-going. Not possessive or controlling like some men can be. He is straightforward, direct. He respects the boundaries that I put in place, acknowledging that my life is more complex than that of other women he's dated. From what I can gather those women did not have careers, just trust funds. They did not have family responsibilities, just frivolous friends. They spent their days in hair salons and spas preparing themselves for him. They were always available. I don't know if he realises I'm more complex than he is. I'm more complex than most people are. He's too lazy to bother trying to work me out, to understand me. He just wants a quiet life. I have to try not to take it personally and remind myself this is a good thing; I don't want him getting too close.

'I love you,' he says, over and over again.

I say it less, but I mean it more because I am risking more. More than he knows, more than he can ever imagine. More than anyone could.

We power through a fast-track course on getting to know one another. Every time I am with him it feels like we're on a particularly successful first date. Each revelation, each discovery, is a delight.

'If you could hop on a plane right now, where would you go?'

'New Orleans. The hospitality, the music, the food. I'll take you one day. You?'

'Bora Bora, French Polynesia. I've never been. I've just seen pictures. It looks like paradise.'

'I'll take you there too,' he says joyfully. I consider my inheritance. The obscene amount of money my father has left me. At least an obscene amount as far as I am concerned. It crosses my mind that I can take Daan to New Orleans or to French Polynesia. I can fly us both there, first class. There would still be plenty left. I could buy property, invest, start up a business. There are a number of things I could do with the money. That's the point of money, it affords opportunities. I haven't told anyone about it yet. Not

108

even Daan. It's only just cleared, and it's sat — currently untouched — in a bank account that I opened specially to receive it. I don't understand the inheritance. The money my father has left me means for the first time in my life I don't have to work. Not if I don't want to. The idea is an anathema to me. When my father left, my mother struggled financially. We lived a life expecting to drown and then he left me enough money to sail off into the sunset. Was it a gift, a way of begging for forgiveness, a way of making up to me at the very end? Or was it a final divisive act? Deliberately calculated to cause destruction and aggro? That thought is so painful whenever I have it, I feel a stabbing sensation in my stomach. I'm training myself not to think that way. Put that idea out of my head. Sometimes not thinking about something is the only way forward. The only way to survive. But the inheritance has caused a schism. It has guaranteed none of my brothers want to continue any sort of relationship with me, they are all hurt and furious. They think I must have schemed and plotted to secure such a chunk. I did not. It makes me wonder, did my father ever like them after all? Did he like any of us?

'What's the best meal you've ever had?' Daan asks.

'In Portugal, on holiday. We had the most implausibly good, deliciously tender, fresh-from-the-ocean octopus. It was sautéed and served in a huge cast-iron skillet bubbling with olive oil, garlic, and spicy sliced purple onions.'

'We?'

'I was with my dad, stepmother and brothers. You?'

'Melt-in-your-mouth steak, eaten outside, cooked on the fire at our safari lodge in South Africa after a game drive.'

109

'Our?'

'My girlfriend at the time.' Not one that earned a name in his potted history. He pulls me close, wraps his arms around me, kisses me. Stopping my mouth so I can't ask any more about the 'girlfriend at the time'. I am 100 per cent aware of this technique; I let it slide. I concentrate on the pressure of his lips, enjoying it gain in force and intent. The getting-to-know-you chats are constantly interrupted by sex. Our bodies are also getting to know each other. We're aerobic, synchronised and insatiable. When we break apart sweating and temporarily satisfied, I ask, 'Did you have a nickname as a child?'

And so it goes on.

Tell me something I wouldn't guess about you.

Who do you talk to the most?

What are you most afraid of?

What do you think your most attractive quality is?

And your least?

I answer as honestly as possible, I think he does too. We are fascinated and fascinating. We charm and excite one another. I look my very best when I am with him. Partially because I try to, partially because I'm in love and don't have to try. Daan has an air about him that is vaguely old-fashioned, almost otherworldly. He is extremely polite. He opens doors and insists, 'After you' — not just to buildings but cars too. He uses phrases like 'You are the bees' knees' or 'Best not to over-egg the pudding.' He then smiles at me, waiting for me to acknowledge his expert control of the English language. He likes talking about the weather — 'It's a peasouper' — and he refers to his umbrella as a 'brolly'. Despite his youth and foreignness, he seems to enjoy presenting himself as some

110

sort of English gent from a time not absolutely attributable, but most probably past. Am I part of that? Does he see me as a damsel who needs to be rescued? Does he see refinement and otherness where really there is simply caution?

My continual insistence that I can't move in with him yet seems to entice Daan. He says he doesn't see the need for delay. He doesn't want a long engagement. His parents give him the deeds to the luxurious apartment by way of an engagement present. 'We can redecorate, make it ours,' he says, excitedly. He hates uncertainty and limbo, which he insists engagement is.

I can't find a decent and robust counter-argument to Daan's insistence that engagements constitute 'limbo' so three months later I walk into the Chelsea register office and marry him. However, despite the efficiency of the getting-to-know-you sessions, I'm not sure how well I do know him. I sometimes think I know what he is feeling, other times I know I don't. But then again, how well does Daan know me?

13

Kai

Twenty-eight years before she met Daan

I like the station waiting room. When I'm in it I think of that TV programme that I used to watch when I was little about Mr Benn. Mr Benn was so lucky. He could just go into a changing room — OK, so admittedly a magic one — and then come out a totally different person, ready for an adventure, just because he changed his clothes. I think that must be really good, although impossible, and Dad says hoping for things that are impossible is pointless and stupid. 'You don't want to be pointless or stupid, do you?' he asks. I shake my head. He asks those sorts of questions using a particular voice. I've thought about the voice a lot. It's kind of fake cheerful. A mix between something like the voice girls at school use when daring you to do something and a telling-off that a teacher might fling out. It's not nice.

Still, I find I do. Hope for impossible things.

I still wish really hard that this station waiting room is like Mr Benn's changing room for me. Even though wishes, even those you make on birthdays, never come true. I have to be a different person when I end my train journey from the one I was when I began it. The waiting room has two doors and I always make sure I go in one and out the other. I don't have to, it's nothing to do with which platform the train pulls in at, or

112

anything logical, it's just a thing I keep doing. To see if things change. To see if I am different. To see if everyone is. I haven't told anyone about my waiting-room habit, Dad would be very angry about it. Dad likes me to think rationally. 'Like a boy, not a hormonal or superstitious woman. You don't want to be a hormonal, superstitious woman, do you?' I knew to say no, even before I had to look up both words. Neither is a compliment. Compliments are words like *beautiful, reasonable, intelligent*. He was not clear about which woman he thinks is 'hormonal or superstitious'. I don't think he means his new wife, Ellie. Most likely he means Mum, although he doesn't directly talk about Mum to me. Not ever.

He once told me that Ellie 'doesn't make a fuss' which I could tell he thought was a really good thing because he said it in his kind, content voice. I guess this must be true because she had my baby brother, Freddie, before she even married my dad and she did it so quietly no one knew anything about it, except presumably Dad. I guess he must have known. He just didn't tell me.

Freddie is very cute, although a bit annoying at times when he doesn't know I'm bored of a particular game and he just wants to keep playing, 'again, gen, gen' is like his war cry. The games he plays aren't proper games, obviously, as he's only two. He likes being swung around in circles, which kills my arms after a bit. He likes kicking a ball backwards and forwards, not exactly between us, because his aim is terrible. And when he's in the bath he likes me pouring a cup of water over his head. He thinks that is hysterical. But once he laughed so hard and kicked his chubby little legs so much, he slipped and then banged his head on the tap and Dad went mad with me. He was really angry. He made a big fuss, but I think it's different with men. If they make a fuss it is not hormonal, it's because they are cross with their stupid wives or stupid daughters. True, Ellie did not make a fuss, but she didn't really speak to me properly for days and kept giving me bad looks. Like the girls at school sometimes do if you wear the wrong jeans.

Ellie must be hormonal though because she is actually pregnant again (gen gen? how many babies are they planning on having?! I wonder). Mrs Roberts, my science teacher, said pregnant women have a lot of 'hormonal changes'. This information was given during the lessons on reproduction education. I wish that had not been taught this year. It is really embarrassing that Dad and Ellie keep having babies because everyone in my class knows they must be having sex when other parents are obviously not. I wish I had parents that just did the same as everyone else's parents. Like telling them off about their untidy rooms, getting a takeaway from the Chinese on Saturdays and complaining about the cost of school trips. To be fair, my dad does do all these things, but he also has sex with his new wife. He has a new wife.

Ellie's belly is so weird. I can't keep my eyes off it. She is really skinny everywhere else but now has this mound to carry around in front of her. She doesn't like me staring, though. She says I am 'unnerving'. I looked that up too. Also, not a compliment. She says I'm weird. Me?! I'm not the one with a Space Hopper up my jumper. I try not to get caught staring though because it makes Dad cross if I upset Ellie. 'She's very good to you,' he says all the time. As though saying it all the time makes it more true.

There is a kiosk in the waiting room that sells teas and coffees and breakfast to people rushing to work in the city. There are no tables though, the place is too small. People have to eat their breakfasts standing up or take them on to the train and hope to get a seat. My favourite breakfast is a bacon buttie. I love the smell of warm fat sizzling and white bread frying; it reminds me of my granddad cooking breakfast for me when I was little. It's usually a woman who serves behind the counter, but sometimes it's a man. They are from Taiwan. I know because I heard the man tell a customer once. I didn't know where Taiwan was, and it took ages to find it on Dad's globe. Most of one Sunday afternoon, but I didn't mind really, because it was something to do.

The Taiwanese couple tune their small radio into a classical music channel which seems to be surprising to the passengers, who always look astonished as they soak up the pianos and violins along with the smell of coffee and fried bread. It is certainly a change because in most shops and cafés only pop songs are played. I like the classical music because that also reminds me of my granddad who had old records of composers that have been dead for ages. I remember him telling me their names — Beethoven, Bach and Chopin — but I don't really know which was which. My granddad died when I was eight which is so sad. If he was still alive, I think I would know which composer was responsible for which bit of music and maybe I wouldn't even be sitting in this waiting room. I'd be sitting with him, most likely. In his lovely warm front room that had too much furniture for its small size but always smelt of sunshine and polish. Which was nice.

Obviously, Mum was more sad than I was about him dying because while he was my granddad, he was her dad and dads trump granddads. My dad said the way my mum grieved was indulgent and that it was disrespectful to the memory of my granddad, who liked people to be happy and would not want us crying. I don't know but I did try not to cry in front of either of them because it upset them both in different ways. Because my mum cried so much, my dad made friends with Ellie. He's explained it wasn't his fault.

I think I must take after my granddad because I like people to be happy too. I think I am a person who is happiest when everyone else is happy. I don't think there's anything wrong with that.

Waiting rooms are not peaceful; people always have a sort of jumpiness about them. I suppose they are worried they are going to miss their train. I know I worry, not if it is late but what if it was cancelled? What would I do then? Where would I go? But I like the place anyway. It feels safe, not one place or the other, just where I get to be me. Today it is rainy, so there are puddles of water on the tiled floor which are always tricky for the ladies in high heels and umbrellas are inconveniently shaken, scattering rain over me. Even so, I think this is where I am happiest because there's no one to make happy here, but me.

The journey starts well. The train is on time. I get a seat with no one next to me, and no one talks to me or so much as smiles in my direction. It is best if they don't because I'm not allowed to talk to strangers, but some strangers are women who look like grandmas; they don't know the rules about talking to children, I don't think. Then it's embarrassing because my choice is to a) look rude by ignoring them or b) talk to them which is against the rules. The journey starts to go wrong when there is no one to meet me off the train. There isn't always. Sometimes I have to get the bus, but I thought today that Dad was going to pick me up. That's what he'd said. So now I have to think do I a) get the bus but what if he is on his way and he arrives, and I am already gone. That will make him cross or b) wait for him here at the station but it is getting dark and it's the last bus, if he doesn't come and I miss the last bus, I'll be in real trouble.

I get the bus.

It's a ten-minute walk from the bus stop to Dad's. 'Nothing at all', he says, although I have never seen him catch a bus ever. He drives a BMW. It's raining hard now so I walk as quickly as possible, sometimes running, although it is hard to run carrying a suitcase. I do it in seven and a half minutes. I time myself.

I quietly let myself in with my own key. I saw a report on the news about latchkey kids. It made me feel a bit sad. Until then, I thought having my own key was grown up, now I lie to my friends about it, so they don't think I'm weird. I pretend there is someone waiting for me with milk and biscuits too.

I take off my shoes and coat at the doorway, because I definitely don't want to drip rain on the shiny tiled floor. I carry them and my suitcase straight upstairs because I don't want to leave anything lying around for other people to trip over, because that's just selfish and asking for trouble. Upstairs I can hear sounds coming from Dad and Ellie's bedroom. I know I have to sneak past their room without them noticing me because I'm not stupid and I know what sort of sounds they are. Making sex sounds is even worse than rowing sounds. Their bedroom door is open. This is bad for two reasons a) because there is a greater risk of them seeing me b) because I might catch a glimpse of them, which would be gross!! I try to keep my eyes on the floor. I really do. Why would I want to see that but somehow my eyes don't listen to my brain and I find myself just quickly flicking a glance that way. I don't even know why I couldn't stop myself. It's utterly awful. Worse than I could have imagined. I can see my dad's hairy bottom thrusting forwards and backwards into Ellie who is not lying on her back, like in the picture of women making sex in the textbook we were shown at school — Ellie is on her knees, bent over. They've got it all wrong. The sounds they are making — grunting, screaming, breathing fast like they've been running forever — prove that it's wrong! He's hurting her.

And something else is more wrong. The woman who Dad is thrusting at is *not Ellie*. She's a totally different shape. She's not pregnant for a start, she has huge boobs and my dad is reaching forward and grabbing at them, with the same enthusiasm as he grabs a handful of caramelised peanuts when Ellie puts them in a bowl as a treat.

'Oh,' I say. I don't mean to. The *oh* must come out quite loud. Maybe I shouted it or screamed it. I must have, to have been heard above their groans. The woman turns my way, she sees me at the door and starts scrabbling away from Dad, reaching for the sheet, pulling it around her. Dad doesn't notice me at first, he lunges after her, laughing, 'Come here, you little tease!' he says.

I run into my bedroom, slam the door behind me.

When Dad comes to see me a bit later, I am not sat on my bed. I feel funny about beds now. I am sat on the floor with my back against the radiator. The warmth is comforting.

'How's school?' he asks.

'Fine,' I say as usual.

'Good, good.' I'm expecting him to tell me to wash my hands, come downstairs to set the table.

'Who is she?' I ask quickly, before I can decide not to. I think I deserve to know. I am not like Ellie's best friend or anything, but if I am going to have a new stepmum, I want some warning.

'She's no one. She's nothing,' says Dad. He doesn't look at me. He looks at the wall above my head.

'Nothing?' I repeat, unsure. Confused.

'There are women you marry and there are women you do that with.'

'Make sex, you mean?' I want him to know I am not a baby. I understand.

'Have sex with, yes.' He corrects and I'm embarrassed that I've shown I'm not really sure about any of this after all. 'The women you marry are something. The others are nothing. Remember that. I don't want a daughter of mine not understanding that.'

I squirm. I feel I've done something wrong, but I don't know what. Surely, he's the one who has done the wrong thing. 'Now wash your hands and come downstairs to set the table. And darling, obviously as that woman was nothing, we don't need to mention this to Ellie. It's between us.'

He doesn't often call me 'darling' and I can't help but be happy about it.

119

14

DC Clements

Thursday 19th March 2020

Back at the station, Tanner returns to his desk, as another senior officer hands him a pile of traffic offences to process. Clements hardly sees her environment anymore; it is familiar to the point of being void. Curling posters on the wall, detailing policies and advertising helplines, no longer catch her attention. She doesn't know if the walls are beige or grey. She still notices smells though — today the station smells of wet clothes and mud; there have been two sudden downpours this morning. Sometimes there is an energy to the place that overrides what she can see, hear and smell; sometimes she can just feel. Feel danger or excitement. Challenge. Lots of her colleagues have their eyes pinned to their phones or screens absorbing the news from European cities in lockdown. Normal citizens being told to stay indoors, doing so. Locked up, not like criminals exactly, but . . . Clements can't process it. It's too wild. A sense of urgency ripples through her body. She needs to find Leigh Fletcher.

Clements walks swiftly to her desk and starts to fill in the paperwork. There is a myth that the police regard any missing persons case which is not that of a child, or where a crime is not obviously suspected, as beyond their remit. It is not true.

Clements wants to find this woman, bring her

home — if that is what Leigh wants. Clements uploads the personal details they collated: name, age, marital status, last sighting, physical description. She attaches the photo, noting that Leigh Fletcher is pretty. It shouldn't matter — it doesn't really — unless the case becomes something bigger than a missing person and ends up in the papers. Then it will have a bearing. The public are always more sympathetic towards a pretty woman than a plain one, although this one is a bit old to fully catch the nation's attention. Women over twenty-seven have to work so much harder to exist, even being murdered isn't enough to incite sympathy, unless you are cute. Clements sighs, frustrated at the world. Frustration is not a bad reaction; it means there is some fight in her, still. Sometimes Clements is furious and wants to kick and punch at the invisible, insidious walls that limit, cage, corrupt. Other days she's just out-and-out depressed. Those are the worst days.

Leigh Fletcher has long dark hair. In the pic the glossy hair has clearly just benefited from a fresh blow-dry. She's wearing lipstick, a pale pink shade, but not much else in the way of make-up. She doesn't need it. Her lashes are thick and fabulous, her skin clear and the only wrinkles on her face are around her eyes. Clements imagines the missing woman identifying them as laughter lines, shunning the miserable description of crow's feet. She's smiling in the photo, a huge beam. But there's something about her big brown soulful eyes that makes Clements wonder. She looks weary. Most working mums are tired — that's a given — but this is deeper. She's drained. Done for.

Clements shakes her head. Sometimes she wonders whether she has too much imagination for a cop. She has to keep that in check. It's perfectly possible that she's reading too much into the snap.

Suddenly, Clements feels the weight of a hand on the back of her chair, someone leaning in far too close — ostensibly to look at what she is typing — in fact, simply invading her body space because he can. She recognises DC Morgan's bulk and body odour instantly. Without looking at him, she knows he'll have food between his teeth or caught in his beard. His shirt will be gaping, the buttons straining to stretch the material across his pale podgy belly that is coated in dark hair. Morgan is not an attractive man anymore, but Clements admits he might have had a charm once. Before his confidence loosened into boorishness, when his mass was the result of muscle not fat. Invasion of body space — and probably much more — is the sort of stunt he has been pulling for twenty-plus years, and no amount of training courses on appropriate workplace behaviour are likely to change him now. In fact, Clements has been on the courses with him and heard him dismiss them as 'political correctness gone mad. Nothing more than the spawn of limp-wristed liberals'. He is a treat. She would probably hate him if he wasn't such a good copper.

'All right, Morgan?' Clements says in greeting. She rolls her chair away from him, narrowly avoiding running over his foot but forcing him to jump back from her.

He straightens up, arches his back. 'Must be the day for it.' He likes starting conversations in an obtuse way, forcing others to ask questions, somehow making him seem more interesting and engaging than he truly is.

'The day for what?' Clements asks dutifully.

'Missing women. I've just had one put through to my desk too.' Clements feels a chill run through her body, her breathing stutters but she manages to keep her outward response to nothing more than raising an eyebrow. So, he was actually reading her screen. That doesn't mean he wasn't trying to secretly rub up against her, though, it's just proof that, despite stereotypes, he is a man who can multitask.

'Really. Who? Where?'

'A Kai Janssen. Her husband called it in. Woman in her early forties, boss.'

Clements is not Morgan's boss. She's not even his senior. They hold the same rank. However, she is fifteen years younger than him and likely to continue to take exams and be promoted, whereas he is most probably done. The use of the term 'boss' is laden with sarcasm. He does not see this 'slip of a girl' so much as an equal. It's her breasts. Not that her breasts are particularly notable. Not especially large or small but their existence — proving she is a woman — is enough to convince Morgan that Clements is inherently inferior. That's why he laughs at the idea that one day she might outrank him. He jokes about it now, so that when it does happen, it won't seem threatening or even important.

'The husband sounded posh, maybe foreign. Dutch? With a name like Janssen. Some foreigners sound so posh they sound more English than we do, though, eh? I'm just heading over there to talk to him in person. To follow up.'

'Do you mind if I take it?' Clements tries to keep the eagerness out of her voice. If he knows she really wants it, then he's doing her a favour. If he does her a

123

favour, she owes him.

'You think they are connected?'

'Maybe.'

Morgan scratches his belly, glances towards the window. It's raining again. 'Be my guest,' he says.

15
DC Clements

Clements doesn't bother taking Tanner with her. She needs a break from her esteemed male colleagues: their sweat, their opinions, their careless assumptions. Not for the first time she wishes her division had more female officers.

It's 3 p.m. by the time she arrives at the address Morgan has given her. The property is on the river, one of those flash, multi-million-pound apartment blocks within spitting distance of the shiny financial district. She is a bit surprised because urban legend has it that no one lives in these apartments, that they are all bought up by Russian oligarchs who don't want to live in the UK but want to protect their cash and so pour it into something tangible overseas. A soulless arrangement. This is a very different part of London from the bit she was at earlier. A few miles in physical distance, worlds apart in reality. Leigh Fletcher's home is slap bang in the middle of row after row of identical Victorian terraced houses, in a street that has yet to be redeveloped. At some point it will probably become another neighbourhood for people with a lot of money but no roots. Clements would guess that the last time the Fletchers' street was transformed was in the 70s. Then, the original features — like stained glass, sash windows and black-and-white tiled paths — were ripped out and dug up.

Replaced by ugly practical solutions — PVC

window frames and doors, cement paths. Their street is not charming or in any way estate-agent 'desirable', but it is not without merit.

It is busy with nose-to-nose traffic, crowded. It's the sort of street where groups of morose teens loll on the low walls at the end of the scraps that pass as gardens, tired parents dash their kids to and from school and football practice, pensioners slowly but determinedly saunter to the corner shop, prepared to pay a bit more for their milk as it guarantees a chat to the person behind the counter. It's an area where the recycling bins overflow, the paintwork on the doors blisters and peels. You get the sense that the people who live on the street are too strapped — by time and money — to bother with DIY. However, there is something appealing about the sense of enduring community. It's the sort of place where all the kids go to the same local school, and the residents don't shoo away the teenagers from the walls because it's silently and tacitly acknowledged, they could be up to a lot worse, elsewhere.

Kai Janssen's part of town is immaculate. The pavements are litter-free, there are landscaped walkways, fountains and green spaces. Although there is not a single soul around to enjoy these features. Clements looks about her and shivers, made cold by a sense of isolation. Personally, she'd rather live with the peeling paintwork and the streets that teem with life. This rarefied atmosphere of wealth is paradoxically suffocating. Clements rings the bell and is allowed into a large glass-and-marble foyer where she is greeted by a man in his fifties sat behind a concierge desk. This makes the place seem more like a hotel than a home.

Clements flashes her badge. 'Can I help you?' the

126

concierge asks, not managing to hide the frisson of excitement he is so clearly feeling on having a police officer visit the premises. Cops don't expect cheers and genial greetings from many people, but they can always depend on a warm welcome from a nosy busybody. Clements asks for Mr Janssen.

'Is he expecting you?'

'Yes.'

'Oh, I hope there's nothing wrong.' The concierge is insincerely obsequious, but Clements doesn't judge. She thinks that arguably it's a necessary quality of the job if you have to suck up to the rich and entitled all the time. Obviously, something is wrong if a cop turns up at your door, unless it's the strippergram variety. There is nothing about Clements that suggests she is a strippergram. She doesn't reply, just smiles politely. She wants to keep him onside, in case she needs his help later; busybodies often make great witnesses, but she has nothing she wants to share with him yet. After a beat he gives up, recognising he is not going to get anything out of her, and calls Mr Janssen. After a brief exchange he says, 'You just tap in the code. It's 1601, the lift takes you right up to Mr and Mrs Janssen's penthouse.' Clements nods her thanks and heads off to the lift.

As promised, the lift doors swish open directly into the penthouse apartment ensuring that any visitor's first impression is that the place is enormous and incredibly luxurious. It is also dark, not pitch black, but lit only by a scattering of table lamps — and because the place is so huge they don't do much to illuminate. The size and sleekness steals Clements' breath away. She doesn't often come across many people who live like this. 'I thought everyone was over the minimalist

127

thing,' she mutters to herself. Sometimes she does that, when she is working on her own. It makes environments less threatening to hear a voice, even if it is her own voice. And somehow this stark space, whilst large and luxurious, is threatening. She automatically scans the mostly open-plan area. There are various living spaces. A sitting area, a dining area, an office and a kitchen. All spacious. There are four doors to closed-off rooms. Bedrooms and bathrooms, presumably.

Most people live like Leigh Fletcher, in amongst a comfortable amount of clutter. They want their homes stuffed full of colour, vintage rugs and mirrors, endless mismatched prints on the walls. Not this place. Although, Clements notes, you would need a lot of stuff to fill this apartment — a lot. So maybe minimalism is the way to go. The walls are painted a dark slate grey. All the floors are a dark wood or marble, the furniture is various shades of graphite. A man steps out of the shadows. Clements doesn't scare easily, but she flinches all the same. The man is tall and broad, bearlike. He looms over her. It is not his physicality that is alarming, it's his emotional state. Clements sees at once that the man has been drinking, perhaps crying, he looks agitated, anxious.

'Mr Janssen?'

'Daan Janssen. Thank you for coming.' He stretches out a hand and doing so, despite his emotional state, underlines the fact he has impeccable, unshakeable manners, the sort of manners that are drilled into a child at an early age and forever trump everything — warmth, sincerity, distress. No doubt some headmaster, or perhaps his father, repeatedly told him that 'manners maketh man'. Maybe they

128

do prevent us from falling into animalistic savagery, thinks Clements.

His grip is firm.

'Come, come in.' He leads her through the open-plan apartment to the kitchen area. Clements knows that even in exquisite luxury apartments such as this, the kitchen is the heart of the home. Although she doesn't find any signs of cooking; all the surfaces are clear from clutter and gleaming as though newly installed that day. There are no condiments, crockery or cutlery — clean or dirty. It looks like a show home. There is a sleek laptop, open and on, emitting an eery blue light into the darkness. The only thing on display that suggests offering any degree of sustenance is an open bottle of malt whisky, with an empty glass next to it. There's ice melting in the glass, it has been used. The rattling ice suggests the alcohol was knocked back at some speed. Daan Janssen pours himself another generous measure and then turns to Clements, shakes the bottle at her. 'Do you want one?'

'I'm on duty, Mr Janssen.' *And it's mid-afternoon.* She doesn't add that.

'Yes, of course. Sorry. Really, please call me Daan.' Clements nods but doubts she will. Best to keep a distance, at least at first. Sometimes, it is helpful to forge intimacy, but she likes to decide when that will be expedient. Morgan was right about something, Daan Janssen's accent is barely perceptible. His foreignness is only detectable by his crisp manner. There's something about his elegant well-cut clothes — he is still wearing the jacket to his suit, even though he's in his own home — and his precise but staccato sentences that suggest a formality, an otherness, that isn't very British. Maybe his particular brand of handsome also marks him out. People think because she is a police officer, and investigating, that she's impervious to the things that matter to other women, but she's not. Clements sees attractive men and notes them the way any thirty-five-year-old woman might. It's just that she also wonders if the handsome men she finds herself face to face with are thieves, arsonists, fraudsters. Killers.

Daan Janssen *is* a very attractive man. He is tall, broad, green-eyed, with blond hair; he wears it brushing his collar, a little longer than most men his age (at a guess she'd put him late thirties). His cheekbones are chiselled. You could lose an eye on them. Even if he wasn't stood in the kitchen of his enormous London penthouse, he would be identifiable as wealthy. If Clements saw him on one of the dating sites that she occasionally — in a fit of optimism over experience — signs up to, she would definitely swipe right. But he'd never be on a dating site. Not this man. There would never be a need. If she wanted to get to this man she'd have to climb over women, a mountain of them. No doubt that's what Kai Janssen did. Clements is keen to look at a picture of her. She's guessing the wife will be a glacial beauty, tall like him, blonde, possibly androgynous. Certainly hard-bodied, lean.

It's been a good day for hot husbands who have lost their wives because Mark Fletcher is also an attractive man. He has brown eyes, dark, almost blue-black hair with only a whisper of grey at the temples. He has a strong, muscular, almost stocky build that makes him appear quite the force. Clements had him down as someone who always enjoyed sport and has never allowed the habit of staying fit to slip. Probably he cycles, runs, possibly lifts weights now, as a boy he will

130

have played rugby and football, possibly captained the teams. There would have been women throwing themselves at Mark Fletcher too, before Leigh. But not women who are seduced by credit cards — women who wanted to have families and to see their husband carry their kids on his shoulders, kick a football with them, pitch a tent. If Clements had to make snap judgements — and she did sometimes — she'd say Mark Fletcher is a family man, whereas Daan Janssen is a ladies' man.

She puts the attractiveness of these men out of her mind and gets back to the job in hand. That is perhaps where she differs from other women, and possibly the reason she has never maintained any long-term relationships, she's never yet met a man who is attractive enough to completely distract her from her work. Family men, ladies' men, none of them can provide a high that equals the one she gets when cracking a case. 'You called about your wife,' she says.

'I should have called you sooner.'

Clements pulls out her notebook. 'Well, I'm here now.' She starts with the standard things: name, age, then, 'So, when did you last see your wife?'

'Last Thursday morning.'

Inwardly she takes a breath. 'A week ago?' She tries not to allow any judgement to leak into the tone of her voice.

'Yes.'

'But you've waited until now to report her missing?' It is impossible not to hear the echo of the same question that was asked of Mark Fletcher earlier today. What the fuck is it with these men who lose their wives? Why are they so slow to become alarmed? Clements thinks that the next time she's romanticising

131

the great institution of marriage, she'll remind herself of these conversations.

'Oh, but she hasn't been missing all that time,' Daan interjects. 'No, of course not. She has been at her mother's. Her mother is very ill. Kai devotes a lot of time to her care. Kai's mother — Pamela, Pam — is in a home, in the north of England. Kai is staying there with her.'

'I see. So, when did you last hear from your wife? Have you spoken on the phone whilst she has been visiting her mother?'

'Yes, we have. We last spoke on Sunday afternoon.'

'But not since then?'

'We swapped WhatsApp messages. I received one at lunchtime.'

'So, you are in contact with your wife? She's simply not at home. That's not missing.' Clements was too eager to come here. She should have called him first, established some facts. She'd jumped the gun on the back of coming straight from Leigh Fletcher's house, thought there was a pattern, a connection. She should be moving on that case, not wasting time here.

Daan puts up a hand to stop her leaving, to hold her attention. 'Only, I don't think it is my wife I am messaging. That's why I came home and decided to call you.'

'What?'

'I think someone is impersonating my wife.' Involuntarily Clements glances at his whisky glass. Is the man drunk? Is he worth listening to at all? 'She called me on Sunday, Pamela had developed an infection, Kai was worried about her. Pam has Alzheimer's. She gets vicious UTIs from time to time.'

There is something about how he explains his

mother-in-law's health issues that makes Clements warm to him. She settles down on the breakfast bar stool and gives him time to finish. 'Then on Monday, when I was expecting her home, she sent a message and it just said, *Can't come home right now.* Very brief. I called her straight away; you know, to see if she was OK. She's an only child. She takes a lot on. But she didn't pick up. I just assumed she'd had to switch her phone off.'

'That happens in hospitals.'

'Yes, but not often in care homes. Never before. I left a message asking if the UTI had got worse. She sent just a one-word response. *Yes.* Again, I called her, again she didn't pick up. Anyway, over the next few days there was some messaging between us. It was a bit off. Not like herself, you know?'

'Her mother is very ill,' Clements says by way of explanation.

'Yes. That's what I told myself too. I called her a number of times, normally we speak every day if she is away, but every time I went through to voicemail and she never rang back. She would just send a message saying things were too difficult, that she was too busy, that she couldn't talk. She didn't give me any detail on what was going on with the prognosis or treatment. She was vague and brief. That's not like her. She likes to talk.' He throws out a smile at his own joke, maybe at the thought of his chatty wife. 'We had a supper party arranged for Tuesday. She never referenced it. I expected her to say whether she'd prefer me to cancel or go ahead without her.'

'With all that she has on her plate, might she have forgotten about it?'

'Maybe. Yesterday, I decided she shouldn't be

dealing with this all on her own; she likes to be independent, but we all need some help sometimes, right?' Clements nods. It is true. 'So, I decided to go and see her and Pam. I texted and asked for the address because I have never visited the place. I realised I didn't know exactly where it was. Somewhere in Newcastle but Newcastle is a big place. No response from her.'

Daan stares at Clements, his piercing eyes expectant of a reaction. Outrage, suspicion? She doesn't know what to tell him. His wife has priorities other than him right now. He has to suck it up. 'Did you call the care home and ask for their address?'

Daan shakes his head impatiently when he gathers that the police officer has not climbed on board with his belief that his wife is missing. 'I don't have the number.'

'You could look it up.'

'I don't know the name of the place.'

'I see.'

'Then I thought perhaps I could find it by going through her stuff. Maybe there's an invoice or some correspondence from the home.'

Clements glances about. 'There doesn't look like there is much stuff.'

'No, we both like a minimalist home so it wasn't really surprising when I couldn't find a paper bill. We are environmentalists. We keep as much as we can online.' Clements suppresses a sigh; he sounds like he is expecting to be congratulated on this very usual practice. Clements tries to be as environmentally friendly as the next person, so she doesn't know why she finds people who declare they are environmentalists so irritating, but she does. 'I logged into her email account, had a poke around there.'

134

Clements raises her eyebrows. It's technically an offence to read someone else's email — admittedly, one that's unlikely to lead to prosecution but it's an invasion. He shrugs, unperturbed. Entitled. 'We have each other's passwords. We're not the sort of couple to keep secrets. I couldn't find any correspondence from the home, or even a file on her mother. I logged into her phone provider and looked up her last phone bill. I thought there would be the number of the home on that. When she is here with me, she calls first thing in the morning to see how Pamela has slept and then in the evening to see that Pam has had a comfortable day.'

'You'd make a good detective.'

He shrugs. He's a man used to being told he's good at things. It doesn't matter to him. He doesn't need to be told; he knows it.

'But here is the thing, on her phone records there are no outgoing calls to *any* number other than mine.'

'What?'

'Well, no personal ones. No care home, no friends, just a couple of restaurants that we've visited, and her hair salon, decorators, that sort of thing. I went through every one of her phone calls — line by line — for the past six months but there are no calls to people she actually knows. Here, look.' He reaches for his laptop, types at the speed of light and pulls up a phone statement. He has all the enthusiasm and urgency of a member of Enid Blyton's Famous Five. Clements is always sceptical of amateur sleuths. She also is starting to doubt his assertion that they are not the sort of couple to keep secrets.

'This doesn't mean much in isolation. I need to check the numbers myself.' Clements' first thought

135

is that Kai Janssen has two phones. 'Does your wife work, Daan?'

'No.'

'Do you have children?'

'No.'

'What did her last message say? The one you received today?'

'*I'm fine, no need for you to visit.*'

'How long have you been married?'

'Three years, last December.' Clements' longest relationship was eight months. She shakes her head, an almost imperceptible motion. She doesn't know how people do it. Live with each other, day in day out, without getting bored or driving each other mad. Without killing each other. But then, she thinks, maybe they don't manage it. Some do kill each other. Daan Janssen continues, desperate to impart his concerns. 'I decided to make a list of the care homes in Newcastle. I collated the information online. I was very thorough. I called them all, one by one. I can give you that list too. I can't find a place with a woman resident by the name of Pamela Gillingham. No one has ever heard of Kai Janssen. I tried all the private ones and the council ones. Nothing. And there is another thing. The Find iPhone app has been turned off.'

'Have you called any of her friends?'

'Without her phone I don't know how to get hold of her friends.'

'You don't have the number of any of them in your phone? Not one?'

'There aren't many. There is someone from her pottery class that she mentions a lot, Sunara. Sunara Begum, I think, but I don't have her number. There are a few friends from her college days — Ginny,

Emma, Alex — but they don't live in London. She sometimes takes spa weekends with them, that sort of thing. They are not my friends. You know? I don't mean I don't like them. I just don't know them. Kai is very busy with her mother. She's devoted and that takes up most of her time. She also supports me in my role. We have a full social life through my work and through the friends I've introduced her to.'

'Have you called them?'

'I don't want to make a fuss.'

Clements nods, trying to appear sympathetic. She doesn't know what to tell him. If Kai Janssen was employed, Clements might assume that there is a second phone for work and that perhaps Kai Janssen isn't as honest as she should be about making private calls on her work phone to the care home but that isn't the case. Daan is right, something is off, but Clements doesn't believe this woman is missing, she is most likely having a cosy weekend away with her lover and it's been eked out longer than she was expecting. Adulterers often have two phones. It's standard practice. Clements suddenly hates her job. In this exact moment it feels like a babysitting service. Women leaving their handsome but self-involved husbands is not police work. She decides the best thing she can do is draw the conversation to a close with promises to make the appropriate enquiries. Sooner rather than later, Daan will receive word from his wife. Maybe a tearful confession that she has met someone else or a hard-nosed 'see ya, don't wanna be with ya'. Either way, this isn't Clements' business. It isn't police business.

'Well, I'll write this up,' she says. 'Check the phone records. Circulate a missing persons report.'

'Do you need a photo?'

'Oh, yes of course.'

Daan immediately pulls one up on his phone, thrusts it under Clements' nose.

'This is your wife?' she asks.

'Yes.'

Clements was expecting someone tall, blonde androgynous but Kai Janssen isn't anything like she imagined. She is a smiley brunette with brown eyes. She is familiar.

Clements is looking at a photograph of Leigh Fletcher.

16
Fiona

Thursday 19th March

When the bell rings, both Mark and Fiona leap off the kitchen stools and speed towards the front door, racehorses out of the gate. Fiona thinks that Mark must be desperately hoping that the police officers were right, that Leigh has come home. Mark called Fiona after the police left earlier, to update her. Not that there was anything solid to report. He told her that the police seem to think Leigh will be home soon. That they are not too concerned. That women — presumably men too — sometimes do take a few days' sabbatical from their families, following a row. They were reasonably reassuring; confident she'll return safe and well. 'Well, that's what everyone is praying for,' commented Fiona, gently. Then she quietly offered, 'Would you like me to come round? We could wait for news together?' She was finding it unbearable sitting alone in her kitchen. But she knew that however terrible she was feeling, however anxious, Mark would be a hundred times more so. The boys would be fretful, lost. She wanted to soothe them if she could.

Fiona loves Oliver and Sebastian; they are almost like family to her. They've been in her life for as long as Leigh has been in theirs. When they were younger, they called the two women Aunty Leigh and Aunty Fi. When Leigh became Mummy, Fiona hung on to

Aunty Fi for a few years, but they've grown out of that now. Still, however much Fiona loves the boys she has to admit they were a challenge this evening. It was clearly a good thing that she had come over. There was no doubt that her presence defused things.

The boys seemed pleased to see her, relieved. Seb, the less complicated of the two, hugged her tightly but then chatted about his day in a relatively usual way. He's naively hopeful that his mum will tumble through the door any moment. Oli's reaction is more nuanced. He's sulky around his father, almost accusatory.

'I'm sure everything is OK,' Fiona said repeatedly because that's what people say at times like this. She wants to appear positive but she's lying to protect the boys. It's obvious something bad has happened to Leigh. Leigh is not the irresponsible sort. She would be here if she could be. If she had a choice in the matter. She hasn't checked in with the boys for days. Fiona suggested to Mark that they call hospitals. 'I don't want to alarm you, but we have to face the facts. It's just not something she'd do. I still can't take it in.'

Mark is in the hallway ahead of Fiona, she looks over his shoulders and sees the silhouettes of a hatted policeman and woman at the door.

'Have you found her?' Mark demands as he swings open the door.

The female officer shakes her head, apologetically. 'Can we come in?'

They all automatically traipse through to their small sitting room. It's a mess but the kitchen is more so. To his credit Mark managed to make the boys a spag bol for supper; however, he clearly didn't have the energy to wash up, so the kitchen isn't the right place to talk.

Fiona is torn, itching to restore order but also not wanting to look like she is interfering. Instead, she's cracked open the bottle of Bordeaux that she brought with her. She thought it was more urgently needed, more supportive. She will wash up before she leaves tonight, though. She might suggest to Mark that she have a bit of a tidy around tomorrow. Everyone always feels better after a tidy around. Well, Fiona certainly does. Leigh is always teasing her about that, saying Fiona is a bit OCD. Fiona suddenly feels an intense pain in her gut thinking about Leigh. It's too awful.

'You have some news?' Mark asks. His face stretched, like his nerves, with anticipation. 'Should we have called the hospitals? Have you?'

They don't answer directly but they obviously do have news, why else would they be here at this late hour? Besides, Fiona notices that there is an energy about them, they seem almost excited. What does that mean?

'What is your wife's full name?' asks the female officer.

'Leigh Anne Fletcher. I told you before.'

'She never goes by any other name?' Mark shakes his head. He looks mystified.

The male officer clarifies, 'No nicknames? No — '

'Well, actually her real name is Kylie. Or it was,' Fiona interjects helpfully. Mark and the police officers quickly turn to her. Fiona doesn't know what to do by way of introduction. She's never had any dealings with the police. She throws out a small, slightly pathetic wave and almost instantly regrets it. She doesn't want to look silly, frivolous, since the situation is obviously anything other. She quickly pulls her hand to her side. 'I'm Fiona Phillipson, Leigh's best friend. We've

141

been best friends for over twenty years.'

Fiona has known Leigh longer than Mark has. She doesn't explicitly add that, she doesn't have to, she knows that the policewoman will understand her claim, her loyalty. Fiona's love came first. The policewoman will get it. Men don't get female friendship. Not really. The exquisite depth of a non-sexual relationship is too much for them to comprehend.

'Kylie?' Mark says, unable to hide his shock. Another hit to his body, his ego. Fiona nods and smiles at him apologetically. She wouldn't like anyone to get her wrong, she thinks Mark is a brilliant guy, a great husband but — well, Fiona is the best friend. She knows Leigh best. Fact. As she has just proven.

The two women have shared flats and been there for one another as they scrambled up career ladders, slid down snakes. Here they are twenty-plus years later — Leigh a respected senior management consultant at an enormous global company and Fiona working for a highly prestigious interior design company that counts amongst its clients many people who appear in *HELLO!* magazine.

'Yeah. She was Kylie, she didn't like it at all. There were too many occasions when we were young and we'd be out, and some random — usually a bloke thinking he was clever and more original than was the case — on hearing her name, would burst into a chorus of 'I Should Be So Lucky'.' Fiona sings the song, in case they need reminding. But then she stops singing abruptly, aware that nobody needs reminding of a Kylie song, ever, and this obviously isn't the place or the time to be singing. 'Sorry. I don't know what's wrong with me. Stress, I guess.' Everyone nods. They understand. Fiona continues, 'Her mum's Australian and it's a pretty popular name out there but not here. It just bothered Leigh to be noticed that way. She's quite a shy person, when it comes down to it. She had it changed by deed poll. About a year before she met you, Mark. Hasn't she ever mentioned that?'

'No, no she hasn't.' Mark sinks back into their comfy sofa. He is a strong-looking guy — usually — but tonight he looks reduced. The sofa swallows him up. He looks dazed. Confused.

'It did take a bit of getting used to at the time,' Fiona admits, throwing him a sympathetic glance. 'I kept calling her Kylie for ages, but it really irritated her, so I had to get used to Leigh. I've come to think she suits Leigh and it rolls off the tongue naturally. I never slip up and call her anything else now.' It is awkward. Who would have thought Leigh would have kept that from him? His embarrassment feels solid in the air.

'I'd like you to take a look at this photo, please.'

The police officer hands Mark a printed sheet. He can't stop himself smiling. Fiona peeks over his shoulder to see what brought the joy to his harried, blushing face.

She looks so pretty!

But then Mark's mercurial face collapses again, he just can't keep a check on his emotions, they are relentlessly assaulting him. He looks up, puzzled. 'Where was this taken?' he asks.

'I'm not certain. Somewhere in London,' replies the police officer.

'When?'

'Some time around Christmas.'

'I don't — I don't recognise the dress,' he stutters.

'No?'

'Or the venue.'

'It was this woman's anniversary.'

'This woman? What do you mean? This is a picture of Leigh.'

The officer moves her head a fraction. Not quite a shake but certainly not a nod of agreement. Fiona thinks there is a level of sympathy in her expression. Mark is the sort of man women feel sympathetic towards, she has long been aware of that. When Leigh first met him, she was always saying, 'I just feel so sorry for him. I want to make things better for him.' As though he was a wounded stray, which in a way he was, as he was a widower with two boys. 'This is a picture of Kai Janssen,' says the police officer carefully. 'Does that name mean anything to either of you?'

'Is she a relation of Leigh's?' Fiona asks. 'The similarity is striking. A cousin, perhaps?' The officer gives a small shake of her head. She keeps her eyes fixed on Mark.

'I don't understand. What sort of anniversary? A work anniversary?' asks Mark.

'No. Her wedding anniversary. I'm sorry to be the one who has to inform you, Mr Fletcher, but there is strong evidence to suggest your wife is a bigamist.'

'What are you talking about?' Fiona demands hotly. Mark says nothing. His mouth is gaping open and closed, open and closed. He looks like a fish on a riverbank gasping for breath. Or maybe waiting for the hammer to bash his head. Stop everything.

'I've just come from her other home. The home she has shared with Mr Janssen for over three years. I'm really sorry.'

The officer says the words 'really sorry' but she does not appear sorry. She is studying Mark carefully.

Working out what he's thinking. Whether he knew this. Fiona wonders: did he? He drops his head into his hands, so no one can look him in the eye. Fiona feels sick, her mind is working overtime. 'I don't understand. Are you saying Leigh is there at this other home with this Mr Janssen?' she asks.

'No, unfortunately she's missing from there too.'

Fiona offers to make tea. She really wants a glass of something stronger. Vodka, ideally. She thinks of the countless times she and Leigh have had a vodka here in Leigh's home — Leigh prefers it with orange, Fiona likes cranberry. She'd take it straight right now. Although, honestly, she feels dizzy enough. A cup of tea is far more sensible, considering everything. The young male police officer follows her into the kitchen, leaving Mark and the policewoman alone. Mark still has his head in his hands. His shoulders are shaking. It looks a lot like he's crying but Fiona can't see his face to know for sure. He could, she supposes, be shaking with shock. Or anger. Fiona looks at the policeboy; her guess is that he's in his mid-twenties. Even so, he is assured, purposeful. She's glad he followed her into the kitchen. She's unsure whether she can manage making the tea, he'll have to do it. She plonks herself on a breakfast bar stool.

'I'm just trying to process what your colleague has just claimed.'

'DC Clements is pretty certain she has her facts straight. She did some checks before we came over here.'

'Leigh has been secretly married to someone else for three years?'

'Yeah. Daan Janssen. He's in bits, too.'

Fiona is pretty sure that isn't information that

should be shared with her, but she files it away to examine later. It might be useful; it might be important. 'Leigh is this Kai? They are definitely the same person?' Her voice is high with incredulity.

'Kylie, you said so yourself. Kai. Leigh.'

'That's fucking madness.'

The policeboy deftly moves around Leigh's kitchen, opening and closing cupboards, until he finds mugs, spoons and teabags. He adds milk and sugar to Fiona's, even though she mutters that she only drinks almond milk, that she doesn't take sugar.

'Drink it up,' he instructs. Fiona is not lactose intolerant; she just prefers the taste of almond milk, but it obviously isn't the moment to be fussy. She does as he says. 'Quite the shock, right?'

'Yes.'

'You didn't know?'

'No.'

He leans closer, lowers his voice. 'Even though you're her best friend? You can say if you did know. You haven't committed a crime or done anything wrong in keeping your friend's secret.'

'I didn't know,' Fiona asserts firmly. He shrugs. Fiona notices that he is wearing a wedding ring; she's surprised, he seems so young. She suddenly feels old and unsure. This boy is married.

He spots her staring at his ring and asks, 'Are you married?'

'No.'

'Hard for you to get your head around this, then. Your best friend being married twice at the same time.'

'Hard for anyone, I should imagine,' Fiona snaps. She doesn't want to sound irritable, but it is undeniably annoying that a child, practically half her age, is

146

guessing at her emotional range. It's true she has never been married even though she's nearly forty-four, but she is aware of the concept. It has just never happened for her. Of course, there have been relationships. She's lived with various partners before, but she's never had anyone drop down on one knee. All three of her live-in relationships ended with infidelity. Theirs, not hers. Two left for other women and she chucked the third one out when she discovered he was being unfaithful. Fiona is no mug. She knows her worth. Leigh often says that men find Fiona intimidating or ultimately inaccessible because she is married to her work. It's certainly true that her work takes up a lot of her time and that she feels passionate about it, but should that be an insurmountable barrier? Fiona wonders how people find it so easy to meet and marry. More and more men Fiona meets nowadays are married and looking for nothing other than a side dish. That is not something she can sign off on.

She briefly wonders whether this policeboy will remain faithful to his wife. He probably is now. He's so young, they are most likely at it like rabbits, totally absorbed in one another, but will they stay faithful? Fiona doubts it, given her experience. The good ones are few and far between. Suddenly, Fiona is aware of the ungracious thoughts swirling around her head. She shouldn't be thinking about the policeman's marriage. She should be thinking about Leigh. What the fuck is wrong with her? She is probably in shock.

Fiona and Constable Tanner take the mugs of tea back into the other room but as soon as the tray is set down, the policewoman stands up and says, 'Well, let's leave it at that for tonight. It's late. We'll be in touch tomorrow. I'll leave you two to drink your tea.'

The moment the door closes behind them Fiona dashes into the kitchen and opens the cupboard where Leigh keeps the vodka.

'What the fuck?' she says as she sloshes generous measures into two glasses.

Mark gives a weak shrug of his shoulders. Lost, defeated. 'I don't understand. I can't believe it. They must have it wrong.'

'They seemed pretty certain. They wouldn't have come round here unless they were sure,' she says carefully. She doesn't want to twist the knife but it's in no one's interest to hide from the facts. Mark stares at Fiona. Glares. His face is stone.

She doesn't like it.

Suddenly, she feels uncomfortable; it is as though the air is being sucked out of the room. She sees the tension build in his face, will it explode through his mouth or fists? He has no control over this situation. Mark needs to be in control. They are too close to each other and yet utterly distanced. It's odd. Normally they get on really well, but he's making her feel uneasy. She straightens her shoulders and reminds herself that everything about this is odd. Off-the-scale crazy. No one is behaving normally. Some women don't get on with their bestie's partners, but Fiona has always loved Mark. She's always thought he was one of the good ones who are few and far between. He looks cold now. Stony. She doesn't know how to reach him.

'They clearly think I have something to do with her disappearance,' Mark continues to glare. His chocolate eyes that bowled Leigh over more than a decade ago bore into Fiona. Alive — not with passion, the way they were for Leigh — but spitting anger. Fiona

148

edges away from him and her back bangs up against the corner of the kitchen counter. She winces. He reaches out a hand towards her, but then hesitates from making contact when he sees her instinctually shrink a fraction. 'Ouch, are you hurt?' His tone is forced jovial.

Fiona shakes her head. 'I'm fine.'

Her voice seems to jar Mark back into himself, in an instant his expression changes. Melts. He looks suddenly vulnerable.

'*You* don't think I have anything to do with her disappearance, do you?'

Fiona holds his gaze, wondering what to say. The truth is no one knows what people are capable of. Who knew that Leigh was capable of being a bigamist, married to two men, running two lives for years and never telling a soul? Never telling her. Fiona thought she knew her best friend inside out. She thought Leigh trusted her. Who can say what secrets Mark might be hiding? What anyone is capable of. It is totally feasible that Mark discovered Leigh's lie. What might that have led to? Crimes of passion are reported in the newspapers all the time. People murder betraying loved ones. It happens.

Fiona takes a deep breath.

She does not believe that about Mark.

'No,' she says eventually. 'No, I don't think you have anything to do with her disappearance, obviously not. My guess is she has run off. Leading a double life must be —' She shrugs, embarrassed. 'Well, fuck, what must it be, Mark? Unbelievably stressful. I can't comprehend it.'

Fiona pours them both another vodka. They knock them back without saying anything more for a moment. They can't find the words.

'It can't be true,' says Mark eventually.

'But she is only here half the time,' Fiona says quietly, trying to convey as much sympathy as humanly possible. 'And the photo.' She shrugs apologetically, although it isn't her that should be apologising.

'What shall I tell the boys?' he asks.

'I don't know. You should talk to the police. See whether they think this is going to hit the papers.'

Mark looks horrified. 'Do you think it will?'

'Well, it might, it's — you know — Juicy. And well — ' Fiona falters, finding it difficult to say any of the stuff that needs to be said. 'It might hit the papers if she hasn't just run off. If there is more to this.' *If they find a body.* 'I hate it that these thoughts are even in my head.'

'This can't be my world,' says Mark. 'It can't be Leigh's world.'

'But it is.' Fiona coughs to swallow the tears that are threatening. 'If the papers pick up on this the boys need to be prepared and protected.' Mark nods. 'Would you like me to stay? To be with you when you tell them?'

He nods again. 'I'll sleep on the sofa, you can have our bed.'

'No, no, Mark. I'll take the sofa. Honestly.' Fiona doesn't want to lie on their sheets. She doesn't want to smell Leigh's sweat, perfume or washing powder, maybe their loving, whereas presumably that is something Mark might need.

'I should have taken the sofa,' he mutters. Fiona doesn't really understand his meaning. She thinks he's not thinking clearly when he adds, 'I want to meet this other man.'

150

'What? No!'

'I have to. I need to see him. See their home. See it all for myself.'

'That's probably not a good idea.'

'Why not?'

Fiona plays with her empty glass, wishing it were full. 'Well, she's missing, isn't she?'

'Yes.'

'So — Well — In cases like these, the husband is always the suspect and we know you didn't do it.'

'You just said you think she's run away.'

'Well, yes, let's hope she has.'

'She's not dead, Fiona.'

Fiona sighs. 'We don't know what she is.'

17

Kylie

Wednesday 18th March

I slept last night. I didn't expect to but the blackness swallowed me. I woke as the morning sunlight crept under the boarded window. I strain my eyes and look around the room for the millionth time. Waiting for something new to jump out at me, something that will help me get out of here. What? I'm not sure. It's not as though a trapdoor is suddenly going to appear. I've checked every link of the chain to see if there is a loose one: there isn't. The zip ties that bind my hand to the chain have chafed the skin on my wrist, but no matter how much friction I create, they are unchanged, immovable. I've scoured the room for a nail or a sharp edge, something I could use to wear away at the plastic but there's nothing. The place is immaculate, bare, barren. Other than the water bottle, which is almost empty now. And the typewritten notes.

As the morning passes, I am forced into using the bucket, and the smell of my own pee now lingers in the room. It's oddly not too disgusting because it is at least human and familiar when everything else is sterile and strange. Although I imagine I will feel differently when I need to do more than wee. Waves of horror and panic slosh through me, leaving me feeling helpless and lost as I wonder how long I might be

152

locked up here for. As I consider being here might not be the worst thing that could happen to me. What is he planning to do to me? I swallow back tears. I try to think about real, physical things, not allow my imagination and fear to take control.

I consider the emptiness of the room. It is not usual. Spare rooms in most homes are stuffed with boxes of old toys or paperwork, unused exercise machines, the ghosts of hobbies — taken up with enthusiasm but not sustained. This room is nothing like that. And the rooms people are kept captive in on TV — on the occasional newspaper report about a real-life example of someone horrendously unlucky — always reveals a squalid, filthy place. Abductors normally live chaotically; the broken and spoilt property reflecting the ravaged lives of damaged, dangerous people.

The empty sterility of this room suggests something much more icily resolute. It has been deliberately cleared, carefully prepared for the purpose of keeping someone captive. My captor has not taken me on a whim. The thought is chilling. I've always believed that anything that has been planned has more chance of success than something that is impetuous. Have I been kidnapped? Does someone think Daan is wealthy enough to pay a ransom for my return? My heartbeat speeds up again. My fingers start to shake once more. I force myself to take a deep breath. I have to stay calm and focused. I'm practised at remaining level-headed and in the moment. Panicking won't help.

I've been trying to remember how I got here. It's tricky to concentrate because my head still aches and I'm beginning to feel the effects of not eating since Monday morning but it's important, so I focus. I remember Monday, taking Seb to school. We walked

153

under a cloud. I was thinking about the row with Mark, what had been said, what was left unsaid, what I couldn't speak of. Seb is generally sunny-natured but I know he resents me walking him to school, so he is never at his best on those journeys. I suppose I have to stop that ritual soon.

I laugh cynically to myself, maybe the decision has been made for me? If I don't get out of here, Seb will have to get himself to and from school no matter how much I want to cling to him. Who will Oli kick against, without his mother to nag him? My sad laugh turns to a definite wail. The thought of my sons left without me lacerates. I push them out of my head. I've trained myself to do that. I'm vulnerable if I think about them, so I mustn't. I am the world's best at compartmentalising. What I need to think about now, is how I got here because it might help me understand where here is and how I can get out. I need to focus.

After I dropped off Seb — a quick squeeze of his shoulder, no chance at all of pulling him into a tight hug or planting a kiss on his head even though I longed to — I walked to the park. On the days my family and friends think I get the late train to Scotland, I meet Fiona and we have a quick coffee and a slice of cake at the café in the local park. I remember meeting her. She couldn't stay long because she had an appointment at the hairdresser's. Her hair is long, like mine — she was going for the big chop, she said she fancied wearing it chin length, but she was vacillating at the last minute about her decision. She showed me a picture on her phone of some Hollywood woman I half recognised but couldn't put a name to, sporting a centre-parted, wavy lob. I encouraged Fiona to go for it. 'I love the soft bends below the cheekbones, it keeps things modern and breezy,' I commented. Or something like that. It seems unbelievable now that we were talking about hair texture and volume. I remember watching her walk away and feeling the usual twinge of sadness that we are not quite what she thinks we are. She thinks we talk about everything, share everything. As I watched her long, narrow back disappear into the distance I felt the space between us. A gap I have created.

Try as I might, I can't remember anything after that. Maybe someone attacked me from behind. The park is generally pretty empty at that time of the morning; the dog walkers have been and gone, as have the school kids trailing into school but it's too early for the young mums with their designer buggies to be heading off to baby yoga or baby music classes. It is possible I was just in the wrong place at the wrong time when this psychopath struck, hit me, dragged me into his car. You do read about such things. I'm more aware than most that life is strange. Have I just been unlucky?

My gaze falls onto the water bottle, it is a supermarket own brand, sparkling. I then pick up the notes and reread them.

I am not the villain here.
Who will come for you? Your husband?

The words make me glance down at my left hand. How have I not noticed before? I'm not wearing any rings. I normally change my rings over just after I leave Fiona. Routine is very important in my world. Is it possible that I was attacked as I slipped off Mark's ring before I put on Daan's? Was I robbed? Daan's rings are particularly valuable. I'm always vaguely nervous when I wear them. The engagement ring is three enormous diamonds jostling for space on a platinum band, the wedding ring is also studded with diamonds. Mark's rings are more modest. A plain gold band for the wedding ring, a small solitaire for the engagement. I always wear my rings.

One set or the other.

The only time I have gone a day not wearing rings was the day I met Daan. My rings were at the jeweller's, because the stone in my engagement ring had come loose and whilst it was being fixed the jeweller suggested he give them both a clean. They were only supposed to be there for an hour, but the day didn't turn out as expected. I sometimes wonder how different my life might be if I'd been wearing my rings that day.

Something occurs to me. Understanding seeps in. It is like icy water being slowly poured over my head, shoulders, arms. It pools around my feet, engulfs me. I might drown.

I am left-handed. If I were restraining someone, anyone, I would chain them up by their dominant hand. Generally speaking, that is a person's right hand, but I've been tied by my left. My captor knows I am left-handed. He knows I prefer to drink sparkling water over still. The realisation is horrifying.

I was not robbed. I was not attacked by a random psychopath.

I know my captor.

Who will come for you? Your husband?

156

'Mark?' Silence. 'Daan?' Nothing.

I feel sick. Weak. My body turns to liquid and shivers crawl through my soul like spiders disturbed, scampering from a dusty corner. I have thought about this moment a thousand times and every time I have thought about it, I've closed my eyes, batted away the inevitable shame, pain, horror. I knew it could not last forever, the life I have constructed.

The lives.

I have always thought I would get found out. Confronted. No matter how much care I took. I assumed one day one of them would find the spare phone, or trail me, that I'd lose track of my supposed whereabouts, slip up when giving an ordinary day-to-day account of what I'd been doing with myself.

I thought I might call out the wrong name during sex.

I imagined that when it happened, I would be screamed at, thrown out, exposed, vilified. I have always been so terrified that Mark would tell the boys, and that I would lose them completely because they'd be utterly disgusted by me. That they would feel betrayed. I have braced myself to face anger, recriminations, hurt. I suppose some part of my brain knew I would one day have to throw myself on their mercy, beg for forgiveness. Forgiveness that most likely would not come. I expected them to hurl abuse, ask me to leave, or to leave me. I didn't think I'd win. Not really, not in the long term.

But I did not expect this.

I shake my head in disbelief. My mind is a mess, mushed and oozing thoughts when usually I am able to be clear and to divide my thoughts into discrete sections.

Could one of my husbands have brought me here?

Neither of my husbands is a violent man.

But they both like their own way.

I have seen both inwardly rage. Outwardly rage too, on rare occasions. Mark when he feels the boys have been mistreated or cheated, Daan because of work stuff. I have seen gritted teeth, clenched fists bang down on tables, fogs of fury, sprays of saliva shower, expletives spat out. But ultimately, both men regain control of their tempers before things ever go too far. They are not thugs. I have never seen either strike flesh. Neither of them would do this to me — bind me, imprison me, practically starve me. Would they?

Honestly, do I know what either is capable of? They have not known what I am capable of.

My body flashes with heat, shame or panic, as I begin to understand what this means. My sweat almost instantly freezes on my skin and I feel both hot and chilled to the bone, an expression that is bandied about but, for the first time in my life, I understand it. I feel so cold, I could be dead. It might be better if I were. I am exposed, stripped. The lack of food is making it difficult for me to think straight. My stomach grumbles and I drop my head into my hands. I wish he'd give me some food. He. Him. Which one?

Which one of my husbands brought me here?

Mark teases me about getting hangry, says that I behave worse than the boys if I am not fed regularly. Whenever we set off for a long walk or drive, he always asks if I have enough snacks with me, commenting that I'll be a bitch when reading the map or that I'll fall out with the satnav, if I am peckish. He sometimes grabs an extra bag of crisps out of the treat drawer

158

and tosses them my way as I fasten my seatbelt. 'Just in case.'

Daan teases me too. He identified that if I am hungry, I lose concentration, that I don't operate at my optimal. Something he exploits, he will sometimes challenge me to a game of chess or cards when I'm waiting for supper. He does so as a joke but also because he likes to win and doesn't have any qualms about utilising an advantage.

They are both right. Same me, different identifiable consequence. Anger. Lack of concentration. Both debilitating. I force myself to stay calm, to concentrate. I need to try to make a plan. I should appeal, say I am sorry. But which one am I talking to? Both men are so different. Not knowing who I am dealing with stops me knowing what to say. Who should I be? The sensible mum that solves everything, looks after everyone, always knows where the lost football shorts are? Or the sexy, cool, independent wife, who has to meet few demands or expectations other than to be interested, interesting, adorable and adoring. I don't know how to start my apologies, my explanations. I don't know who to be. I don't know who I am.

Frustrated, frightened, I begin to shake so hard I think he might be able to hear my bones rattle. 'I'm sorry. I'm so sorry,' I whisper through the door, through the walls. That is true. Whoever I am talking to, that much is true.

Rat-tat-tat. The typewriter keys spring into action. I listen as the paper is pulled from the machine, there's shuffling as it is pushed under the door.

You are going to be.

The words punch me. My tears seem to dry instantly on my cheeks, no more fresh ones fall as terror surges through my body, great waves like passion but spiteful. So brutal, so raw. This is more than a threat; it is a promise. Of course. What did I expect? I never thought it could last forever. That would require infinite luck. I should have listened to my mother, who always told me I am not a lucky person. But I wanted my father to be right. He held the opposite view. He dismissed that acceptance of one's lot with a bored impatience. He declared that you could make your own luck, and you should. All it took, he said, was courage, determination and resilience. My dad pleased himself. My mum pleased no one. My dad was untouchable. My mum was described by nosy neighbours and exasperated distant relatives as 'touched'. An old-fashioned word for mentally ill.

So, I tried my father's way. I tried to make my own luck.

I think my mother was right.

I suppose some people might believe I deserve to be locked up, and maybe I do because what I've done is a criminal offence but not like this. Not chained, not starved.

Which one of them hates me so much he would do this to me?

Which one of them loves me so much?

'Take me to the police!' I yell. 'I'll face it, I'll admit everything. I won't tell them you brought me here.' I listen carefully, but the typewriter stays silent. All I hear is the sound of footsteps, someone walking away.

I am alone.

18

DC Clements

Friday 20th March

'Did I wake you?' Detective Constable Clements asks
as the doors of the lift gently swoosh open and she is
faced with Daan Janssen bare-chested, wearing nothing other than tracker bottoms. He yawns, stretches,
raises his arms above his head, treating her to a flash
of blond thatches of pit hair. Other than those,and a
gentle trail that disappears down from his navel, he is
smooth. Her preference is for smooth men. She can
smell his pheromones, it disconcerts her.

'I haven't slept. Coffee?' He doesn't wait for an
answer but walks through to the kitchen. She follows.
She already has the sense that this man leads, others
follow. She mentally adds it to the profile she is drawing of him. 'I haven't slept well for days,' he tells her as
he starts to move around the kitchen preparing coffee
in a big, shiny, no doubt top-of-the-range Nespresso
machine. 'Normally when my wife is away visiting her
mother, I throw myself into my work, take the overseas meetings, visit the gym, catch up with one or two
people to keep myself busy. But this week it has been
different. I've been agitated. First, because I thought
Pam was ill and then because I became increasingly
certain something was off. I am not wrong, am I?
That's why you are back here.'

Clements chooses not to answer the question

straight away, instead she asks one of her own. 'So, Kai is regularly away from home?'

'Yes. Most weeks she's away for half the week, looking after her mother.'

'How do you both manage? Her being away so much? It must affect your relationship.'

'You know, our friends occasionally ask the same question. I am quite used to it, normally I even enjoy it. Truthfully, I guess we're a little smug about it.'

'Smug?'

'We're secretly convinced that somehow we are in a better place than couples who need to live in one another's pockets. You know? Cooler than people who do not respect each other's independence.' He grins, almost apologetically, probably for using a word like 'cooler', thinks Clements harshly. 'The space between us works well for us.'

He hands Clements a coffee. He hasn't asked her how she takes it. She likes an Americano. She sees that is what he has prepared for her. She takes one sugar. She sips. It is sweetened. She doesn't know how he guessed. Is she that predictable? Or is he that brilliant? There is something about him that makes you believe he knows you, understands you — which is always seductive. This power is both flattering and bewildering. Clements is glad she has clocked it, armed herself against it. Could he perhaps be drawing a profile on her, the way she is on him? Clever people do that with one another: assess, surmise, in order to stay in control, stay a step ahead. It's a talent. A skill.

A problem?

Clements watches him very carefully as she explains how much his charming skill of knowing a person — staying a step ahead — failed when it came to

162

his own wife, the person he should be most intimate with. She breaks it to him that it is not just a matter of him not knowing where Kai is, it is a matter of him not knowing *who* she is.

His wife's name is not Kai Janssen. She is Leigh Fletcher. Formally Kylie Gillingham. Daughter of Pamela Gillingham who does exist but does not live in the north of England and is not beleaguered with Alzheimer's. She lives in Perth, Australia — moved back there two years ago — and is in hail health. Clements tells him, as gently as is possible, that rather than tending her mother Kai, Leigh, Kylie — whatever you want to call her — was living just a few miles away, for half the week, every week with her other husband, Mark Fletcher. Clements concludes, 'But she is missing from that home too.' And as she is revealing this information, Clements is carefully studying Daan Janssen as though he is a cell under a microscope. Because Clements wants to know, is this news to him? Or was he already aware of his wife's treachery?

He doesn't react. He doesn't move or break eye contact, he doesn't swear, punch a wall, or cry. Clements notes his remarkable self-control. When Clements stops speaking there is a silence that stretches for two or three minutes. He breaks it. 'I see. Another coffee?' Clements nods. Not because she wants another coffee but because she recognises his human need to do something, occupy himself. When his back is to her and he's putting water into the machine he asks, 'Are there any children?'

'Two stepsons. She adopted them when she married Mark Fletcher as their birth mother is deceased.'

He turns to her. Excited? Relieved? 'You see, that can't be right. Kai has never wanted kids.' Clements

163

waits a beat. Doesn't have to add, *she didn't want them with you. She didn't want any more so as to avoid complicating things further*. He is a clever enough guy to work it out. She watches his face as he takes just a fraction of a moment to reach the realisation.

'You're sure about all this you are telling me?'

'After you showed me Kai's photo last night, I went back to the station to do some digging. We've checked phone records, employment records, birth and marriage certificates, National Insurance numbers. There is no room for doubt. Kai and Leigh are one and the same woman.'

He nods, draws himself up a little taller. Other men might have collapsed, deflated. Daan grows.

'Why do you think she did this?' he asks.

Clements doesn't know the answer. She doesn't even think it's the relevant question. 'I'm more interested in where she is now.'

'Well, isn't it obvious?' His mouth twitches in irritation. Clements gets the feeling this man thinks everyone is a little slow for him. His pride must be deeply wounded to know he has been the slow one, he will want to reassert himself. 'She's found the whole thing too stressful, so she's thrown in the towel on us both. Most likely moved on to someone new altogether.'

Clements nods. 'It's a possibility.'

'A probability,' Daan Janssen asserts. He passes the DC her second coffee, which she sips hurriedly even though it is too hot and scalds her mouth. 'I suppose, as the second husband I'm not a husband at all so this matter no longer concerns me.'

'Well, it's not as simple as all that.' Clements remembers how Janssen presented himself on their first meeting, he was distraught. She doesn't feel comfortable with his ability — real or feigned — to file this away so neatly and quickly.

'I'll consult a lawyer, but I imagine it is. I was with a woman, she has gone. A grown adult walking away from a duplicitous relationship can't be a police matter.'

'A crime has been committed.'

'I have no interest in pressing charges. Anyway, how can we? She has vanished.'

'Yes, she has.'

Daan Janssen picks up DC Clements' cup, it is still half-full.

He throws the coffee in the sink, rinses the cup, places it carefully upside down on the drainer. 'I'll walk you to the door.'

The police officer is not used to being ejected from buildings; it is usually her job to move people on. She tries to reassert herself as they wait at the lift. 'You will contact us if you hear from her?'

'Of course.' The lift arrives, the doors swish open. Then Daan says, 'And be sure to let me know if a body turns up.'

19

Kylie

Wednesday 18th March

I doze off and when I wake up — bleary-eyed, still woozy, scared — there is food and more water. The relief is prodigious even though this time the water is still, and the tray is laden with all the food I like least. Liver pâté, cucumber batons (I note they actually came in a pack with carrots, which I do like, but the carrots have been removed), cheese and onion crisps (which are the only crisps I don't like to eat) and three cold, tinned hot dogs. I stare at the tray for a nanosecond, surprised by the petty cruelty. This meal has been selected to bring me the least possible comfort or pleasure. These are foods both men know I actively dislike. Which of my husbands would go to the effort of shopping for food that I hate? Then I wonder at myself for being surprised. Whichever it is, he has locked me up; clearly, we're not friends.

I am starving. My best guess is that it's Wednesday lunchtime but it's hard to be sure. The room is really dark, some light comes from around the boarded window and from under the door. There are two small, recessed ceiling lights, but I can't reach the switch. I last ate on Monday morning; I didn't even finish the entire slice of cake then. I hungrily bite the hot dogs. There is no cutlery. I'm not sure if I'm being denied cutlery because I might make a weapon of a fork,

166

or to dehumanise me. I feel filthy using my fingers to eat as I've been forced to pee in the bucket and there is obviously no place to wash my hands. I use the cucumber to spoon the pâté into my mouth and although the taste makes me want to gag the hunger is stronger than either preference or fastidiousness.

'Thank you for lunch,' I yell at the door. I try to sound pleasant, at best I achieve neutral. I can't let anger or fear leak into my voice. 'Who am I talking to?' My question sounds reedy, needy, pathetic but it does at least get a response. I hear the keys of the typewriter being struck.

It doesn't matter which one of us, does it?
It has never mattered to you before.

This is not true. This is so far from the truth. If it didn't matter to me which one I was with, I could have picked either one. That's the whole point. I couldn't choose. But how do I explain that?

I cram a second hot dog into my mouth. I swallow it without tasting, then I force myself to slow down, chew carefully. I might make myself sick, besides I don't know when I'll be fed next. Something about my hunger after the enforced fast reminds me of the first time I dealt with Oli being sick. It was about four months after Mark and I married. He picked up a tummy bug at school, the way kids do. I remember him vomiting all over the lasagne I had carefully prepared for their tea. It was like *The Exorcist*. I was grossed out — the smell, the mess — but then I saw the small boy's big watery eyes, shocked, scared, and I stopped thinking about what I was feeling. I stopped being horrified. I just wanted to fix him. I leapt up from the table, caught a lot of the vomit in the salad bowl, in my hands, down my jeans — I didn't care. I stroked his back, murmured, 'I've got you, it's OK. You're OK, better out than in.' He vomited for twenty-four hours.

Who knew such a small boy could have so much stuff in him? Certainly not me at that point. New to parenting and dealing with sick kids, I was terrified. I thought the doctor's advice not to let him eat anything other than dry toast, maybe a spoonful of rice, was barbaric. Naive, I thought he should be rushed straight to hospital and wondered why everyone else wasn't as panicked as I was. I guess Mark had been through it so often by then that he took it more in his stride. I changed sheets, mopped Oli's hot body with cool flannels and refused his requests for Coco Pops. 'But they are like rice, Mummy,' he pleaded. It was the first time he called me Mummy.

Suddenly, I don't feel hungry. What have I done? I picture Oli and Seb, mops of dark hair, tanned skin and long lashes in common. Seb skinny and angular, all elbows and feet that in the last few months have grown too long for his body which has yet to catch up. Oli is filling out; he wears a hint of the stocky strength of the man he will become. I envisage them as I usually do, huddled over their phones or eyes glued to the TV, oblivious to everything else around them, including me. This is an image I have often been assaulted by in the past. When I am with Daan. On those many occasions I have immediately forced the thought of them out of my head, slammed the door on the room in my brain where the boys sat. I have to sectionalise and bracket, it is the only way. Shut down, blank out. I trained myself so it was as though once I was away from them, I viewed them through tracing paper. The memory of them a pale and poor copy of the original. So far away and indistinct, they did not quite exist. The thought of them did not have the force to rip through the tracing paper, insist on their reality, their notability. I feel awash with shame that I have ever shut a door on them, even mentally. Now I ache for my boys. My children.

And they are my boys.

If either Oli or Seb ever woke in the middle of the night with a terrible dream or a high temperature, it was always me who climbed into their beds to comfort them. Mark would have done it, in a heartbeat, he had done it before I came along, but he knew that if he went into their rooms, I wouldn't sleep alone in our bed anyway. I wanted to be involved, I wanted to soothe and comfort. I wanted to feel needed. So he let me tend them. Joking that he wouldn't 'fight me for a night with a kid in a single bed'. I have made their beds, picked up Lego, built papier mâché volcanoes, shopped, cooked, cleaned bathrooms. Stove to loo. In one end, out the other. Relentless. I've performed these daily devotions, this worship, uncomplaining, with joy, mostly. I have watched them grow. These small beings, stretched out, reached me in a way no one else had until I mothered. And I've listened to them. Heard their funny observations turn from charming to challenging, but not always wrong or rude. Sometimes very thought-provoking. I've been with them as their vocabularies became more complex, their friendship groups more unknown, their desires more secretive. As they've grown, I have tried to store them up but because they constantly changed, my memories are unreliable, they spilt, seep away. I want them to be less liquid, more solid.

And I've wanted all of this, felt all of this, whilst leading a double life.

It's a comfort to think that the boys won't even know I'm missing yet. They won't have cause to be scared. That's something. I wonder, is there a chance this could be over by Thursday? How long does Mark or Daan, whichever, think he can keep me like this? Obviously not indefinitely. Neither man is a killer. I am their wife. The sentence makes my scalp crawl. The wrongness of my situation has lurked in my sub-conscious for years, a dark stain on the peripheral of my vision, a small catching in my nostrils that meant I chose to breathe through my mouth. I'm not used to articulating it even to myself.

I am Mark's wife.

I am Daan's wife.

I belong to them both.

They both belong to me.

If Mark is my abductor, Daan will already know I am missing as he was expecting to see me on Monday. If Daan is responsible, then because of the way I've constructed my life, Mark won't know I'm missing until Thursday afternoon. But this is madness. They will have to let me go eventually. Exposed, humiliated, brought to my knees, lesson learnt but he — which-ever he it is — has to let me go. Doesn't he?

'Mark?' I call out. I scramble on all fours, as close to the door as the chain will allow and listen. I know someone is on the other side of the door. I can't see or hear them, but I can tell there is someone there by the way the light falls. 'Mark, is it you? I think it is. I understand. I'm sorry.' I start to cry. I don't want to. I don't want to appear weak, defeated or pathetic, but I am. I'm all three. 'Think of the boys. I know, I know, you always do. I *should* have. That is what you are thinking right now, isn't it? That I should have thought of them. I am so sorry. Don't let this get out of hand, Mark. Please. If you let me go by Thursday, they will never need to know this has happened, we can carry on as normal.'

The words tumble out, without me really thinking about them. How can we carry on as normal? What is my normal? Two husbands. Mark is never going to agree to that. That isn't even what I mean. Is it? Am I asking him to take me back? Am I saying I'll give up Daan? I don't know. I don't know. I just need to get out of here.

The typewriter throws out a short, angry-sounding burst. I should wait to see what it says but I don't, I talk over the clatter, desperate to get my point across. Desperate to convince. 'Is that what's happening here? Will I be given a choice? A chance? I'll have been taught my lesson without the boys being affected. Mark, I know that matters to you. They above everything, matter to you.'

The note slides under the door.

Wrong.

Reading the word. I clamber, scamper like an animal, back towards the radiator away from the door. As though the word has burnt me. Shit. The room seems to tilt, I'm on a rolling ship in a storm. Wrong husband? Wrong that I'll get a choice, a chance? Wrong that the boys matter above everything? Maybe not above anger, jealousy, fury. My heart is beating so fast now that I can feel it in my throat, in my gut.

171

'Daan?' I realise that calling both men's names is likely to further infuriate whoever it is who is out there but I'm beyond being rational. I slam my hand into the floor. 'Let me explain, let me out. Daan? Daan?' Nothing. I scream, 'I hope to God it is you out there, Daan, because if I've driven Mark to this point of madness, the boys will lose both parents!'

The typewriter clatters. I scramble for the note.

Don't pretend to care about the boys.
You only care about yourself.

I do care about the boys. I love them. It might not look that way right now, considering everything, but I do. I always have. That fact has never changed. It's unalterable.

Suddenly, I feel a familiar but rare gurgling low in my gut. I can't reach the bucket quickly enough; the waste starts to pour out of me before I can pull down my trousers and pants. Steaming shitty liquid runs down my legs. I look around me helplessly. I snatch up the sheets of paper and try as best as I can to use those to clean myself, but the waste keeps flowing from my body. I've barely eaten anything these past few days but anything I have eaten is now on my clothes, my legs, the floors, the bucket. It's even on my hands — steaming, stinking, humiliating. The food must have been covered in a laxative.

I peel off my jeans and pants throw them in a corner, I'll put them on when they dry out. I can't afford to use my drinking water on cleaning anything other than my hands and legs. I sit in the corner furthest from the door, back against the wall. Half-naked. Sullied. Degraded. My stomach screams with hunger, but I can't risk eating anything else, my arsehole is raw.

I start to cry. To sob. My pity is mixed with fury. 'Thank you for lunch, fuckface.'

20

Mark

Friday 20th March

Mark doesn't know where to start with telling the boys their mother is a bigamist. Whether it is even something he ought to do. Isn't it bad enough that she's missing? That she's gone? Isn't that enough for a child to process? Oli might know the word but Seb would probably sigh and ask, 'Do I have to look it up?' Leigh makes the boys do that — look up in a dictionary words they don't recognise or understand. She only allows them to google if there isn't a dictionary close to hand. She says the process of researching etymology helps with remembering the meaning better than just being told. Yesterday, the government announced they are closing schools and cancelling exams. Mark thinks his head is about to explode. How the fuck is he supposed to home school Seb on top of all of this? Leigh would have relished that task. She'd have immediately reached for pens, drawn up timetables, researched resources, downloaded the Duolingo app.

He's furious with her. Loathes her. Feels betrayed in a way that makes him want to shed his own skin. Slither out of it like a snake. Cast aside who he is and start again. That particular thought winds him. Was that what she felt every time she left their house? Did she shed them?

Fiona is at the supermarket. Mark has noticed that

when the three of them are alone together, the house descends into a fog of recriminations; spiky anger — or maybe fear — stains the atmosphere. Largely, they all hide out in separate rooms. So Mark is surprised when Oli strides into the kitchen, goes directly to the fridge, opens it, peruses the contents, takes out a plastic bottle of milk and starts to drink.

'Get a glass,' says his father. Oli tuts, rolls his eyes but does reach for a glass.

'I think Seb is crying,' says Oli. 'He just can't comprehend how Mum might leave him like this.'

'No.' Mark knows he needs to go and comfort his youngest. Try to stop the baffled, hurt tears but he's hesitant. What can he say? He heaves himself off the breakfast stool.

Oli looks pleased that his dad has broken through his inertia and is going to do some parenting. He wants to try to gee him up. He fishes his phone out of his back pocket. 'Look at this meme, Dad.'

Mark almost bats away his son's phone, he's not interested — Leigh was always better at feigning attention to mindless memes — but he digs deep to find some level of patience. If it matters to Oli, he should try to pay attention.

Mark doesn't understand what he's looking at. There is a man walking around his house, muttering about being all prepped for lockdown. He has a six-pack of beers tucked under one arm, the remote control in his other hand. He opens cupboards and shows piles of loo rolls and packets of dried pasta, neatly stacked. He nods, approving of his own planning. Then he opens the door to his understairs cupboard, there is a full wine rack and his wife. She is bound and gagged. Struggling to escape. The man

175

on the video says, 'Yup, all ready for lockdown.' He nonchalantly selects a bottle of wine from the rack and closes the door on his wife, trapping her in the dark cupboard.

'What the fuck, Oli!' yells Mark.

Oli looks startled. His father doesn't usually swear at him. 'Funny, right?' he says, but there's no certainty in his voice, or stance, or eyes. Oli seems to understand his mistake now. He turns red and starts to walk hurriedly out of the kitchen.

'No, that's not bloody funny. Do not show that to your brother, do you understand? Do not show that to anyone. Do you hear me?'

Oli doesn't reply but Mark hears his bedroom door slam. The rage surges through his body. It has nowhere to go. It isn't Oli's fault. Mark shouldn't have shouted at him. This is all her fault. But she's not here. Not stood in front of him. That's the problem.

Mark looks under the kitchen sink and grabs the roll of black bin bags. He bounds up the stairs, taking them two at a time. The house seems to shake. Anger is charging around his body like a highly combustible fuel. He might explode. He opens her wardrobe door and starts to wrench her clothes off their hangers and shove them into the sacks. Dresses, tops, jeans tumble into the binbags and settle like twisted limbs in a mass grave. The process isn't fast enough for him, he stops wasting time and throws garments into the sacks with the hangers too. He tries not to remember when he last saw her wearing each piece, he refuses to recall how she filled her clothes, sometimes twirled in front of him, happy with her look, or on other occasions groaned she had nothing to wear. The gap that opens up in the wardrobe is satisfying. He wants rid

176

of her. All traces of her. The sack fills up quickly, he grabs a fresh one. Then a third. Everything must go. He wants to wipe her out. He yanks open the drawers where she keeps her underwear and starts to push her pants, socks, bras into the sacks too. Carefully coiled belts, folded scarves and even make-up are tossed away. These things are part of her sham, part of her deception.

'What are you doing, Dad?' Mark jumps as though he's been scalded. He turns to see Seb staring at him, wide-eyed, scared.

'Just having a clear-out.'

'Of Mum's things?'

'Yes. I'm taking them to the charity shop. She doesn't need them.'

Seb looks like he wants to cry again. 'She might need them, when she comes back.'

'She's not coming back,' says Mark. He turns away from his son, because he can't bear his expression. The pain he radiates punches Mark over and over again in the stomach, the head. He wishes he'd never brought Leigh into their world. He can't bear the fact his boys are going to lose two mothers. 'There is some ice cream in the fridge. Why don't you go and get some? I'll be down in a moment. I'm nearly done here.'

Seb glares at him but leaves the room.

Mark always had more space in his wardrobe and as a consequence she stored her wedding dress there. It is not enough to throw that out, donate it to charity. He snatches at the pretty floaty fabric. It's easy for him to put his big hands on it and rent it apart. Each tear, rip, slash, slakes his thirst for obliteration. Only when the dress is in tatters does his breathing start to slow.

Her clothes are now nothing more than chaotic snarls of junk, trash. It strikes him as funny that something can alter in value so significantly, depending on how you view it. He carries the black sacks downstairs. He is red in the face, his back is clammy, but he feels a bit better. He doesn't feel so much of a fucking fool.

21
Fiona

'What do you think he's like?' Mark asks.

'Who?' Fiona is pretty certain she knows exactly who Mark is referring to, but she doesn't want to make a mistake by bringing his name into this home before Mark does.

'Him, her other husband,' he spits out the word. Fiona reaches for the plastic basket in which laundered, but yet-to-be ironed, clothes lie tangled. Mark had pulled the items from the dryer earlier but hadn't thought to fold and smooth them, that was the sort of thing that only the person who finds themselves responsible for ironing remembers to do, knowing it makes the job easier in the long run. Fiona does all her own ironing — obviously — and it seems like Leigh does all of the Fletcher family's. Fiona tips the contents of the basket onto the kitchen surface, that she has just cleared and wiped, and then methodically starts to fold the laundry.

'What does it matter what he's like?'

'Oh, come on, Fiona,' Mark sighs impatiently. Of course, it is mad of her to pretend it doesn't matter. Other than where Leigh is right at this moment, the only thing that can matter to Mark is the all-pervasive question: what does the other man have that he doesn't? What had seduced his wife into becoming not another man's lover, but another man's *wife*? It has to be pretty spectacular to instigate a treachery

179

so complete and absolute. Like anyone who has ever been betrayed, Mark is most likely stuck in that deeply disgusting and disturbing place where he is eaten up with a need to know everything about the other person he has been betrayed for. Yet Fiona knows that every piece of knowledge will whip, sting, inflame his sense of inadequacy, confusion, shame. Mark perhaps even knows as much too but he won't be able to stop himself forensically googling and trailing all the social media accounts he can track, examining any morsel of information he can glean. What does the other man look like? What does he do with his life? Why did she pick him? It is a dark, destructive compulsion. But then most compulsions are.

'You know, it's not like she's just left me for another man. That sort of jettisoning goes on all the time. That's commonplace, manageable. What she has blown up is not just what we had, but who we are. My past, the boys' childhood, it is all annihilated. It never existed.'

It is late, the boys are asleep, or at least in their rooms, faking sleep and playing on their phones. Fiona has spent most of the day at the Fletchers' but even so she hasn't been alone with Mark. This morning she went to the supermarket, this afternoon he said he needed to take a walk, to clear his head. She offered to go with him, but he asked if she would stay with the boys. 'In case she comes home,' Fiona suggested, trying to keep him hopeful.

'Yeah, right, that,' he muttered. He didn't seem to believe it was a possibility.

He was gone all afternoon, but Fiona didn't mind. She hung out with Seb, helped him with his geography homework and then watched banal YouTube

180

videos with him that she had pretended to appreciate, and did in a way because they made him genuinely giggle. Oli had heard them laughing and eventually joined them on the sofa. The three of them sat closer than they might normally.

There was something comforting about the tangy smell of Lynx body spray oozing off one boy, and fried food and pop off the other. From time to time, Fiona surreptitiously turned her head to catch the scent of them.

Mark returned just before supper, which Fiona had prepared, and they all ate together. She didn't ask him what he'd been doing all afternoon. Where he had been. Both boys trudged back to their separate rooms after they'd cleared their plates, conversation exhausted. Being together they felt obligated to appear hopeful. It was wearying.

'I'll come up and turn your lights out later,' Mark offered. He wanted to tuck them in, maybe kiss their foreheads, like he did when they were younger. Nowadays bedtime was more often about negotiating the relinquishing of phones. Oli didn't respond at all, Seb shrugged. No one wanted to perform any of the usual bedtime rituals that marked the end of another day when their mum hadn't come home.

'The boys just need some space too,' Fiona comments.

Mark nods. 'Thanks, Fiona, your being here really helps.'

'Oh, I'm doing nothing.' She knows this isn't true. She's done the shopping, laundry and cooking; she's being a surrogate mum but it's not very English to brag about one's usefulness in a crisis. Mark raises a small grin, understanding the code. 'You've done everything. Not least simply keeping the conversation going at supper. A supper you made. The boys are a bit calmer around you.'

It hasn't been discussed but it seems to be tacitly agreed that Fiona will stay on the sofa again tonight. She reaches for a bottle of Merlot that she bought this morning. She's pretty sure it's Mark's favourite. She holds it up. He nods. She pours two large glasses.

Mark sits down in front of the family computer that is on a small desk in the corner of the kitchen, where the boys are encouraged to do their homework. Fiona smiles as she remembers talking to Leigh about this. 'Is it so you can oversee their homework while you make tea?' she'd asked.

'No, it is to minimise the chance that they lose hours watching porn whilst pretending to do home-work,' Leigh had replied with a wink and a grin. Leigh knows the boys inside out. Fiona had often enough witnessed Leigh intuitively understand that whilst one of the boys may appear sulky, they were in fact nerv-ous about something; then she'd offer to run through Seb's lines for whatever school play he was rehearsing or she'd give Oli a pep talk about the likelihood of him being picked for the football team. Mark was more likely assuming the kids were just being a bit 'teeny' and morose. He often demanded that they 'Turn that frown upside down'. Not that Mark is a bad parent, far from it. On the scale he is somewhere between better-than-most and good. Leigh is excellent. She has also always been an excellent friend too. If Fiona is ever feeling lonely or a bit depressed about a lousy date or the prospect of a long weekend alone, what-ever, she never has to admit as much to Leigh. Leigh just seems to sense it and will immediately issue an invitation for Fiona to join them for Sunday lunch or maybe just to stand on the sidelines and watch Oli's match.

It is unbelievable to think that lovely Leigh has done something so wrong. Something illegal, immoral.

Evil.

Because looking at Mark now, splintered with grief and heartache, it is hard to think of Leigh's actions as anything less than evil.

This evening, Fiona had explained to Oli that Leigh was a bigamist. Seb is too young to understand it all, but Fiona thought it was fair to bring Oli up to speed. He is not a baby and he'd resent it if they treated him like one. Oli said he felt he was Luke Skywalker discovering Darth Vader was his dad. That seemed about right to Fiona. The whole thing was such a colossal shock.

Fiona doesn't want to judge. Relationships are a morass of dos and don'ts; broken rules and hearts. Her own acidic experiences prove that. How many times had she discovered she was dating a married man, for instance? Not by design. She would meet someone on an app and they always say they are single at first, then when she started to care (always after sex) they would admit to being married. Fiona remembers chatting about this to Leigh.

'They don't want to hide it for any length of time. They want you to know, so you understand their level of commitment,' she'd explained.

'Or lack of it,' Leigh had pointed out. Eyes wide.

'Precisely.'

'I'm sorry.'

'Well, it's not your fault.'

'You know what I mean,' mumbled Leigh.

183

'You are so lucky to have Mark. Shall we clone him?' Fiona had asked with a laugh. She didn't like to appear mopey.

'No. Yes. I mean no, we probably shouldn't try to clone him but yes, I am lucky. I see that. I know that.' Was Fiona just misremembering things now, filtering? But was Leigh confused, defensive? Fiona recalls her adding, 'But he came with his drawbacks.'

'The children?' Fiona had gasped.

'No, not the boys. I'd never describe the boys as a drawback. His steadfast insistence that we couldn't adopt or foster. That was hard.'

'But you have two anyway,' Fiona pointed out.

Had Leigh blanched, blinked slowly? Fiona was sure she had. She wasn't misremembering or rewriting history. 'Oh yes, two *children*,' Leigh had confirmed. Did she momentarily think Fiona knew more than she did?

Leigh has two children, that is two more than Fiona has; she should have counted her blessings. And now it turns out she has two husbands as well. It is unbelievable.

Fiona brings herself back to the here and now. 'Do you think her parents are to blame?' she asks Mark.

Mark shakes his head. He admires Fiona's loyalty but has never been a fan of the therapy woe-is-me culture that allows people to blame mummy and daddy for their own fuckedupness. Fiona clearly sees as much reflected in his face because she tries to explain. 'I'm just saying, from what she's told me, her dad was emotionally disinterested — hell, every which way disinterested — and her mum tried too hard to please him. Or to be seen, or something. She was split between their two homes, wasn't she? After they divorced, she — '

Mark cuts Fiona off impatiently. 'Look, maybe you're right. Maybe everything can be explained but nothing can be excused.' He isn't ready to unearth any understanding. Mark lets out a deep breath, pulls on a mask that radiates grim determination and taps the keyboard. Fiona abandons the folding of the laundry and plonks herself down on the bench next to him; she is just as curious as to what Mark's search might throw up. Mark's fingers quickly fly over the keyboard. Tap, tap, tap. Mark taps in *Dan Jansen*.

'He's a fifty-four-year-old Olympic speed skater?'

'The police said he was Dutch, that's unlikely to be how you spell his name,' Fiona points out.

'How do you think you spell it?'

'Dan will be double 'a', maybe. And Jansen could be double 's'. Try that.'

There are a number of Daan Janssens but some are too young, others don't live in London; it is an unusual enough name to quickly and easily identify the right man.

The real Daan Janssen is just as impressive as an Olympian. Maybe more so. He is CEO in some trading division in the city. Mark clicks through to the company website. His suave, smooth face shines out from the top of the 'Who We Are' page and the same image is at the bottom of the mission statement which Fiona and Mark read in full although, having done so, neither of them is really any the wiser about what the company does. Something important, powerful, lucrative. That much is obvious.

Mark cannot take his eyes off the image. The pixels begin to separate, dance in front of him as he stares at the blond, chiselled man with green eyes and an easy,

185

confident smile that seems to say sincere, serious but also entertaining, invigorating. It is just a head-and-shoulders shot but somehow the man's mass and self-assurance radiate off the screen and punch Mark in the face. Mark is shorter, darker, more hirsute. His smile is generally hard won, tighter. 'She clearly doesn't have a type,' he mutters darkly.

Fiona doesn't know how to respond. If she speculates that the men might have similar personalities — perhaps they are both ambitious, hardworking, courteous? — she is wading into murky waters. If she suggests the contrast is the appeal, she is as good as holding Mark's head under the water, until he drowns. She stays silent as they trail through Daan's social media accounts. He has Facebook, Insta and Twitter but it appears that he rarely posts on any of them. When he does, it is with photos of breathtaking scenery taken in far-flung exotic places: mountains, lakes, waterfalls. He — presumably they — obviously travelled a lot.

'All those times she said she had to work away for a week, do you think they were real?' asked Mark. 'Or do you think she was with him?'

'I was just wondering the same thing about that trip she had with her mother last year. You know, when the two of them supposedly met up in Dubai to celebrate Pamela's seventieth birthday,' sighs Fiona. 'Did that happen or was it another lie? I remember thinking at the time ten days in Dubai seemed a lot. There are only so many glitzy malls you can trail through and Pamela isn't a sunbather. Maybe Leigh spent a bit of time with her mum and then the rest with him.'

'I'll need to talk to Pamela and check the dates,' mutters Mark grimly.

Fiona flashes him a smile that she hopes is sympathetic and supportive. 'At least there are no pictures of beaming faces, his or hers.' Although on four or five of the photos there are two shadows dripping across the scene. A man and a woman holding hands. Mark flinched when he first saw the shadows. He obviously recognised Leigh's as easily as Wendy would know Peter Pan's.

Kai Janssen has social media accounts too. Ones where she displays photos of artfully arranged books, cups of coffee, cocktails and flowers. Her hands, legs or feet are often in shot but never her face. She's been very careful not to risk being recognised, no doubt aware that the six degrees of separation that are supposedly between everyone are often pinched to just two or three degrees on social media. Mark slowly and systematically clicks on the profiles of everyone who follows or has even liked her comments. 'Should I reach out to each of these people?' he asks.

'I don't know. To what end?'

'I just want to know about her life. Her other life. I need to understand it.'

'But would these people even respond? The few men who have liked her posts are likely to be couple friends — you know, Daan's friends, really. They are unlikely to want to talk to you. And women are generally reluctant to interact with men they don't know who approach them through Instagram.'

Mark sighs again, deeply, as though there is a storm inside him that needs to escape.

'I could do it for you,' Fiona offers.

'Will you?' He brightens.

'Yeah, leave it with me. The women at least are more likely to respond to me.'

Fiona starts to tap on her phone while Mark continues to search for information about Daan. It doesn't take long to find details of where the other husband's office is and where he lives. People are unaware what information telephone directories and electoral rolls hold.

'I'm going to visit him,' he announces firmly.

'I don't think that's a good idea.'

'I have to. I need to see her home, to know this is real.'

Fiona wants to put her arms around Mark and give him a friendly hug the way she had on countless other occasions, but she stops herself. Obviously, the gesture would just be intended to reassure but it seems a weird thing to do if Leigh isn't in the vicinity. Loaded. Open to misinterpretation. 'It is real, Mark. I'm sorry but it is,' she says, carefully. 'And honestly, I think we both know you are too angry to meet up with him. It might, you know, end badly.'

Mark turns red; it isn't clear to Fiona if it is embarrassment or a deepening fury. She knows a lot about the Fletchers' lives. She knows about the time Mark held a guy up against a wall by the scruff of his jacket, legs dangling, even though the guy was taller than Mark. The incident had happened at one of those children's adventure parks, a place with trampolines, rope ladders and ball pits. A family place. The guy had lifted Seb off a rocking horse so that his own son could have a go. Seb had just got on the horse after queuing for it for twenty minutes, and when Oli — protective of his younger brother — pointed out that was unfair, the guy had yelled at him. He made both boys cry. They were very young. Leigh had been there and from her account, the guy did sound like a prick.

'Mark was terrifying,' Leigh had laughed, not really afraid. 'I thought this bloke was going to pee himself.'

'What did Mark say?' Fiona had wanted to know.

'I don't think it was what he said, it was how he said it. He was all quiet and threatening, proper psycho.'

And there was that time when a neighbour complained about the boys playing football in their own back garden, he said they were annoying and too noisy. He called them brats. Mark tore a strip off the neighbour. Even though he was elderly. He just snapped. 'Where the hell do you think they should be, if not in their own garden? Hanging around the corner shop? Drinking in the rec?' He's never spoken to the neighbour since.

Fiona has witnessed his fierce over-protectiveness first hand. Once, when they were all on a day trip to Bath, Leigh bumped a car as she was parking, a tiny bump, no damage done. She was full of apologies but the other driver called her 'a silly careless cow'. Mark was out of the passenger seat in seconds; he threw the guy against the car bonnet like he was in an episode of *The Wire*.

'I'll go and see him,' offers Fiona.

'You? Why?'

'Well, first because, like you, I am curious but, unlike you, I'm not furious.'

'Hey, that rhymes. You are a poet and you don't know it.' Mark treats Fiona to a tired grin. It strikes her that hard-won smiles have their charm.

'I can report back. We can't risk you going over there and losing it but maybe we do need to know more about him. I said before, one or other of you is a suspect.'

'Well, I haven't hurt her.'

'I know that, silly.'

It was an uncompromisingly childish word, designed to beguile and pacify. Mark used it on the children when they were much younger. Still, he appreciates it. Some part of him wants to be infantilised. It is too much. Too tragic.

'How will you make contact?'

'I'll call on him, tell him the truth, I'm a friend of Leigh's and I want . . .'

'Want what?'

'I want to get to know Kai.'

22
Oli

Oli sits at the top of the stairs in the dark and listens to his dad and Fiona talk in the kitchen. He often does this, listen in on adults. It's not because he's sneaky. It's because they are. Normally, there is not much to hear. Normally, his parents talk about what to watch on TV or whether there is enough milk for breakfast. Tonight, obviously there is a lot more being said. There was on Sunday too. His parents really went at it. He was surprised at the time and also he wasn't. Not really. His dad really downplayed the scale of the row to the police. You can't blame him for that, though. He'd be mad to admit to what was really said. Considering everything.

He is glad she has gone. Bye bye, skank. Who needs a fucking mother, anyway? He's nearly sixteen, he's three inches taller than her already.

What a day! Fuck. He is buzzing. There is a weird energy running through him. Like he's nervous, anxious but also like he's just won a match or something, scored a hat-trick. He can't believe his life at the moment. For ages he's been just the same as everyone else really; thinking about exams, his hair, football, his mates, who he should ask to the prom — all that normal stuff, and that was OK, but now this! He can't get his head around it.

The police are investigating his mother's disappearance. Bad. No matter how chill he wants to appear about it, he knows that is very bad. But then GCSEs have been cancelled! Good, no matter how shit he is feeling about everything else. That is a result! It looks like they are going to work out grades on coursework or something, which is pretty neat for him because his mum — he catches himself — Leigh helped him on quite a bit of that.

Oli has lots of friends and is popular at school, with everyone except the teachers, that is, who think he's lazy, disorganised and not trying hard enough. This might all be true, he doesn't know. He just thinks exams suck, he's crap at them. He had started to think they were probably right, the teachers. Most likely he would struggle to get to a good sixth form and eventually a good university, or even a shit one, come to that. So why bother?

He remembers saying that to Leigh, quite often. She actually never calls him lazy, or disorganised. She just says things like, 'There's a knack to exams, we just have to work on developing that.' She made it sound easy, and as though they were in it together. When he was getting into knots with some impossible homework and close to losing it, she'd say, 'Maybe we should find a different way of looking at this problem?' She'd let him dictate his thoughts into his phone and then help him write up what he'd recorded as a structured essay. It sort of worked with the way he thought about stuff.

Thinking about her being this thoughtful and patient, makes his stomach spasm.

So yeah, his coursework was OK. He might get some seven and eight grades now. Even in the non-science subjects. Leigh always said he was a seven and eight sort of kid. She didn't agree with the teachers. She

192

said he'd find his own success, his own way. It was a pretty good thing to hear.

Until, that is, you know she's a liar. Then it doesn't really matter what she said, *ever*.

If the exams hadn't been cancelled, Oli would have had to spend the next few months revising. Even the thought of cramming the facts into his head, being sure as he pushed one in another one fell out, scares him, but now he doesn't have to worry about any of that. It's the biggest break ever! He would have spent nights lying awake thinking about that airless school gym, him sweating, his head fuzzy with facts that swam around, weak and vague. He would never have been able to remember the difference between attrition and abrasion when it came to the erosion of coastlines, and all the different French verb endings. It made his scalp itch to think about it, his palms clammy, throat dry. But all that was gone now. Thank fuck.

Still, he must remember not to look too pleased about it in front of his dad because his dad is behaving like a mental case right now. Yeah, OK, his wife going missing is clearly a blow, but Oli thinks his dad should have some pride. Considering everything they've discovered. Oli would never let a girl get to him so much. And even if she had, he would never let anyone know. He'd just get his revenge on her. He wouldn't be left looking like a total dick. His dad should have sex with Fiona or something, to get even.

His dad is not having sex with Fiona though, instead he's behaving like some sort of jailer with him and Seb. Monitoring his every movement, making it harder to simply get in and out the house, FFS. He wonders if they'd notice if he slipped out now. He really feels a need to get away. Just out. Away from here. Away from her absence. The lack. He could go down to the embankment. It's a really cool place to hang out and practise tricks. Although she's sort of ruined the place now.

That is where he saw her, with him.

Six months ago. They were just walking along the street, hand in fucking hand, as though it was the most natural thing in the world. She looked comfortable, entitled. She should have been checking over her shoulder, nervous about who might see them. It was so arrogant not to be jumpy, cautious.

She looked really beautiful. It was a weird thing to think about your mum and not something he did think generally. His mates sometimes said his mum was fit. When they were younger, she had been identified as a MILF, it was just something that was said when they were playing video games in the safety of their own bedrooms. The confession spilling out amongst all the cussing and trash talk that was routine whilst shooting up Russian mercenaries. Oli hadn't liked it and told everyone to 'fucking shut up' which they had. Sebastian is still young enough to say his mum looked pretty and he sometimes wants to take a photo of them all when they are heading out somewhere, but Oli outgrew that mum/son adoration thing a while back. So it surprised him that he couldn't help but notice she was glowing, shimmering. He honestly didn't recognise her at first, she looked like someone else. Besides, she was supposed to be at work in Scotland.

Then they fucking kissed, in the street. Totally gross. The man was nothing like his dad. He was younger, taller, blonder. He was wearing a suit. Oli had never

194

seen his father in a suit, other than on his wedding day which Oli could barely remember but there were photos all around the house.

His mother was having an affair.

He isn't an idiot. Loads of his friends' parents are divorced. Usually their dads started banging someone else, usually younger and usually someone they met at work. That was the pattern. He didn't know of any mums who had affairs, though. It was so weird. What was wrong with his dad? How dare she? He had followed them. It was nuts but what else could he do. He didn't want to look at them, but he couldn't take his eyes off them either. They walked for ages. It was a hot day. The bloke took his suit jacket off, threw it over his shoulder. Oli scooted along on his board, sweat pooling at the base of his back. Following someone isn't as easy as they make out in the movies. He kept his distance, but he was scared he'd lose sight of them. Unlikely though, as the man was a fucking giant. He was sure his mum was just going to turn around and spot him, but she didn't. She was too absorbed in the giant. It made him fucking sick.

They went back to this really flash apartment block. He couldn't work out if it was a hotel or what. It looked like apartments but there was a bloke at the reception desk. What was that about? They went inside. Through the huge glass wall, Oli watched his mum chat to the receptionist. They were all friendly, not in a rush. She should have been ashamed, she should have been skulking. Hoping not to be spotted. But she was so relaxed.

He waited for ages for her to come out. She didn't. He'd have waited all night but the bloke on the reception desk came out and asked what he was hanging around for. 'Get along home, or I'll call the police.'

'What have I done wrong?' Oli yelled back. Fucking loser. He hadn't done anything wrong, but he moved along anyway. He had a feeling his mother wasn't going to come out of the apartment block any time soon.

Oli didn't know what to do with the information. He got up every day and wondered, is this the day she tells Dad and leaves us? He didn't want it to be. Yet he did. It made him nervous, angry. He watched her to see if there were any signs that she was more or less happy than usual. There were none. She was just the same as ever. Just as reliable. Just as interested in his friends, school and football, just as uninterested in his Insta, his obsession with trainers. She didn't change and that should have reassured him, but it didn't, it worried him. He started to wish she would act differently, say something. Rowing or crying or something, maybe even leaving, would be better because her not changing meant this was her norm, and he began to wonder just how long it had been going on?

He couldn't look at her in the same way. He hated being alone with her. He backed off and that was desperate because it just made her try harder with him. She cooked his favourite meals, turned up to every match every weekend, she was constantly asking, 'You OK, Oli? Anything worrying you?' What was he supposed to say to that? He felt embarrassed that he knew this weirdly intimate thing about her. It made him feel mad, alone, cheated and he didn't know what to do with those feelings. He started calling her Leigh. He didn't want her to be his mother anymore. She had poisoned his home. His life.

She was so smug. Going about her life as usual.

Tricking them all into thinking she was a nice person. That she loved them. He wanted to spoil things for her. He wanted her to taste some of her own poison.

23

Kylie

Wednesday 18th March

The room stinks. I stink.

Here's the thing. I have been a better wife to both of them because I have two husbands.

Or is that just what I've always told myself?

When I was a child, it was always clear when my father was seeing other women. Unlike some sorry-assed adulterers he did not try to smother his culpability with compensatory acts of sorrow or regret; he did not buy my mother guilt flowers. He did not recognise his own fault and responsibility. Far from it. Instead he blamed my mother for not being enough for him. He punished her for making him stray. My father did not like to see himself as a bad person, an adulterer. He reasoned that she made him behave worse — be worse than he wanted to be — because he was somehow, on some level, forced into adultery because of her failings. Madness, I know. But his own particular brand of madness and we all have one.

Guilt and unacknowledged self-loathing meant he itched for opportunities to blame her, to find her lacking so that he didn't have to blame himself. A poorly ironed shirt, a teabag left in the kitchen sink, a differing opinion on a TV show could lead to a humdinger, knockout, nasty knuckleduster of a row. A fight. He never physically hurt her, he didn't have to, his words wounded. Mortally. He would accuse my mother of being cloying and beneath him. This confused me later, after he told me there are women you marry and women you fuck. My paraphrasing. He said there are women who are something, others who are nothing. But in that case, what was my mother after he stopped being married to her? An ex-something? Was Ellie really the only something?

It didn't matter what he said to Mum, how much he insulted her, blamed her, ignored her, he couldn't make himself feel better, he could only make her feel worse which was what he was running from in the first place; hurt feelings.

My mother was strongly disinclined to fight back. She often said, 'Hush now, Hugh, you don't mean that. Stop saying things you'll regret.' But he would rail anyway, yell, blister, bark, squall for hours. Eventually, she learnt not to fuel his fire with platitudes which he thought were cowardly, and over time she resorted to silence or tears. It was cruel. Hard to watch.

I would not be like him. I refused to be. That much I have always been sure of. I know what the universal opinion is of people who have affairs. They are unilaterally dismissed as bad, undisciplined, selfish. I love both men and I have always been good to both men. I married them to be something better than a common adulterer. People who have affairs always think they are so special, so ground-breaking and different, but they are not. They are ordinary, predictable, boring.

At least I am not that.

I would not have a constant see-saw of affection. Favouring one man because he was the first, the next because he was a novelty. There was no hierarchy. No other man. Not that such a concept exists for their gender. We hear of the other woman, not the other man. No one thinks a man can be anything other than centre stage. He is never just a bit on the side. He is never called a homewrecker. But there are names, humiliating tags that I would not permit. I would not have a cuckold and a lover, both labels marred with preconceptions. One pitiful, the other unstable. And I would not blame Mark for not being enough, Daan for being too much.

It is not much of a defence, I know, but I did at least take onus. I owned the guilt and grief, I absorbed it all. I rarely row with either man. In fact, things that Mark and I might have usually argued about, had indeed previously and reasonably bickered about — like whose turn was it to go to the supermarket or where we were going to go on holiday — I have let go since I married Daan. I smile. I brush it aside. I let him have his way. I always go to the supermarket. He always chooses our holiday destinations.

The stench of my waste lingers in the air. I can't get used to it. I can't ignore it. I'm so hungry again.

'Please, this is enough now,' I wail out loud.

I am a better wife to Mark because I am married to Daan.

I am a better mother too. More patient, more fun, more alive. I am better because there was an excess of energy, garnered from my other life. I never mummy-slump. When out for a family walk, I don't leave them to trail, heavy-footed behind Mark and me, heads bent over phones or earbuds in, trapping them in a world I can't access. Instead I walk alongside them, sometimes I hop or jump, behave childishly. Which they enjoy. It diminishes the difference between us,

200

moves me closer to them. I set challenges. 'Race you to that tree.' 'Race you *up* that tree.' I build camps in the woods with them. At home I play *FIFA* on Xbox with Seb and *Warzone* with Oli, I talk to them about more than schoolwork. Our conversations flit from rappers to YouTubers to haircuts, friendships, girls, travel, sport. My absences from my boys are inexcusable. I know it. Possibly inexplicable. But when I am with them, I am at least 100 per cent with them. I do not spend my time nose buried in my phone or out on long, private runs. All parents have outlets. Everyone needs an escape.

I have never confided the particulars of my situation to anyone. How could I? But if I had, they would have asked, 'Why not just leave Mark? Why not just divorce?' There are a myriad answers to those questions. I still love Mark. I thought that would change but it didn't. I trust Mark. I have a life and a home with Mark. The boys. I don't always trust Daan. I can't have children with Daan. Or anyone. I owe Mark. I am indebted to him for giving me his sons, children I'd never have any other way. I couldn't bear to hurt Mark. Daan doesn't need me as much as Mark does. Mark doesn't want me as much as Daan does. The reasons collide, mesh, mash. They never stop flooding my brain. There is one reason.

The boys.

I've loved them with every fibre of my soul since the moment I clapped eyes on them. They fill me up with so much love and meaning that there are times when I've thought I might explode with the joy of being their mother. And I fill them too. They need my love, they need me. I know that it was part of my appeal to Mark that I loved them so entirely. He wanted a lover,

201

maybe even a wife but he *needed* a mother for the boys. Someone to unfurl his boys. I put my cool hand on the heat of their grief and drew it away, soothed. What you need and what you want being perfectly aligned is a rare and wonderful thing. Mark grabbed it with both hands. The boys blossomed under my care. When I married Mark, I officially adopted them.

I reach for the water bottle; the label is smeared with my diarrhoea. It's disgusting. I'm disgusting. I carefully tear off the label and then take some sips, regardless.

The worst days are the ones when Mark thinks I am away with work and really, I'm just sat in Daan's flat. Sometimes, when I'm certain Mark isn't going to be working from home, I do sneak back to the house to put on a load of washing so that the chores don't add up at the weekend. On Wednesday afternoons the boys often play sports. I'd like to go to those games, but I can't because how would I explain being away on a Wednesday night and how can I justify to Daan living away from him for more than four days a week? He is patient enough giving up every weekend of his life because he thinks I am nursing my sick mother. I have to be strict. Disciplined. I have a lot to lose. Twice as much as the next woman. I see the boys play football at the weekends. That's enough. It has to be.

The boys were aged seven and eleven when I met Daan. They had just started to break away from my tight and constant maternal clench. I realise now, that as all boys turn into tweens, teens and ultimately young men, they have to push their mothers away. It's natural. It is still hurtful though. I couldn't help but feel saddened when they quickly turned their heads away from me and a kiss might land on their ear or simply die in the space between us. The boys had started to edge into the stage when all they needed me for was to locate a stray trainer or charger cable, cook a meal. I still needed them.

My arms felt empty.

It was around that time I suggested to Mark that we consider fostering or even adoption. 'Maybe a girl,' I said hopefully. 'A toddler, someone who needs a loving home.' Someone who would accept my kisses without question. He instantly dismissed my idea, not giving me or my needs even the dignity of a debate. 'I don't want to go back to nappies and broken sleep, Leigh. Besides, adoption's such a risk. If you are not genetically related, you don't know what you are getting. How can you be sure you'll bond?'

'I'm not genetically related to Oli and Seb,' I pointed out.

For a moment Mark froze, he looked caught out, afraid. Then he pulled me into a hug. 'God, I forgot. Isn't that wonderful?'

And it should have been wonderful. If maybe, momentarily, Frances wasn't sat in the shadows of our relationship and Mark had thought of me as the boys' mother — simply that, not the stepmother, the stand-in or make do. But I didn't really think that was what was being said. When he'd said that if a parent wasn't genetically related to the child, you couldn't be sure you'd bond, Mark was not talking about my relationship with a future child or indeed the children we had, Mark was referring to his own feelings on the matter of nature versus nurture. So, in fact, it was far from a compliment. Really, he was revealing that he didn't believe my bond with the boys could ever be quite as strong as his. It was as though he'd stabbed

203

me. Then left me to bleed out.

Two or three weeks later my father died. It was a very intense time.

My reflections are punishing. Stopping, examining, recalling is something I've studiously avoided over the past four years. I change track. Pull to mind the thoughts that I've always used to console myself.

I never got behind on the washing, no one ever opened the fridge and despaired that there was no milk for their cereal. When I went to Daan's to become Kai, my last act before I walked out of the door was to check in the freezer, count the Tupperware tubs of bolognese and shepherd's pie. Checking there were always organic meals made from scratch by me, enough to last until I returned.

No one was neglected.

I close my eyes. Let the darkness of the room take me. Sleep isn't restful, but it's better than the nightmare I'm living.

204

24

DC Clements

Friday 20th March

When DC Clements returns to the station after visiting Daan Janssen, she is immediately called into her boss's office, she doesn't even have time for a fag. She tells herself that is a good thing, that she should give them up soon anyway. Filthy habit.

'Where have you been?' Her boss doesn't normally keep tabs on her in this way. He respects her judgement, her work ethic — besides, he is swamped himself and doesn't have time to micromanage. However, when she explains, he looks irritated, impatient. 'I see. Look, Clements, we're too busy for this. File the report, put out an alert but other than that, drop it. I'm not giving any more man-hours over to it. There isn't a body, so there's no case.'

Clements is being given an order. She should accept it, but she feels her mind and body resist slightly. No, there isn't a body, but there is something. The woman with two husbands — two lives — flung herself forward, jumped up and down, insisted she was interesting enough to be noticed. Clements is fascinated by her. Mystified by her. She doesn't even know what to call her. Leigh Fletcher? Kai Janssen? Maybe Kylie Gillingham is best. The name she had before she had any husband. Before she got herself into this mess.

'I just feel, sir, that there might be more to this

than — '

'We work with facts, DC Clements, not feelings, as well you know.' He only ever gave her the full-title thing when he was reminding her of rank, her place. 'Most likely the woman has run off to ruin some other man's life. From her profile, I'd say she's quite the survivor, not the sort to get into danger. She's the sort that looks after herself.' Clements stiffens at this. Women frequently find themselves in danger, irrespective of what 'sort' they are. 'If she turns up, we'll press charges for bigamy. She might get a few months inside. Most likely just a fine, but I don't suppose we'll see her again anyway.'

'But there's no indication that she planned to leave,' Clements points out. 'Neither husband can recall anything out of the ordinary in her behaviour before she disappeared. Neither man believes any clothes to be missing, both her passports are in the drawers that they usually lived in.' One of the husbands could be lying, though. Probably was. Maybe both of them. The thought skitters across Clements' mind.

'Two passports?'

'Yes.'

'One in each name?'

'Yes.'

'Well, she's clearly wily.' It isn't a compliment. 'It takes some cunning to have two passports, two names on the go. If she ever does turn up, that charge will need to be answered to as well.'

'How do you think she managed it, sir?' Clements has already considered the matter, she's drawn her own conclusions, but she wants to draw in the Detective Inspector, get him to engage in the case. Not actively, just enough for him to give Clements the nod to continue investigating.

'It's tricky but not impossible if she had deed poll documents, wedding certificates, household bills in different names. If a person creates enough confusion around such matters, then they can generally find a loophole. No system is infallible. She probably benefited from appearing middle class, middle-aged, female, respectable.' Clements knows her boss is currently going through a divorce, his middle-aged, middle-class, respectable wife is taking him to the cleaners. He resents it. Everyone resents everything nowadays.

'Or perhaps she simply bought a second passport. Kai Janssen probably has enough money to find fraudsters, even if Leigh Fletcher doesn't. Who knows who she knows?' Clements suggests, wanting to haul the woman out of a comfortable, familial setting just for a moment and place her somewhere more terrifying. It isn't a comforting thought, but it has to be looked at. Kylie Gillingham might be mixed up with the wrong sort of people. All possibilities deserve an airing. Clements presses on with the facts that strengthen her belief that the woman has been taken rather than done a runner. 'No money has been withdrawn from any of her bank accounts since Monday morning when she paid for coffee and cake at a café in the park. A contactless transaction. That fits in with what her best friend told us. That was the last time anyone saw Kylie. The last time this made sense to anyone. What is she doing for money if she's run away?'

'She probably has several bank accounts. There's probably a complex trail of cash moving from one account to another, criss-crossing freely.'

'Well, I'd like to request the bank statements for

all accounts going back some years, to unravel it. To see if it came to an abrupt halt on Monday.' The Detective Inspector raises his eyebrows, sceptically. Clements changes tack, puts an alternative on the table, one with which her boss is more likely to hold truck, anything to be given permission to request the bank accounts, devote a little more time. 'Or to see if there is evidence of an escape fund being established.'

'Yes, you'll probably find money has been siphoned off to fund a flit.'

'But what if I don't? I mean, sir, questioning has not revealed any reports of obvious signs of stress or anxiety. There were no fluctuations in her routine, no sudden eruptions of temper. She was organised, controlled, careful. A cool customer, that much was certain. Mark Fletcher talked about some strain between her and their oldest boy, but that seemed pretty standard stuff in terms of parenting a teen, nothing that strikes me as a reason for a woman to bail on her life.' The DI looks uninterested. He keeps glancing at his screen, checking emails.

Clements cannot believe a woman who immaculately planned her life — her lives — with such precision would have left without money, passport, clothes if she could have helped it. So, even if she has done a runner, it is most likely impromptu. Under threat or fear? Possibly? Probably? What was the straw that broke the camel's back?

The Detective Inspector sighs. 'Not sure if you are aware, DC Clements, but we are facing a global pandemic. Things are going to get rough imminently. There might be riots and revolt once the government announces plans to curtail the nation's movements. There will be those who will use this to cause a fight,

208

gain a foothold, exploit the vulnerable. We will be waist-deep in looters, thugs, gangs, pushers. They'll all come creeping out of the woodwork soon enough.'

Clements knows it is true. 'But, sir, if we go into lockdown like the Europeans, any leads we have will go cold.'

'What leads do you have, Clements?' he asks impatiently. Clements doesn't reply. He answers for her. 'None, just hunches. What's your plan? Knocking on every door in London and asking if they've seen her? Stop wasting police time. You know that's an offence, right?' Her boss chuckles at his own joke, trying to show her he isn't entirely unsympathetic to her, one of his key team members, just pushed for resources: time, man-power, funding. 'Look, when lockdown begins, we're going to have more than enough on our plates without chasing around looking for a grown woman who doesn't want to be found. Conversation over.'

Non-religious bigamy cases are rare. Clements has come across just two in her career, in both instances the men had more than one wife; her online research last night suggested that was the pattern. The jokes those cases spawned when being investigated were along the lines of, 'He wants to plead insanity,' or, 'What is he going down for? Didn't realise sadomasochism was a criminal offence.' Had a female bigamist created an unarticulated but tangible sense of resentment? It annoys Clements that sexism drips into every part of her world. She wonders whether her boss's reluctance to invest any time in this missing persons case was a misplaced sense of indignation against a woman who had dared to break not just the law, but the rules too. How dare Kylie Gillingham dupe men?

Clements returns to her desk and starts to fill out a Section 28 Data Protection form that would give her access to the bank records. Morgan comes to find her and takes it upon himself to offer an uninvited opinion. 'It's obvious, isn't it?'

'Is it?'

'She was no longer able to maintain the deception. Perhaps she was even bored of it.'

'Bored?' It just doesn't sit right. Clements can't imagine getting bored of either man, let alone a situation where you had access to both. She is slightly annoyed with herself for having this thought, it is shallow, slick, borderline silly. Yet it came from her gut and Clements has learnt to trust her gut. The life Kylie had constructed was many things: illegal, complex, dangerous, challenging but it was not boring.

Only young Tanner has a differing view. 'Which one of them do you think did it?' he asks, not quite able to hide his excitement. 'The frazzled dad or the hot he-man?'

'Do you operate exclusively in stereotypes, Tanner?'

'I try to,' Tanner affirms with an unselfconscious grin.

Clements huffs irritably, even though she has been asking herself a variation on that same question. Did either of them know more about her disappearance than they were letting on? Were either of them responsible? If they had discovered her betrayal, there would be motivation. Humiliation, fury and desolation fuelled many crimes of passion. Jealousy was a poison.

Both men were insistent that they had no clue that she was betraying them. But that in itself blew Clements' mind. How was it possible that they had no clue? She thinks perhaps the issue is that healthy,

210

rich, white men are dangerous because they are disinterested in everything other than themselves. Women, people of colour, poorer men are still trying to work out the world. They are still asking why it is unfair. What can I do to make it fair? How do I ask for a pay rise? How do I get heard? Or believed? The people still asking themselves these questions observe what is going on around them, because everything around them is a potential threat. Clements has a theory that handsome, rich white men have nothing to work out and so they rarely bother with introspection, let alone inspection. The husbands assumed she was fine: busy, happy, trustworthy. And in this instance the self-absorption of the handsome, rich white man worked in Kylie's favour.

Until of course it didn't.

Everyone in the station is playing a waiting game. The air is electric, like it is just before a storm. Despite orders to drop the case, Clements decides to make some more phone calls. She calls Kylie's mother in Australia, who says she last saw her daughter last year, they had a three-day break in Dubai. Kylie paid for it. 'I wanted it to be longer. It was a long way to travel for just a few days,' the mother complained. Clements — who was guilty as charged and did operate on hunches, although not instead of facts but as well as — thought the mother was self-involved, hard work. If Kylie wanted a sanctuary, somewhere to escape to and cut free of the mess she has created, Clements doubted her mother would offer that. 'You'll get in touch if you hear from your daughter? It's important.'

'Of course, poor Mark. How could she do this to him? And those boys. They've always been like grandsons to me. She's an ungrateful girl.'

211

Another couple of calls unearth the fact that Kylie did not have a high-powered job as a management consultant. She had done until four years ago, when she resigned. 'We were surprised when she resigned, sad, you know. She was really good at her job. Great team member,' explains her old boss.

'Did she give any explanation?'

'She said she wanted to spend more time with her family. Said it was getting too much for her. There is a lot of travelling. Women with families often find it hard to strike the balance.' Clements bites her tongue to avoid asking if men with families also struggled to find the work/life balance. She considers her jab is less likely to score considering Kylie had two lives to balance with work. That sort of ambition is hardly laudable.

Obviously, both the sick mother and the flash job were fictions, created to allow Kylie to move between the two men, the two homes. Clements wonders how she financed it if she wasn't working. Mark Fletcher had said that there was a salary going into their joint bank account every month. Daan Janssen isn't stuck for cash, but was Kylie going as far as to allow Janssen to pay for the mortgage with her other husband? Was this what it was all about? Money? That thought turns Clements' stomach. Weirdly, she sort of admires the woman who independently flouts the rules, flicks the finger to the patriarchy and finds her own path, but if it is just for money it somehow seems more layman, normalised. More criminal. Was she simply exploiting one man to prop up the other? That position was pitiful. Understandable, but lacking the exciting notoriety of rebellion.

Clements and Tanner pore through the bank

212

accounts and phone statements. They discover that Kylie is independently wealthy. Her father had died very close to the time she met Daan Janssen. The father left her a fortune. Clements is immediately intrigued once again. This woman wasn't doing it for the money. She didn't need Daan Janssen to prop up the Fletcher household finances. She didn't need either man at all.

She wanted them.

Clements calls both husbands again to bring them up to date on her findings. Mark Fletcher sounds fraught, broken. Daan Janssen sounds maddened, peeved. They both claim that she hadn't told them the truth about the timing and circumstances of her father's death. Mark knew he had died, but had no clue about the inheritance she'd benefited from. 'They always had a very difficult relationship. She barely spoke of him. Why would he leave her money? Are you sure?'

Daan thought the father had died many years ago, when Kai was a child. 'She didn't often speak of him. She said she couldn't remember him. Hardly knew him.'

Kylie Gillingham carried around alone the grief of losing her father in order to finance her double life. Clements doesn't know whether to be disgusted by the woman, pity her or what. She marvels at the case. She has seen the weird and wonderful in her line of work — well, mostly weird really — but this! The audacity of the woman was almost admirable; the planning involved certainly was. Clements sometimes struggled to keep her one, relatively straightforward life ticking along, she can't imagine the logistics involved in being two women.

Clements is aware that she feels something faintly unsavoury towards this woman too. Unlike the male officers, it isn't judgement, it is something she tries to avoid in her life — jealousy. Not full-blown, tie-you-in-knots, green-eyed-monster but something akin to what she might feel when she saw a picture in a magazine of a celebrity with a perfect life and a perfect figure, a couple of perfect kids. And Clements would ask herself, why her? Why that woman? Why not me hanging out by a swimming pool?

But then DC Clements reminds herself that Kylie Gillingham's life wasn't perfect, was it?

It couldn't be if she's run away from it. Or worse, been taken from it.

Clements calls two of Kylie's three half-brothers (she can't yet track the third, apparently he's on holiday in Malaysia). They don't have much to add. They haven't seen Leigh since their father left her the bulk of his wealth, they offer assurances that they will contact the station if she gets in touch. They sound remote, disinterested. Again, Clements doubts that these family members would offer a sanctuary to Kylie if she needed one.

Clements rings a few of the numbers recently dialled on both phones she had owned. Leigh's last tracked phone calls included a call to the school secretary to ask if she could rummage through the lost property box to try to locate Seb's missing school coat, she'd also rung the dentist to book regular check-ups for both the boys. They were scheduled for next week. Kai had called her hairdresser, to make an appointment for a trim, an appointment she'd failed to show up to. 'Is that unusual?' Clements asks the woman who answered the phone.

214

'Yeah, I can't remember her no-showing before. She's really nice, tips well. Is she OK? I hope so.'

'Most likely. Did she seem OK when she spoke to you?'

'Yes. Totally.'

Everyone Clements talks to agrees that neither version of Kylie Gillingham was showing any obvious signs of stress, nothing out of the ordinary.

Finally, at just before 7 p.m. Clements calls the best friend, Fiona Phillipson; 7 p.m. is her cut-off on a Friday for making enquiries. She plans to stay for a few more hours at the station, get a takeaway delivered, there isn't anything to rush home to because she isn't mid-season on any TV show at the moment, but she doesn't like calling people too late on a Friday because other people have lives.

'You didn't see any change in her behaviour?' Clements asks. As the person who last saw Kylie, Fiona's testimony is key.

'No, none, but then we've established that she has quite the poker face,' Fiona comments sharply, not able to hide her anger. 'Who knows what she was thinking.' Clements gets it, Fiona is hurt. She thought they were close. Besties. All Kylie's friends and family are reeling, coming to terms with the fact they don't know her, no one knows her. They are, naturally enough, enraged. Clements is just sad. In her experience, the unknown are the most vulnerable. And dangerous.

'Leigh is one of those really busy women — you know, never still for five minutes, two minutes, always dashing about, somewhere to go, someone to see, something to do,' offers Fiona. 'It made the rest of us feel left behind. Sort of rooted.'

215

'Being rooted can be a good thing,' comments Clements.

'True, yes, of course it can,' Fiona rallies. Her voice has a defensive edge to it. Clements recognises it, empathises with it. A single woman exhausted with justifying her choices. Her lot.

'I suppose it must have finally got to her. The deceit and everything. Years of it, from what you say. Maybe she just couldn't handle it anymore,' murmurs Fiona.

'So, you think she's run away?'

Fiona falls silent. Clements wishes she was conducting this interview face to face. She is good at reading people and knows that often a lot is said inside silences. 'I don't know. It's one thing to think, isn't it? Possibly the best thing.' Fiona's voice cracks. Not just angry then, worried for her friend too? The police are unfortunately used to bearing the brunt of people's worry in the form of aggression. It doesn't surprise Clements when Fiona throws out the heated challenge, 'Isn't it your job to take the educated guesses?'

'It's our job to find out everything we can.' Fiona sighs. It isn't clear if the sigh is one of frustration, anger, grief. 'Is there anything at all you can think of that may be relevant? Anything to help us understand her state of mind?'

'She was depressed.'

'Are you sure?'

'No, not certain. Maybe you should check with her doctor. I think she was on tablets at some point.' Fiona admits this reluctantly, aware she is betraying a confidence, not wanting to paint her friend in a bad light. Clements doesn't judge, half the people she knows are on antidepressants, popped them like vitamins, but if Kylie was depressed and taking

216

antidepressants, she would be classed as vulnerable and maybe the missing persons case could be escalated.

'That's helpful, I will.'

'I remember her talking once about how she couldn't see any joy anymore. That she was blind to it.'

Clements doesn't know how to ask the question but doesn't know how she can avoid asking it either. Time is running out. They might be locked down by Monday. Other cases might come along and take precedent. It is a sickening thought, but lockdown is bound to lead to an increase in domestic violence. She wouldn't be able to solely focus on this once lockdown was announced. Not without a body. But she doesn't want a body. A body is so final. 'Do you think she could have taken her own life?' Clements probes. She tries to keep her tone neutral. Any hint of sympathy, empathy, shock, or judgement can be leading. She wants to know what the best friend thinks.

'I don't want to think that but it's possible and maybe —'

'Maybe what?'

'Well, maybe that's better than the alternative, you know. Someone taking her. Someone hurting her.'

25

Kylie

Thursday 19th March

I wake up because I sense movement. The lack of food has made me sluggish now, and I only manage to shake myself fully into consciousness as I hear the door bang behind him. The opportunity to identify which husband is doing this to me is lost. One moment I am sure it is Mark who might accuse me of not caring for the boys. The next I wonder, is it Daan who might declare I only care about myself. I don't know. I can't hold on to my concentration long enough to chase a theory thoroughly. I am so hungry. So scared. I see there is another food tray and more water. I pull at the edge of my jumper. Trying to cover up. I'm not being modest, that wouldn't make sense; both men have enjoyed those parts of my body many times, and besides I'm alone in the room now, but my nakedness and the foul bucket leave me exposed, vulnerable, like a badly treated animal, caged by the circus ringmaster.

I crawl to the food tray and examine it. Two bananas, a protein bar, an M&S superfood salad and a bottle of iced tea. It's Honest Tea, organic, Fair Trade, honey green, gluten free. Everything is in unopened packaging or its skin. It can't have been tampered with. It's safe to eat. I almost laugh. One of my husbands has drugged me, imprisoned and chained me, starved,

218

then poisoned me but has now taken the time to shop for my favourite iced tea. If anything demonstrates how messed up this situation is, then my food tray does.

The shopping could have been bought by either of them. Although I run two separate lives, there is an element of crossover. Sometimes this is uncomfortable. Sometimes it feels very natural. These particular products span both my worlds so the tray doesn't offer the answer to who my abductor is.

Leigh Fletcher does not eat protein bars, but her oldest son, Oli, does.

Kai eats them after an intense workout.

In the Fletcher home, this iced tea is a treat.

Daan buys it as a matter of routine.

Both Leigh and Kai like an M&S salad.

I don't usually talk about myself in the third person — in two third people. I know I am both women. I know both women are me. I am not insane. I'm not even self-deluded.

There is another note on the food tray.

Choices have consequences. Weren't you ever taught that?

I know I should be nothing but penitent, but the sanctimonious nature of the message irritates me. I suppose it's not that surprising that I can be repentant and irritated at once; I'm the master of complex schisms. Of course, I am aware choices have consequences. It's one of my mantras that I find myself repeating to the boys. I have never been blasé about what I've done, the choices I've made. I didn't really think I would avoid the consequences. Not really, not forever. But

219

this? This is madness, it is disproportionate and cruel. Frightening. My fingers shake as I unwrap the protein bar. I take a small nibble but then hunger cravings overwhelm me. I shove it in my mouth, barely chewing, almost gagging. I swallow it down. What day is it now? I think it is Thursday, but it feels as though I have been here forever. My God, how long might this go on for? I turn my jeans inside out and then pull them on. They are stiff with my waste, so crawling into them is disgusting. I retch at the smell but feel less exposed wearing them.

Before Daan, I had never been tempted to be unfaithful. There were occasionally men that I'd meet at work or even other school dads who threw out suggestive looks, flirty comments and invitations that could have led places. I had no interest whatsoever.

Then Daan.

I tried to keep away from him at the beginning. I broke it off time and time again, every day.

In my head.

Over and over again, I planned the things I would say to let him down gently but when I was with him, it was lightning, a bolt through my body, my being. Penetrating, blazing, exhilarating. Like lightning, once in a lifetime, and like a scar left by lightning, irrevocable and permanent.

I just couldn't let go.

I thought it was simply a case of a lawless body. He sparked inside me a level of lust that I could not control. Possibly, I didn't want to. I was arrogant enough to think that wasn't really a problem, that it would eventually fade away. An infatuation. Inconvenient, but not necessarily devastating. But I was not in control of anything. I started to care. I couldn't put the brakes on that. Couldn't? Wouldn't? I thought I'd get used to him. Maybe then become bored of him. But familiarity did not blunt him.

The confusion is unbearable. I suppose it always has been.

I married both men for clarity. I divided myself for clarity. That sounds paradoxical but it's not, it's simple, clear cut. They each got me half the time but at 100 per cent capacity, and how many marriages do much more? I have seen other women at the school gates who spend half their time at the gym, or with their friends gossiping, drinking chardonnay over a long lettuce lunch. Didn't I give as much to my marriages as they did to theirs? Many of the school mums work and their situation is even harder. I've been a wife with a demanding office job, and I know how that pans out. When those women are at home, in their husband's company, often their minds are still at work: did they reply to that email? Have they proofread that document? Are any marriages more than 50 per cent commitment? At least I was not guilty of letting my mind wander. No matter who I was with, they got my attention. I couldn't afford to dwell on the other.

When I was with Daan, it was painful to think of Mark and the boys. Awful. I did not want to drag them into a world where I was on all fours, begging another man to take me. And when I was with Mark, and thought of Daan, he seemed incongruous. He was delicious and glamorous. Sometimes, in the early days, he did drift into my mind as I shoved dirty clothes into the washing machine, when I scrubbed ovens or loos, but imagining him seeing me do these grubby household chores was uncomfortable. I didn't

221

want even the ghost of him near the domesticity, in case he was at all supercilious about the drudgery. I couldn't allow an imbalance. One thing could not be better than the other. They were equally brilliant. Just different.

I peel one of the bananas. I know I should eke out this food. Ration myself, but I can't resist. I suppose that has always been my problem. I nibble on it, try to make it last.

I call both places home. Home is where I feel needed and essential to the boys, to Mark; where I am the linchpin. Home is where I am desired and enjoyed by Daan. But the two places are not mutually exclusive in what they supply to me. Mark also desires me. Daan also needs me.

To lessen the confusion, I tried to compartmentalise completely.

To hermetically seal one life off from the other. But it wasn't the answer, not really. I must have thought there was something missing between Mark and me, for Daan to be able to ease his way in, settle and find a place. The glamour perhaps? The freedom. No matter how hard I tried to keep Daan out of the life I shared with Mark, his existence took something from that original life. Something was lost. Innocence, simplicity. However many barriers I placed between them, I couldn't hem that in. It drained away. It drained away when I bought a second phone, when I opened up a new email account. It disappeared altogether when I agreed to marry him.

I look around the small, rank, locked room. The very antithesis to glamour. To freedom.

I am jolted from my thoughts by the sound of paper being threaded into the typewriter. The sound is a taunt, a threat. Yet somehow, it is a chance too. I scramble towards the door and listen to the keys being struck. A short blast, like gunfire. A sheet of paper is shoved under the door. I perform the usual acrobats to drag it towards me with my feet.

Why a second marriage?
Why not an affair like everyone else?

I consider the question, how it is phrased. Who does it sound most like? Daan? Who would ask this? Mark? But I realise that the important thing right now is to answer the question, keep him talking. It is the way I'm most likely to bring about a resolution. I can think about who is behind the notes when I am alone. I open my mouth but my voice cracks. I don't know where to start. Words stutter in my throat. I am tired, dehydrated, but that's not the problem. The words I've swallowed for so long have to be spat out. My survival used to depend on my silence. Now I think it depends on what I say. The truth that is unpalatable to Mark might soften Daan — but dare I risk confessing it? I could cause more pain, more anger depending on who is on the other side of that door.

People talk about the value of truth all the time. The importance of it. They pursue it as though it is the elixir of eternal youth, as important as life itself. It is not. It's just not. Often the truth is brutal, which is why most of us avoid telling it most of the time. I have regularly been more frightened by the truth than by a lie. A lie, undiscovered, keeps people safe. A lie can be quiet, non-violent.

You want the truth?
I could not walk away from him.

223

Every time my phone buzzed to say a message or email had arrived it was as though he had tugged on the rope that bound us. Pulled me back to him. Every moral code I had ever lived by told me not to reply and respond. Yet I did. Rational thought insisted I simply stop visiting his flat, stop agreeing to his dates and yet I didn't. And instincts that normally facilitate my self-preservation demanded that I did not turn up at the register office; yet, something bigger overrode all that. Longing? Lust? Love? I don't know. I just couldn't stop myself.

I am addicted to him.

'I didn't plan to go through with the second wedding,' I admit carefully. Even as I let Daan push his engagement ring onto my finger, I thought it was impossible, a game. A sick game, I suppose, but one I was somehow compelled to play, unable to quit. 'I thought we might row and break up.' We did sometimes row, but only as a precursor to a passionate making-up, we would bounce back together, iron filings clasped to a magnet. 'I thought I could disappear before the wedding. Ghosting is cowardly, I know. Cruel. But I thought it was all I had the strength to try.'

I knew Daan wouldn't be able to find me, to track me. I could disappear from his world, he would never be able to track down Kai Gillingham. There was no paper trail under that name. And he would never have been able to track down Leigh Fletcher, he didn't know she existed. 'Every day I woke up knowing I had to pull out, sooner or later, I had to call it off.' I had to disappear back to my old life, my real life. I had got carried away, what I wanted was impossible. But God, how I wanted the impossible. I wanted them both.

Yet, at the same time I wanted it to stop. More contradictions. More paradoxes.

I didn't know how to make it stop. I just could not walk away from him and know he was in the world, continuing. Seeing other women, speaking to them, favouring them, kissing them, fucking them, maybe ultimately even loving them. I couldn't bear to think of that. I guess that was selfish of me. Well, it was, I know, but it was hard enough thinking about the life he'd had before me. The women he'd had before me. I couldn't stand for there to be anyone after me. I just couldn't give him up. Besides, then he got a job in the UK. He did so much to be with me. I didn't know how to get myself out of it.

Daan keeps me busy and amused. He always has a bunch of ideas about what we could do, how we can spend our time. It stopped me thinking. I did things with Daan that I'd never have done with Mark. I don't mean in bed, both men got fairly equal attention there. Or at least, both men got what they wanted there. I mean, I have had different experiences with Daan. I've been places, heard stories, met people, seen countries that were beyond Mark's and my reach, or even imagination. Daan and I are a busy couple. Always occupied. It's tricky to pin us down for a dinner or theatre date. Our schedules are booked up for weeks in advance. Maybe, if Daan's personality type was closer to Mark's, I might have had more time to think about what I was doing. To regret it. As it is I have been too busy for regrets. Being busy is a lot like being fulfilled.

Daan wanted a big wedding too, but his vision was nothing like Mark's. It was impossible not to compare. Daan didn't want a marquee in the garden, kids running around, wildflowers in jam jars, he wanted something sophisticated, oozing London chic. He had a number of friends who had married a year or so before we got engaged; the wives in those fresh couples rushed to give us recommendations on the hippest venues, the most sought-after florists, dress designers and pastry makers. Daan's friends are all extremely stylish, they are the beautiful people that run the sort of Instagram accounts that terrify the rest of us. However, they were friendly enough with me from the off, they seemed delighted that Daan had finally found someone he wanted to marry. There is no doubt in my mind that before me, he'd been what my mother would call 'quite a womaniser', he'd never been in a relationship longer than six months. Daan's friends gave me the impression that, before we met, he was the sort that bobbed and weaved in and out of many lives, avoiding the punches, leaving nothing worthwhile behind. He never wanted to be tied. He didn't like to make plans that reached forward into the future, a future he wasn't prepared to gift to anyone. But, by the time we met, that must have been quite exhausting for him and frustrating for his friends. Not to mention heartbreaking for all the women who had fallen in love with him and yearned for more. His intrinsic independence meant he didn't want to be caught. I suppose that is why my repeated absences worked for him. He also didn't want children. So my barrenness worked too. When we are polishing our meet-cute story — bringing it out in company and burnishing, buffing it — we don't tell our friends about the joint or the sex acts in the disabled toilets.

I don't tell them about the other husband.

'So eyes across a crowded art gallery?' they ask.

'Gallery steps to be accurate,' I reply with a smile.

'How romantic.'

And it was romantic.

His friends were delighted that he had found someone he was prepared to change his ways for, and that he'd chosen someone who appeared down-to-earth, normal. His female friends placed soft, manicured hands on my arm, squeezed conspiratorially and whispered that his exes had all been high-maintenance or shallow. They thought he had grown up. Picked wisely.

They had no idea.

Thinking about it now, all this time later, I suppose Daan sensed in me something not quite reachable and he found that fascinating. Some men always want what is just out of their grasp. I offered him a perfect blend of intimacy and detachment that most clever people find intriguing. He likes my tight bodycon dresses that say I want his attention, combined with my laissez-faire attitude and general abstraction that suggests I don't — or at least if I *do* want it, I don't need it. I am a challenge. Or I was. I wonder what I am now? A disappointment. A regret. A failure. Daan doesn't like failing at anything.

You can meet a lot of people, spend a lot of time with them but still not know them. They do not know you. Sometimes that is the aim. Daan is a talker. He tells stories constantly. His whole life is divided like a book into chapters. His sporty school days, his idyllic family life, his interesting time at Harvard, the wild party years. The anecdotes all ooze a sense of accomplishment and happiness. They are well-rehearsed, often recited but still chime with sincerity. His life has been blessed, fortuitous. Until meeting me, I suppose. I know one hundred times more about him than he

227

will ever know about me. I wonder how this chapter of his life will be served up in the future. The period when his darling wife went missing, was torn from him, or perhaps the time when he imprisoned his bigamist whore of a wife. Although, who would he tell that story to?

26

Daan

Friday 20th March

'Oh, Mr Janssen, it's you.'

Daan freezes. He is not in the mood to chat to anyone and certainly not Alfonso, the officious concierge. Daan would prefer to keep all interactions with Alfonso brief and at the main reception desk. How can he explain being on the back stairs of the building?

'You're still here, Alfonso, it's late. I thought you'd have clocked off,' Daan says with a tone he hopes is full of bonhomie and ease, and does not betray the levels of stress he is under. Both men glance about. The back stairs are not dirty, they are befitting of the luxurious apartments, so the walls are painted and there is decent-quality coir carpeting, but neither man expected to see the other and can't help being a little taken aback. Feeling vaguely wrong-footed.

'Heading that way,' Alfonso replies.

He doesn't seem to be in a hurry. Daan always rushed home from work Monday to Wednesday when he knew Kai would be waiting for him, he tends to linger longer in the office on a Thursday and Friday, clearing admin until someone suggests a drink or something. Daan has never considered Alfonso's homelife. Now he finds he is curious about how other people live, manage. How they negotiate their way through intimacy. Until very recently Daan thought he had everything on lock, that he knew more than the average person about being a successful man. Now he just feels like a bloody fool; the humiliation burns inside him. Who does Alfonso return to of an evening? How does he spend his weekends? Daan thinks back to the rare occasions that he and Kai spent the weekend together. He would book exquisite restaurants, get great seats at the theatre, sometimes arrange for them to go backstage and meet the stars, because often he knew someone who knew someone, and those sorts of things were within his grasp. He would tenderly make love to her. Kissing her body over and over again, almost worshipping it. He thinks about how excited he always was about those precious weekends, how hard he worked to make them perfect from start to finish, certain that he was treating his wife, indulging her, rewarding her for all the time she devoted to her ailing mother.

It makes him sick.

Alfonso looks up at Daan with a quick hopefulness. He'd like to chat.

Daan wonders, is Alfonso married? Does he have children? Grandchildren? Is he divorced? Lonely. Is that why he keeps such odd and long hours? Does he like being here in this building more than he likes being at home? Daan is surprised these questions have occurred to him now. He has known Alfonso for years, cheerfully greeted him morning and evening, discussing the weather, a parcel, the delivery of white goods. Alfonso is a fixture in Daan's life and yet he has never felt curious about him until this moment. Daan doesn't get too involved in people's private lives. As he was brought up with staff, he knows the dangers of becoming overly familiar with them and blurring the lines, it is tricky to pull back when necessary. And at some point, it is always necessary. Of course, he is friendly, polite. He tips well at Christmas, most likely the best tipper in the entire building by some way. He wants Alfonso to look out for him, take care when receiving deliveries, making hotel bookings, monitoring the external security cameras but he doesn't want Alfonso to be his friend. His home has to be a sanctuary; he doesn't need those boundaries flexing. He doesn't need Alfonso popping up to his floor just to make conversation, he doesn't need his inquisitiveness, keenness, nosiness.

'Haven't seen much of Mrs Janssen this week,' says Alfonso.

'No,' says Daan revealing nothing.

'Everything all right?' Alfonso's gaze slips down the length of Daan's body. Does he notice the dirty tracksuit, are there tell-tale dark patches of sweat on his T-shirt? Daan thinks he can feel sweat on his top lip, his hair is greasy, his eyes are probably bloodshot, he can't remember when he was last entirely sober. Daan thinks Alfonso's question is impertinent, or his gaze. Both. His face turns icy to allow Alfonso to know this is what he is thinking and therefore to close him down, swiftly. Alfonso does clock Daan's irritation and colours slightly. 'Oh, sorry, don't mean to pry. It's just with the police being here, I started worrying about her. She's such a nice lady, your wife. Always asks about mine.'

Daan doesn't want Alfonso to be his friend, but nor does he want him to be an enemy either. Typical that Kai knew Alfonso was married, that she took an interest. She always did appear to be interested in everything and everyone. Bitch.

Daan doesn't want to answer the question and he learnt long ago that you don't always have to, so instead he comments, 'I'm just getting a bit of exercise, taking the stairs rather than the lift. Trying to hit twenty thousand steps a day.'

Alfonso whistles, 'Twenty thousand? I'm lucky if I hit five thousand. Very sedentary job, mine.'

'Yes, mine too, but I try.'

'You wouldn't find it easier just working out in the gym?' Alfonso asks.

Daan tries not to look startled at being challenged. 'Of course, that's where I've just come from.' It would at least explain why he is sweating, breathless.

'Oh, I must have missed you. Normally I notice who is working out or swimming.' Alfonso meets Daan's gaze. 'You know, the cameras.'

Daan has forgotten about the internal security cameras. Casting his mind back now he remembers at one residents' committee meeting an argument between residents as to whether internal cameras were an important security measure or an invasion of privacy. There were enough residents with nefarious goings-on who didn't want their every move monitored. They'd take the risk of dealing with burglars. Daan hadn't got involved in the argument, he didn't much care. He vaguely recalls that the compromise reached was that cameras were installed in the gym and pool but not in the corridors. The argument being something about health and safety in communal areas. He hadn't understood the reasoning at the time, thought perhaps Alfonso was the only one to benefit because he could ogle the fitties as they exercised. Daan is glad now that

232

there aren't any cameras in the corridors.

'I didn't stay long today. Got there and realised I just didn't have the energy to work out. Just turned straight back around at the door.' Daan flashes Alfonso a big smile. Then he remembers that the best form of defence is attack and asks, 'So why are you skulking around the back stairs, after hours, Alfonso? Anything I need to be concerned about?'

It was bolshie, rude, but it does the job. Alfonso looks defensive. 'I'm not skulking, just checking about. Doing my job. Seeing everything is OK before I clock off for the weekend.' He is self-justifying which makes a person appear shifty. 'One of the residents said she's heard things.'

'What sort of things?'

'Well, she wasn't sure. Some shouting or crying, she said. It might have just been someone's TV.'

Daan and Alfonso meet one another's eyes and neither likes what they see. 'What do you make of this pandemic business?' Daan asks.

'I don't know what to make of it.'

'My guess is we will all be locked down next week.'

'You think?'

'Most likely. You'll probably be better staying at home. I'll send out an email to the residents, if you like, confirming that.'

'Well, we'll see, shall we?' counters Alfonso. 'No need to action anything yet. I'll come in if I can.'

'Oh, I think it's better to be safe than sorry.'

Alfonso nods, as Daan knew he would and he turns away, heads back down the stairs. Daan waits until he hears his footsteps fade to nothing, the sound of the door opening back to reception, then carries on upwards.

233

27
Kylie

Thursday 19th March

I need to keep communicating. I need to answer the questions asked and even those that haven't been put to me yet. Carefully, I push on. 'I realised that planning an enormous, expensive wedding was not only cruel but unsafe,' I admit. 'Even though I was going under a different name, there was always the risk of being physically recognised. You both moved in different circles but the further I widened those circles, the greater the risk of being found out. I had to draw in. Make both lives smaller.'

Daan had lots of family, friends and people from work he wanted to invite, he assumed I would want the same, I immediately vetoed colleagues, that was the easiest win.

'I don't want to get married in front of a room full of co-workers,' I'd argued.

'Why not?'

'It doesn't feel intimate enough. Co-workers are transient, they are not friends.'

'OK, if that's how you feel.' He looked a little bit disappointed but wanted me to be happy. Brightening, he added, 'I'm really looking forward to meeting your friends, though.' He never had and he must have thought that was odd. He was the sort of boyfriend women would generally want to show off.

234

'They're looking forward to meeting you too,' I lied. 'It's just my closest friends don't live in London, and they all have young families so are pretty absorbed in their own lives.'

'Tell me about them again. So, there's Ginny, who you met in college. She's married with two kids, right? And Emma is a single mum. Tell me a little more about Alex, you hardly talk about her.'

I hardly talked about any of them. Despite his probing questions, I tried to keep them at a distance. These women he named are my actual uni friends, but they all know Mark well, and there was no way I could ask any of them to the wedding; they were all at my first one. Why did he have to be a concerned and interested sort of boyfriend? I remember kissing him to distract him. Leading him to the bedroom.

'I kept telling myself that there wasn't going to be a wedding and yet I found myself arguing for one that would be possible, feasible.' I told him my preference was for an intimate gathering. I told him my mother was too sick to attend, I'd already said my father was dead. I said that I was an only child, never once mentioning my three half-brothers.

I remember him asking, 'Are there any aunts or uncles? Cousins?'

'No, none. Both my parents were only children too.'

'God, that's awful, Kai.'

He wrapped his arms around me, his sense of protectiveness heightened because he thought I was all alone in the world. I pushed on. 'Besides, it's not about the big day, is it? It's about us.'

Daan agreed to a small wedding in the end. He loved me, was wild about me back then, which is sometimes bigger than love and he softened. I loved him deeply too. Love him.

I love them both. There's another inconvenient truth.

Yes, even now. I don't know which I should hate for locking me up, so I continue to love them both.

I have sometimes wondered, perhaps I should have insisted on a massive do, one that necessitated a two-year engagement to secure the perfect venue, to have a dress handmade in France and shipped to me. If I had done that there would have been an opportunity to walk away. Wouldn't there? But I didn't do that. I booked a private room for twenty at The Ivy, I bought a dress from Harvey Nics, sent out invitations. I made it happen.

I wanted to be his wife.

'I hired a bridesmaid. Who knew that such a service even exists? But it does. I found a discreet advert nestled in the back of a glossy wedding magazine,' I confess.

I called the mobile number. A polite young woman named Jess answered. 'Who needs to hire bridesmaids?' I asked her. I had carefully worked out what I planned to say my reasons for calling were; I wanted to check that my lie was within the realms of possibility. Besides, I wondered what other shadowy reasons people had to justify hiring a woman to do the most intimate job a girlfriend could do. I couldn't believe there were many women committing bigamy who needed to keep their wedding on the downlow.

'Women who want their actual friends to enjoy the wedding and not be burdened down with too many tasks,' Jess replied lightly and brightly. 'Or maybe to even up the numbers, if you have, say, three close friends but want four bridesmaids to make the

236

photos symmetrical. It is a flourishing business.' She had a sweet, sing-song voice. I guessed she was probably born and bred somewhere like Surrey, she was most likely gifted a pony when she was five, her father loved her and her mother. Her reality was light years away from mine. Even the sanitised reasons for wanting to hire a bridesmaid seemed peculiar to me, but she appeared to accept them. Her trustfulness made it easier for me.

'My family don't approve of my husband,' I told her, 'so they are boycotting the wedding. My sister should have been bridesmaid. I can't bear the idea of anyone else doing her job.' It was a complicated lie because I had no sister and if she said anything to Daan, my cover would be blown. 'I'd need you to be one hundred per cent discreet. I don't even want my husband to know they are not a real friend.'

'OK.'

She didn't ask but I felt compelled to plod on. 'Because I don't want him to feel any more awful about coming between me and my loved ones. He knows my family have boycotted the wedding, but not my friends.'

'Wow, your friends too.' It was clear she was now wondering what my fiancé had done to upset everyone so thoroughly.

'My friends are mostly from my childhood, my family are making them choose sides.' I knew I should stop talking. The more I said, the less convincing the story was. I've since learnt that the best lies are brief and rooted in truth. I've got better at being bad.

'My family have very niche issues,' I commented.

'Takes all sorts. I'm not here to judge. So, let's get some details about this wedding, shall we?'

Once I revealed the budget, Jess gently suggested that she could put me in touch with a couple of actors who 'regularly play the role of wedding guests'. I realised her sing-song voice was deceptive. Maybe her father hadn't loved her mother. Maybe she knew more about the dark side of the world than I initially assumed.

'How does that work?'

'Well, they are given roles and characters before the wedding, much like you do at a murder mystery evening.'

'I see.'

'It's no biggie. It's just a way of evening up the seating.' When I hesitated, she added, 'It helps avoid any awkward or potentially embarrassing questions. They can be such a downer at a wedding.'

'What might it cost?'

'Well, for my services, the bridesmaid and say five guests were looking at — ' She named a sum that made me inwardly gasp. 'Good value for money when you consider what's at stake,' she added, leaving me in no doubt that she understood that I was far from a normal bride, concerned with something borrowed, something blue; I was submerged in a world of subterfuge and dishonesty.

And after the wedding, there was the honeymoon. I told Mark I was away with work. My previously demanding role afforded me a cover. Daan wanted to spend two weeks on a remote island somewhere, drinking cocktails, rolling around on white sand. I agreed to five days in Venice, said I couldn't leave my sick mother for longer than that. I felt superstitious about saying my mother was ill when she was well, but she'd always been quite wearing as a parent, not especially supportive. I told myself she owed me this. When she moved back to Australia I grasped at the convenience her absence offered me.

Lie after lie stacked up but the lies stopped tugging on my conscience. They became easier. They became part of me. I never thought of telling the truth. Leaving one or the other of them wasn't an option for me. And it went smoothly. I was able to glide through weeks and months, into the first year. Beyond.

I realise that I've stayed in my head, confessed very little to my captor when I hear the typewriter keys being bashed again. It's as though he has kept track of my internal monologue and drawn the same conclusion.

You're a fucking liar.

The anger and impatience bleed from every word. 'Yes, I told lies, but I didn't break hearts! I didn't abandon my children. I didn't hurt anyone!' I yell back. It sounds selfish, maybe even unhinged, but the ease of the situation allowed me to believe it was OK. What I was doing was OK. And wasn't it? For four years? Wasn't it? Mark thought I was working harder than ever, heading towards a promotion and a larger salary, which we needed as a family, but he could never provide and Daan respected my commitment to my sick mother. My absences stopped him from getting bored of me, made him hungry for me. I gave them the marriages they wanted. I reach for the cold tea on the tray, but I am weak and shaky. As I unscrew the cap the bottle slips from my grasp. It spills over me and the floor. 'No, no, no,' I moan. Fleetingly I consider licking the floor, like a beast. I just stop myself in time because the smell of my own faeces hits. Frustrated, unthinking, I fling the bottle at the door. It's plastic so doesn't smash. 'What harm was I doing?' I demand. 'What fucking harm? The old adage is true. Right? What you don't know can't hurt you.'

I hear the keys of the typewriter once more.

But I do know now.
And I am hurt.
So I am going to hurt you.

28
Fiona

Fiona doesn't know how, or even if, she should tell
Mark that she recognises Daan's address. His name.
She could explain that she once pitched for a client
who lived in the spectacularly impressive block. The
exclusive apartments in that development are worth
millions. The place is serviced and pet-friendly on
the fashionable border of the financial district. It is
dreamy. Telling Mark about Daan's extreme wealth
can't help. It would just add fuel to the fire that was
so obviously raging inside him.

The apartment that she pitched to transform was
on the fourteenth floor. It was big but not quite the
star of the show. Within just half an hour of being
in the potential client's company, it became clear
that Mrs Federova was obsessed with the penthouse
apartment and Daan Janssen, the 'very handsome'
man who lived in it. She spoke about 'the masterful
design and modern luxury uniquely embodied in the
three-bedroom, four-bathroom duplex penthouse'.
She repeated the facts as though she was reading
them from a brochure, her accent thickening as she
practically salivated when sharing details about the
wraparound terrace that offered 'truly unparalleled'
views. What Mrs Federova seemed to covet most was
the outside space that the penthouse boasted. 'There

241

is a wood-burning fireplace, a fully equipped outdoor stainless steel kitchen, a sun deck, hot tub, private outdoor shower, a jacuzzi and a sauna,' she informed Fiona, with ill-disguised jealousy.

To think that had all been Leigh's. It was mind-blowing.

Fiona pitched for the job although she doubted she would ever be able to completely satisfy the client. Fiona couldn't gift Mrs Federova the biggest pad, which is what she really hankered after. Fiona had noticed that about rich people, they were rarely content with their own wealth however much that was but often obsessed with the greater wealth of others. Why couldn't people be more grateful? she wondered. If she had a fraction of what others had, she would be gratified, gladdened.

Fiona takes the tube to Daan Janssen's apartment. It's not an especially pleasant journey. People are becoming increasingly nervous about the media attention on the virus. She doesn't know what to believe. Is there a real threat? It sounds like something out of a sci-fi movie. The reporting of the origin of the disease seems smeared with prejudice and designed to create fear. The Asian passengers on the tube are wearing facemasks, other passengers stare at them with a mix of envy and resentment. Anyone who coughs is glared at. Fiona stands for the journey. She spreads her legs and bends her knees to find balance as the tube judders, she doesn't want to touch a railing.

Fiona recalls the apartment she had pitched to transform. The floors were a decent-quality hardwood but pocked by small rugs that, whilst charming in a cottage, looked provincial and out of place in the spacious, urban dwelling. It never failed to surprise her how many people with a lot of money had no taste at all. She'd noted with some pleasure that the furniture was quality but dated, knowing she'd be able to make inroads and improvements easily. Quick wins tended to lure in clients.

Fiona remembered Mrs Federova proudly showing her the communal areas. 'To help set tone.' In fact, to show off. The swimming pool, covered with silver mosaic tiles, and the communal gym with all the best equipment on hand to help bodies stay toned, were impressive. Desirable. Every detail was easy to recall. Exquisite opulence abounded. She couldn't tell Mark that. Or, if she was going to tell him, she should have said something straight away.

The other thing that she recalled about the development was the number of apartments that remained empty for sizeable periods of time, as they were bought up by people with multiple properties and choices about where to live. It wasn't just Mrs Federova who was looking to employ an interior designer, many of the properties were under construction. Floors ripped up, kitchens and bathrooms ripped out in a constant quest for the latest must-have top-social-status decor. Fiona wasn't complaining, she earned a living through other people's ambition, other people's discontent.

The development was very private, quiet. The apartments were exclusive, practically deserted. There was something else that Fiona didn't want to say to Mark. Fiona thought they were the perfect place to stash a captive.

Or a body.

243

29

Kylie

Friday 20th March

I keep drifting into a peaceless sleep and then waking
again, shivering or sweaty. Hungry, unrested. Each
time I wake there is a split second when I forget I am
in this room and I think, am I with Mark? Am I with
Daan? The usual question that I ask myself whenever
I wake. Usually, whichever answer presents itself,
unrolls into some level of organisation and I take
control. But now when I wake up, it takes a moment
to remember, *I am alone*. Time sloshes around me. I
might drown in it. What can I do other than wait it
out? I think it is Friday. If it is, then no matter who
is responsible, the world must know I am missing by
now.

The world must know I am a bigamist.

All I ever wanted to do was give the boys a happy
home but now they will know their home was faulty,
fractured.

In most marriages there is a problem with time.
There often is not enough of it, sometimes there is
too much of it. Naturally with two marriages I have
this problem doubled, intensified. However much I
plan, compartmentalise, organise, sometimes the two
worlds blur, they collide. At Christmas, for example,
I can't be two people and I have to be in one place or
another. I have to choose. Until this past Christmas

244

I always chose to be with the boys, with Mark. How could I not? Christmas is for kids. Daan is not a kid. But he is my husband, so it hurt being away from him. I told him I needed to be with my mother on the actual day, that we could celebrate another day, what did it matter to us? And he agreed. So on the twenty-fourth we drive up to Mark's parents' home, sit on the motorway for long hours, nose to tail with all the other cars full of people trying to get to their families; compelled by love or duty, or a blurred blend of the two. Love and duty can be smudged together like two different coloured packs of playdough; once teased, mauled, handled they can never be completely separated. Both bright colours smirch into a duller shade.

Our Christmas Days pan out very much like everyone else's we know, I suppose. An early start, the kids bouncing on our bed, bony knees and elbows landing indiscriminately, stockings already opened, a chocolate orange quickly consumed, the evidence of which is smeared on their faces. There are paper hats and too much food, too much drink, a polite pretence that new slippers are the ideal gift from my mother-in-law. I drown in a mass of plastic and tantrums, and sulks and laughter. Then it is all over by 4 p.m. By that time, Mark's parents are usually dozing on the sofa, not replete, stuffed. The boys are huddled in the corner of the room playing with new toys, sometimes contentedly but most likely low-level bickering abounds. A full row might erupt or be avoided because the turkey sandwiches and trifle are served. Food none of us need or really want but we have to have it because, 'Christmas isn't Christmas without turkey sandwiches and trifle, is it, pet?'

Mark's parents are nicer to me at Christmas than

245

they are at any other time of the year. They are never horrible or mean to me, but they are — despite stereotypes about northerners — cool towards me. They see me as an interloper. To them, I am not simply Mark's wife. I am Mark's 'second wife' or worse, his 'new wife'. That is how Mark's mother once introduced me to a neighbour. We'd been married six years at that point. Longer than he and Frances were ever married. But at Christmas, a morning sherry, Frank Sinatra crooning, maybe my elaborate, well-thought-through gifts seem to soften them. I might get a kiss on the cheek or be pulled into a hug. I don't blame his parents for their coolness though, their distrust. They are right not to trust me, aren't they? The other stereotype about northerners — the one that specifies that they are a canny bunch, and that you can't pull the wool over their eyes — that may be true. Maybe they sense something in me. I always think his mother can see right through me. I wonder what she thinks about my disappearance.

Good riddance, perhaps.

Daan and I make more of the season generally, because we can't focus on the specific day. Our celebrations are very different. We have never done late-night trolley dashes around Toys R Us, nor do we get stressed about booking our supermarket delivery of the Christmas shop around mid-November, because Daan and I do not shop as though the apocalypse is coming. Which is a relief because who would opt to do that twice? By contrast, we glide around Harvey Nichols food department, slipping delicacies into our basket: New Zealand Manuka honey, Jamon Iberico crisps, large hunks of pistachio nougat. Our groceries are delivered by a series of local artisan

246

food experts: greengrocers, butchers, bread makers, fishmongers. We celebrate Christmas on the twenty-seventh or twenty-eighth, depending which day Christmas has fallen on. I tell Mark I need to be back at work, he stays with his parents, so they get to see a bit more of the boys and I get to travel from York to London by train. I love that journey, it is transitional, hopeful, crammed with anticipation.

However, last year, as early as October, Daan started to make noises about how he really wanted us to have a Christmas together. 'I don't mind how we do it exactly. I can come up to your mother's care home with you. I just want us to be together.'

'No, that's not much of a Christmas. You are better spending it with your family.'

'But you are my family. You are my wife. I want to spend it with you. And from what you say of your mother it is not even clear she knows it is Christmas Day. You could go to her the day after. Just one Christmas. Is that an unreasonable ask?'

Of course it was not. Or rather, it should not have been. So, I agreed.

We woke up late and ate smoked salmon on rye bread, sipped vintage champagne, until we started on the oysters and bloody Caesars, which Daan introduced me to, explaining that they are the same as Blood Marys but with a splash of clam juice added. We ate the meals in bed. There was no plastic, or novelty dancing Santas, he did not gift me a sandwich toaster or a new Dyson. He bought me a diamond pendant. As he fastened the clasp, I felt his breath on my neck. I missed the boys and Mark and the smell of sprouts so much I wanted to howl. They believed I was stuck, because of weather, at one of my half-brother's homes. Suddenly, I was awash with an overwhelming need to get back to Mark, Oli and Seb. I couldn't have Christmas there with Daan. The routines, the patters, everything could fall apart.

I played with the idea of telling Daan that I'd had a call from the nursing home, that my mother needed me, that I had to leave. But I knew he would rally, offer to come with me. Of course he would. Wouldn't any considerate husband? He would want to drive me to Newcastle. But I wasn't planning on going to Newcastle. There was no care home to visit, no sick mother. I wanted to go to my boys. I was stuck. I couldn't do anything. If I did, I would undermine, I'd destroy everything that I'd so carefully constructed. I felt sick for the entire day. The delicious food, the vintage champagne stuck in my throat as I fought tears. Daan repeatedly asked if I was OK, 'You are not yourself.'

'The early morning drinking has gone to my head, I'm already fighting a hangover,' I muttered.

When I returned to my home with Mark and the boys on Boxing Day night, the house was gloomy. They arrived half an hour after me and made it a home. They'd had a great Christmas, apparently it was the same as ever. I wasn't really missed.

And that was terrifying.

Are they missing me now?

I am beginning to wonder, even before I was brought to this room and locked up, made to shit in a bucket, was I trapped? Was I already being punished? Why can't I tell who it is behind the door? Why can't I distinguish between them? Haven't I been paying attention? I thought they were so different, so distinct. Two completely separate lives. Two completely different men. I can't deny it was a thrill discovering another man. His body. His brain. I was curious. With Mark I had been looking for a soulmate. I thought I'd found it. But now, I have to wonder, does such a thing even exist or is it made up by songwriters, novelists, film-makers to comfort the masses? To give us something to search for? The truth is, Mark didn't answer *every* aspect of my being, it's maybe an impossible ask. I yearned to be carefree, but I never could be with Mark. Not entirely.

Because we're the sort of people who are aware that things don't always turn out well. I know this because my entire childhood proved it, he knows it because his wife died young. Daan offered me a rose garden of a life. His vast wealth and confidence (both earned and inherited) formed a protective bubble that was so deliciously tempting. With Mark I am always aware that in every garden there are stinging nettles, biting insects. There is a sadness to Mark, a seriousness. Even now, all these years later, he can't quite allow himself to be completely joyful. I realised when I first met him that things were still raw, I thought it would wear off. I thought I'd make him happy. But I didn't. As the years went by, I accepted that whilst Mark is indeed a lovely man, he is not a happy man, not entirely and he never will be; I can't change that. He is slightly depressed. The world disappoints him. I wonder whether he thought the world was rosy when he first met Frances. Did she have that? Something else she beat me to. As the ultimate people-pleaser, this hurts me; that I can't make him entirely happy. Consequently, I can't be entirely happy when I'm with Mark.

I married two men in an attempt not to be lonely,

yet I have destroyed the intimacy between Mark and I, and I can never build intimacy with Daan. I am not who they think I am. I am just a version of her. They each have a version of me. The problem is not just that no one knows *where* I am. No one knows *who* I am.

I am lonelier than ever. My loneliness pulls me under. I close my eyes again. Allow my mind to shut down, my body to preserve energy. My sleep is broken. I keep jolting awake, scared by my dreams, horrified when I land in my reality. On the second or third time I wake up, I find there is a fresh bottle of iced tea. I glug it back gratefully. Fall back to sleep. The next time I wake is in the dead of night. The room is airless, the blackness drenches me, chokes me. Something is not right. Something else.

I sit up full of dread. I can't breathe. I can't see. I realise that I'm wearing a hood of some kind. It's been taped around my neck, a fraction too tightly. I'm choking. I panic and take a deep breath which draws the fabric into my nostrils, I start to pant, shallow breaths are safest. I can't see anything but he's here. I know he is here in the room with me.

'Darling?' I daren't use a name. I don't want to inflame him. But the endearment infuriates. He stamps down on my hand. Holds his foot there, grinds harder, I think I hear a bone snap. I scream in agony, pain shoots through my body. He lifts his foot, I try to roll into a ball. He kicks me once, twice. Swift, punishing. It's controlled. One man is huge, the other compact, both are strong. The kicking winds me, hurts like hell but I know either man could have broken ribs if they wanted to. 'Please, please no,' I beg. Another swift choppy kick lands on my shoulder this time, as though I am a dog that's got underfoot. But kicking a dog is unequivocally cruel, I've always believed only sadists mistreat animals.

'Please, Mark, Daan, think. Stop,' I beg. But he strides out of the room, bangs the door behind him.

What was that? Dear God, what have I done? What have I driven them to? How could either man have done that to me? I have started this, but the response is madness. I thought I was waiting it out, being humiliated, forced to think about my actions. Maybe choose. Maybe lose both. I don't know. Now I see this is far, far more. Am I going to survive this? Will he kill me? Could either man kill me? I start to frantically pick at the gaffer tape around my neck that secures the hood. I pull off the hood and gasp at the air, taking in big gulps, recognising breathing freely is a luxury. Even breathing the air in this rancid room. I scrabble towards the door, momentarily forgetting the chain, until it yanks me back, causing the shoulder that has just been kicked to burn with pain. My right hand is throbbing, my ribs bruised. 'Let me go. Please let me go,' I beg. 'I'm sorry. I'm sorry. OK? Is that what you needed to hear? Well, of course I'm fucking sorry.'

No response. There are different kinds of silence, of quiet. Sometimes it is peaceful. Like a child sleeping, their steady breathing a comfort. The silence between two strangers is awkward as they flail around looking for common ground, small talk — but the silence between two lovers, content in one another's company, reading newspapers perhaps, or completing a crossword, that can be a space of calm and reassurance. The silence between a disappointed husband and wife mid-row is the worst. That is the silence I have spent my life avoiding. The silence that is tense, angry, threatening. And now there is that exact silence between us. He is that side of the door with his type-writer and anger, and I'm this, with my chain and empty uncertainty.

I scream. I let out one long, continuous scream. I howl, a wounded animal. Then I wait, but nothing happens, there is no reaction. No one comes, even though the scream is real and loud and still burns in my throat. Where is everybody? Why are the streets so silent? I can't look out of the window but am beginning to wonder whether I'm a long way off the ground, away from traffic and life because the silence is eery, London streets are never empty. It grows dark again and no one comes back.

I sit motionless. My eyes straining to focus through the darkness. It's hopeless. Time passes and I lean back against the wall. Then lie on the floor. More time. I roll into a ball. More time. My eyes flutter. My hands throb. The only sound is my growling stomach.

30

Oli

Saturday 21st March

Oli picks up his skateboard. 'Are you going out?' his dad asks.

'Might as well, nothing else to do.' Oli sounds bored by the fact because appearing bored is habitual. Showing enthusiasm or having something particular to do, admitting that anything amuses or interests him is not dope. Oli is not bored. How could he be bored right now? But he has worked out that it is best if he acts bored in front of his dad, because that is what's expected of him. And any emotion bigger than boredom might trigger his dad. His dad is acting crazy. Storming about in and out of the house, so moody. He's like a faulty firework — you just don't know when he is going to catch or where he is going to blast and burn. Like when Oli showed him that meme and he went off it. He was only trying to lighten the mood. OK, in retrospect, suggesting they watch *Baptiste* was a bit off, but all his mates had seen it, and he didn't know it was a spin-off from a show, *The Missing*.

Or maybe he did know. But what the hell.

When Oli made the mistake of saying he was pleased that exams have been cancelled, his dad yelled, 'How can you be thinking about that right now?' Pretending to be bored is safe.

He just wants to help keep things calm, on track.

253

Oli is worried about his dad. He's worried about everything.

'Where are you going?' his dad demands now.

'The skate park.'

'Which one?

'Does it matter?' Oli doesn't know why he said that. He should just tell his dad he is going to Regent's Park. He isn't, but that's not the point. It's not a good idea to rock the boat and draw attention to himself. All his dad wants is an answer, it's stupid not to give him one, it will just lead to a scene. But sometimes Oli does stupid things. Like pre-ing too much before a house party, or saying stuff about a girl that he doesn't mean, or not saying stuff he does, other things. His head decides one thing, but he goes and does something completely different anyway. Leigh would usually excuse it. 'He's just a kid, he's just finding himself.' She was generally the easy-going parent, the good cop, so to speak.

Until she wasn't. Bitch.

The pain of the betrayal sears through his body again. Scalds him from the inside. That has happened a few times this week. He is ashamed that he feels this way. That he misses her. He doesn't want to. He *doesn't* miss her, not really. How could she? How could she? His own mother. What a total bitch.

'Wear your helmet,' says his dad but he doesn't push for the answer to his question about where Oli is planning on skating. It's not usual. Nothing is usual.

Just as he is about to leave, the house phone rings. His dad leaps up out of his chair like he is some villain in the Bond car, ejected from the passenger seat. Oli waits to see if it is the police with news.

He hears his dad say, 'Oh, hi, Fiona,' Oli decides

254

to linger a little longer. Fiona only left their house about half an hour ago, he can't think what she's calling about already but he is OK with the fact that she is always calling or hanging around. She seems to cheer up his dad and Dad deserves that, yeah? After everything. Because it has turned out to be worse than he could have imagined. Not an affair. A whole other world. He hears his dad tell Fiona that Seb is upstairs in his room and Oli is going skateboarding. His dad calls to him, 'Fiona says if you are going on the tube take some hand sanitiser.'

Oli shrugs. 'We don't have any.'

'He says we don't have any,' his father repeats into the phone, he sounds exhausted. He nods and then looks up at Oli. 'She says she bought some yesterday, it's near the bowl on the table where I put my car keys.' Oli isn't going to use it. But it is sort of cool of Fiona to look out for him. At least she is keeping her shit together, so he goes into the kitchen, finds the sanitiser and puts it in his pocket. His fingers graze the card the policewoman left him, the corner accidently scrapes underneath his nail. He flinches like he does when he is woken by an alarm. She gave it to him in case he ever wanted to talk to her. 'If you think of anything, *anything at all* that might be relevant. Anything that might give us an insight into your mum's state of mind.'

He hasn't called, even though the cop had said 'anything' three times. Probably because of that. That desperate urgency she was trying to convey felt like a lot.

He has been wearing the same cargo pants for days now. No one nags him to put clothes in the wash basket. Leigh made a big deal about that. Pretty chill most of the time, washing was the thing that she could go a bit obsessive about. Nothing would be washed unless it was in the basket. She would basically conduct a stand-off until he complied, she'd watch him go around the room picking up T-shirts and stuff, like some sort of washing Nazi. Fiona cooked an awesome burger and chips supper the other night so it's not as though he's being neglected, he's just not nagged. Fiona says she likes to keep busy and to have something to do. She put a wash on. He noticed because not only did she pick up his clothes from off the floor, but she changed his sheets too. Bit weird that, TBH. Leigh left him to strip his own bed because it's a privacy thing, sheets and stuff. But Fiona means well. Probably Leigh just didn't care so much and what looked like consideration at the time was in fact disinterest. Right?

He doesn't know, it's possible.

He doesn't know Leigh. None of them do.

His head aches with thinking about it. He has to get out the house.

He walks out of the front door, letting it slam loudly behind him. He doesn't want to turn around or glance up as he expects his brother's face will be stuck to his bedroom window, like it has been since Thursday morning. Eyes alert, scanning the street — left, right, as though he's watching a pro-level tennis match — looking for his mother. Sad. Hopeless. His brother is taking this pretty badly. The front door slams again, which makes Oli turn around. Seb is not in his room, he is standing awkwardly on the step.

'You're not coming with me,' Oli says automatically.

'I didn't ask to.'

'No, but you were going to.'

'No, I wasn't.'

'What have you got in your backpack?'

'Nothing.'

'Clearly you have something.' Seb is wearing his school backpack. It looks almost as bulky as when he is going to school and it's full of a day's textbooks.

'I'm going to my friend's for a sleepover.'

'Which friend?'

Seb hesitates. He is not used to lying to his older brother. He is quite a straightforward kid but he clearly is about to lie because he has a tell, he juts out his chin when he's being dishonest. Leigh identified it years ago, when he wasn't much more than a baby. Everyone in the family knows when Seb is lying. 'I'm going to Theo's.' He sounds like he's trying the name out. Asking Oli a question. Sort of, 'Might I be going to my friend Theo's house? Does it sound feasible?' Oli wonders if he's running away. Off to try to find Leigh. It's the kind of thing Oli himself might have thought about doing if he was twelve and none the wiser.

'Does Dad know?'

'Yes.' Seb turns pink. Pretty clear evidence that not only is he lying but he is ashamed to be doing so. Oli sometimes wonders how his brother survives at school.

'Don't let me stop you.'

Seb sets off down the street, Oli watches him get smaller. He stops at the corner where their road joins the busier high street. He hangs about the lamppost for a while. Oli can't see what he's doing. Might he be waiting for Theo after all? When Seb eventually turns right, Oli sets off after him. He has a lot going on, but he can't just let his little brother wander off into London on his own. As he approaches the

257

lamppost on the corner where Seb was hanging about, Oli spots it immediately. A poster, one of several. A plea. Oli's heart contracts and swells. He can actually feel it beating.

HAVE YOU SEEN MY MUM?

The question is, he has to admit, bold and arresting, it will probably get more attention than a simple MISSING. But it is exposing, horrifying, for Seb and somehow for Leigh too. Oli acknowledges that Seb's computer skills are pretty good. There is a picture of Leigh, a good one. She looks happy and sparkling. Not the sort of woman who would want to go missing at all. Seb took the photo eight days ago just before they all went out for a family meal. It's the same one the police have. The next line spells it out, in case a passer-by didn't understand.

SHE IS MISSING.

Oli almost laughs at the innocence, the naivety, but the laugh catches in his throat, and sounds suspiciously like a sob.

REWARD FOR RELIABLE INFORMATION

What reward? Seb has about £24 to his name, and it's only as much as that because he's saving for the latest FIFA to drop. Seb had also put his own mobile number on the poster. Stupid kid. He'll have endless weirdos ringing him.

258

The posters are not laminated. They will tear or the ink will run once it rains, Seb obviously hasn't thought about the fact that they will become illegible pretty soon. They are attached with zip ties. Oli recognises them as his own zip ties that he keeps under his bed. Zip ties are useful things to have, you can make keyrings or fix binder files with them. Seb has probably rooted about and found them. Oli got them out of his dad's shed in the first place so he can't complain that Seb nicked them. Besides, Seb saved a couple of quid by doing so and he needs all his cash for his reward. Oli is being sarcastic because that is how he behaves with his brother, as a matter of routine. Teasing, sort of scrapping, but they are always on the same team really. Even though they are three years apart, they've always been close. The posters are killing him. He can't believe Seb has made these alone and that he feels he needed to lie about what he was up to. But then, everyone has their secrets it seems. Presumably, Seb is not planning on going to Theo's at all but instead trailing the streets of London putting up these miserable, desperate posters. He could get lost, he could get into trouble. He can't go about plastering his phone number everywhere. Oli tears at the poster, crumples it up.

Oli follows his brother's Hansel and Gretel trail from lamppost to lamppost, ripping down the posters, faster than his brother can pin them up. He has to hang back, lurk in shop doorways so as not to be spotted. He watches his brother carefully, laboriously tie the posters to the lampposts. Other people are watching his brother too. Some give him a sympathetic smile; others give him a wide berth. Oli tears the posters into small bits and throws them in rubbish

259

bins. Their work carries on for a couple of hours. It becomes apparent that Seb has run out of posters when he allows himself a rest. He goes into a newsagent's, comes out with a Coke and a Snickers bar.

Oli is waiting for him.

'Oh.' Seb jumps, blushes. Oli feels bad for him. He's not the one who should feel guilty. He's just trying to do a nice thing. He's just trying to find his mum.

'I thought you were going to Theo's,' says Oli.

Seb juts out his chin. 'Oh, he sent a text to say his mum said no.'

Oli thinks it's a weird thing listening to someone lie to you but pretending you believe it. It makes you feel powerful but also sad. 'I was just thinking of going over to Aunty Paula's,' he says. His Aunty Paula. Their mum's sister could be a bit intense, clearly she never got used to the idea of losing her sister, but he sort of gets that. He's not sure he got over it either and he barely remembers her. Is it possible to get over such a thing? Still, despite her intensity, Oli likes Paula, he knows she always has his back. Neither he nor Seb can do any wrong in her eyes. They practically have papal status. She has called a couple of times since Leigh went missing, but she's only spoken to his dad. Leigh always denied that there was any beef between her and Aunty Paula, and maybe that was true. But there wasn't any love between them either. He really needs to see Paula. 'Do you want to come? You know she always has like a mountain of treats. We could maybe stay over at hers.'

Seb's face lights up. 'For real? Yeah.'

They head towards the tube together, Oli stuffs his hands deep into his low pockets, hunches to glue his eyes to the pavement. It hurts to look at his brother, who is overly grateful for the offer of company. He hasn't been a very good brother since Leigh went missing. He should try harder. Seb is clearly a mess. He needs this to be over. He needs some answers. Everyone does.

Oli's fingers move around the cop's card and the hand sanitiser. Is it time to make a call? Surely it isn't necessary. Everyone now knows about Daan Janssen and where he lives, so Oli admitting he'd known about her other life before isn't going to help, it is most likely only going to get him into trouble. The cop said call if there was anything that might give them an idea about Leigh's state of mind. And him knowing about her thing for months doesn't really reveal anything about her state of mind, does it? Although, maybe it reveals something about his. He shivers. That is the last thing he wants to do. But he does want them to look closely at this Daan Janssen. The cops must be doing that, right?

31

Kylie

I need food and drink. Especially drink, a body can survive weeks without food but only a matter of days without drink. Light is sliding under the board on the window, another day. Saturday? Time has dictated everything I've ever done, for so long I've lived with strict timetables, appointments and commitments; not having it as a frame pushes me closer into free-fall. I have to fight against that feeling. I have almost become used to the stench of the bucket. Proof of my filth and frailty. It frightens me, what I'm able to become used to.

I wish everything could have stayed as it was, in the weird false state of suspension that I had created. I know I was living in a place on Earth that did not follow the laws of the land but after all, laws are simply things written by someone or other — often a very long time ago — and handed down, demanding obedience. Who is to say a woman can only love one man at a time?

A man, probably.

Sometimes it felt as though I was defying not only the law of the land but also laws of physics too. My life somehow defied gravity. I was floating. I refused to acknowledge that for every action there is an equal and opposite reaction. But there is. For every moment of bliss I've had, I have to pay. I paw helplessly over the discarded food tray, the plastic bottle has some water left in the bottom, there is half a browned banana remaining. As I pick it up, I unsettle a fly. It buzzes away and I vaguely wonder how it got into the room. I don't care that I once read that almost every fly that lands on food vomits on it too. I'm too hungry to care about anything. I eat it slowly, carefully chewing each mouthful. I listen for the sound of footsteps or the typewriter. Nothing.

The day crawls. He doesn't bring any more food or water. My mouth is so dry, my lips are cracking. The typewriter stays inactive. I find myself longing for it to start up again. I am reminded of all the times I swapped illicit WhatsApp messages with whichever husband I was not with. If I was with Daan and saw Mark was '**typing . . .**' my stomach would squeeze with love and anxiety. I always anticipated a message detailing some sort of problem: a sick child, lost homework, a fracas with a teacher. When I was with Mark and saw that Daan was '**typing . . .**' my stomach would slosh and slide with love and a delicious anticipation. I long for the typewriter to clatter. Like a lab rat I've been trained to respond to the sound of its keys and I find I want to be challenged. I want to be held to account. It would almost be a relief.

Frustrated, I kick the wall opposite the door. It's a hell of a kick. The pain of it shoots up my leg, into my hip and I instantly regret it. The last thing I need right now is more pain and further injury. But then I notice it, a dent in the wall. I have made a dent in the wall! I stare at it in surprise. After days of being so weak and powerless I feel a surge of invigoration carouse through my body. I made a dent in the

263

plasterboard. I made a difference! I kick the wall again and again, with my toe and then I turn and kick with my heel. Then I lie on my back and stamp both my feet into the wall, because that seems more powerful still. After half a dozen blows, I hear the plaster crack. The wall starts to sort of crumble and cave in front of me. I laugh, surprised at how lightweight and fragile plasterboard is. I start to claw and grab at the pieces, tearing the wall away. There's a cavity and then more plasterboard. I punch through that relatively easily and I find I can get my hands through to a new space. I start to pull at the board, bringing bigger pieces down until I have made a hole in the wall that is big enough so that I can easily see into the next room.

It's a larger room than the one I'm in. I'd guess its original purpose is another bedroom. But, like the room I'm being kept in, whilst the walls are plastered and painted, the floor is concrete, and there is no furniture. A work in progress. Still, it is space, it is air that is less putrid than that which I've been breathing. I move as close to the new room as the chain will allow and breathe deeply. I sob with relief and delight, but I'm too dehydrated for there to be any actual tears. My chest lurches up and down, dry heaving. I am so relieved to have this progress. I can't go anywhere, even if I make the hole bigger, I am still chained so can't crawl through it, but it feels like I've done something, changed something. I feel some control and maybe even hope.

That feeling increases as I see past the hole I have made there is a small window and it is wide open. I stare at it amazed. I take a moment, a beat. Compute everything this means. I stand up, move about as much as I can. I see that I am high up.

264

Oh God.

I can see a river, houses, some blocks of flats. It's dark in both the room I'm in and the one I'm looking through and I'm at a distance from the window but even so, I think I know where I am. I recognise the view. I may not be as high up, but I think I am in my own apartment building. I am almost certain.

Daan.

My head is fuzzy now. Memories, thoughts, reasons are loose, scattered. I'm losing my grip.

I freeze for a moment. Not sure if I am devastated or relieved.

There couldn't have been good news. Whichever one I discovered was responsible for this would have broken my heart. At least this way the boys are safe; their father is not a madman. Daan, of course. I understand. More than anyone probably.

I needed something of my own. I wanted someone to love me more than anyone else. It's not an excuse, but it is my explanation. My mother loved my father most. When he left, she seemed to step out of the world. Or at least step away from me. My father loved his new wife and new sons more than he loved me. He didn't even love me enough to disguise the fact. Mark loves his children most. My children love their dead mother. That is the hardest, dead people are easy to love and impossible to compete with.

Having a favourite child is frowned upon. Poor parenting. The goal is to love them equally, even if it is differently.

I love Seb because when I am around him, I can soften, I can be still, peaceful, complete. He makes me laugh out loud. I'm always throwing my hand over my mouth and erupting into the sort of laughter that

265

ultimately makes my ribs ache. He's funny, irreverent, fast.

I love Oli because he is a challenge. He doesn't care whether he makes me laugh or not, but I care whether I can draw a smile from his handsome full lips, whether I can ease out a grunt of approval. If I can lessen his seemingly endless mistrust of the world, his pain.

I love both my boys equally but otherwise. No favourites. Any right-thinking parent would rather die than admit to having a favourite.

And my men? My husbands? It is the same with them.

Thoughts whirl in and out of my head as my eyes rest on the chaos and rubble at my feet.

I wanted to be loved exclusively. Daan loves me more than he loves anyone else. Daan loves me so much but what did I offer him? Not the same singularity, not exclusivity. Of course, it is Daan who brought me to this, Daan is not a man who would accept sharing.

Nor is he a man who will forgive.

My instinct is to yell for help, but I doubt I'll be heard on the street even through an open window, not from this height. I'm more likely to be heard by Daan, who is presumably close by. I pick up a piece of plasterboard and throw it towards the window. My aim is off, it hits the wall. I bend, pick up another piece and try again, this time it falls short. However, the third piece of debris sails out of the window. The relief is enormous. It isn't a big piece, but I imagine it falling to the ground, maybe even landing on or near a passer-by. They'll look up and wonder where it has come from. Excited, I reach for another piece

266

of plasterboard. I throw that, it flies. The next doesn't and I'm bitten by a sense of panic. I know I have to stay calm and focus. Systematically I hurl the pieces of debris out of the window. Eight, nine, ten scraps hit the mark and find freedom. I continue to break pieces of plaster from the wall and hurl them out the window. I imagine the debris collecting in a pile on the pavement below. Surely someone will notice that. Alfonso the concierge won't like a mess around the building, he'll want to investigate. The hole in the wall is now sizeable — I've snapped off every part I can reach. I'm getting tired and more of the debris is missing the target of the window and just coming to rest somewhere in the other room. My hands are cut, scratched, bleeding.

I need water.

I slump down against the radiator again and wait.

As the day leaks away, the cold night air comes through the window and the hole in the wall and chills me. I try to wrap my arms around myself to keep warm, but it's uncomfortable because of the chain and the injuries. I carefully tuck both hands between my thighs instead. My fingers are freezing but trying to warm them leaves them smelling of my shit. I sit in silence. And wait.

But waiting is not enough. I have to do more. My progress with the wall has given me some hope. I have to keep trying. I slam my chain against the radiator. It makes a clanking sound in the room. Maybe the sound will somehow reverberate through the pipes of the building. The sort of neighbours I have will not like being disturbed, they will investigate. I slam the chain again. Crash. And again. Clatter. And again. Clang.

I will do this all night if I have to.

I will crash and clatter and clang. I will not be silenced.

32

Daan

Sunday 22nd March

Daan pulls apart from the body tangled in the sheets
next to him and rolls onto his back. He stares at the
ceiling. Her breathing is a touch under a snore, but
heavier than he is used to. It is distracting. He could
never live with it. Not that he's thinking of living with
it. Obviously. He never intended to even allow her to
stay over. It isn't like him to deviate from a plan, but
he isn't thinking clearly. When she turned up at his
door it was just easier to let her in than send her away.
On some level it was good to see her, she is so separate from everything else he is going through. She
has no idea he is married to a woman who is married
to another man. That mess, that humiliation and the
subsequent consequences, are light years apart from
this — an uncomplicated shag, a bit of companionship.

He can smell her now, warm and alive. Here. It is
some comfort. It is something. She starts to stir, rolls
over to face him, her hair spilling like waves across the
silk pillowcases. Kai insisted on them having silk bed-
ding, she read somewhere that the pillowcases helped
preserve a blow-dry. He too liked the silk sheets and
everything they did between them. They had a good
sex life, excellent. He always thought it was kept hot
because she was away for half the week, not quite

269

accessible, not quite available. Unlike other women who were always throwing themselves prone at his feet. When he first met her, she was a career woman with a job she loved, that was hot. When she suggested giving up work to nurse her mother, he'd been a bit disappointed, care homes were not erotic, but he did admire her sense of duty and commitment. She still offered him space.

Of course, since he's discovered what Kai had really been up to when she was away from him, it isn't at all sexy. It is demeaning. Unforgivable. He is not beyond reproach when it comes to fidelity, but the other women he took were just ways to pass time. Not dissimilar to drinking a decent glass of wine or going on a challenging run. Fun diversions. Not important. She was married when he met her. There was no way to look at that fact without thinking it is important. Vital. *Everything*. She was never his. *He* was the diversion. He was not important. It was unbelievable. Insulting. How could this have happened to him? Fury burns in his stomach, like a fire. Jealousy, a desire for revenge and answers billow through his mind like smoke.

The woman next to him wakes up, rolls towards him, smiles. He can't think what to say to her, so kisses her to buy some time. As he pulls away from her hot lips, and the slightly anxious, needy glint in her eyes he comments, 'Well, I wasn't expecting that.'

'But you were hoping for it.' She plasters a grin on her face. He has seen this sort of rictus grin before; it is entirely fake. The women he dated pre-Kai all wore it. A pseudo-brazen *I'm tougher than I look* grin. An expression that is supposed to convince their lovers that they are not insecure, clingy, desperate, or even, good, old-fashioned hopeful.

It was a lie, of course; those women were all those things. As he fears this woman is.

Sex makes people vulnerable. It might be fashionable to pretend women can hop into bed and keep the sex there, as just that — a human instinct, a need like thirst, or hunger, something to be satiated, but he hadn't yet met one woman that could really do that. They always allow it to leach into their heads, their hearts.

Except perhaps for Kai as it has turned out. Apparently, she was capable of compartmentalising. *World champion*, he thinks bitterly.

He had not been hoping for sex with this woman specifically, he never thought of her in between their hook-ups which were irregular, not coveted but pleasant enough. He would never have reached out to her, he never had, she made it easy for him. Last night she literally brought it to his door. What was he to do? Of course, he always had a vague hope to have sex. He was a normal man. He thought it might take his mind off everything. And it had for a time. But now he wants her to leave. He doesn't need this complication.

'I guess,' Daan replies, throwing out a wolfish grin. He can make any woman think she is the only woman in the world for him, that he has been thinking about them, maybe even longing for them, when he hasn't. The only woman he ever thought about in her absence was Kai.

Now, more than ever.

Ironic that he'd spent so much time and effort on Kai, making her feel she was the only woman in the world for him, when she didn't really value fidelity anyhow. Well, lesson learnt. *Everyone has lessons to*

271

learn, he thinks bitterly.

Daan will give this woman breakfast because he likes to think of himself as a gentleman, and throwing her out without breakfast after he's come in her mouth is not a very gentleman-like thing to do, but he has things to do today and what if the police come back? It wouldn't look good if he were found entertaining like this. Of course, technically, he has every right to do as he pleases, but it is about the optics. He bounces out of bed, picks up his jeans that lie discarded on the floor, pulls them on, without looking for boxers. 'I'll make you a coffee. You like cappuccino, right?'

'No, black.'

'Right.' He nods, clicks his fingers, as though that is what he said in the first place. 'And eggs, how do you like them?'

'I shall resist the pun of saying I like them unfertilised,' she replies. He grins, pretending to appreciate her joke but he's heard it before, many times. She holds his gaze. 'Poached. Softly poached.'

'Coming right up.' He marches into the kitchen with the sort of determination that encourages her to follow him. He won't be serving breakfast in bed. He doesn't want to do that. He wants to be as efficient about this as possible. Obligingly, she does follow him. As usual, as expected, she keeps swivelling her head from left to right, taking in the impressive apartment. Doesn't she do something connected with design or interiors? That rings a bell. Or maybe art or film. He can't recall. Whether she does or doesn't, she must appreciate the place. Be impressed by it. Who wouldn't be?

Kai. Apparently. Fucking bitch.

272

'This is such an exquisite apartment,' she says. 'But you really need to get your concierge guy onto sorting out those waterpipes.'

'Waterpipes?'

'Didn't you hear them clanking all last night? I mean, I'm no plumber, but it sounded like hot water going through pipes or something. It kept me awake. Haven't you noticed it?'

'No, can't say I have.' He wants to move the conversation on. He wants to move her on. As the egg is poaching, he says, 'Look, it is great to see you again but I have to tell you, I'm going through some heavy stuff right now, so it is not really a good time for me to start something up.'

He expects her to look hurt, or perhaps she'll rush to assure him that she isn't looking for anything heavy either, most women would rather lose anything than face. She surprises him when she asks, 'What sort of heavy stuff?'

'You wouldn't believe it if I told you,' he replies.

'Try me.'

Daan shakes his head. He doesn't know how to tell this woman that he has a wife. Let's face it, that is something they haven't discussed so far. And now he would have to confess to a missing wife. A wife with two husbands, so not really his wife at all. He doesn't know how to get into that. He walks around the break-fast bar to where she is standing, and kisses her lips, cups her breast. He finds that usually gets women to stop talking. As he gently squeezes her nipple, he feels it start to stiffen. He also starts to stiffen then he remembers that he has a lot to accomplish today; he doesn't have time for this, he breaks away. 'So yes, really heavy stuff and I haven't the space to start this up.'

273

'Start this up *again*, Daan.' He hears the accusation in her voice.

'Well, yes,' he shrugs and hands her the plate of eggs and toast. He hasn't made one for himself. He hasn't got any appetite at the moment. He watches her eat which she does unhurriedly and deliberately. He thinks she is drawing out the process on purpose, which annoys him. He glances at his watch.

'Are you going somewhere?'

'What?'

'I saw your case in the bedroom, I wondered if you are going on holiday.'

'No, well. Probably. I was thinking of it. Maybe I'll take off next week. I need a break.'

'Because of the stuff you are going through?' she asks, smiling.

'Right. Do you want to take a shower?' He's struggling to be polite now. He needs her to take the hint.

It appears she finally has when she replies, 'I think I'll shower back at my place.'

He watches her start to slowly gather up her clothes, her bag, get dressed. He counts the seconds. He's never good with women who want to outstay their welcome, but he's finding it particularly trying today. It takes all his self-control not to shove her down the lift shaft.

'Daan, tell me something, and be honest about it. Are you married?' She throws out the question when she is at the door. She has clearly sensed his impatience, his indifference. He sighs, what does he have to lose now.

'I was,' he replies. 'Yes, Fiona, I was but I'm not anymore.'

274

33

Fiona

Fiona had wanted to die the moment she realised she had been having an affair with her best friend's husband. Literally, she wanted to curl up in a ball and stop breathing. Stop being. It was too much. It was so unfair. So cruel. She didn't know what to do with the information. Who should she tell? Who could she tell? Under the circumstances, who could she trust?

She first met Daan when she went to pitch for Mrs Federova's interiors project. It was in the foyer, just as she was leaving, he was arriving. 'Met' is probably a generous description of the interaction. She clapped eyes on him as he swept past her, he gave her a polite nod of acknowledgement that she was sharing his space. It took everything she had not to openly gape. It was as though he cast a spell.

The moment she left the building she'd started searching through her dating apps that made suggestions based on geographical vicinity. She didn't really hold out much hope that he would appear on any of the listings. Not a man like that. Too rich, too handsome. He wouldn't have to try to find women online, they would be queuing up to date him in real life. Yet she searched because she felt compelled. Even a minuscule chance was some sort of chance. She swiped past face after face; ruthlessly her finger moved left, left,

275

left behind. Then, when she was searching her third app, she found him. She could hardly believe her eyes, but it was definitely him. She might have only seen him for a moment, but he was hard to forget.

He had posted three pictures. One of him on a boat, all tanned and vibrant; another in a suit, serious but no tie, open-neck shirt, the suggestion of rebel; the third a close-up. She zoomed in. Examining his perfection in every pixel. She didn't use this particular app that often. It was known to be one where people looking for uncomplicated hook-ups tended to post. Fiona wanted more than uncomplicated, despite what she told Leigh and all her other friends, despite her insistence that she was married to her job and was way past 'all that romance nonsense'. The truth was, Fiona remained hopeful that she would find a proper boyfriend, a soulmate, a partner. Yeah, it was a case of optimism over experience, but she had never quite been able to crush the dream. Fiona ached for what Leigh had. A devoted husband, a cheerful home, maybe even kids. Not biological ones, not anymore, that was unlikely as she was in her forties but there was adoption, fostering, stepchildren. She was open. So, Fiona didn't often use this app because whilst it wasn't advertised as such, her own experience and anecdotal evidence from her other single friends suggested the men on this site didn't want commitment. Worse, some already had it, elsewhere. Fiona chose to ignore the red flag, and she swept right.

She waited outside the luxury apartment for over an hour hoping against hope that he might respond. She stared up at the building shimmering in the sunlight and marvelled at the fact he was inside, so close, but felt thwarted that he was still so far. Unless he responded, he would remain forever out of reach. Would he respond? If so, when? Should she wait here or go about her business? A watched kettle never boiled and yet wasn't this fate? What were the chances of seeing someone as delicious and then being able to track him down so swiftly? Slim. Negligible. But she had; she felt it was meant to be. That is what people said, didn't they? In their wedding speeches and things. *In the end. It was meant to be.* The feeling was bolstered by the fact that particular day she happened to be wearing a very flattering dress from Reiss and high shoes. She rarely bothered with heels in London nowadays, but her legs were her best feature and she'd been waxed yesterday. That all seemed a lot like fate. Or at the very least luck. She would take either. Her profile picture was flattering. Her hair fell in waves across half her face, which was at once slimming and provocative; she peeped out from the curtain of hair, like a burlesque dancer might peek out from behind heavy, scarlet, velvet drapes.

She really needed to get back to her desk, start thinking about tackling Mrs Federova's pitch proposal but she held her faith, screwed up her courage and stayed put. She waited patiently for a further twenty minutes, telling herself she would give up at half past. There had to be a cut-off point. She almost exploded with delight when she saw the tick and the icon asking if she was available to chat.

Did we just meet?

She dithered. Would he think she was some sort of stalker if she admitted they had? Would he be scared off? Or would he admire her efficiency, her opportunistic nature? No one was overly syrupy about dating apps nowadays; pragmatism beat romanticism every

277

time, so she replied:

Yes. I was in your foyer earlier. I have a client there.

She didn't, not strictly speaking, she had a *potential* client, however, that level of nuance had no place in dating-app chat. She wanted to present herself as successful and purposeful, trusted. She waited a moment, but he didn't respond. She wondered whether she had lost him. Already? It was possible. Bitter experience had shown that the first few moments of online chat could smother things before they had even spluttered into life. People were ruthless. Impatient. Quickly she tapped:

I saw you in the foyer and thought you were worth hunting down.

The use of the word 'hunt' was a gamble. Would it excite him? Intrigue him? It was a thin line between sexy, go-getting woman and desperate weirdo.

Are you a genuine redhead?

She did not hesitate. **Yes.**

I suppose I have to take your word for that.

I can prove it.

He replied with two love-heart-eyes emojis. One might have shown some level of sincerity, two showed appetite.

Are you free now?

It was hard for Fiona to tell herself that their first liaison met her expectations, which whilst only recently formed, were crystal. On the plus side, he was polite, he offered her a drink, she accepted even though she normally avoided drinking through the day. She accepted because she needed something to calm her nerves; yes, she was game, but she was also human and this whole encounter whilst entirely exciting was vaguely terrifying. He made her a gin and tonic. A

278

strong one. He was breathtakingly handsome, and the apartment was one of the most impressive she had ever seen even in her professional life, and so much more impressive than anything any of her other dates had ever lived in. She knew she was getting ahead of herself, yet she could not help imagining waking up to the view, making supper in the kitchen, drawing a bath in that onyx bathroom and sharing it with him.

She was giddy with nerves. Not because she was breaking all the online dating rules by going to an unknown man's home without alerting anyone to her whereabouts — which was dangerous, stupid — instead, her nerves came from an almost debilitating fear that she might put a foot wrong. That she would blow this opportunity. Fiona never came across good-looking, affluent, single men. It was a stunning opportunity. She had to get it right. Her loneliness had been all-pervasive for some time. Maybe years. A constant. White noise. A low drone, irritating and overwhelming. She tried to shake it at work, at book cubs, by talking to Leigh, her hairdresser or strangers in the shops. The more she tried to shake it off, the tighter it clung. It seeped into her, into the marrow of her bones. It became part of her. She was her loneliness.

But less so when she was with Daan.

She didn't normally have sex with men the first time she met them. She had rules about meeting for coffee first, then for lunch or an alcoholic drink. Sex, if it happened at all, only ever came after the third date, which had to be dinner. But where had the rules got her? She was single at forty-three years old. Her rules were outdated, they were holding her back. The rules were obsolete when applied to how adult relationships worked nowadays. People wanted to know if they were sexually compatible before they wasted too much time on dating. Indeed, last year, she'd dated one lovely guy several times before they finally fell into bed, only to discover they didn't really do it for each other, everything was a bit tepid. It was a shame. She had no more time to waste. Besides, she had said she would prove she was a natural redhead. Everyone knew what that meant.

The sex was not tepid. It was technically perfect. Ideally, Fiona would have liked more kissing, a little foreplay perhaps and she'd have liked to have been lying down. Clothes off. But she couldn't complain because her screaming orgasm was real. She'd faked hundreds in her lifetime, even when there *had* been kissing, foreplay, a bed. So it was crazy to feel disappointed when she came bent over the kitchen table. Besides, the important thing was that there would be follow-up, an actual date, with conversation and a chance. He said, 'See you again,' as she left. She hung on to that.

There have been three more encounters since then. Four including last night. It doesn't sound many, Fiona concedes, not over five months, but there was messaging too, phone calls, pictures. He likes her to send pictures. She can't say they've dated exactly, not in a traditional sense. They haven't ever visited a restaurant, or the theatre or even the cinema. But on two occasions, afterwards, Daan ordered food to be delivered (Thai), and last night, afterwards, they went to a local bar (and then back to his apartment for a second round of sex). Things have been progressing.

But he has been married all along. She has been used. Daan is married to her best friend. It is such

280

an enormously overwhelming fact to try to take in. Shocking. It has left her reeling.

Her *missing* best friend. The thought sends chills through Fiona's body, flashes of panic seize her and almost paralyse her limbs. She feels heavy and stupid one moment, energetic — almost raging — the next. She is not being rational. Staying over at Daan's last night was a stupid risk. She hadn't planned on staying but she had needed to see for herself how he was reacting to Leigh's disappearance. Suspicion always fell on the husband. It was just a fact. Statistics. He looked terrible. Broken, splintered. Then he'd smiled at her in a way he'd never smiled at her before. As though she was the person he most wanted to see in the world. Although she couldn't be, could she? Surely the person he most wanted to see in the world was Kai. He asked her in, it all seemed simple, normal; she didn't feel frightened at all, even though anyone looking on might think she ought to be. Before she'd clapped eyes on him, she had been stretched with anxiety, aching with concern, apprehension, fear, but then he kissed her — she could taste the whisky he'd been drinking on his lips and all that melted away. He kissed over and over again, and she felt better. Quite simply that. Soothed. So she stayed.

This morning he looks completely different. There is no point in kidding herself. She couldn't if she tried. It's as though the scales have fallen from her eyes about everything, now she knows what deception her best friend is capable of. His eyes search her face, but not in a lust-dazed way, his eyes have a sadly all-too-familiar morning-after hardness. He wants to know when she will leave. Whether she will leave without a fuss. That look used to make Fiona feel

281

ashamed, then it made her despair. Now, her despair has stiffened to something closer to resentment. She shouldn't have slept with him. He doesn't care about her. He does not see her as a girlfriend, a lover. Not even a mistress or a temptation. She means nothing to him. She leaves.

Without a fuss.

Like he wants.

Fiona doesn't know how to tell Mark about her involvement with Daan. It is too weird, too much. She hadn't asked to be in this position, she just found herself in it. Honestly, she had started to suspect Daan might be involved with someone else around Christmas time, their second hook-up. The suspicion hung about in the shadows of her mind. The infrequency of their dates, the way he never let her move around the flat; they fucked in the kitchen and then she'd leave. His casual, dismissive way with her was hard to ignore completely and especially during the season when everyone was supposed to be merry and bright. She hadn't wanted to confront him. Like a child, she thought if she ignored her problem, it might go away. How could she have imagined who his wife was? She could never have imagined her best friend was married to two men. Who did that?

Fiona should have confessed to Mark that she already knows Daan. Now she has complicated things by promising she will find out more about him and report back. She is getting herself into hot water. If Leigh has taught her anything, it is that lying is not the answer. Fiona should try to avoid that as much as possible, she should tell the truth when she can. Obviously, there was no real need for Fiona to go to Daan's to find out more about him. She was already able to

282

tell Mark that Daan is affluent, charming, accomplished, that when he speaks to you it is as though a spotlight is being shone on you and you are stood on the stage at Carnegie Hall. Established, important, spectacular. Had Leigh felt that? Of course, she must have. She had been his leading lady for years. And Fiona? Well, Fiona had been nothing more than a chorus girl, no matter what she might have once believed or hoped.

Daan has been a delicious secret that she has nursed for five months now. A secret that she brings out whenever she is alone, to be examined gently, carefully. Furtively. She's never spoken to Leigh about him. She has wanted to, on about a hundred occasions. She wonders now what would have happened if she had. Imagine if she had mentioned that she was dating a rich Dutchman, would Leigh have blanched? If Fiona had photos of Daan, and had shared them with her best friend, would Leigh have broken down? Confessed? Fiona doesn't have photos of Daan though, the photos only went one way between them and there were no occasions when it would have seemed reasonable to take a couple shot.

Fiona had not mentioned Daan to Leigh when they first hooked up because she knew Leigh would have been dismissive, even supercilious. If Fiona had confided the details of her relationship with her friend, Leigh would have insisted on saying that Fiona was nothing more than a booty call and heading for trouble. Fiona knew Leigh would have concluded that her rich mystery man was probably involved with someone else because, in truth, all the indicators were there. Leigh had done that before. She believed in tough love and never had any problem with telling

Fiona if her lovers were losers or likeable. She didn't hold back.

Fiona had always struggled with Leigh's brutal dismissals of her romantic involvements. It was humiliating, patronising. Leigh seemed a bit smug; she clearly enjoyed playing the happy wife, able to dole out advice, offer guidance to her hapless single friend. Fiona used to have to bite her tongue. She wanted to demand, 'What do you know about it? Dating has changed since you met Mark.' But she didn't, because whilst part of her felt belittled, hurt, another part of her hoped Leigh *did* know more than her, and might somehow magically guide her to the happily ever after. But it has turned out that Leigh was a liar, a cheat. She really was only *playing* being the happy wife. Leigh was far from the perfect wife and mother, the perfect friend that she portrayed. She had no right to offer advice. Her life was a sham, a fraud. She had caused so much pain and confusion.

How could Leigh do what she had done and not tell Fiona? They were supposed to be best friends. All those years. All those lies. To think Fiona had felt bad about keeping quiet about her thing with Daan for a few months. Sleeping with a man who she suspected was involved with someone else was hardly a moral crime in comparison. She hadn't even planned to keep quiet about that forever, only until whatever they had was a bit more established. Just until it was robust enough to withstand Leigh's scepticism and scorn.

Daan. What is she supposed to think about him now? Having sex with him, actually sleeping with him last night was a mistake, it has clouded her judgement again. Stopping over was so much more intimate than a hook-up. She now knew what his breath smelt like in the morning (annoyingly still attractive), it had been something else feeling his warm, rhythmic breath on her neck as he slept.

Still, she has to look at the facts. Daan isn't a faithful husband. Should she tell the DC that? Is it relevant? She doesn't want to be drawn into this quagmire. But if it helps the police build a profile of Daan then she probably should tell.

One thing Fiona is clear on is that it is essential Mark does not meet Daan. What Mark is dealing with is monumentally painful, confusing and cruel. She understands — more than anyone — how viciously hurt he must be. Her pain is tearing her into pieces, what might Mark's pain destroy? If anything kicked off between the two men, it would just add to the misery.

Fiona does not go straight back to Mark's. She needs some time to think about what to do next. She calls him, says she'll pop over later this afternoon, or early evening. She buys some more groceries, noting the shelves look like the mouth of a seven-year-old who has lost baby teeth, black gaps stand stark. Fiona feels a swell of impatience at people's selfishness. There would be enough to go around if no one hogged more than they needed. She does a few errands, returns home for a shower and, even though it's a Sunday, she calls her boss to confirm she'll be continuing to work from home for the foreseeable future. Her boss is flexible, less interested in the tragedy of her missing best friend than she would be in normal circumstances because a lockdown of the city seems imminent. It's all anybody is thinking and talking about. Hospitals are being prepared for an influx of patients, the police are being drilled for potential rioting and looting. All resources are being redirected that way.

'Stay safe, yeah?' says her boss. It is said with self-consciousness but sincerity.

Fiona feels her stomach contract with anxiety. What will a locked-down city mean for Leigh? She knows she has one more call to make. Yes, obviously being unfaithful is a long way away from being someone who might hurt his wife. Fiona isn't saying Daan is capable of that, she'll leave that decision up to the police. All she can do is give them the information she has.

34
DC Clements

Sunday 22nd March

Despite the alert that was issued on Thursday, no members of the public have reported a sighting of Leigh Gillingham. Not one. This is unusual. Pre-Coronavirus the general public seemed to be much more interested in missing people. Whether their concern was genuine or because they are busy-bodies who believe they can do the job better than the police Clements can't be sure, however routinely someone — many someones — would have called in a sighting, which may or may not have checked out, but would have at least stopped Clements feeling like she was shouting down an empty chasm. Now, everyone up and down the country has problems of their own. Loo roll and pasta stockpiling has become the national hobby. People, bloated with suspicion, skirt around one another, unwilling to look another being in the eye. Maybe this is the reason no one has seen a forty-three-year-old, five-foot-seven brunette in black jeans and a camel-coloured coat, anywhere.

Kylie was last seen on Monday the sixteenth. It is Sunday the twenty-second. A week. Clements feels the pressure of the days dissolving in front of her. She feels cheated that they weren't alerted to Kylie's disappearance until four days after she'd vanished. A handicap. Clements and Tanner sit in the almost deserted station, poring over the facts, files, information and hunches; determined to wring every moment out of the time they have left on this investigation.

There isn't a reward for information, which doesn't help. Daan Janssen hasn't offered to fund one, even though he is in a position to do so. Nor has Mark Fletcher, although coming up with the cash would presumably be more of a struggle for him. That said, Clements knows of cases where people have taken loans, mortgaged their houses, sold their cars to be able to offer rewards for information on their loved ones. Not that the police unilaterally encourage this, it can lead to all sorts of confusion and attract the wrong type of person coming forward with inaccurate information. Normally, the police have to spend time discussing the pros and cons of offering a reward. Normally, relatives are desperate and willing to try *anything* to bring their missing home. Even missing people that left mid-fight, mid-crisis, mid-trauma.

Normally.

Neither man has made posters to pin on notice boards of cafés, libraries or community centres. There are no laminated photocopies of a favoured photo of Leigh or Kai zip-tied to lampposts. Posters that beg passers-by for attention and help. Posters that rip at hearts, and as often or not, fade in the sun or smudge in the rain before they yield results. Neither man has nagged for a press conference, a radio appeal. As far as she is aware, they have not spent hours walking the streets in hope of spotting Kylie. It puzzles and bothers Clements that neither husband seems interested in following the usual patterns or protocols to help find the woman. Clements has known cats that have gone astray to cause more concern. Yes, the circumstances are unusual, and Kylie has clearly fallen from grace in both their eyes, but shouldn't they care more? Frustrated, Clements voices her thoughts to Tanner. 'Shouldn't what they once had inflame if not concern, then at least curiosity as to her whereabouts? Shouldn't they want to fight for her, to fight *with* her? If they loved her a week ago how could it all have vanished so instantly, so completely?'

'Well, obviously their indifference indicates guilt, an involvement in her disappearance. Maybe they are not niggling for a thorough search because they don't want it to be fruitful. Maybe they already know what happened to her.'

'What — both of them?'

Tanner shrugs and grins, 'You're the one always saying keep an open mind, boss.'

So far, Clements has considered a number of theories including one or the other husband discovering the truth, perhaps threatening Kylie with exposure, with violence, and her running away afraid. Or, one or the other husband discovering the truth and hurting her, perhaps in a moment of fury, perhaps something planned.

She could have fled.

She could be dead.

It depends on how far either man might be prepared to go. Marital homicide is frighteningly common. Every week, two women in Britain die because of violence in their home. *Every week*. The person these women presumably loved and trusted most in the world — once upon a time — kills them. It is hard to believe in fairy tales in Clements' line of work. There ought to be protests, banners, placards, marches, even riots. She'd understand riots, venting anger and frustration at that statistic. There are none of these things; there is silence and sometimes it feels like indifference.

Clements sighs and rubs the back of her neck. Rolls her head from left to right and back again to release tension; her neck cracks out a tune like a glockenspiel. She shouldn't let herself think this way. She gets carried away. Frustrated by the enormity of the all-pervasive problems when really, she ought to concentrate on the micro level. Finding Kylie Gillingham won't stop the relentless march of fear, or violence, or misogyny, but she might help one woman see her kids again.

'I suppose, since there have been no sightings, no leads, we have to consider the theory most favoured within the station,' says Tanner. He can't hide his disappointment.

'What, that neither of the husbands has hurt her, that neither of them was aware of her bigamy?'

'Yup, that she has simply run away.'

'Well, the stress and impossibility of carrying on two lives concurrently must be enormous,' Clements admits. 'Still, even if that is the case, it doesn't mean she's safe,' she adds grimly. 'What's not to say someone else out there might not have brought her to harm? The world is full of violent, unstable, cruel men.' For generations, since time began, men have picked up arms and picked a fight. They've chosen land, women, resources and various illusions of power that they've deemed excuse enough to savagely battle for. Clements wonders, is it in their DNA or an environment thing that leads to this constant vehement ferocity? And without armoured wars, for nebulous kings, that allowed sword wielding on battle fields,

290

there seemed to be a few favoured outlets for that pugnacious anger: video games, fascism and hurting women. Considering the options, Clements thought video games provided a national service.

'What if she hasn't run away? And what if nobody has hurt her? What if it was all too much and she's taken her own life?'

Clements scowls at Tanner. This thought depresses her the most. She has become hardened to many things, but not suicide. Dealing with suicide wrung her out, mangled her inside. The waste, the hopelessness, the helplessness.

'Well, you can never be one hundred per cent certain about who might take their own life, who might be so desperate to think that was the only way, but I don't feel Kylie fits the profile. She is too heretical, too unconventional.'

'But the best mate was right. Leigh Fletcher's doctor has confirmed she was prescribed antidepressants.'

'Yes, but a while ago and at a very low dose. She hadn't renewed her prescription in months which suggested she didn't feel the need for them anymore.'

'Or maybe she had come off them too suddenly — that could create problems.'

Clements nods, it is a possibility. 'But we've checked hospitals, refuges and the Jane Does in morgues. No sign.'

Tanner has been surprisingly keen and helpful in continuing to make enquiries for this case. Clements thought his interest might be pulled towards the totally novel prep for the pandemic, that's where all the buzz is, but he has remained keen to help pursue the matter. Clements wants to think his diligence comes from a good place; she tries not to think that he is hopeful of finding a body. A body that would push this inquiry into something high profile and macabrely juicy. Still, even with his help, they are no closer to knowing where this woman has vanished to.

'Thing is, Tanner, I'm no quitter, but I'm beginning to wonder, should we simply accept that Kylie Gillingham is a woman who tends to do things in her own inimitable way? Maybe she doesn't want to be found and maybe she's right to have come to that decision, considering both men have given up on her so easily. It is unsettling.'

Just as Clements is thinking no one has anything else to add to Kylie Gillingham's story — that maybe she will have to let it lie as everyone seems to want her to do — there are two phone calls, almost back-to-back, that allow her to keep the lighthouse lamp lit. First, Fiona Phillipson calls to say she has had sex with Daan Janssen. Clements is open-minded, it is helpful in her line of work and as she always doubts the fidelity of incredibly hot men, she isn't shocked or judgemental when she hears this confession. She is curious, though. When? Where? How often? She doesn't need to ask why. She's met him twice.

'Obviously, I didn't know he was married when I got involved with him,' says Fiona, there's heat and shame in her tone. Clements thinks she may or may not have known. Most single women like to think they are not the sort to have a crack at a married man. No one believes they have 'homewrecker' on the list of their character credentials. But the truth is, it's lonely out there. Women who should know better do stumble down that path. Clements herself had once snogged a married colleague at a Christmas party. It is embarrassing to think about. So clichéd; a quick grope in

292

a quiet corridor on the way to the cloakroom at the end of the night. Yes, it was after everyone had had a bit too much to drink. She'd been going through a dry patch romantically and working on a depressing human trafficking case; she wanted to grab at any comfort that came her way. His warm lips, solid body that smelt of sweat and a tang of a citrus aftershave was that — momentarily. A comfort. It hadn't gone far because she was wearing high-waisted, super-shaper tummy-control pants and she just didn't have the energy to crawl out of them, couldn't face the mortification of being exposed in them. She'd called herself an Uber, left the party alone. But if she'd been wearing better underwear, who knows where it might have gone? She is a policewoman not a saint.

'I should have said something the moment I made the connection,' admits Fiona apologetically. The regret and pain in her voice loud and clear, even though she's mumbling.

'And when was that?'

'When your colleague — Tanner, is it? — and I were in Mark's kitchen. He mentioned Daan's name. You had already said that Leigh was going under the name Kai Janssen but I wasn't looking for the connection. It didn't click. I wasn't even certain you'd said Janssen, I thought most likely Johnson. There was so much to take in. But in the kitchen Officer Tanner said Daan's name. I didn't want to believe it. I wanted to think it was a horrible, strange coincidence; after all, everything about this is off-the-scale strange, isn't it? I wanted to think that there might be more than one Daan Janssen.' Clements is all too aware of people's willingness to kid themselves. 'But Mark and I did some digging. We googled, it quickly became apparent that there aren't many people with the same name, fewer still living in the UK, there was only one contender to be Leigh's Daan Janssen. It's not like he's called John Smith — ' she breaks off — 'I didn't want to believe it. But now I'm sure. I have to face facts.'

'And when did you last see Mr Janssen?' Clements asks.

Fiona hesitates and sighs. 'This morning.' Clements allows the pause. Gives it power and space. 'I wanted to check it was definitely him and to see how he was doing, I suppose. I certainly wasn't looking for a hook-up. I, I — ' Fiona stumbles. Clements waits patiently. 'Obviously, I now realise I hardly know the man. I mean, I thought he would be devastated since his wife has gone missing. I thought maybe he'd talk to me about it and I'd glean something because he doesn't know that I know he's married, let alone that I'm his wife's best friend.'

'And was he?'

'Was he what?'

'Devastated.'

'No, I don't think so,' Fiona admits. The silence sits between them again, this time scratching, burrowing at what needs to be said. 'I mean, he seemed pleased to see me.'

'And did you?'

'Did I what? Glean anything?'

'Did you hook up?'

'Is that really a police matter?' Fiona asks indignantly.

'You don't have to answer. You called me. I'm just trying to understand the man. I want to help your friend. That's what you care about, right?'

294

'Of course it is. That's why I'm calling.'

'You are, I suppose, saying that you don't trust him now you realise he was not faithful? *Is* not faithful?'

'I'm not saying anything about anyone. I'm just giving you the facts,' Fiona snaps.

'I'm sorry if this is awkward for you, Fiona, and I'm not taking a formal statement — anything you say is completely voluntary but if you can answer the question it might help me. Did you have sexual relations with Daan Janssen when you last encountered him?'

'Yes,' Fiona whispers. 'I went to his place, I stopped over. I know that makes me sound pathetic, or heartless, or just plain stupid but I did, yes.'

'And yet you are ringing me now to say you don't trust him?'

'I am.'

'Why? What went wrong?'

'Nothing went wrong as such. I'm just trying to be honest. I'd had a glass or two of wine last night, it's been a very trying time. I wasn't thinking straight but now, in the cold light of day, I'm trying to do the right thing. I assume you do meet some people who are still keen to do the right thing, Officer?'

'A few.'

'Well, I'm one of them. Daan and I were — well, it was a casual thing. We had a few dates in London. He once came to my cottage on the coast for a weekend, but I've known Leigh for twenty-three years. I love her. I'm furious with her for lying to me but at the same time I'm really sad that she had no one she thought she could confide in. I could have helped her. Or at least comforted her. We're best friends. I'm scared for her. Why didn't she turn to me?' Clements doesn't have an answer to that either. Fiona adds, 'I

295

asked Daan if he is married.'

'And what did he say?'

'He said he *was*. Past tense. And, it's just, well, that building. It's so quiet and empty, right? Big parts of it are deserted. Someone could be hidden in it relatively easily, don't you think?'

'We'd need a warrant to search it.'

'Well, get a warrant.' Fiona sounds frustrated, indignant.

She probably thinks the police are working too slowly on the case. It's a common misconception of the general public that the police can always be doing more and doing it faster. The truth is investigation is a laborious business, all about perspiration and perseverance. Even the rare bright spots of inspiration need to be backed up with evidence which is inevitably slow to surface.

'We need evidence to place Mr Janssen under suspicion and to justify a search warrant.'

Fiona sighs. 'Well, get evidence then.' She hangs up.

Clements relays the call to Tanner, he looks jubilant. Clements reins him in. 'Fiona's information does not place Daan in the frame for Kylie's disappearance.'

'No, not exactly but it certainly casts a new light on the situation. Or perhaps more accurately the same light but simply with a higher wattage.'

'I have been wondering about the fact that the texts that were supposed to be from Kai to Daan dried up as soon as the bigamy came to light. This leads me to believe that Kai never sent the texts, just as Daan claimed.'

'Because how would she know the game was up and when to stop pretending she was with her sick mother?'

'Exactly. Why wouldn't she continue to try to keep up the pretence? It bothers me that the texts stopped at the same time as both men were made aware of her bigamy.'

'So the question is, who had the phone? Was it the hot dad and was he buying time before her absence was revealed by texting the he-man? Or was it the he-man and he was creating an e-trail alibi by pretending to be in touch with her?'

Clements nods. 'Stopping the texts was a mistake. Who made the mistake?'

Clements hadn't liked the way Daan Janssen was able to turn his emotions off like a tap. One minute, he was all passionate concern, demanding they find his beloved wife; the next he was the epitome of icy indifference, as he shrugged off all association. Clements had almost understood the vacillation when she thought he was deeply in love and hurt, but if he is shagging around (and there is no reason to believe Fiona is the only woman he's having extra-marital sex with) then he is not such a clear-cut candidate for the husband-of-the-year award. If he isn't heartbroken, then his plunge from impassioned to indifferent simply seems unstable. Clements needs to unpick this, ponder it. However, she doesn't have time right away because her phone buzzes again.

'Detective Constable Clements.'

'It's Paula Cook here. I'm Mark Fletcher's sister-in-law. The sister of his late wife.'

'Hello.'

'My nephew had your card.'

Clements gave her card to both of the Fletcher boys but takes a guess, 'Oli?'

'Yes. Look, I don't know how this can possibly be

297

relevant to you. But I thought I had to mention it.' Her voice is loud but quivering; a contradiction. Almost aggressive with assertion and yet the sort of aggression that comes from a sense of anxiety or apprehension.

'I'm listening.'

'You know my brother-in-law and I are close. He's a good man. A great father.'

'OK.' Clements is curious as to where this might be going. It sounds exactly like a sentence leading up to a 'but'.

'And you need to know I'm not close or anything with Leigh, or Kai or whatever the hell her name is.'

'Right.'

'But that's natural, since I'm Frances's sister, I think. Leigh came along very soon after my sister's death. I just don't think I was ready for her.'

'OK.'

'Oli and Seb are here at mine right now and they've been telling me all about you, and the investigation, the things you asked them. Oli mentioned that Mark had told you Frances died of cancer.'

'Yes. That's right.'

'Well, she didn't.'

'She isn't dead?'

'She's dead but she didn't die of cancer. She fell down the stairs. She had cancer. She might have died of that eventually or she might have recovered.' Paula says the word with a hint of breathy hope. Then, more staunchly, she adds. 'We will never know. She fell down the stairs and broke her neck.'

'But Mark Fletcher said it was cancer.'

'He always says that.'

'Why?'

'I don't know. You'd have to ask him that. She was

298

very weak. She was undergoing chemo treatment. Apparently, she had tried to get to the bathroom on her own and just wasn't strong enough. Mark was downstairs making a cup of tea.'

Clements wonders whether her investigative powers are a little off. Was it an error to have accepted the first wife's cause of death at face value? She wonders: does she need a holiday? A change of diet? Or was questioning the cause of the first wife's death out of her remit? Should receiving this information now be seen as a win, rather than a few days' old mistake? She doesn't know. Sometimes it is hard to know and easy to doubt herself. She is determined to be thorough now, though.

'Who else was at home with them when this happened?'

'They were alone together. I was looking after the boys.'

'Why are you ringing me to tell me this?'

'I don't know. I hate myself for doing so, I'm not trying to cause trouble for Mark. I really don't think he is involved in Leigh's disappearance, but I think you have to know the facts. Oli is messed up. Really not himself at all. So angry. I'm worried about him.'

Of course the boy is messed up — his bigamist stepmother is missing — but Clements asks, 'In what way particularly do you think he's messed up?'

'He told me he knew that his mother was having an affair.'

'He knew?'

'Yes, he'd spotted her with the other man about six months ago. The poor kid has lived with the weight of that secret for all this time. I was just wondering, if a child could discover her secret, maybe one of the husbands could have. Maybe she wasn't being as clever and careful as she thought she was.' Clements can hear contempt and concern in Paula's voice.

'What are you saying? Do you think Mark Fletcher is capable of violence?'

'No, no not really. He's a really good bloke. I don't know what I'm saying. I shouldn't have called.' She hangs up abruptly. It doesn't matter, a statement as such isn't needed, the lead is enough. Clements updates Tanner and tells him to call up the coroner's report on Frances Fletcher's death.

'Thing is, you always wonder, don't you? Slipped or pushed. You know the pressure of caring for a terminally ill family member is immense,' Tanner says, he is practically rubbing his hands together with undisguised glee.

'Well, even if you are right about that, which I'm not saying you are for a minute, there's hardly a pattern is there.'

'Two dead wives.'

Perturbed, Clements says, 'We don't know Kylie is dead.'

'We don't know she's alive.'

'There's no body, no one pushed her down the stairs. Stop it, Tanner, it sounds like wild speculation to me.'

'I'm not speculating. I'm theorising.'

'Stick with the facts, Tanner,' but even as she delivers her rebuke, Clements tries to recall how big Oli Fletcher is. Is he a man or boy? The net — far from drawing in — is widening.

And the clock is ticking.

35

Kylie

Sunday 22nd March

Last night I was freezing, today I feel I am suffocating. The weather is glorious, I can see the blue sky through the window of the next room and even feel the heat of the sun scorching through the boarding that covers the window in this room. It's only March, how can it be so hot? How long have I been here? Weeks, months? I know this isn't true, it can't be. But maybe it is. I am confused. I don't know what is true anymore.

Maybe I never did.

I long for water, food, a flushing toilet. I lie on the floor, put my head through the hole in the wall I have created and feel the luxury of the breeze from the window. I ache with the effort of crashing my chain against the radiator. No one has come. I need to rest from the repetitive action, just for a while.

I need water.

I'm so tired.

I fall to sleep. I don't fight it. I sink into it, gratefully.

When I am asleep, I dream I am making a list of what it means to be married to Mark. I present the list to the Father Christmas in the Harrods grotto. We used to take the boys there when they were younger. A wondrous place where sweets and treats are handed out freely, and by some magical process Santa knows the names of the children. Something to do with the elf in the queue having a headset and chatting to the children, repeating the info so Santa is prepped. Mark and I were fooled for a moment. We laughed, delighted to be enticed into the make-believe. It's charming. I miss it as a Christmas ritual. Why did we abandon it? Oh, I remember. When Oli was about ten, he insisted on telling all the children queuing that Santa wasn't the real deal, that he was a different bloke every year. 'Just tug his beard.'

Not the real deal. Not the real deal.

It's hard to pull the wool over Oli's eyes.

The list, the list. As I hand it to Santa, I think it might save me. But he looks at it, frowns, shakes his head, tells me I am on the naughty list. I am not nice.

I wake up, or at least I think I do, I'm bleary, dreary. It's hard to stay conscious in this hot room, with so little sustenance and the pain from the assault pulsing through my body. The list swirls around in my head. What is it like being married to Mark? What does it really mean? I close my eyes again, but I can still see the list, it's tattooed on to the inside of my lids. Or maybe I can hear it. Who is reading the list to me? Mark? Oli? Santa?

A home that feels like a big smile every time I open the door. Everyone else adoring my man, endorsing my choice because of his deep all-year-round tan and his big biceps. Help with putting on bedsheets. Lots of jars of spicy chutney and cheese in the fridge. Wet towels on the bathroom floor. A constant supply of Merlot on the rack. The sound of football matches blaring through the TV. Being bought Bailey's year after year for birthdays, Mother's Day, Christmas and Easter because I once mentioned it was a guilty pleasure. Giving away those bottles of Bailey's to neighbours and the school tombola; my tastes have changed, I don't like Bailey's anymore, I can't find a way to tell him. He hasn't noticed. The alarm going off before the boys need to be up so we can have fifteen quiet minutes lying in one another's arms. No leaky taps, flickering lightbulbs, wonky shelves ever, he is handy around the house. No one noticing my new underwear. Or my old underwear. Hanging baskets that are the envy of the entire street. Dad jokes. Someone who will listen to me retell a plot of a book but will not read that book. Drinking cans of cider in the back garden on hot summer nights. Being encouraged to plunge into a cold lake to swim. Liking the swim. Singing along to country and western music on long car journeys. Feeling safe.

My throat is dry and scratchy. It hurts but not as much as the thought: he used to make me feel safe. Is that why Santa is shaking his head? Is he sad too?

I crawl around the room to see if anything has been delivered. Close to the door, there is a tray with a chicken sandwich, an apple, water. When did that arrive? I don't know. I hate myself for not checking sooner. It might have been there for a while, maybe even before I started pulling down the wall. I could have helped myself sooner. Or have I been asleep again, did it just come? I don't know. I'm scared about how many things I have no idea about. I drink the water. Sips. Sips. I know that now. Three trays in a week? Careful. Careful. Slowly, I start to eat. Chewing every mouthful as if it were my last. Because it might be.

I am alone. It should be a relief. I suppose I have some chance of escaping if I'm not guarded. If I can work my way free of the chain, if I can break down the door, if I can stand by the window and call for help. But I've had those ideas for days now. It is impossible. I am not getting out of here unless someone gets me out. So somehow the aloneness is terrifying. What if he never comes back? What if there is no more water or food? I stop eating. I have to ration. The thought makes me want to cry. I'm so hungry I could die.

I might very well die.

36
Fiona

Fiona rings the bell. Mark almost instantly flings open the door, he must have been waiting for her. She imagines him crouched in the hall, ready to pounce. Not on her exactly, but on the information she brings. He has a near-empty wine glass in his hand and a sharp, shrill energy about him.

Not standing on ceremony, she steps inside, slips off her jacket, slings it over the banister. She doesn't want to be the first to speak because, despite grappling with the problem all the way over here, she still isn't sure what she's going to tell him, so she gets her question in first. 'Any news?'

'No.'

'You haven't heard anything from the police?'

Mark shakes his head impatiently, not bothering to conceal his need to know what she has discovered. 'So? Did you go to see him?'

'I did.'

'What's he like?'

She doubts she can tell him. But then, can she afford to lie to him? It's likely to come out at some point anyway, now she's spoken to that officer. It is best he hears it from her.

'He's everything you might imagine him to be,' she admits with a sigh.

'How do I know we imagine the same thing of him? I imagine him to be arrogant, slick, supercilious.'

305

Fiona nods. 'Yes, he's those things. To an extent.' She glances about her, buying time. 'Where are the boys?'

Mark looks a little surprised to be asked, as though he hasn't thought about them for a while. 'They're staying overnight at their aunt's house. She's going to drive them home tomorrow. She didn't give a time.'

'You've been on your own all afternoon?'

Mark shrugs. 'Where am I going to go?' Suddenly, he seems to remember that they are hovering awkwardly in the hallway and that he is holding a wine glass. 'I've a bottle open, join me?'

'Yes, please.'

Fiona follows Mark into the kitchen. She takes advantage of the fact he is busy finding her a glass and filling it, therefore not staring at her intently as he was when he first opened the door. She garbles, 'Look, Mark, there's something I need to talk to you about.'

'About Daan Janssen?'

'Yes.'

'Do you suspect him of hurting her?' He immediately sets down the bottle, glares at her. The brief liberation from his intense need to know what she is struggling to tell sputters and dies.

Fiona reaches for the wine bottle, fills up both glasses, takes a sip and a deep breath. 'I don't know.'

Mark looks something approaching excited. 'But maybe and you've only just met him, yet you have your suspicions of him. That's something. That's huge.'

'Well, that's just it. I haven't only just met him. I've actually dated him. I knew him before.'

'What?' Confusion floods Mark's face.

Fiona rushes on. 'Obviously, I didn't know he was married and even if I suspected he was, I certainly did

306

not think it was to Leigh. How would I know that?'

Mark, normally so tanned and robust-looking, turns pale, she thinks she can see through him to the wall behind where the kitchen knives are displayed on a magnetic block. 'I don't understand. When did you date him? I don't remember you ever talking about dating a Dutch millionaire.'

'Well, I don't tell you all about everyone I date. I do have a private life.' Fiona knows she sounds defensive and more importantly she is not being honest with him or herself. She sighs and gestures towards the sitting room. 'It's a long story, can we sit somewhere comfortable?' She feels she might collapse.

They sit at either end of the couch and she tells him about the dates she had with Daan Janssen. It's humiliating, far from her finest hour, so she is vague. So vague Mark is eventually compelled to ask, 'So did you have sex with him? Look, I don't want to be indelicate here, Fiona, but I need to know what sort of bloke Leigh was mixed up with.'

Fiona blushes, it feels very close to the conversation she had with the police officer. Why is everyone so obsessed with whether they had sex? She knows she is being disingenuous. Sex is nothing. Sex is everything. Sex disrupts.

Detonates.

'Yeah, we are adults, we had adult dates. For God's sake, Mark, what do you want me to say?'

'So, this man was betraying her? He's not to be trusted.'

Even though she has just called the police, pointing out the same, she wants to appear composed, reasonable in front of Mark. 'Well, he wasn't faithful, but that doesn't mean he's responsible for her disappearance.

It's dangerous to jump to conclusions.'

Fiona can't quite read Mark's face. He seems to be calculating something. Piecing things together. He swallows back the rest of the wine in his glass, bounces out of his seat, goes into the kitchen. Returns with the bottle. Fiona senses he'd like to swill the lot down from the neck, but he shows restraint, shares what's left between their glasses. 'And you knew this straight away, the moment the police mentioned his name? You knew who he was? You knew it all the time we were looking at his profile and social media accounts?'

Fiona nods, embarrassed. 'I didn't know how to tell you.' She pulls her eyes to meet his. 'You needed me. You've been hurt so badly by Leigh. I thought I would be twisting a knife.'

'By admitting that not only my wife, but my friend too had been seduced by this Daan Janssen?'

Fiona nods again, contrite. 'I am so sorry.'

Mark's face softens. He realises that she was simply trying to protect him, trying to be a friend to him. He's grateful to have someone on his team. 'You have to go to the police with this. It will help them understand what sort of man they are dealing with.'

'I've already spoken to them.'

This at least pleases him. He nods, allows a smile to slide to parts of his mouth, not a full commitment but some level of grim satisfaction. 'Good. Good.'

Fiona can't see any good in this.

It is an unreasonable hope — because Mark is naturally focused on Leigh and on his own trauma — but she is disheartened that he hasn't noticed or recognised her disappointment, her disillusionment. She was in a relationship with Daan, OK not a decade-long marriage admittedly, but there had been something.

308

Even if it was only on her side. Even if it was illusory. She'd like her loss to be acknowledged. She knows Mark has been reeling since Leigh's disappearance, but she too has lost Leigh. Her longest, most meaningful relationship.

Fiona gives him the information he craves. She talks about the penthouse apartment, the jacuzzi and swimming pool. She imagines hearing details about the other man's extreme wealth is concurrently irritating and a relief. If Mark can square this away by reasoning Leigh was attracted to Daan's wealth — a wealth Mark could never attain — then maybe that is easier than admitting to any nuance about why else she might have needed both men. However, as Fiona describes the expansive rooms, the hardwood floors, she notes Mark hasn't asked any questions, he's barely nodding along. He doesn't seem interested.

He cuts her description short and asks, 'How could I have lived with her for all that time and not known what was going on behind her eyes, behind her smile? I thought we were an exceptionally close couple. We used to laugh and mock couples who were not as close as we were. Or as close as I thought we were. I was the one she was laughing at really.'

Fiona is out of her depth. She knows Mark feels humiliated, idiotic. She wants to comfort him, she'd like to be the one to do that, but she doesn't know what to say because in all honesty how can she defend her friend? She treads carefully. 'I guess it's possible to be close, you know, to see each other all the time, and yet not be aware. I mean, she was taking pains to hide stuff from you. You're not a mind reader. It's not your fault.'

'I thought what we had was not only meaningful,

309

but everything.' The confession hangs raw and exposing in the air. 'It turns out we were just a couple of strangers exchanging views of school timetables, what we should eat for dinner,' he adds bitterly. He grips his wine glass so tightly his knuckles turn white. Fiona clocks his angry hands and is just about to ease the glass out of his grip when the stem snaps. 'Fuck.' He is cut. Scarlet blood bubbles on his hand, and red wine spills on the carpet. Mark stares at his wound and the mess but doesn't react. Fiona jumps up, dashes to the kitchen, comes back with salt, kitchen roll and a tea towel.

'Let me look at your hand.' Mark remains inert as she checks there is no glass embedded in the gash. 'Press tightly,' she instructs. She clears away the broken glass, mops up as much of the mess as she can and then pours salt on the stain. She roots out a bandage from the first aid tin and binds his injury. The cut isn't big, but it must be quite deep as his blood quickly blooms through the dressing. Finally, she doesn't ask but just goes into the kitchen, opens another bottle, brings it back to the living room with a fresh glass for Mark.

They fall silent, each deep in their own thoughts of how they have been fooled, deceived, betrayed. They drink in a morose fog. There's music coming from somewhere, a neighbour's house. It's a poppy, non-descript tune. It should cheer but it doesn't, it jars. It seems meaningless, taunting. It seems peculiar that ordinary things like music playing from a radio station can be happening, considering everything. The windows are open because it's been an unseasonably hot day but it's still March and the night air hasn't held any warmth. Fiona shivers, stands and pulls the

310

window closed. As she sits back down on the couch, she reaches for a throw. She recognises it as one that Leigh bought when they were on an IKEA shopping trip together, about two years ago. Fiona had picked it out. Leigh always wanted her interior design advice but would cheerfully say, 'Just remember I don't have your clients' budgets.' But she did have, didn't she? She had access to enormous wealth, just not in this life. Leigh lied about everything, even which throw she could afford.

The throw is grubby, a bit frayed but it is warm, comforting. Fiona stretches it over her legs and reaches to pull some of it over Mark's too. He doesn't seem to notice. She wonders what he is thinking about exactly. If not a shopping trip to IKEA, then what other small domestic detail — that formed the bricks and mortar of their relationship — might he be looking at from a different perspective? Fiona finds she does that a lot, on dates and things: wonders what men are thinking. She is never sure; they always seem so inaccessible. So far away. She breaks the hush when she comments, 'You know, I always thought she was the most honest person I'd ever known.'

'Clearly not,' mutters Mark, dryly.

'No. You're right. Turns out she was the most honest person I've ever known up until the point she stopped deceiving me. Hilarious.'

'I miss her,' Mark says. It's hardly a confession. It's to be expected yet he seems ashamed, distraught admitting as much. 'The boys miss her.'

'I know. I do too.'

'I thought we were a team. A two-person, handle-everything that might ever come-along team. Not just the big stuff. Not just house moves, the kids' friendship groups, illness.' His voice catches. Fiona thinks of Frances. This man has lost two wives. 'But the little stuff too. You know, like taking the cat to the vet, doing the shopping, and repainting the hallway, all that boring, essential stuff was just not so bad because we did it together. It was actually sometimes fun.'

It's been a long time since Fiona has had someone to share life's mundane tasks with. Though she remembers clearly her ex Samar calling her his cheerleader, and before him Dirk called her his partner in crime. She used to be feisty and roll her eyes when people referred to their partners as their 'other half' or worse yet, their 'better half', but over the last few years her cynicism has become tired, exhausted. Exhausted in the true sense of the word: sapped, wearied, depleted. Now Fiona thinks the idea of having a better half is edifying. People need support. There are worse things than to be propped up. You could be left alone to collapse.

Being married is about legal rights and shared financial goals and responsibilities, yes, but really it is about the other stuff. The nebulous, nuanced stuff like secret in-jokes and pet names — 'you had to be there', 'Oh, it's just something we say to each other' — having a private, non-verbal language whereby a single look might say 'let's get out of here' or 'he's a wanker' or 'I love you'. Different looks, obviously. Creating family traditions — 'We always go to Salcombe for the May Bank holiday. The crowds are a nightmare but it's our thing.' Fiona has heard them all.

She takes another slug of her wine, to swallow down the bile in her throat. Those are the things she yearns for. She absolutely understands Mark's dependence on being married. She respects it, craves it.

Mark's eyes are glassy, he's a bit drunk. He's been a bit drunk, or very drunk, every night since Leigh disappeared. No one can blame him. Maybe she should talk to him about abstaining for a while, but honestly, she hasn't got it in her.

'I miss her laugh. She had a weird laugh. Fast and loud,' he muses, mushily. The drink means he bounces about emotionally. One minute furious, the next wistful. No one could expect him to be stable, though, considering the circumstances. 'Leigh made the house warmer and happier. Her absence was always felt, you know, when she went to work. What we thought was work,' he adds. Fiona bites her tongue. She hasn't really heard Mark talk about Leigh this way before she vanished, or at least not for a very long time. He sounds sentimental, syrupy. It is the sort of tone reserved men use when they are forced to make public declarations — at their wedding speeches, for instance. No less sincere for that but slightly awkward to listen to. Mark's usual tone with and about Leigh is more pedestrian as a rule. He is sometimes teasingly affectionate, but never mawkish. Fiona has heard him use the syrupy voice often enough though, about Frances. His ex-wife. His dead wife. Does he think Leigh is an ex-wife?

A dead wife?

He carries on, 'The boys should be used to her not being here, since she was always gone half the week but they're not doing well,' Mark continues. 'It's different now, obviously. No one is expecting her to walk through the door at any moment.'

'Aren't they?' Fiona asks.

Mark shrugs. 'No, not really.' He takes another swig of alcohol. 'You can feel their anger in the air.'

313

Fiona thinks this is true. You can almost taste it, but it is not just the boys' anger. It is Mark's too. Without her, the house is drenched in an ominous vibe. 'God, she was manipulative. Right? I mean, she had us all fooled. What a bitch, hey, Fiona?'

'Yeah,' Fiona admits. 'She's my best friend but she's a bitch. I can't really deny that.'

'She's my wife but I was the first to say it.' He looks around as though surprised by her absence, all over again. Then he buries his head into the throw. Fiona thinks he's crying at first, but he's not. He is taking a long, deep breath in. Perhaps trying to soothe himself. Perhaps trying to catch Leigh's smell on the fabric. A theory that is confirmed when he sits up. Slick-eyed, but not vacant, he is alert; twitching like a dog that listens for footsteps on the street, a squeak of the gate that indicates his mistress is home. But there are no footsteps on the street, Leigh is not home. Mark mumbles, 'I can still smell her in the rooms. That's something.' He sighs, admitting that it's not much really.

'I do understand,' says Fiona. Mark flinches, looks sceptical. 'Well, not completely, obviously, but I feel betrayed too. I can't believe this is happening, that something has gone so horribly wrong in our worlds, when we were all just going about our business, you know? How has she kept me out of her life like that, so absolutely?'

'Half her life,' says Mark with a sardonic smirk.

'Her *life*,' Fiona insists. 'She's a bigamist, so I'd argue she's defined by that. That is her life. I didn't know I was out of her life. That I didn't exist for her. She's left me feeling, I don't know, sort of less. Do you know what I mean? I feel cheated.' Mark nods ruefully.

314

'Oh crap, sorry. I'm going on about my feelings. I can only imagine how diminished you must feel.' Mark shrugs and holds Fiona's gaze, and something flitters between them. Not just comfort or empathy. Something more stirring. The air is tight, brittle. Fiona feels one wrong move or word, and it would all shatter. Quietly, carefully, she asks, 'Would you take her back? You know . . . if she came back. If she walked through that door right now, would you take her back?'

'She's not coming back, Fiona,' says Mark and then he leans forward. The tight, brittle air explodes as he kisses her. It takes a moment and then she kisses him back.

37

Kylie

Daan is stood in the room demanding I make a list for him too. 'Keep things fair!' he is shouting which is out of character. He's normally supremely confident and would not demand, or even acknowledge, the need for an even playing field, happy to play all odds, even if the odds are stacked against him, which in all honestly, they rarely are. Tall, handsome, rich, male — normally all the odds are in his favour.

But of course, that was him before he knew about Mark. Now he has discovered he doesn't know me, it's fair to assume I don't know him. That he is other.

'Get on with the fucking list!' His mass and blondness swell and fill the room, he's pulsing with vitality and irritation. I am reminded of how it is to be with him when people are late, and he feels they undervalue his time. Normally generous and charming he becomes irate and struggles to hide his annoyance. Except, he is not in the room. He has gone again, and I can't be sure he was ever here. Was it just my imagination?

Am I hallucinating? Lack of food, dehydration?

The room sways, puckers as though it is being folded away like a concertina fan. One moment voluminous, the next cramped. Have I been drugged again? Something in the chicken sandwich or the water. What can I trust? What do I know? My head is pounding, pulsing with pain. But then so are my hands, my ribs, my shoulder.

316

The list. The list. What is it like being married to Daan? What does it mean? Upgraded body consciousness, so intense and regular workouts. Trying to turn back time, or at least the effects of it on my body and face. Not because he asks me to or because he is younger than me, but because he thinks I am beautiful and he tells me so all the time. I like basking in his praise. I want that to last as long as possible. Expensive restaurants. Well-cut, beautiful clothes. A feeling that there will never be anything that he can't tackle, that he can't win. Cleaners, a concierge, a personal coach, staff to cater for dinner parties. Dinner parties! Jo Malone candles. It strikes me that the list seems to be mostly about the things he can buy, but he is not that at all. I focus.

A sense of humour that is like mine. Dry, sharp. We spar intellectually. Freedom. Time. A big but autonomous family who are in equal parts frighteningly competitive and successful. They demand nothing of me beyond glossy hair and straight teeth so that I fit in; other than that they come free of all obligation including love or hate. Rooftop terraces. Champagne and cocktails. Lots of phone sex. Text sex. Anticipated sex.

The memory is simultaneously urgent and yet distant. I can't imagine desire right now. Lust. I know it was there, a force to be reckoned with or capitulated to but I can't feel the breathless pressure of it anymore. The list. The list. What else is on his list?

A willingness to hear the plot of a novel I enjoyed but, like Mark, an unwillingness to read the damn novel. A sense that when I'm with him everything is possible.

It is not possible to leave the room. I am not beautiful, right now, bruised and foetid.

I am in hell. He is the devil.

317

38
Mark

Monday 23rd March

Mark gets up early and leaves Fiona sleeping. Both the boys being out of the house provides him an opportunity. Since Fiona confessed to her involvement with Daan, he has known exactly what he has to do. He needs to do it quickly. No one else can do this for him.

Mark finds himself carefully studying Fiona as she sleeps. The bridge of her nose, the crown of her head, her usually well-maintained lowlights — that subdue the copper of her hair — are growing out, there's a smidge of hair striped through with grey. He finds it moving. Honest. He notes that sleeping Fiona looks vaguely anxious. What a shame. He wonders if that is because of what happened last night between the two of them. He shouldn't have kissed her. Or maybe he should. He doesn't know. Nothing is clear cut anymore. He no longer has any idea of what should or should not happen, what he should or should not do. Most likely, her look of anxiety is due to the fact she is worrying about Leigh's whereabouts. Or maybe, she lives with some ever-present level of concern — work, money, ageing parents, the drag of unrealised ambitions. Most people have something.

Fiona has been kind and helpful. Great with the boys. She is attractive too. Not a knockout, like Leigh, who is one of those rare, lucky women who continue

318

to get more beautiful the older they get. Mark is now a bit shamefaced to admit that when he first met Fiona, he'd noted she was a redhead and wore a sort of perma-angry face but didn't really give her much more consideration than that. He'd secretly dubbed her 'Ferocious Fiona'. She had softened since then. He hadn't noticed exactly when that had happened, but she seemed to have found her style and stride.

Looking at a person sleeping is undoubtedly incredibly intimate, even if that person is just asleep next to you on the train. Mouths gape open, words are muttered under breath, undignified drool slips and glistens on the chin. Sleep is an act of trust. He can't understand why Fiona never married; she'd make a great wife and mother, although the chance of being a mother is slim for her now, he supposes. Fiona moves in her sleep, twitches, maybe she has sensed him in the room. He doesn't want her to find him towering over her, it would be weird, so he silently backs away. Yes, she is sweet and caring. He hopes she'll stay in his life, even though Leigh is out of it now. Especially because of that.

But what he has to do next has nothing to do with Fiona.

He catches the tube. It's unusually quiet, ghostly. The city is awash with a sinister sense of dread and fear. When he arrives at the apartment, he finds it is not quite as sleek and swish as he was expecting; there is a slight air of neglect and desertion, only just perceptible, better disguised than in less affluent areas but Mark can identify it. There's no one about, he imagines the residents have all scurried away to their homes in the country or even abroad by now. If London closes and theatres, shops, restaurants are boarded up, its lure is muted. He steps over a pile of rubble and debris on the pavement outside the luxury building. His first thought is to wonder if there have been any lootings or break-ins, but glancing about he can't see any other sign of a disturbance so assumes the mess is a result of a burst bin bag or careless fly-tipping. The smaller pieces of plasterboard catch on the wind and are lifted, scattered along the street.

Inside the building, Mark finds the concierge clearing out the drawers behind his reception desk. The man looks agitated and although Mark doesn't ask, he confides, 'Been sent home. Got an email from the residents' committee. They're saying it's because of the pandemic. Most residents have cleared off and they are saying it's better for my health. But — ' He stops himself, draws in his mouth as though someone has sewn up his lips. He shrugs. It is clear he wants to say more. Maybe confide something, have a bit of a grumble as though they are old friends. Mark isn't in the mood; he is polar opposite of being in the mood. 'The cleaners haven't come in,' adds the concierge with a sigh. Mark glances at the marble floor and concedes they are perhaps not as shiny as expected, the endless glass walls are a little smeared with hand and nose prints from where people outside have pushed their faces against the glass and peered in. Mark is glad. He wants Daan Janssen to feel the pinch of neglect and desertion. At least that. A pinch. Actually, he wants him to feel the knockout punch. Mark concentrates on his breathing, not allowing it to become shallow and panicked, not allowing it to appear too deep and menacing. He has to seem normal. Calm. Although what the fuck is that anymore? Normal. His normal is insanity.

He isn't sure if Janssen will agree to see him. But he has to be curious, doesn't he? The concierge makes a call, announces him; Mark is relieved when he receives a nod and is pointed towards the lifts. 'I know where I'm going,' says Mark, gruffly.

The lift doors glide open with a whisper. The air conditioning is brutal. Mark shivers which he regrets as he finds himself toe to toe with Daan Janssen, and he doesn't want to look as though he is quaking in his shoes. To meet Janssen's eye, Mark needs to look up and he hates that this man is looking down on him. Hates it. He wants to thump him. Feel the force of his fist smash into that chiselled jaw that she must have caressed, must have kissed. One swift punch wouldn't satisfy him. Mark wants to bash away the handsomeness of his face. Ruin him. Punish him. Vent his fury and frustration. His instinct is to drop blow after blow on Janssen's stomach, chest, head. He wants the man to drop to his knees and even that wouldn't be enough; he wants him to collapse, crawl into a ball. Then Mark would stand over him and kick the shit out of him. Kick him in the shins, the back, the balls. Blood, spittle, cries to *stop, stop* would sputter all over the dark wooden floor. The violence creeps through his veins like a pervasive weed. Poisoning him. He clenches his fist. Janssen's eyes flicker for less than a fraction of a second to the readied hand and then back to Mark's face. Mark can see the dare in Janssen's eyes, the desire for a punch to be thrown. Mark breathes out. Slowly. He hadn't realised he was holding his breath.

He has to fight the fury. Keep it under lock and key. He's not here to beat up Janssen.

Neither man offers a hand to shake. It would be

ludicrous. Janssen does offer, 'Drink?'

'No.'

'Sure? Water? Coffee? Vodka?' Mark shakes his head. He could do with a water, his throat is dry and swollen, he could do with a stiff drink but he's not going to accept a thing off this man, considering everything he's already taken. Janssen shrugs. 'Well, I want one.'

Mark follows Janssen through to the kitchen, where Janssen pours himself a vodka and drinks it back, a fast shot. That's when Mark notices Janssen's eyes are bloodshot, his skin has a filmy grey sheen to it, symptomatic of a lack of sleep. He's not a well-looking man. How could he be? It's only 10 a.m. and he's drinking vodka. Mark doesn't care if the man drinks himself to death, he just wishes he'd done so five years ago, before he met Leigh.

Disappointingly, inside the apartment there is none of the neglect Mark identified in the communal areas; obviously the cleaners are still letting themselves in here. It is so tidy and neat that Mark struggles to find something to rest his eyes on. He needs a photo — although that might break his heart — bookshelves, a print hung on the wall, something to distract. He forces himself to focus and notes that there are these things, not crammed, higgledy-piggledy in every nook and cranny like in their home, but artfully displayed on spacious shelves and walls. Restful, deliberate. He concentrates on a print of a black woman wearing enormous glasses and a green coat. It's a hip, powerful picture, he is glad of it. He latches on to it and counts the model's eyelashes.

'So, you want to look around?' asks Janssen. Mark nods. Ashamed that he wants anything at all from Janssen; he doesn't want to be in his debt, but he craves to look around, see where they lived. How they lived. He can't pretend otherwise. He needs it. 'Go ahead.' Janssen waves his hand that is holding his glass, expansively. A man with nothing to hide.

Mark wants to stride purposefully, show he is not daunted or uncomfortable, but he finds himself mooching, creeping because he is both. He moves from room to room, opening cupboards, looking behind doors. There are a lot of cupboards, Mark assumes it is the only way to keep the place looking so minimalist. Hide everything away. Janssen doesn't ask him what he's searching for, nor does he stop him opening cupboards, looking behind doors. It's a big place. Mark tries to imagine Leigh sitting on the large cream leather corner sofa, no doubt it's a designer brand that would mean something to people who care about brands. Mark doesn't; he cares about herbaceous plants and soil drainage. He tries to imagine her in the industrial-looking kitchen, at the sleek dining-room table, perched on one of the bar stools. He can't. He can only see her tied up in an empty room. That is the only way he sees her now.

Mark longs to see an overflowing basket of dirty washing, fridge magnets that clasp desperately to pizza delivery fliers and money-off coupons, stray debris such as hairbands, Sellotape, newspapers, Bic pens, junk mail, mugs of half-drunk tea. Something familiar. Anything. This place is sparsely furnished, impeccably clean. Nothing is out of place. They must have an army of cleaners, he thinks. There's no way Leigh would have a house this gleaming. Then, momentarily, he feels hopeful; a random thought occurs to him. This place is neat to the point of absurdity. This is not Leigh's place. She would *never* live in a place like this.

323

There has been a mistake. His Leigh is not Kai after all, his wife is not a bigamist. It has all been a horrible, disturbing, disgusting, sickening mix-up. But he can fix it, it is not too late.

He blurts out his thought, hopeful and pathetic. 'Leigh would never live here.' His tone is scornful. He is no longer jealous of the wealth Janssen has, he's contemptuous of it. All the edgy, well-thought-through objects, all the rich fabrics and clean lines mean nothing. This is not her life. This is not Leigh's world. He is no longer angry with her, he is sorry. Sorry that he thought she could ever betray him. She is a woman who happily sits amongst cat hairs and stray sneakers to eat spag bol off a tray in front of the TV. 'Leigh would never live here,' he says again with more certainty and excitement.

'Leigh didn't though, Kai did.' Janssen's tone is iron. Mark's certainty and excitement evaporates instantly. Janssen has thrown the first punch after all — intentionally or otherwise. Mark feels a slackness in his gut, a bearing down on his sphincter. He wants to ask where the bathroom is but won't give Janssen the satisfaction of seeing his frailty. He clenches, straightens his shoulders, draws himself up to his full height, ignores the spasms in his stomach.

'So, you are saying what? She was only ever half a person with me?'

'Half a person with either of us.' Janssen shrugs and reaches for the vodka bottle again. Something like pity snags Mark's conscience. He's been drinking too much himself as well but only in the evenings, and usually with Fiona for company. He has the boys to think about; he's had to retain a semblance of keeping it together.

'I will have a coffee with you,' he says. Janssen takes the hint, puts down the vodka and reaches for two pods, two cups.

Whilst Janssen prepares the coffee Mark continues to roam around the vast apartment. This time, instead of denying her occupancy, he looks for her tastes and influence. He looks for her. He examines the bookshelves to see what she read here and the art on the walls to know what she looked at. In their home they have a few framed mass-market posters. Ones with inspirational or funny messages. Leigh chose them all. Mark tries to recall what each of them says. In the hallway there is one that reads *Don't grow up, it's a trap*. One in the bedroom, *I'll be ready in five minutes!* In the kitchen a poster declares *Cook, dance, laugh, live*. In the downstairs loo, there is one that has just a single word. *Breathe*. He has never given that one much thought before. Now he wonders whether that was the most pertinent. The one she looked at every day as she checked her make-up before she dashed out the door, the one she saw on her return when she dashed in the house desperate for a quick pee as she transitioned from Kai back to Leigh. Janssen's walls are covered in numbered prints that suggest exclusive, limited runs. There are oil paintings, modern ones, huge and undoubtedly expensive, possibly privately commissioned. Did Leigh choose these works? Is this what she would have liked to hang on their walls if they could have afforded it?

He opens the door on to their bedroom. He holds his breath, takes in oxygen through his mouth because he doesn't want to smell her, not here. He looks at the bed. It's enormous. Mark wants to ask Daan what she was like in bed, this woman Daan was married to, this

325

woman Mark was married to. He doesn't yet believe they are the same person. Well, he believes it, but he can't process it, not quite. Not entirely. He swallows the question, pushes it back down his throat. The answer might kill him.

There are three doors off the bedroom. The first is the bathroom. Their bathroom at home was refurbished last year. They picked new grey-and-cream tiles and did away with the bath so they could fit in a larger shower. The result is quite smart. Admittedly there are nearly always hardwater marks on the shower glass and taps. Open tubes and bottles of shampoos, body washes, toothpaste, Leigh's various lotions and potions are scattered about like confetti. Hidden intimacies — like verruca cream, iodine tablets and sweat block wipes — are rarely returned to the cabinet that was installed to store such things but instead expose them as a couple — as a family — that are less than perfect but totally human. Still, it is fine. A decent place to grab a hurried shower in the morning, although it is best if you leave the window open because despite the refit there is always a faint lingering smell of mildew.

This bathroom is incomparable. Of course it gleams, that is to be expected considering the rest of the apartment, but there is more than that to appreciate. This bathroom is a sanctuary; it is sensual, classy. No one grabs a rushed shower here. The mosaic tiles shimmer. The copper bath is enormous, two can easily bathe until they wrinkle in there. There are no bottles or packets lying around, just fat candles, perfectly stacked piles of towels and beautiful decanters full of what Mark can only presume to be bubble bath — no not here, not bubble bath — oils. The room smells

326

of something woody and dark. Ginger or citrus. He can't see a loo brush or a bottle of bleach. He tries to imagine her weeing in here, shaving her legs, taking off her eye make-up. He can't, because it lacks her trail of mess. And maybe not being able to imagine her is a boon after all.

He goes back into the bedroom and opens another door. He was expecting a wardrobe. It is a wardrobe, if an entire room of shelves and rails can be described as something so humble. This walk-in wardrobe is the same size as Oli's bedroom, a little bigger than Sebastian's. He stares at the racks of shoes neatly lined up behind the glass sliding doors. He's seen something similar in very posh restaurants, for storing expensive wines, but row after row of shoes being displayed like art? This blows his mind. At home Leigh has a normal-size wardrobe, it is heaving — or at least it was before he set to with the scissors and the bin bags. That wardrobe had been full of high street clothes that were often creased when retrieved, sometimes a button was missing. The clothes and shoes in this room are ordered by colour. Two soothing rainbows of style and luxury fan out in front of him.

He counts eight navy bodycon dresses. *Eight*, more than one for every day of the week. They are not identical, he can see that, but they are similar. He recalls the number of times when thrifty Leigh gazed admiringly at say, a blue striped shirt and then decided against it because 'I've got something similar in grey, who needs two striped shirts?' He can't believe she has so much, such excess, such choice. That thought stings. Inflames. Of course she has choice, he remembers bitterly. That is the problem. He can't get his head around it. He stretches out his hand and tentatively

327

strokes one of the dresses. It's a dark red colour, and silky, undoubtedly sexy. He can't think that there was an equivalent in her wardrobe at home. Not even a cheaper, synthetic, high street version. Leigh dresses practically, not sexily. The fabric of this dress feels like moisturised skin. He imagines her in it. He imagines he is touching her. His hand trembles.

A green long-sleeved wool dress catches his eye. Green is her favourite colour. At least it is Leigh's. Who knows whether Kai had her own favourite colour. He moves closer to the green dress, instinctually buries his head in it and inhales. He expects it will smell of dry-cleaning fluid, or maybe an expensive unfamiliar perfume. But no. There she is. In every fibre. Leigh. The smell of her deodorant, perfume, body, so faint it is just a breath but so familiar that it's a typhoon. She was here. She is Kai. Of course, he knows it, but now he *feels* it. He has been ravaged by such anger this past week, fury, uncontrollable, unstoppable. He hasn't been able to think clearly, plan properly. His actions have been irrational. The boys have been neglected, barely spoken to. Thank god for Fiona. For a moment he considers ripping every garment from its hanger, clawing at them, tearing at them, destroying her, or at least this embodiment of her — just as he did with Leigh's clothes, but he doesn't. Instead, he takes the green wool dress off the hanger, holds it close to his body and drapes the sleeves over his shoulders as though she is embracing him. He starts to sway from side to side, dancing with her. Like she had wanted him to.

His heart breaks.

He thinks he can hear it crumble, the destruction rolls through him like an avalanche. The last time he cried was at Frances's funeral; then as now, over-whelmed by regret and sadness, a yearning for things to have turned out differently. Fat tears slide down his face now for the same reasons.

'Your coffee is ready.' The firm, foreign voice star-tles Mark back into himself. He is glad he has his back to the door and whilst Janssen must have seen him swaying, and quite possibly saw the dress too, he could not have seen the tears. Mark wipes his face on the dress and then drops it on the floor. He follows Janssen back into the kitchen and never wonders what is behind the third door.

They sit at the breakfast bar, staring at the cups of coffee. Mark wishes now he had said yes to the vodka. Fuck it, what does he have to lose? What *more* does he have to lose? He reaches for the bottle and splashes a generous measure into his coffee. He's glad Janssen doesn't comment but just reaches for the bottle and mirrors the action. 'Did you find what you were look-ing for?' Janssen asks.

'I don't know what I was looking for. I found something.' Mark isn't normally cryptic. He consid-ers himself an easy-going, straightforward bloke but he doesn't know how to explain what he's thinking. The anger is no longer pulsing in his throat, an emo-tional hairball threatening to suffocate him. He hasn't swallowed it down, or spat it out exactly, but he's no longer choked with fury. It is some improvement.

'Can I see your home?' Janssen asks. He then tries to clarify or be more tactful perhaps. 'Her home. The home she has with you?'

'No, I don't think so,' replies Mark gruffly. 'You know, the boys. It wouldn't be fair on them.'

Mark knows he's not playing ball. It ought to be

quid pro quo, but he can't do it. He can't be that generous. He can't let this man into his home. This man who has been inside his wife. This man who is *married* to his wife. He doesn't want to see his eyes flicker with judgement, curiosity or superiority and surely there would be at least one of these things. The cork pinboard, with curling scribbled notes pinned to it, muddy shoes tumbling out of the understairs cupboard as though they can walk on their own. The gleaming cleanliness of this place had been enlightening, all the mess and chaos of his would be exposing.

'Well, will you tell me about it at least?' Janssen pursues.

Mark is momentarily irritated that this man hasn't googled him and looked up their address, turned Google Maps on to photo mode to scope out the streets she spent half her time in, as Mark had done for the section of her life that was a mystery. The lack of interest is somehow a snub, a sign of superiority or laziness. What else has Janssen had to do with his time this past week? Mark considers, maybe he has searched but as Mark Fletchers are more abundant than Daan Janssens possibly the search wasn't fruitful.

He takes a deep breath and says, 'It's nothing like this. It's — ' He breaks off, he doesn't want to call it ordinary, although it is. Or scruffy, although it is. The scruffy normality is not the heart of the house that Leigh lives in with him, and presumably that is what Janssen needs to hear about. The heart. Would telling him comfort him or torture him? Mark doesn't know which he wants to achieve. 'Lots of the houses in our street have cigarette packs and empty bottles pocking the small area from front door to road, others

330

have well-kept gardens and hanging baskets. It's varied. Disinterest lives cheek by jowl next to pride.' He is circling, starting wide and then getting closer to the target. 'It is amazing how contrast can cohabit, coexist.'

Janssen gives one quick little nod, his long blond hair falling over his eyes. It irritates Mark. Leigh always swore she didn't fancy blond men. Bitch. Liar. The spiteful words slice through his consciousness. He is startled by them. He thought he was feeling calmer. He barely feels responsible for the spite. He is not responsible, is he, if it is in his subconscious? The fury has not gone, it's in flux. Mark should not be surprised. Deep wounds take a long time to heal and some scars never fade.

'Where do you live?' Janssen asks.

'Balham.'

'A Victorian terrace?'

'Yes.'

Janssen nods again, no doubt quickly able to visualise where his wife spent half her life. People know what terrace houses in South London look like. Imagining her life here had been harder. Mark doesn't know where to start. He clings to small details, unable to supply a broad picture. 'I walk past a supermarket trolley every day, a different one. Sometimes Oli and Seb push them back to the supermarket, to collect the pound. Oli does that less now. A quid isn't worth the walk and effort once you're sixteen.'

'Oli and Seb? Those are your boys?'

'Yes, our boys — my boys. Oliver and Sebastian.' Mark colours. He hadn't meant to talk about them. He doesn't want them in this place. He realises he can't do this. He can't talk about his home to this man. He owes him nothing. It's better to focus on getting

331

answers, rather than providing them. He decides to change the subject. 'Did you think you were going to get old and die with her?'

'I don't think about getting old,' replies Janssen. 'You?'

'No one knows when they are going to die,' Mark comments. Janssen raises his eyebrows. 'My first wife died of cancer. I've never taken long life for granted.'

'I see.'

'You know the police will be looking at one or the other of us right now, and thinking we are responsible for her disappearance?'

'I do.'

'Well, I didn't hurt her,' Mark says.

'You are bound to say that,' points out Janssen.

'You haven't said it,' counters Mark. The men meet one another's gaze and try to read the rules of the game they are playing. Mark notices Janssen is sweating; there are dark patches under his arms. It looks like he slept in that T-shirt. Seeing the man dishevelled, chaotic and vulnerable is a relief. Mark has been imagining that he'd still be crisp, confident, in control; most likely continuing to wear pristine white shirts and sharp dark suits. It helps to think they are levelled; equally disturbed, distraught, desperate. 'What I can't work out is why she stayed with me, considering all this luxury.' Mark gestures around. 'Coming here must have been quite the holiday from her real life.'

Janssen's upper lip curls slightly, probably objecting to the implication that her life here, his life, isn't real. 'Are you implying she was with me just for my money?' He laughs, the laugh is a little forced and goes on a little too long. It's hard to believe it reflects any real mirth.

'I'm just saying it would have been easier for her to divorce me and then to marry you, if she had wanted you.' Mark knows Daan must have had this thought too. He must be furious. How furious?

'And if she had wanted you, why did she even notice me?' asks Janssen coolly. 'You can't point score. We are in the same boat.'

Mark sighs, nods. 'Shit creek without a paddle.'

Janssen nods. 'I know this expression. Exactly this. The English always have the exact phrase.' He sighs, Mark doesn't know him well enough to understand if it's impatience, regret, sadness. 'Anyway, I guess the wealth didn't mean all that much to her, in the end, because she was able to leave it. Walk away.'

'If she left,' Mark challenges.

'Of course she left.'

'You believe she walked away from you. From all this?'

'What other explanation?'

Mark shakes his head. 'I don't imagine her leaving the boys.'

'Face it, we weren't enough for her. All four of us combined, not enough. She was a very greedy woman.'

It's a sad condemnation. Janssen doesn't trust in Kai's love the way Mark trusts in Leigh's. Is it easier for Mark because he knows Leigh would not have left through choice? He feels grimly smug. He loves her more. Of course he does. His actions prove that. 'If you think she walked away, where do you think she went?' he challenges.

Janssen shrugs stiffly. 'I don't know. I don't care.'

'You are very cold.'

'I am very hurt.'

'Did you kill her?' Mark wants to see how Janssen responds to the question, asked straight out. What might the DC see if she asks the same thing of him?

Janssen meets Mark's eyes. 'No. Did you?'

'No.' They stare at one another both aware that either of them might be lying.

39
Fiona

Fiona didn't want the kiss to stop. His lips were warm and soft and urgent. Yes, urgent. He wanted her. Needed her, that might be better still, more reliable, more enduring. Even so, the cool air from the window breathed on to her cheek, the non-descript pop music needled, the blanket no longer felt soft and comforting, but instead started to scratch. She pulled apart.

'God, sorry, sorry. I shouldn't have done that,' Mark said immediately. He rushed the words out, like vomit. The retraction, more urgent than the kiss. Even though she was the one that stopped the kissing, she felt disappointed that he so quickly scurried into an apology. Into regret. She wished men would kiss her without regret more often. He scuttled back to the other end of the sofa.

'No, no. Don't apologise.' She wanted to tell him it was nice. Not to be sorry for it, but to do it again, that she regretted stopping him, but she was too embarrassed. From the look on his face — panicked, nervous — he obviously was glad she'd come to her senses, brought him to his. So instead she said, 'It's just that I'm not sure it's really what you want.' She glanced at the empty wine bottle, to indicate her reasoning. 'And even if it is something you might want one day, it's too soon.' She hadn't been able to resist adding that. Leaving the door open just a little bit. A crack.

335

Mark got to his feet; he was swaying a little. He asked her to stay over again, pointed out she'd also been drinking too and shouldn't drive. She hesitated. He said she could have one of the boys' beds if the sofa wasn't comfortable. He would put on clean sheets; she didn't think that was necessary, she'd only just changed them herself the day before yesterday.

'I can get an Uber back or I can walk, it's not far.'

'It's late, though.' His concern for her safety was probably just that, normal friendly concern but it felt just a bit more. A little insistent. In a good way. 'You've been really good for the boys. I don't know what we'd have done without you.' It was a familiar chant. Fiona remembered he used to say it to Leigh when they first met.

She didn't know what to do. It was late. He'd spoken about Leigh in the past tense and he'd seemed categorical when he said, 'She's not coming back, Fiona.' How could he be so sure? She needed to think that through. It might mean nothing. It might just mean that he was simply talking about what she did before — 'Leigh made the house warmer and happier' — it didn't necessarily mean that he thought Leigh was dead. Maybe just gone. Gone for good. He saw her in the past tense. Fiona had drunk quite a bit; he was right about that. She couldn't reason. She was being wild, leaping to crazy conclusions. She agreed to sleep on the sofa. Was that sensible? As she fell to sleep, she thought that she was living Leigh's life a little. One night with one husband, the next with the other. The thought was disquieting. Leigh was no longer someone anyone in their right mind could aspire to be.

Though this morning, Fiona is glad she stayed.

She woke up to find the house empty. Wherever Mark had gone to, he was not home to greet Oli and Seb when they returned from their aunt's. But she was. She makes them a sausage, beans and bacon brunch, even though they both say they've already had breakfast. 'A bowl of cereal isn't much of a breakfast at your age,' she comments.

She doesn't point out that prepping food and eating it fills the day. They all need that. The day to be filled. After the fry-up, they debate whether to have pancakes too, that's when they hear Mark's key in the lock. A hush descends. The boys are nervous of their dad, unsure when his temper might flare up again, what they might do that will trigger it. Fiona is embarrassed after last night. She decides the only option is to front it out. She smiles brightly. 'Oh, great timing, Mark. We're just in the middle of a massive blow-out brunch,' she smiles. 'To pancake or not to pancake? That is the question.'

He is pale, black bags gather like clouds under his eyes, but he smiles back at her. She thinks she can see the smile reach his tired eyes. The first time since Leigh went missing. She's pretty sure she's not kidding herself but the doorbell rings again and the moment dissolves.

It is the police.

Fiona tells the boys to go upstairs. No doubt they will listen in from the landing, but she can't do anything about that. She sits down on an armchair in the living room, while Mark answers the door. Is this the moment? From now on will life be divided between before and after? She wonders what they know exactly. What they have come to say. That they have found Leigh? That there is a body? That they have arrested

337

Daan? There must be something because why else would they be here? Time slows. It pulls at her skin, drags her down. The room feels too full. Oppressive.

It's confusing. They start to question Mark about his first wife. Details around her death. It makes no sense to Fiona. Why are they talking about Frances? And then, slowly, she begins to understand. They are saying Frances didn't die of cancer; it transpires she fell down the stairs. Fiona turns to face Mark. It's like driving in a fog, she is disorientated, stressed. She grips tightly, peers closely but can't recognise anything familiar.

DC Clements glances at Fiona. Fiona can feel heat rise through her body. She feels they want to ask why she is here. Again. She wishes she hadn't stayed last night after all. Her head is too hot. She's relieved that they don't ask her anything but instead continue to direct all questions to Mark. 'Why did you lie to us?'

'Did I?'

Tanner pulls out his notebook, flips through it. The sound of the turning pages cracks like a whip. 'When DC Clements was talking to your oldest son you said, 'My first wife died of cancer when Oli was five years old. I suppose he remembers Frances a bit. But Leigh has been his mother since he was not quite seven.' ' The policeman snaps closed his book.

Mark looks surprised. Didn't he know they would be taking notes? They are the police, for God's sake. That's their job. To investigate. 'She did have cancer. She would have died of that — that is the sad truth,' he says. 'Then she slipped.'

'Slipped.'

'Or tripped,' he says firmly. 'I didn't actually see the accident. I assume you've read the coroner's report.'

'Yes, yes we have,' says the detective. Fiona can see Mark looks frozen to the chair. A statue touched by the Queen of Narnia. 'Did Leigh know how Frances really died?'

'No.' His voice cracks with the admission.

'You didn't tell her?'

'It never came up.'

'Oh, come on, Mark. All those years?' Tanner doesn't try to keep the exasperation or disbelief out of his voice.

'It was an impossible thing to tell her.'

'What? The truth was impossible?'

'Yes.' His voice is steady, neither defensive nor regretful. The lack of emotion unnerves Fiona more than his previous displays of anger have. What will the police make of it? He plods on. 'The thing is, it was all to do with how we first met. You'll remember, Fiona, you were there at the play park, the day Seb fell off the slide and cut his head open.'

Fiona nods. That much is true. 'Do you remember, I froze? It was because I was thinking of Frances and her bleeding out at the bottom of our stairs. Later in the hospital when I told Leigh I was a widower I couldn't bring myself to say my wife died of a head injury following a fall. It was too much. Especially in front of Oli, I didn't want him thinking Seb might die like his mother.' Mark sighs. 'I was trying to protect Oli and so I said she had cancer. Which she did. I thought I was just saying something that wasn't a lie as such, just a less uncomfortable statement to a stranger. I never expected the stranger to end up being my wife.'

Fiona wants to believe him. A less uncomfortable statement, not a lie. She can understand that. She wants the police to believe him too. 'But afterwards?

You had years to tell her the truth,' the detective points out.

'Well, how do you come back from that? How do you say, 'Oh, by the way I got it all mixed up about how my first wife died'? It was easier all round to just stick with the original story.' He is getting impatient.

'So, you lied to your sons, too, about how their mother died?'

'Well yes, I had to be consistent.'

'Jesus, Mark.' The words tumble out of Fiona's mouth. She is shocked, exasperated. Clements and Tanner turn to her. Fiona doesn't know whether she wants to collapse on the sofa and put her arms around him — this poor man who didn't have the confidence to correct a simple lie and has therefore made things very awkward for himself all these years later — because obviously the police have some level of suspicion of him now. Or, ought she make a dash for the door? Because one dead wife is a tragedy until a second goes missing and then it is a genuine problem. Why stay and support this man, this liar?

Clements allows the interruption to sit with them for a moment and then she says, 'Well, that's all we wanted to clear up for now. We'll be in touch.' Fiona sees the police officers to the door. She doesn't know what to say to them, so she stays silent. Clements simply comments, 'Nice to see you again, Ms Phillipson. It's good of you to keep such a close eye on your friend's family.'

'The boys,' Fiona mutters, by way of explanation.

Clements smiles briefly. Fiona gets the sense Clements knows her concern extends beyond the boys. Fiona returns to the sitting room. Mark hasn't moved a muscle. It is tricky negotiating the intimacy of sleeping on this man's couch, feeding his children, kissing him; this man who is her best friend's husband. Yet she owes her best friend nothing because Leigh has lied to her too, to everyone, for four years. Why is the truth so hard to pin down and offer up? She should probably grab her jacket and walk out, right now. The problem is she wants to stay, to kiss him again. She does neither thing.

'Why didn't you tell her? Trust her to understand the initial lie in the hospital.'

'You're saying I should have trusted my bigamist wife more?' Mark's voice is spiked with indignation. He sighs. 'Is there anything you need to ask me?'

Fiona can hear the challenge. 'Yeah. Did she make you happy?'

He looks surprised; that was not the question he was expecting. 'Yes, she did. Does,' he corrects himself hurriedly. Then he shrugs and says deliberately, 'She did. Past tense. I'm using the past tense because she doesn't make me happy any longer, not because I think she's dead. God forbid. Just to be clear.' Fiona blinks, remains silent. 'I didn't kill Frances or Leigh. OK? I guess you need to hear it from my own lips. I guess you must have trust issues too, right now. I don't know where Leigh is, and I didn't hurt her. Do you believe me?'

Fiona doesn't know what to do or say. She sits quietly, perfectly still and considers. After a few minutes she says, 'Let's have a cup of tea, then I have to get back to my flat.'

'So, you're leaving?'

'I just need to get back to my flat for a bit, Mark.' Fiona tries to keep her voice level. She'd do well to ape his emotionless state. Not to give anything away.

341

'I haven't been there for a couple of days. I need to put a wash on. Go through some emails. You understand.'

'Yeah,' he says with another sigh, 'I understand.'

40

Kylie

My stomach cramps, spasms of acute hunger cause me to crawl into the corner of the room. I pull my knees up, tight to my body, trying to flatten out the cravings. I think he has decided to let me starve to death. My head swims. I fall to sleep, for just moments and then jerk awake. Or maybe it's longer. I don't know. Both men are waiting for me in my dreams, my nightmares. The two men are completely unalike. Almost nothing in common. Other than me, I suppose. Yet they are both waiting for me. Furious.

The water is all gone.

Having two husbands, two lives, is very time-consuming. Something had to give. I chose to sacrifice friendship. I took Daan's phone calls before friends. If he suggested we meet on a date where I was already tied up, I pulled out of the prior arrangements. The lovely women I met at work — who I had joked with in the staff canteen, swore with when bosses were unreasonable — all fell by the wayside. As did my mummy friends, the mothers of the boys' friends. I turned down invitations to join book clubs or spend the evening with someone enthusiastically selling beauty products or kitchen utensils. The only friend I could not give up was Fiona. She has always been like a sister to me. The thought of her comforts me but in some ways hurts me too. I lost her anyhow because I couldn't tell her. Of course not. So the honesty and

343

intimacy between us faded and then disappeared altogether.

There is nothing honest about a second bank account, about a second phone. It's complicated. Strangely, it wasn't the things I kept apart that stung — the separate things were a shield — it was the crossovers that were painful. The near misses fling themselves into the front of my awareness now. They itch uncomfortably around my wrist where I'm chained, they sit in my parched throat. I can't swallow them back.

I recall walking down the street. Kai walks with an arresting fluidity. She rolls, languidly, like a cat. Leigh bounces, much more of a puppy. This me, is bounding. So I am Leigh, heading towards Mark, Oli and Seb, keen to rest my eyes on them, to feel the boys roughly bury into me as they hug me hello. There is a supermarket trolley lying across the pavement. I bend to stand it up and park it to the side so that it doesn't obstruct those with strollers or in wheelchairs. That is when I notice it, the bracelet glinting against my skin. Relieved I've spotted it, I slip it off. Not that Mark would guess they were real diamonds, he'd imagine I'd splashed out at Swarovski at best, more likely Accessorise. I slide £4,000 worth of jewellery into my handbag. Noting that I should take more care. I slip in and out of consciousness; in my dreams, my nightmares, I'm chained by a row of diamonds.

My head throbs as I recall an especially busy week when I took clothes from both my wardrobes to the same dry cleaners and then had them delivered to the penthouse for ease. I didn't think an extra dress and suit would be noticed; I planned to take them back to my home with Mark on Thursday. But Daan did spot the dress Leigh had worn to Mark's parents' wedding anniversary lunch. 'That's very fashionable,' he commented. I knew it was a criticism. He is not fashionable and doesn't aspire to be. He is classic. He liked me to be classic too. Classy. I didn't take offence. I was simply relieved he hadn't seen Mark's suit from Next.

I suppose there is only so long you can choke back a secret like this. Bliss like this. Pain and stupidity on this monumental scale will out.

I sacrificed myself. I wasn't twice as interesting or busy or complete. I was half the person. In my dreams I hear the typewriter hammer out another note. The paper is slipped under the door.

Too late for regrets.

Then there is another, it flies around the room.

Too late for explanations.

And then a third. A flock of paper birds swoop and swarm, surrounding me. Pecking at my hair, my head, my eyes. I manage to read one or two of the messages.

Too late for excuses.
Too late.

And I close my eyes because he is right. It is too late for me. I do not know how to be or who to be. I'm no longer the woman I was or even the woman either of

345

them thought I was. I'm no longer anyone. It will be easier if I allow myself to slip into unconsciousness. It will be easier if I let go.

346

41

Mark

The moment Fiona leaves the house Mark bounces up the stairs and charges into Oli's room.

'You knew?' he demands.

'Don't you ever knock?' Oli is trying to sound bolshie, confident but Mark can see in his eyes he is scared. Scared of Mark? The thought is like a punch. Another one. His son gets up off the bed, draws himself up to his full height. Chest out, man to man, eye to eye. He glowers a challenge. He's taller than Mark now. Maybe two or three inches. When did that happen?

'Why didn't you tell me?' Mark demands.

'Because you'd have gone off it.'

'What do you mean?'

'You know what I mean. You'd have gone all hulkman and started tearing our lives apart. It was better I just dealt with it my own way.'

'And how was that exactly?' Mark's spittle hits Oli in the face.

He doesn't acknowledge it. He doesn't wipe it away. Slowly, he replies, 'I decided to do nothing. You know the teachers are always calling me lazy. I decided to do nothing.'

Mark wants to believe him.

But he doesn't.

347

42

Kylie

Someone is shaking me roughly. 'Kylie, Kylie. Kylie, wake up.' It's just another dream and I don't want to wake up. But the voice is desperate, frightened and insistent. They won't let me go. 'Kylie, open your eyes.' I feel a water bottle being pushed to my mouth, water dribbles down my chin and it feels real. The wetness on my top is true. I flicker open my eyes.

'Fiona?' I try to say her name, but I can hear it comes out as little more than a moan. Still she looks relieved. She gently puts the bottle to my lips again and this time I manage to sip. She kisses my forehead. Fiona, who for a long time I loved more than anyone else in the world. Until I had a husband and kids. Then another husband. A thought skitters through my mind. I am still the person Fiona loves most in the world. She will save me.

'Oh God, Kylie, what the fuck have they done to you?'

She's calling me by my old name. The name I was when we met. The name it took months of training to get her to kick, but I don't chastise her for using it as I did when I first applied for the deed poll, instead I'm glad. I am grateful. Kylie is the woman I was before. Whole, complete. Singular. I cling to Fiona, even though doing so causes spikes of pain to throb through my injured hand.

I start to sob, inelegant, hiccupping, hysterical sobs

348

erupt from my eyes, mouth, nose. The feel of her flesh, after nothing but space and brutality, makes me feel dizzy, untethered. I thought I was going to die. I thought I wanted to die but I know now I don't. I want to live. I want Fiona to rescue me. She gently prises her way out of my grasp. Stares at me for a moment, probably taking in my wounds. 'Kylie, love, we haven't got much time. They know what you did. Both of them do.'

'I am in Daan's building, aren't I?' I mumble.

She looks at me carefully, presumably weighing up what I'm capable of dealing with. 'Yes, you are in Daan's building,' she confirms gently.

'Daan did this to me,' I assert. I've surmised as much but still, hearing it confirmed hurts, wounds.

'No, well, maybe. I don't know. I thought it was him. He's — well, let's just say he's not what you think.' She looks embarrassed, awkward. 'But I'm not so sure now who did this. I think maybe Mark put you here. You know, if he found out what you'd done and who with then — '

'You think he is setting up Daan?' I croak.

'Maybe. I don't know.' She sounds desperate. 'Or maybe they planned it between them. Maybe they are in it together.'

'Both of them?' I'm stunned although should I be? They have shared so much unbeknown to them, is it such a leap to think they might share this, unbeknown to me?

'We haven't got time to think about this now,' she says hurriedly. 'We need to get you out. I've brought pliers, they're in here somewhere.'

In fact, she has a whole bag of helpful stuff; she tips it on to the floor and rummages. I lie back against the wall, too weak to be of much help. She hands me the small bottle of still water and a chocolate bar. It is all I can do to slurp back the water. My fingers are shaking too badly to manage to tear open the wrapping on the chocolate. She notices, stops rummaging and opens it for me. She snaps off a small piece and puts it in my mouth. 'Here you go, baby bird,' she says with a sad smile. Her eyes are wet. It's a thing we used to say to each other, way back when we lived with one another. If one of us was sick and needed pampering, or maybe just hungover and too idle to move, we would hand feed each other Haribo jelly worms and make jokes about baby birds. The tender words feel like hugs. Fiona returns to rattling around with the contents of her bag. She has clean clothes and first aid equipment. I look at her wide-eyed in astonishment.

'I didn't know what you'd need, how I'd find you. You know, what sort of state you'd be in, once I worked it out.' She grimaces. 'You are going to be OK, Kylie. I know this has been shit, but you're safe now. I'm going to get you out of here.' She picks up the pliers and cuts the zip ties that hold me to the chain. My hand flops to my side. I look at it almost surprised. Momentarily unsure what to do with this freedom. 'I am going to take you to my beach cottage first. I think you need to hide out until the police come and sort it all out.'

'Why don't we just go straight to the police now?'

'We can, Kylie, of course we can. It's your call. But you are a bigamist, that is a crime. I just couldn't bear it if they arrested you straight away, made you go straight to a cell, to court. How do these things work? I thought you'd want a decent night's sleep first. I thought we could try and get hold of Oli and Seb, so you could talk to them, you know, before the police take you.'

I am so grateful, if I had more energy I'd cry. Instead I mumble, 'How are they?'

'Oh, they are doing fine considering everything. I guess the test is going to be how they cope when this salacious tale is spread all over the tabloids.' I drop my head into my hands. 'Sorry. God, this is all too much. You can't think straight right now. Let's get you somewhere safe and clean. We can call the boys and the police after a good night's sleep. We just need to get a move on now, we really do. If he comes back, I don't know what he'll do to either of us. Please, let's get going.'

43

Kylie

Fiona talks to me in a low, soothing voice as she leads me out of the apartment, to the lift and through the reception.

'Where's Alfonso?' I ask.

She looks confused. 'Alfonso?'

'The concierge.'

'Oh. I never found out his name,' she says, distracted. 'Probably they've moved the switchboard to his home and he's working from there. Jesus, Kylie, you have no clue what the world is like now. There's a pandemic, we're in lockdown, you know — like in Spain and Italy.' I nod, remembering the fear growing before I was abducted. 'Besides, Alfredo's duties — taking in packages, dry cleaning, that sort of thing — will soon all be on hold. I told you, lockdown.'

'Alfonso,' I correct.

'Right, yeah.'

'How did you get in?'

Fiona looks sheepish. 'I had a client here a while back. She gave me the key code.'

I lean on Fiona, weak with gratitude for this coincidence. Once outside, I gulp the air, wildly appreciative of the heat of the evening sun, the breeze, its freshness. Fiona is parked close by, the few snatched minutes in the fresh air aren't enough; the moment we are in the car I press the button to lower the window and lean, like a dog with my head sticking out, breathing in deeply. Fiona concentrates on weaving through the streets. It is deathly quiet, eerie; shops and restaurants are being closed up, some are already boarded up. It makes my escape more dramatic. If anything could be more dramatic than what I've been through.

'It's like the apocalypse,' I mutter.

'Let's hope not. The good news is that the lack of delivery lorries, cars and even bikes does at least mean we will make good progress through London.'

She's right about that, soon we are on the motorway heading for the Jurassic coast in Dorset. Fiona bought her place about six years ago. Not a romantic wreck of a cottage, but a nineties bungalow. Pretty soulless initially, but a brilliant, covetable seafront location. She made a project of gutting it and redecorating it. Unlike just about every beach cottage I know there is not a starfish motif in sight, nor any anchor motifs or sailor stripes come to that. The place is decorated in blush pinks, peaches and vibrant oranges, homage to the sunset she enjoys watching from the comfort of her enormous couch, through the wall of glass that allows the most beautiful views. We've often made this journey together — usually with Mark and the boys too — to enjoy long weekends where the sea breeze tangles hair, salt sticks to skin and toes can bury into the warm sand. It's a place where I've always felt peaceful and happy. I long to be there, cosseted. Safe. I realise my body is still taut and primed for an attack, for something else awful. I take a deep breath and let my head fall back against the rest.

I'm so grateful that Fiona had the foresight and kindness to decide to take me there first, rather than straight to the police station. She is right, I do need a chance to recoup, maybe even try to relax. Of course, I must face everything sooner rather than later — what I have done, what has been done to me — but Fiona has shown her best friend credentials by caring most for what I need and giving me that, valuing it above even what is expected of her as a law-abiding citizen.

Fiona keeps glancing my way. Concern oozing out of her, she must be desperate to know exactly what I've been through since I saw her last. I get the feeling she is biting back her questions. She doesn't say much other than urging me to drink and eat. 'You are so thin,' she murmurs.

'What day is it? I ask.

'Monday.'

I have been locked up for a week. It's felt like years. I close my eyes and allow myself to drift to sleep, knowing I'm safe. Fiona has my back.

44

Kylie

Fiona gently shakes me awake. 'We're here.' She smiles kindly. 'You were out for the count.' Dazed, I stumble out of the car. The cottage is a welcome sight against the dark sky. Fiona gathers up bags from the boot of the car and then opens the back door. Dumbly, I follow her into the kitchen, not quite capable of helping myself, needing her to tell me what to do next. The place has a cool, empty feel to it. It smells a bit musty. Fiona flicks on the lights, smiles at me. 'I'll light a fire, but I think the first thing you need is a bath, right?'

How bad must I smell? Fiona draws the bath as I carefully strip off. I wonder whether we should have gone to the hospital, whether my hand is broken but the lure of a hot bath and a night's sleep in a comfortable bed is too much for me to resist. Fiona has lit candles in the bathroom and poured a generous amount of some lovely scented oil into the bath. It's a sanctuary. I carefully lower myself into the water. I lay still, the warm, sweet-smelling water gently laps my body. I can hear Fiona move around the kitchen below preparing supper. The idea that I'm going to be clean and fed causes me to weep, quietly.

Fiona knocks on the bathroom door. 'Can I come in?'

'Of course.' As we shared a flat for so many years, we've seen one another's naked bodies often enough before, but today I feel shyer because of the purple-and-brown bruises blooming on my ribs, wrists, chest and back. I expect her to recoil or look shocked; I'm grateful for her strength when she simply picks up a sponge, dips it in the water and starts to carefully clean my back for me.

'Do you want to talk about it?' she asks. 'I mean, only if you feel up to it.'

'You must have been wondering how did I get myself into this mess?'

'Well, yes.' She pauses and then murmurs, 'Oh Kylie, what made you think it was OK?'

Until this past week, I have always worked hard at minimising the time I spend thinking about my situation and I've made sure I *never* talk about it, not so much a whisper. However, whilst I was locked up memories, thoughts, causes for my choices clambered into my head — elbows out, demanding to be noticed. All that time alone and nothing to do, it was impossible not to feel the jabs at my conscience and reason. At my heart. I think I do want to talk about it. I want Fiona to understand me as much as it is possible to do so.

'You know as a child I lived half a week with my mother, half a week with my father.'

'Yes.'

'Their divorce meant I became a baton stick, hurriedly handed over on doorsteps, that is until I was old enough to take myself to and fro on trains and buses. You know, no one ever asked me if I liked living divided between them.'

'Well, I suppose you were lucky that both parents wanted you.'

'The thing is, I don't think both parents did want

me,' I admit. 'I think they just wanted the other not to have me. A very different thing.' My childhood was complex. Pitted and pocked with pain. Marred by a sense of anxiety about the future and regret about my short past that seemed to already be so solidly wrong that I doubted I could ever fix it. Fiona gently dips the sponge and then squeezes the water out on my shoulders. The rhythmic action is comforting.

'As I lived between my mother and father, even the simple task of getting ready for school was challenging. I often struggled to find a clean uniform, the thing that signals to a child that she belongs, fits in. Invariably, inevitably, the piece of kit or bit of homework I needed was in the wrong house.'

'That's tough on a kid. Awkward,' Fiona murmurs sympathetically.

It was more than awkward. I'm not explaining it well enough. I push on. 'Neither of my parents bothered to develop routines or take ownership of me and my needs. It was a good day if I found food in the fridge. I was often hungry. I didn't have my own room at my father's, I used the guest room and was forbidden to put up posters or customise it in any way. I was allowed to leave one bag of personal belongings there, but I had to stash that under the bed in case the room was needed.'

'But you had a room at your mother's, right?'

'No. We shared a room. In some rentals, we shared a bed. She was always telling me my father didn't give her enough money to 'live properly'. Although, she was never hungry enough to look for a job.'

'Your mum has always been a piece of work,' Fiona comments.

It's confusing that I feel the stab of disloyalty as

always when I allow anyone else to criticise my mother, however mildly. Despite everything, she is my mother. I carry on though because it's a relief to finally be talking about this to someone. To Fiona. 'The worst thing of all was the way they each questioned me about the other. My father always wanted to know if my mother was up to scratch. He wanted to catch her out. Find fault. Even if that meant I was hurt or neglected in some way, he didn't seem to mind the cost as long as he could say, 'Ha! I said she was unfit!' Something he yelled if I missed a dentist appointment or when I scalded myself preparing supper. 'How many meals has your mother cooked this week?' 'When did you last eat a fresh vegetable?' The truth caused trouble for my mum. Admitting she was in bed, lying in the dark and in her depression when I scalded myself was snitching, as was admitting we ate tinned carrots and sweetcorn.'

'It can't have been easy,' Fiona says.

'My mother's questioning was more like an interrogation. When I returned home from my father's house, she would be waiting for me at the door. Breathlessly keen. She wanted me to recount every moment I spent there. Who said what to whom? Who wore what? Did they look happy? Were my brothers well behaved? Had my father and Ellie bought anything new in the past week? What did they eat? Drink? What music did they listen to? Sometimes she would hiss angrily, roll her eyes and comment, 'All right for some. Tuna steaks? They cost a fortune.' She would get me to describe or even sketch what Ellie was wearing and then manically scour shops to find a similar outfit. Other times she would silently turn back to her bedroom. Defeated, distant, distraught.'

The water in the bath is getting cool now. I stand up and reach for a big towel that Fiona has had warming on the radiator. I climb out of the bath and wrap it around me as I carry on talking.

'Over time, I learnt that it was easier not to feed either of them the answers they hungered after. When my father asked about my life with my mother, I simply said, 'It's boring, I don't want to talk about it.' I said that over and over again until he eventually stopped asking. After that, he barely spoke to me at all.' Fiona tuts. 'With my mother I insisted, 'I don't remember.' 'But you must!' she would yell, irritated. I'd shake my head. 'Nope. Nothing. I remember nothing.' I stayed stubbornly silent until she declared me useless. I learnt to lock up both lives, build a wall between them.'

I finally dare look at Fiona. I stand dripping on the bathroom floor and hoping for some understanding, some forgiveness. She looks pale. She is biting her bottom lip. Her stress tell.

'So this is why living two separate lives as an adult hasn't been as weird for you as it would be for others,' she comments. 'Not as weird as it should have been.'

'I guess,' I admit with a shrug.

45
DC Clements

It is Tanner who draws her attention to the plaster-board on the ground. He impatiently kicks it as he strides towards the luxury building. 'Bloody litter louts. I hate them. They have the right idea in Singapore. Three-hundred-dollar fine for dropping a fag end or sweet wrapper. Crap like this would get a court appearance. Stringent enforcement.'

Clements looks up. She can see light bouncing and glinting on most of the windows above. But one, on the fourteenth floor, is opaque because it is open, and the light is being swallowed. It's a possibility. She grasps at that because sometimes, a possibility is enough. 'We need to get up to that floor,' she says.

The place is deserted, no sign of the concierge but they find his number, pinned behind the desk, conscientiously left for residents who might need his help. Within twenty minutes Alfonso is at the building and he is happy to let them in. He seems pleased to be needed. Irritated that the residents have sent him home.

'I saw that mess, wanted to sort it out, but they wouldn't give me the time. Mr Janssen said I had to get on my way ASAP.'

'Everyone is being asked to work from home now. I'm jealous,' says Tanner. 'Don't worry about it.'

'We're glad you are here though. Very grateful,' adds Clements.

The man straightens his shoulders, purposeful. 'Well, the apartment with the open window belongs to the Federovas. Russian couple. Rarely here. Haven't seen them for months. They have workmen in and out now and again. Doing it up. Haven't seen many of those for a while though either. Normally Mrs Federova emails me in advance because I sort out access. Can't think why a window might be open. They may have loaned the place out to a friend, I suppose.'

'Can you let us in?'

'Happy to.'

They knock on the door of the apartment, out of courtesy but there is no answer, so Alfonso presses the key code and the door swings open.

They swiftly walk through the rooms. The only thing that initially seems out of place is a typewriter and a pile of paper on the floor outside a bedroom door. They open that door. Clements' eyes jump from one thing to the next, taking it all in in an instant. The hole in the wall, chains attached to the radiator, debris, empty water bottles, food wrappers, a stinking bucket of crap.

'Call it in, Tanner. We need to take prints, or maybe tests of the waste in the bucket; we need proof she was in here, but I think it's — '

'A safe assumption.'

'I was going to say a decent lead. There's no such thing as a safe assumption.' But Clements feels something scorch her belly: adrenaline. This is something. This is big. She has to admit, this is the closest you ever get to a safe assumption.

'No body though. You think he's done her in and got rid of her?' Tanner asks.

'I hope not but we need to find Daan Janssen. Let's

pay him a visit right now.'

Alfonso is holding a handkerchief to his face. He looks pale, shocked. 'I'll take you up. I can let you in there too, if he's gone.'

362

46

Fiona

Fiona is trying her best to be as sympathetic as possible. Kylie is her best friend. Well, she was; everything has changed irredeemably. It is very hard to see her beaten and broken body. Clearly, she's been through a lot. Yet Fiona can't help but feel just a bit irritated by Kylie's continued self-justification of her bigamy. She wants to yell, 'Own it!' Kylie has been alone for a week, locked up with nothing else to think about, yet she still does not appear sorry; she just wants to keep explaining why she's done what she's done. Fiona thinks about Mark's pain, the boys' fear, Daan's anger. Why can't Kylie see that what she has done is unforgivable, unjustifiable? Fiona bites her tongue and offers to bandage up Kylie's hand. She straps it close to her chest which means Kylie has to eat supper one-handed but as it's the right hand that's damaged, it doesn't cause her too much of an issue.

Fiona has prepared a basic pasta dish with a jar of tomato sauce. She expected Kylie to be ravenous, but she is just listlessly picking around the edges of the hearty serving. Kylie is taut, brittle. It's understandable but hard to negotiate. Fiona wants to feel on solid ground. She wants to be able to recognise her friend and their friendship, however, she isn't sure she knows Kylie anymore. It's disconcerting to have a stranger in the kitchen. Has she done the right thing in bringing her here after all?

She nods at the pasta. 'Sorry it's nothing special but obviously I packed in a hurry, I just grabbed some groceries out of my cupboard.'

'It's great, honestly,' Kylie assures her, but she continues to poke the pasta with her fork, not quite managing to shovel it into her mouth.

This won't do, thinks Fiona. She needs Kylie to relax. She needs to relax too. 'I'll open a bottle of wine. I think I have a few quite decent ones stashed away.'

Kylie knocks back the wine quickly enough. Once she has sunk a glass she loosens, her limbs lose their contorted hardness. Her eyes become a little glazed and slippery. Obviously, the alcohol has gone straight to her head. Fiona doesn't know where to start in bringing Kylie up to speed. Should she mention that she dated Daan? That Mark's first wife did not die of cancer? That Daan was planning on leaving the country? That Oli knew about Daan? That she kissed Mark too?

It seems like a lot to load on her at once.

Instead, she decides it is safest to put the conversational onus on Kylie. Fiona asks, 'So tell me, which one would you choose?'

'Really? Now, you're asking me this?'

Fiona giggles. 'Well, I might not get another chance if you go to prison.'

'Very funny.'

'Which one of them are you hoping did this to you, or maybe it's easier to recognise which one of them are you hoping didn't?'

Kylie shivers. 'I was in Daan's apartment block. I think it's pretty clear cut.'

'Yes, but like I said, maybe Mark set him up.'

'You really think that's a possibility?'

364

'Would you want it to be?'

'I just want the truth.'

'That's a bit of an ask from someone who has lied for so long,' points out Fiona sharply. 'Sorry, I don't want to sound unsympathetic, but seriously, Kylie. Talk to me. Tell me.'

Kylie reddens, looks awkward. No doubt aware of all the thousands of times she could have told Fiona, her best friend, what was going on in her life and didn't, but instead chose to lock Fiona out. Exclude her. Fiona wants to know how Kylie managed to stamp on her principles and judgement, spit out lies, choke down the truth. But again, that seems a bit much. It's more palatable to ask, 'I mean, you were married to Mark for ten years. He's your real husband, right?'

Kylie pushes her plate away but picks up her wine glass. 'They are both so different. Mark is, you know, at heart cautious. With one man I tried to do more and more and more until I eventually realised no matter what I did, I couldn't make him happy. I couldn't square away his pain at his loss of Frances. I'd never replace the dead wife. With two men, I found I gave each slightly less attention and for some reason that worked out well. It shouldn't have, but it did. Mark seemed relieved that my happiness wasn't entirely dependent on his and Daan admired my independence; he'd had his fill of needy, clingy, weepy types. Both men got what they wanted.'

Fiona is wide-eyed. 'I'm not sure they did.'

'With Daan, I was sexy, elusive, frivolous. I played a role, lived out a fantasy.'

'But just a fantasy?'

'Who is to say our fantasies are any less real than our actuality?'

'Oh, Kylie. For fuck's sake. That just doesn't make sense,' Fiona snaps.

'I loved Daan. OK. I loved them both. I didn't plan to. If you'd ever met him, you might understand.' That is Fiona's cue.

She could say she has met him. She too has fucked him, but she doesn't. She gets a strange sense of satisfaction knowing something that Kylie doesn't for a change, so she stays quiet. Kylie continues. 'He had something different, something extra.'

'Tell me about it. Help me understand.' Fiona gets up to refill Kylie's glass.

'In the early days we met in his apartment; it was serviced, slick, very like a hotel. That alone was, you know, fun. But it was more than fun. The longing, the needing between us was palpable. When I was meeting him, I had to force myself not to run. Sometimes it seemed a wonder that we resisted having sex in the lift as we headed towards the apartment.'

It is black outside now and has started to rain. It seems like they are completely alone in the world. The scene feels familiar. Fiona and Kylie have often shared confidences over the years, swapped stories about flirtations, crushes and seductions, sexual conquests and interludes. But besides that, Kylie's words feel familiar because Fiona has also felt that urgency — that desire — as she approached Daan's apartment. Although in her case, it had been one way. Daan had never asked her to go to a restaurant, let alone to marry him. 'So, was he good then? In bed?' She isn't sure why she is choosing to torture herself this way.

'So good,' Kylie replies, a small smile playing on her lips. The memory not quashed, even after everything.

Even though she's been chained to a radiator, starved and beaten. It is unbelievable. 'The moment we entered the apartment, he would throw me against the wall, his lips on mine, his hands everywhere. He'd want to hitch up my dress and pull me on to him right away, but we tried not to, we would try and make ourselves wait just a little bit longer.'

Fiona reaches for a glass of water. Her throat is so dry, she can't swallow. 'Describe it to me. Make me understand.'

'No.' Kylie laughs, embarrassed. Finally embarrassed. But not embarrassed that she has had this glut, this overabundance. Embarrassed to share it with Fiona, who she no doubt pities. Who she assumes has no clue.

But Fiona gets it. She can see it. Imagine it, even though it wasn't the same for her. He bent Fiona over the kitchen table. She imagines it was different for Kai. He'd back Kai on to the bed, as she fell flat, he'd move swiftly, quickly rooting out her wetness, delving in with his brilliant tongue, bringing her close to climax within moments as he went deep and she pushed her hips into his face, willing him to do whatever he wanted with her, take whatever he needed. Clothes would be shed; hands, fingers, tongues everywhere: on her tits, her arse, her neck, her waist, tits again, arse again; exploring without limits. They couldn't get enough of each other. She would find her way to his cock and flick her tongue up and down, take him in her mouth and suck, drawing him in. She'd do this until he moaned that it was the best fucking blow job of his life, that he wanted to come in her mouth. Of course, he wouldn't. Throbbing with desire he'd slip inside her and she'd sigh, scream and yelp with utter uninhibited pleasure. They would both be wet, hot, needy. Finally, she would quiver and tighten, he would feel her utter surrender. Then, and only then, would he come, deep inside her.

Fiona can barely breathe. Her head is spinning.

47

Kylie

My head is spinning. The kitchen is hot, clammy. I want to feel a breeze after the week of being trapped, starved not only of food but oxygen and hope. However, I feel too exhausted to even stand up, stretch up to open the window. I'm completely sapped, drained. I should eat more of this pasta. I am allowing myself to get weak and lightheaded. Drinking is a mistake. Talking to Fiona like this, about this, is a mistake. Fiona is looking at me in a peculiar way. We've known each other forever. I can read every one of her expressions. She looks furious. That can't be right. Just curious, maybe? Confused? She keeps urging me to carry on. I should include Fiona in this, however difficult it is for me to explain. That's what she wants. If she is angry at all, it is because she has felt left out.

'At first everything between Daan and me was exciting and unreal. I told myself it had nothing to do with Mark, with my family. A discreet hook-up in a posh apartment once a month. Not honourable but not unprecedented. Minimal communication in between. Just sex. It was never meant to be serious, yet people can't be contained. Feelings can't be capped or controlled.'

'No, they can't,' admits Fiona. I smile, grateful to her for trying to understand me.

'He had this power over me. The desire I felt. The force of it was irresistible. And it never stopped. It

369

never went away. Even in the moment I was sated, I'd want him again. I couldn't ignore it.' Confessing such intimacy is hard but I'm drunk and that helps. 'It started with a drink on a trendy rooftop bar and specifically an incident in a toilet.'

'Classy Kylie.'

I shrug. I know how it sounds. It sounds awful but it felt like something different altogether. Something brilliant. 'I did not plan to see him ever again. After the first time. Of course not. I woke up waiting for the shame and guilt to kick in with the hangover.'

'It didn't?'

I shake my head. 'I got out of bed and banged on the door of the boys' bedrooms, made everyone's breakfast, showered, went to work on the tube. I did everything I had done the day before as though nothing had changed. I did not feel guilty. It would be easy to say I wish it had felt guilty, because if I had I might have stopped. It'd certainly be more normal. More expected. But I don't think that is what I wish. Even now.'

'Even though you ended up chained to a radiator as a consequence?'

I take a gulp of wine. I don't believe I asked for this. I don't believe the response was justifiable or proportionate, but I almost understand it. I think I do. I shrug, 'When I spoke, he listened. I felt more heard than I have ever been.'

'I don't know what to say,' comments Fiona. We both fall silent. She stands up, clears away the plates, tops up my drink again.

'I knew it was wrong. Obviously. Moral compass rule number one. But as it didn't *feel* wrong it was hard to believe it was.' My heart is beating exceptionally fast. The confession is causing panic, or maybe the memory is churning up a familiar, formidable delight. 'It just didn't feel wrong. I should have felt bad, but I didn't.'

'I suppose you thought you were going to get away with it.'

'I thought maybe if no one ever knew, then it wasn't awful.'

'That's just something you told yourself to make things easier for you. It was convenient for you to think so. All lies are convenient.'

I feel the tender sting of my bruises under my clothes, the throb of my hand. It wasn't as simple as that. There was more to it. Can I make Fiona understand? I blurt, 'The thing is, in marriages, in all relationships, sometimes, we do things badly. We are in the wrong, we make mistakes. Life is full of small, undignified moments, insignificant like grains of sand but when they start to add up, to stack up, you make entire beaches of pain. I didn't want a marriage like that full of tiny failures of character on my part — on his. I guess I chose a double life so that I could make both shinier.'

'But neither was real.'

'They felt real,' I insist.

'You can't have it all.'

'But I did. For a time, I did.' We both sit in silence. I am reminded of the silence of waiting for the typewriter to clank into action behind the door and it makes me feel uncomfortable. 'I need fresh air. I've been inside too much recently. Can we take a walk?'

Fiona looks outside, the wind is agitating the branches of trees in her garden, causing them to whip the air. It's too dark to see the sea but we can hear the waves crashing. It's inhospitable. I'll understand if she refuses my request. She smiles and jumps up. 'Sure.'

48
Daan

Daan is on his way to the airport when he gets the call; his passport in his jacket pocket, his smart Tumi luggage neatly packed, just carry-on size. He needs to be swift, can't afford any potential delays. If everything goes well, he can have the rest of his belongings shipped to him. If he has to leave them behind, he can always start again. It's just stuff. Suits, shirts, shoes, shit. It's not real.

Not like she was.

Whoever is trying to get hold of him is being persistent. It rings out and then immediately starts up again. He doesn't care who it is. He doesn't want to talk to anyone.

She's gone. It's a fucking mess. The whole lot. He wants to leave it all behind him. The pain, the humiliation. He wants to get out of this country while he can. Put it all behind him.

It is an unknown number and he never answers those. It's always just some scammer trying to tell him he's been in an accident and is due compensation or some idiot asking about his most recent dining experience. His entire life is a car crash, now that he's been taken in by the world's biggest cheat. He can barely recall a time when it mattered to him what he ate, let alone who served it and what the ambience was like. That life has gone.

She destroyed it. Twice over. Once when she

373

invented herself as the perfect woman and tricked him into falling in love with her. And now this. Humiliation, anger, disappointment burn through his body. He has no choice. He has to run away.

The unknown number could belong to the DC or Mark Fletcher. He concludes that, whoever it is, it will be trouble. He doesn't want any more trouble. He doesn't want to have to talk to the DC whilst he's on British soil. He'll feel better once he's back at his family pile in Holland. Protected. He supposes it might be his boss, who will have got his email by now, the one saying he wants to resign. Not that he did *want* to. He *had* no choice. She took away his choices. He could have asked for relocation maybe. But at some point, he would have to face everyone. Explain that his wife was a bigamist. It is too humiliating. Better he just disappears.

49

Kylie

Despite my limbs being unused to exercise recently and therefore being at once heavy and frail, my knees almost crumbling beneath me, it feels incredibly good to walk outside. We set off up the incline, intending to follow the path that takes us along the cliff edge. It's utterly invigorating, to enjoy a freedom that I have never quite understood or appreciated until it was taken away from me. I think about Oli and Seb, calling them, calling the police. I have to do both things tomorrow, but right now I just need to clear my head. The wind lifts my hair. I don't even mind the rain on my face.

Fiona and I have done this walk together a number of times before and we automatically headed this way without discussion. We've never attempted it at night, though. The narrow, winding path is harder to navigate in the dark and the ground is wet underfoot. The wine probably isn't helping. Fiona insisted on bringing another bottle along. I reached for a can of Diet Coke, but she overruled me. I should probably slow down but am at that point of drunk when what I want and need is greater than what I am thinking or reasoning. I take sips from the bottle neck, occasionally remembering to offer it to Fiona. But she just smiles, 'It's all yours. After everything, no one can blame you for wanting to let your hair down.' The wine is slackening my shoulders, that are scrambled up around

375

my ears, it is also loosening my tongue.

'He never asked me if I was married and I didn't know how to tell him. I didn't dare, in case he ended it. Because ending it would have been the worst thing. Or so I thought.' I sigh. I'm not sure she hears the sigh. It's probably drowned by the sound of the crashing waves somewhere below us. My feet slip and slide under me. I am wearing a pair of Fiona's scruffy old trainers. As we left the house, I found them under a bench at the door and pushed my feet into them, not taking the time to lace them properly.

'Whoops. You need to be careful,' she says, catching hold of my arm. Her clasp is tight. She will keep me steady. Safe.

'I never imagined it would last any length of time. Every time I was with him, I thought it was the last. Told myself it had to be. But I just couldn't say no.'

'Bullshit,' interrupts Fiona. 'Absolute fucking bullshit.' I blink, surprised at her eruption. We do have a relationship where we call out one another on things from time to time. I've often been in the awkward position where I've had to point out that Fiona's latest fling is a non-starter for instance, but I'm surprised by the ferocity of her curse at this moment, during this intimate confession. 'There must have been a thousand times where you could have said no to him. Before you walked into the restaurant to meet him for the first time, before you sat down at his table, before you accepted the second glass of wine, stepped into the cab, walked into the lift, slipped between his sheets. Before you walked down the aisle, for fuck's sake.'

'Well, yes.'

'But you didn't.'

'No, I didn't.' I shouldn't be surprised by Fiona's anger. It's going to come from every quarter. My sons, my brothers, my mother. I shall need to brace myself for it. Bear it. I think of the moment I slipped between his sheets. And afterwards, the views of the Tower of London, London Bridge and HMS Belfast that I enjoyed from our apartment window. These were places I had taken the boys. Trailed with them in ever-decreasing circles of interest. Crows, murders, battles — unable to enthuse them the way a YouTube video can.

'Were you drunk?' Fiona demands. The rain is clinging to us both now, not heavy but persistent, undeniable. Causing a film, like cellophane, that somehow separates us. My wet hair is getting in my eyes, I am carrying the wine in my one working free hand so I can't push it away. Fiona persists, 'Were you drunk when you first slept with him? When you started all of this?'

I glance at the bottle in my hand and realise I feel very drunk now. Blurred. Uncertain. I let the bottle gently slip out of my grasp onto the soft ground. In the dark, Fiona doesn't notice. I reach for the truth. 'No, I wasn't drunk. I can't use that as an excuse. I wish I could in a way. People would understand it more. Find it more forgivable, but I wasn't drunk — or if I was, it was not on alcohol, it was something more. Maybe possibility. Maybe inevitability.'

'You were greedy.' Fiona raises her voice, to ensure I can hear her above the noise of the sea and the wind.

'Yes, I was,' I admit. Because that is it. In a nutshell. I was greedy.

'I don't get it. You had a permanent sing-along, dance-along, lifelong-adventure buddy in Mark but that wasn't enough for you. You had to hoover up another guy.'

'Well, I don't see it that way. I — '

'You don't get to live two lives. You are just one person. One body. You have to pick a life. Why wasn't one enough for you? You stupid bitch. You already had it all.' Fiona's insult is pushed out with a smile, but I can't pretend to myself that she isn't having a go. She clearly is more than confused. She's not shouting to be heard above the sea, she's shouting because she thinks I need telling. I stop and face her, it's the least I can do. I've seen Fiona lose her temper before, many times. She is the epitome of the fiery redhead. Yet I'm shocked that her face is almost unrecognisable, twisted and split with what I now see is fury. 'Do you have any idea what a freedom it is to be able to send a text, just a simple bloody text about what is on your mind, without having to second, third, fourth guess how he might take it?'

'What?' I ask.

'Once you're married, there is no such thing as coming on too strong, is there? You can't be the crazy intense woman. That's such a bloody luxury. Do you know how lucky you are that you got to be totally, one hundred per cent yourself because that's what it means to be married?'

'Well, not really for me,' I point out. She splutters out a sound of indignation from her nostrils. She's raging but a moment's reflection must reveal that it was never that for me. The opposite. Having two husbands cost me the opportunity to be myself.

'Which one of them were you planning to get old with?' she demands. 'Or were you going to hobble on your Zimmer frame backwards and forwards between

378

the two?'

'I don't know,' I stammer. 'I hadn't thought that far ahead.'

'You hadn't thought at all, had you? What about when you were sick? Who looked after you? One of them would, that's for sure. You were never on your own. You never had to crawl out of bed and drag yourself to the chemist for tissues and paracetamol. They probably think the sniffling, snotty version of you is cute, do they?'

It obviously isn't the moment to tell her that I haven't been bedbound-ill once in the four years since this started. Mums rarely get the chance to be bedbound; bigamist mums have no chance at all. I had to push on. Instead, I remind her, 'When you were ill, I brought you chicken soup. I went to the chemist for you.'

It is true: sometimes Fiona was like my third child. I'd drop everything to help her. As I know she would me. Even now. Wouldn't she? She is furious with me at present, but I just have to ride out the storm. She'll forgive me. Of course she will. Why else would she rescue me and bring me here to safety?

'I'm struggling with this, Kylie. Because I don't know who you are. What you think and feel, what you say, what you do. There's no consistency about you! And without consistency, you are nothing. You might as well be dead.' I recoil from her. *It's just a phrase*, I tell myself. People say it, they don't mean it. Except in this past week, for me, that seemed a scarily real possibility. I might very well have ended up dead. How can she say that to me now? She glares at me and adds, 'You can't be on two teams. You've got to pick a side. Tell me which one of them you loved the most?'

'I don't know why it matters. It's not as though I'm going to get to choose between them. One of them abducted me. The other no doubt hates me just as much. I'm not going to be able to save either relationship.'

'Just pick one!' she shouts.

'I took immeasurable risks for Daan, I lost friends for him. That shows I love him.'

'You don't know what love is.'

'But I do. Twice over. I love them both.'

'That's not allowed.'

'I know, but who decided it wasn't?'

She raises her hands and for a moment I think she is going to hit me. Instead she pulls at her own hair. I guess she is trying to make me choose between them as some sort of therapy. Facing up to things. I'm frustrating the hell out of her. We stand on the cliff edge, drenched, incensed, bewildered. I imagine Daan walking away and I feel all the things I am going to miss about him. They hit me like stones. His loud, low, long laugh, his funny stories, his promise of the unexpected, a bright future. Then I think of Mark. His pride in his children, his solid, steady work ethic, his earnest interest in the land, our shared history. My bones snap.

'Mark,' I blurt. 'Mark, Oli and Seb outweigh Daan. I guess they always did. I was never able to leave them. I'm glad it was Daan who abducted me. I choose Mark.'

'Right, good, I'm glad we've got that cleared up. Finally.' The dark night, the noise from the waves smashing, the wind whipping is disconcerting, overwhelming. Her breathing is as fast and shallow as mine. But something skitters across her face that looks a lot like triumph. We look at each other and it is as though it's the first time we've ever really seen one another.

And I suppose in a way it is.

We see one another for what and who we really are. It's hard to know who is most disappointed, disgusted. 'Do you see what you have done?' she asks. 'Because you have tried to run two lives in parallel, you've shortened the one you really have. Sort of used them up, you know? You've run out of time. Do you see that?'

I feel the force of the shove a nanosecond before I anticipate it or understand it. I don't know why I've been so slow. The wine? Something in the wine? It's too late now. My knees crumble under me and I am flying. The grassy verge, the edge of the cliff, the black sea below are somersaulting into one. Round and around I spin. It's a fraction of a second. It's forever. I am plummeting. I am done.

50

Fiona

Fiona walks quickly back to the house. Her head is whirling. Twisting. She takes deep breaths. This isn't the moment to lose her cool. She's been so careful all along. She can't afford a slip-up at this late stage.

She had expected Kylie's eyes to be wide with horror and anguish, her face to be distorted. She thought there might have been a moment of realisation when she would beg to be saved. At least for the boys. But she didn't do that. She stared, eyes wide open (finally!), as she understood what she had done and what it meant, which just goes to show how selfish she is. Was. She can use the past tense. Kylie should have wanted to survive at least for the boys.

Bitch.

She looked almost peaceful. That annoys Fiona, that Kylie found peace. That isn't what she wanted to deliver.

Still, at least now she knows which man Kylie would have wanted to hold on to. Which she ultimately valued the most. It was as Fiona had guessed. There is some satisfaction in getting it right. Knowing Kylie better than she knew herself. Fiona guessed months ago. People are always assuming she knows little about intimacy, because she hasn't ever married — it's so insulting, so patronising — she knows more about any of them than they do about each other.

Fiona carefully but rapidly packs up the house.

Removes any evidence that she — let alone Kylie — has been here tonight. Then she drives back to London. She hasn't had a drop to drink. She was very careful about that. Not that she'd have touched the wine, of course. Not after what she'd put in it to ensure Kylie's reactions were slowed. The drive should take just less than three hours. She wants to hurry but forces herself to keep below the speed limits for the entire journey; she cannot afford to get flashed by a camera.

By now, DC Clements will have searched Daan's apartment block. It would be lax of her not to, considering Fiona told her he is unfaithful, an accomplished liar. They will have found the room. Well, Fiona wasn't able to keep it secret forever. Kylie was getting rebellious. That stunt with the plasterboard, that annoying clanking of her chains. Fiona couldn't keep drugging her and starving her, one thing or the other, so a move had become necessary. When they dust the room for fingerprints, they will find empty water bottles and protein bar wrappers with Daan's fingerprints on them. When they search Daan's apartment they will find the cash receipt she planted, for a chain and zip ties, a plastic bucket purchased at B&Q ten days ago. Eventually, if they search well enough — and DC Clements will because she strikes Fiona as the thorough type — they will find Leigh and Kai's phones hidden in the back of Daan's wardrobe.

Fiona stole the protein bars and bottles of water from his kitchen, not on her last visit to his flat but on the one before. This whole escapade had taken quite some planning, quite some organisation. Fiona is rather proud of herself, how thorough she has been. How she has thought of everything. Kylie always believed she was the smart one, as she was a management consultant and a bigamist too, but in fact Fiona has outwitted her. Tortoise and Hare.

Fiona isn't a lawyer though, and there's only so many things a person can sensibly google so she's not absolutely certain whether this amount of evidence is circumstantial, or more robust. She believes Daan will be arrested and trialled for Kylie's abduction. Of course there is a possibility that he's left the country by now but that won't look good either. He will naturally protest his innocence and no doubt hire brilliantly cunning lawyers who will draw out the case for his extradition to the UK; even if he has to stand trial, he may or may not be convicted, again because he can pay for decent lawyers. Without a body, it will be hard to make a case that will carry a long sentence. But there may be a body. Fiona expects Kylie's body will wash up. She's already told the DC that Daan has visited her cottage on the coast, it will be assumed he returned to a familiar place to dispose of Kylie. He hasn't ever visited her home, of course. Nothing so cosy, nothing so committed. Still, that's not a problem. She has planted enough items around her place to convince a jury he has been there. A single cufflink, the partner of which is still in his own apartment, a glass with his lip and fingerprints, his toothbrush, a pair of boxers. Bits and pieces she picked up from his place when she stayed over on Saturday.

Kylie smiles, confident that Daan will go down for Kylie's abduction and murder. Yes, he might get a lawyer to argue him out of a long sentence or he might rot in jail. Who knows? Who cares? It doesn't matter either way. Even if he gets away with a couple of years, his reputation will be ruined. For the rest of his life he will have scandal and shame attached to him. Staining him. People will shun him, whisper about him behind their hands, behind his back. He'll no longer be the golden boy. The Man. Maybe, in the future, he will think twice about nonchalantly entering into extra-marital sex; casual, indifferent sex with hopeful women. Because what he has done is cruel. Vicious. He needed to be taught a lesson.

Fiona is gripping the steering wheel, her knuckles are almost transparent. She thinks of Kylie describing that overwhelming lust, her smug explanation of her aloofness which made Daan hot. He'd had his fill of 'needy, clingy weepy types', had he? Well, it is unlikely any woman is going to cling to him now. A man drenched in infamy and suspicion.

Then there is Mark. What of Mark? Mark who Kylie finally chose but could not settle for when she had the chance. Silly girl. Well, Fiona has done Mark a favour, obviously. Yes, she was a bit blindsided by that mix-up over the cause of Frances's death. That had confused things, almost sent the police the wrong way. But that will smooth out, in light of the evidence against Daan. Fiona plans to help Mark pick up the pieces. She will slowly but surely mend his broken heart. Fiona hadn't thought she'd necessarily step into Kylie's shoes with Mark, she'd assumed he was too devoted. But it is interesting what pain and betrayal can spawn. He kissed her! She hadn't wanted the kiss to stop. She thinks now of his lips: warm, soft, urgent. Yes urgent. He wants her. Needs her. He isn't in love with her yet, obviously. She's not stupid! But there is *interest*. A kiss shows interest. Besides, he likes having someone to mother the boys. That had been Kylie's in, way back when. He isn't a man who does well on his own.

When the time is right, Fiona will step in. She will comfort the boys, guide them through the next stage of their lives: exams, universities, relationships. She will be a grandmother one day! She can hear Mark's voice ringing in her ears, 'You've been really good for the boys. I don't know what we'd have done without you.'

Yes, she will become Oli and Seb's stepmother, she will become Mark's wife. Third time lucky for him! She will be patient, careful but she'll make it happen. Hasn't she proven anything is possible if you focus? She is glad Kylie chose Mark in the end. It is deeply satisfying knowing she is going to finish up with exactly what Kylie had finally worked out she wanted.

She will ultimately have one of Kylie's lives.

Fiona really has thought of everything because she has had plenty of time. She's known about Kylie's bigamy since just before Christmas. She was over at Daan's, he had just done his usual wham, bam, thank you ma'am in the kitchen, and was making noises about Fiona getting on her way. When he popped to the loo, she'd taken the opportunity to have a quick snoop around. She had started to suspect a wife or at least a significant other and wanted to find evidence. Actually, she wanted to be proven wrong, but even then she thought it was unlikely that she would be wrong. There was always a wife. Some part of her always expected a wife. She hadn't expected it to be Kylie, though. She really had wanted to die the moment she realised. A closet full of women's clothes told her he had someone, the wedding photo by his bed told her who. She was paralysed with shock and shame. She wanted to curl up in a ball and stop breathing.

She followed Kylie for weeks. Tracked her every

move to be certain. It seemed so unlikely, there had to be another explanation. Twins separated at birth seemed more plausible than a double life. But after she had trailed her from one home to the other for weeks, months, and there was no room for doubt, Fiona began to realise Kylie was the one who deserved to feel shame. To stop breathing.

Initially, she hadn't planned on killing Kylie. Killing is so extreme. Just teaching her a lesson. Getting her to think about everything she had done. But she would not think. She would not own it! All that bleating on! That justifying. All week. It drove Fiona mad. The plan had been to punish Kylie for stealing Daan away from her. For being greedy, hoovering up two husbands when Fiona hadn't even secured one. She thought Kylie might come to her senses, ditch Daan and maybe he would turn to Fiona. But Kylie would not pick one of them, no matter how hungry, beaten or scared she was.

And then Mark kissed Fiona.

She got closer to the boys.

Things shifted.

It was obvious that there was no chance for her with Daan, he was cold and indifferent towards her. He was in love with Kylie, but Mark moved on — surprisingly quickly. She didn't want to think of herself as rebound — who did? — but she was a woman of a certain age, time was running out for her, she didn't like dating married men, so options were limited. If she had allowed Kylie to live and simply had Daan brought into disrepute, as she originally intended, she may still have ended up alone, because Mark might have taken Kylie back. He was kind-hearted like that. To a fault! She couldn't risk it.

387

Mark deserved happiness.

Fiona wanted happiness.

Kylie had been happy, twice. And, Fiona thought, that was enough.

Acknowledgements

Thank you, Kate Mills, my utterly brilliant editor and publisher. You are a unique combination of grit, enthusiasm, integrity, and ingenuity. I am so unbelievably fortunate to have you. The same goes for Lisa Milton. How magnificent to have such a wonderful, wise woman at the head and heart of HQ. It is a joy working with you both, it really is.

Thank you, Charlie Redmayne, for being an engaged, inspiring and pioneering CEO.

I'm so delighted to be working with the very best team I could possibly imagine. I am thoroughly grateful for, and appreciative of, the talent and commitment of every single person involved in this book's existence. I know you all work with passion, perception and supreme professionalism. Thank you *all* very much. Anna Derkacz, Fliss Porter, Harriet Williams, Sophie Calder, Izzy Smith, Joanna Rose, Claire Brett, Becca Joyce, Rebecca Fortuin, Becky Heeley, Darren Shoffren, Kelly Webster, Agnes Rigou, Aisling Smyth, Emily Yolland, Kate Oakley, Anneka Sandher, Anna Sikorska, Laura Meyer and Abdu Mohammed Ali. This book is dedicated to Abdu because it is true to say, without him it would not have existed!

I want to send massive thanks across the seas to the brilliant teams who publish my books worldwide. You really are making my dreams come true. Thank you Sue Brockhoff, Adam Van Rooijen, Natika Palka, Loriana Sacilotto, Margaret Marbury, Nicole Brebner, Leo McDonald, Rebecca Silver, Lia Ferrone,

Carina Nunstedt, Celine Hamilton, Pauline Riccius, Anna Hoffmann, Eugene Ashton, Olinka Nell and Rahul Dixit. There are many others who I have yet to meet but I am so grateful that incredible professionals worldwide are giving my books their love and attention. It's so ridiculously exciting. Thank you.

Thank you to all my readers, bloggers, reviewers, retailers, librarians and fellow authors who have supported this book.

Thank you Jimmy and Conrad, for putting up with living with an author for another year! I know doing so comes with its challenges, but I hope we can agree that — on balance — living with my weirdness is tolerable. Love you both.

We do hope that you have enjoyed
reading this large print book.

Did you know that all of our titles
are available for purchase?

We publish a wide range of high
quality large print books including:
Romances, Mysteries, Classics
General Fiction
Non Fiction and Westerns

Special interest titles available in
large print are:
The Little Oxford Dictionary
Music Book, Song Book
Hymn Book, Service Book

Also available from us courtesy of
Oxford University Press:
Young Readers' Dictionary
(large print edition)
Young Readers' Thesaurus
(large print edition)

For further information or a free
brochure, please contact us at:
Ulverscroft Large Print Books Ltd.,
The Green, Bradgate Road, Anstey,
Leicester, LE7 7FU, England.
Tel: (00 44) 0116 236 4325
Fax: (00 44) 0116 234 0205

Other titles published by Ulverscroft:

JUST MY LUCK

Adele Parks

For fifteen years, Lexi and Jake Greenwood have participated in a lottery syndicate with their friends, the Pearsons and the Heathcotes, playing the same six numbers every single time. Over dinner parties, fish-and-chip suppers and summer barbecues, they've discussed the important stuff — the kids, marriages, jobs and houses — and laughed off their disappointment when they failed to win anything more than a tenner.

But then, one Saturday night, the unthinkable happens. There's a rift in the group. Someone doesn't tell the truth. The syndicate falls apart.

The next week, Lexi buys a lottery ticket using the same six numbers.

And, on Saturday, those six numbers come up in the draw.

Lexi and Jake now possess a lottery ticket worth almost £18 million. And their friends are determined to claim a share of it . . .

LIES LIES LIES

Adele Parks

Daisy and Simon's marriage is great, isn't it? After years together, the arrival of longed-for daughter Millie sealed everything in place. So what if Simon drinks a bit too much sometimes? Daisy's used to it: she knows he's just letting off steam. They are a happy little family of three — perhaps soon to be four, if Simon gets his way. But when a visit to the IVF clinic reveals disturbing information, their family life is thrust into a spiral of destruction. Has Daisy been lying all along? Simon embarks upon a steady decline as pieces of his life fall to ruin, until one night at a party things get out of control, and disaster strikes. The happy little family of three will never be the same again . . .

I INVITED HER IN

Adele Parks

When Mel hears from a long-lost friend in need of help, she doesn't hesitate to invite her to stay. Mel and Abi were best friends back in the day, sharing the highs and lows of student life, until Mel's unplanned pregnancy caused her to drop out of her studies. Now, seventeen years later, Mel and Abi's lives couldn't be more different. Mel is happily married and has a chaotic but happy family home with three children. Abi, meanwhile, followed her lover to LA for a glamorous life of parties, celebrity and indulgence. Everything was perfect — until she discovered her partner had been cheating on her. What Abi needs now is a true friend to lean on. And what better place than Mel's house, with her lovely kids, and supportive husband . . .